P9-DUH-038

DATE DUE

BORN WITH
THE CENTURY

BORN WITH
THE CENTURY

by

William Kinsolving

G. P. PUTNAM'S SONS
New York

The author gratefully acknowledges permission from the following sources to reprint material in this book:

Bourne Company for lines from "Whistle While You Work," words by Larry Morey, music by Frank Churchill. Copyright © 1937 by Bourne Company. Copyright renewed.

Alfred A. Knopf, Inc., for material from "Sunday Morning" by Wallace Stevens from *The Collected Poems of Wallace Stevens*, copyright 1923, renewed 1951, by Wallace Stevens.

Random House, Inc., for material from "Shine, Perishing Republic" by Robinson Jeffers from *The Selected Poetry of Robinson Jeffers*, copyright 1925, renewed 1953, by Robinson Jeffers.

Charles Scribner's Sons for quotations from the works of F. Scott Fitzgerald and Thomas Wolfe, which are fully protected by copyright.

Siquomb Publishing Corporation for lines from "The Circle Game" by Joni Mitchell, copyright © 1966 by Siquomb Publishing Corporation. All rights reserved.

Venice Music, Inc., for lines from "Tutti Frutti" by Dorothy LaBostrie and Richard Penniman, copyright 1955–1956 by Venice Music, Inc., 8300 Santa Monica Blvd., Hollywood, California 90069.

Warner Brothers, Inc., for lines from "Let's Fly Away" by Cole Porter, copyright 1930 by Warner Brothers, Inc.; and for lines from "You Must Have Been a Beautiful Baby" by Johnny Mercer and Harry Warren, copyright 1938 by Warner Brothers, Inc.

—Acknowledgments—

I wish to thank Twentieth Century-Fox for taking a gamble.

My gratitude to Michael Gruskoff for suggesting "something about the liquor industry" and for his continuing encouragement.

Several friends gave support and lucid advice: Carol Buck, Robert Baumann, Robert Fitzpatrick, and Sara Anne Fox.

Lisa Doermann did impeccable research.

Faye George typed the manuscript many times, always with stimulating enthusiasm.

My editor, Phyllis Grann, thoughtfully applied to the manuscript her conspicuous talent and well-honed skill, for which I thank her.

W.K.
1979

For Susan

May 3, 1971

Magnus Macpherson came out of a coma in the VIP unit of the American Hospital in Paris. Doctors and nurses were surrounding him, prodding, bending his appendages, and muttering to each other in French. Then they left, telling Magnus nothing.

He tried to yell at them but his mouth wasn't working. The one nurse who remained took the oxygen tent down. She smiled kindly, gave him an injection, then adjusted his catheter. Magnus watched carefully; he wasn't sure he could feel it. When she finally went across the room and sat down, he tried to move various parts of his body to see which of them still worked. The strain quickly exhausted him and he fell asleep. Most of the day, he slept; he was awakened once by a nurse who put a tube through his nose and down into his throat. Then he slept again.

On the second day, just after dawn, Magnus' daughter, a woman in her mid-forties, arrived from the United States. Despite her trip, she looked elegant with her tailored suit and stylish red hair. She smiled when she came into the room, a smile which remained in spite of what her eyes expressed. After standing at the end of the bed and looking at Magnus, she sat down next to him and said, "Father."

Magnus opened his eyes; he made no sound. His daughter reached over and took his hand. He did not feel anything; it was the bad side.

A short time later, Jamie Macpherson, in his early forties, appeared at the door. He stopped when he saw WeeDee and looked at her for a moment without speaking. She held her smile.

"Hello, Jamie."

He nodded.

"WeeDee . . ."

Magnus Macpherson made a noise of greeting. Jamie turned and moved to the other side of the bed. He looked at Magnus intensely, then glanced away, as if embarrassed.

Magnus looked neat; his nurses had seen to that. But he knew the left side of his face, particularly the cheek and flesh around his mouth, sagged noticeably. He could not contain the small flow of saliva which ran down his chin and fell on a towel the nurses placed on his shoulder. But his eyes were all right.

Jamie tried to see how badly his father had been affected by the stroke. When Jamie noticed Magnus was watching him, he looked away. Then self-consciously he crossed himself and seemed about to kneel down.

Magnus gave a violent guttural outburst. Jamie took an awkward step back from the bed. Then his face seemed to close and he said, "That's right, I don't have any prayers." He watched as Magnus choked to silence, the saliva dripping from his chin. "Certainly not for you."

WeeDee stood up quickly and said, "Jamie, if your flight was as long as mine, you need some coffee."

Jamie blinked and nodded. Both turned back to Magnus, whose eyes switched from one to the other, recognizing their hospital exit. Then he made a sound, a falsetto groan, which only the nurses recognized as his equivalent of laughter. They turned away and went out the door, glancing at the nurse but saying nothing.

They returned twice during that day. Jamie ordered that no one be admitted to the room besides the doctors and special nurses. Private guards in plain clothes were put outside the door around the clock.

On the third morning, the cardiologist came in to examine the patient.

"*Bonjour,* Monsieur Macpherson, you are feeling better today?"

By then, Magnus felt the stroke had smashed him like a rat trap, the crooked crossbar of which had crushed down on him, dividing his body in two. One piece was dead, the other was itchy, uncoordinated, and subject to spasms and cramps.

Magnus knew the stroke could mean death. God had never been subtle with Magnus Macpherson through almost three-quarters of a century. He had the stroke on La Sheachanna, the Dismal Day, always a bad day for a Highlander. But to Magnus, death was life's last big surprise, and speculation was a waste of time. Time was valuable to Magnus; his only concern about death was: when?

The cardiologist had turned away to write on the chart. The nurse was standing near the bed. Magnus reached his good arm out and put his hand on her flank. She looked down at him, startled, then quickly at the doctor's back. Then she didn't move at all. Magnus saw her face flushing and slowly moved his hand over her polyester white uniform to the top of her thigh, his thumb gracefully brushing the slight rise made by her pubic hair.

He forced his sound for laughter, and dropped his hand as the cardiologist turned around. The nurse quickly moved to straighten the bottom of the sheet, but Magnus Macpherson laughed again, his eyes looking to heaven, his hand indicating to God and the nurse that his catheter had been cast off.

Outside the door an argument broke out. One voice was demanding entrance in English, another refusing in French. With a sense of Gallic chivalry, the cardiologist gestured for the nurse to stand away from the entrance. The shouting in the hall grew louder.

"I'm going in there! Ask him. He'll tell you he's my father."

Immediately Magnus began making noise, hitting the bed with his right arm, then jerking his finger back and forth toward the door. The cardiologist watched, then went to the door, opened it, and spoke rapidly in French. The security guard and two male orderlies were holding a young man of about thirty against the wall. They let him go after the doctor spoke. The young man came into the room without regarding those who had been restraining him. When he reached the side of Magnus' bed, they exchanged looks that joined like a Chinese puzzle.

"What's going on, Magnus?"

Magnus gestured with his good arm the way one calls for a check in a restaurant. The young man pulled out a pen and said to the cardiologist, "Give me something to write on."

The doctor volunteered his prescription pad. The young man held it as Magnus began to write. He was left-handed and held the pen awkwardly in his right. The room was silent for a few moments while he slowly drew words. Then the young man started to laugh, and was joined by Magnus' falsetto groan, a strange harmony which brought the security man to the open door. The pad fell to the floor, and the young man put a hand on Magnus' shoulder. Then he turned to the doctor.

"You speak English, don't you?"

14

"Yes."

"O.K., Doctor, what do we have here?"

"I'm not your father's . . ." He hesitated, then corrected, "Monsieur Macpherson's doctor. He'll be here . . ."

The cardiologist's hesitance to use the term "father" was caused by the records indicating that Magnus Macpherson had only two living children. He had already met them and was not sure who this young man might be.

"But you know what's going on?" the young man asked.

"Yes."

"Tell me. And don't worry about his hearing bad news. He can deal with it."

It was said quietly but with force.

"Monsieur Macpherson has had a cerebral thrombosis, which is a clotting in a blood vessel in the brain. We have determined it is not an intracerebral hemorrhage, or a tearing of the blood vessels, which is fortunate. How serious the thrombosis is, we cannot tell. Monsieur Macpherson arrived here in a coma, but he reacted quickly to an injection of procaine hydrochloride at the base of the spine, which is a good sign. He is receiving anticoagulants and cortisone to thin the blood so that no further damage can be done, and with the hope of dissolving the clotting."

"Prognosis?"

The doctor looked down at Magnus and decided to stick to the truth. "It is the veins. Monsieur Macpherson is seventy-one. At that age the veins can be sclerotic, brittle. Under too much pressure they can break; then we have the cerebral hemorrhage. The drugs can also cause damage; we can only use so much of them. Another problem is that a large section of the body is not working, and we cannot be sure to what extent that will, with time, affect other parts of the body. Any prognosis must include all these variables, and consequently . . ."

Jamie and WeeDee Macpherson came in the door.

"Hello, Gus," WeeDee said. Her green Chanel suit set off her red hair. Jamie said nothing. He was wearing the same dark suit as before, and looked as if he hadn't slept.

Gus looked at them with a smile through half-open eyes.

"Well, well, Jamie and WeeDee. Together, as you love them, folks!"

No one changed a look. Gus continued. "We were listening to the doctor give his prognosis. You two came in just on cue, as always."

WeeDee went over to Gus with a kiss, which he accepted but did not return.

"The executive terminal called us when your plane arrived. We've already heard the prognosis."

All three of them glanced down at Magnus, who met their eyes with a dangerous look.

Gus turned to WeeDee and Jamie with the same look.

"I get a feeling you two have been making all kinds of plans. Do we get to hear them?" The "we" referred to Magnus Macpherson and himself.

The cardiologist gestured for the nurse to follow him out, but WeeDee stopped him.

"Doctor, we'll need your advice about how soon my father can travel. Gus, the plane's being fitted with a bed so Father can fly back to the United States as soon as he's able. We want him to be as comfortable and as well cared for as possible." She gave a quick smile to Magnus. "And we want him near us. He'll go to Columbia Presbyterian as long as he needs to be there, then to Alabaster House in Connecticut."

"That's a nursing home, WeeDee."

"It's a private convalescent hospital. The best."

Gus was getting angry, but he controlled it and turned to Jamie, who had not spoken a word.

"And I'm sure there've been some plans about Macpherson Industries?"

WeeDee answered.

"Plans had to be made, Gus." She looked at the two watches on her wrist. "An announcement of Father's stroke was given to the wire services three hours ago in New York in time for morning editions. The full story will appear in my paper and the New York *Times*. It will say that I'm going on M.I.'s board of directors, and that Jamie and I will become co-chairmen of the Macpherson Foundation, that there will be no appreciable change in management or policy of either, and that we look forward to Father's speedy recovery. We figure the stock will dip five points at the most and recover two or three of those by the end of the week."

Gus quietly gave in to his anger.

"Very neat. Why the hell couldn't you have waited a few hours until I got here? You knew I couldn't leave Mexico City; we'd damn well have lost that Pemex oil. You knew that, so you—"

"Excuse us, Doctor." It was Jamie Macpherson. His voice was as colorless as his clothing.

"Of course." The cardiologist looked at the nurse, and she began to follow him out. But Magnus gagged, then groaned. His good leg had suddenly jerked up and locked, the muscles badly cramped. The nurse went immediately to the bed and began massage, gradually straightening the leg.

"The nurse can take care of him now," said the doctor. "She speaks very little English." He smiled ingratiatingly. "As to flying your father across the Atlantic, Dr. Bourget, of course, will have to give his official opinion. But *entre nous,* for your . . . 'plans' . . . I would guess in three more days." He gave a slight bow, and with a sense of being very discreet, glided out the door.

Gus went on, his anger growing.

"You knew damn well if you waited, I'd never let you even think about sticking him in a nursing home and waiting for him to die. I'm on the board, too. Aren't you pushing things a little? . . . And, by the way, what's happening to *his* stock?"

WeeDee looked at Jamie and sighed.

"Our lawyers went to court today in Manhattan to ask that power of attorney be granted to us as his children."

"Who?"

"Jamie and me."

Gus looked from one to the other with a bitter smile as he nodded at them.

"After all these years, you're finally calling me a bastard."

Jamie started talking, his words smooth as ice. "We had to move quickly, you know that. Your relationship would have taken time in the courts. Nobody's trying to do you out of anything that's yours."

"Yes, Jamie. But everything's got 'Macpherson' all over it. When the big hurry is over, are you and WeeDee going to give me a third of everything? I doubt it, don't you?"

WeeDee and Jamie were silent. Gus watched them for a moment; then, shaking his head, he turned to Magnus.

"Seems they have us both by the short hairs, Magnus. You aren't of sound mind or body to the courts, and I'm not a Macpherson to the courts."

"Gus, you're dreaming up phantoms to hate, just like you used to." WeeDee was smiling as she spoke, very calmly, like a mother rather than a sister. "No one's trying to cheat you. No one's using the word 'bastard' except you. We're doing what has to be done for

Father"—she included them all in the phrase with a look—"and for what he spent his life building."

"There it is. 'Spent'! You're thinking of him in the past tense. He isn't going to die. Does that fit into your plans?"

"We have no plans for Father dying." She glanced quickly at Magnus. "Only for his recovery."

"Everybody dies," Jamie said. He stood at the foot of the bed looking at Magnus Macpherson without emotion.

Gus smiled. "Well, that's true, Jamie. Everybody dies. And we sure as hell know all about it, don't we?"

Jamie barely glanced at him. "Your perverted attempt to take the place of a dead son by this fraudulent rescue attempt is transparent greed, Gus. We—"

"I'm not taking anyone's place except my own! And the dead son bit is your problem, Jamie. It always has been."

"Oh, shut up, Gus, both of you." WeeDee turned away and went to sit down. "Stop trying to shock us. We all know about death in this family."

The three of them were quiet, looking into the shadows in the room. Then Gus said, "I'll bet triple the points Macpherson stock advances when the Mexican deal is announced that Magnus is going to live to take it all back from you. And then he'll give it all to me."

He looked at Magnus, and again they laughed together.

"You closed the Pemex agreement?" Jamie asked, his monotone slightly higher than usual.

"Yeah, signed with a lot of fancy Mexican seals."

WeeDee stood up. They were all quiet and moved toward the bed.

"So," WeeDee said as she again lifted the hand on Magnus' bad side and held it, "Macpherson Industries is going to change whiskey into oil."

"It's a miracle," said Gus. "We could start a religion on that, and *really* get rich."

Jamie did not join in their exhilaration. His face had no lines for smiles.

As he groaned his laughter, Magnus Macpherson signed for the prescription pad, which was on the floor. The nurse picked it up, tore off the used sheet, and held it out. Magnus watched to see if she could read what he'd previously written to Gus: "I'll live. The nurse gave me a hard-on." She was blushing, so he knew she understood English. He wrote again, scrawling the letters carefully, and held it up for them to see: "Macpherson Industries *is* a religion."

The three of them read it. WeeDee squeezed the bad hand and put it under the sheet neatly.

"Get some rest, Father. We'll take you home in three days."

Jamie did nothing but turn away and walk out. WeeDee followed, asking the nurse to come with her. Gus whispered to Magnus, "They're ready for you to die. I'm not, so that makes two of us, and to hell with them. When you're ready to die, I'll take you home to Scotland."

After a final look, Gus turned away. At the door, WeeDee put her arm through his, and together they went into the hall.

Magnus Macpherson watched them go; he was alone again. The look on half his face relaxed to sardonic bemusement. He felt no pride, other than that they had all come. He knew their reasons were complex; each of them felt conflicting degrees of affection for and alienation from him. Their reasons involved all the usual excitements which flow around a rich man dying: money, power, possession, survival, the future.

But Magnus was certain he was not going to die. He was going to live; however, he was going to need some help. He wondered who was going to give him that help. Jamie, not one bit. WeeDee probably, but help as she saw fit. And Gus? Yes, Gus. Why? Because Gus needed Magnus alive and well. The other two didn't.

Home, Magnus thought. He wished for a glass of pure malt whiskey.

I
The Creation
1900–1933

"It's a complex fate, being an American."
—HENRY JAMES

1

Ane's sorrow, two's mirth,
three's a burial, four's a birth.
Five's a wedding, six brings scaith,
seven's money, eight's death.
—OLD SCOTTISH RHYME

They'd be looking for him; Magnus knew that. In the three days since his mother died, one or another had been looking for him. He had to decide the linen around her, the place in the back room for the board for her, the wooden platter to be placed on her breast for the salt and the earth. He had not cried once, not since she breathed the last phlegm-clogged breath through her rotten lungs. He had not cried when her eyes, which she had kept on him through the last of her dying, turned to their blue-marbled milk, nor when his older sister, Kath, cried out: "Mother!" and his younger sister, Kristin, thought by all to be touched by the fairies, sank to her knees with a sad queer grin on her face.

His father, the Reverend James Macpherson, reached slowly over and closed the dead eyes of his beloved. He had not been able to save her with all his entreaties to his God. He fell into a black silence which everyone knew to respect. Young Magnus, twelve at the time, was relied on for decisions. He made them, even about the killing of the cat which was seen jumping over the body by the women sitting through the long night. A cat passing over a corpse was accounted ominous of evil; it had to die.

The day of the funeral, before dawn, he had climbed to a favorite tor of Ben Rinnes from which he could look down at Dufftown and see the crooked cross of its two main streets. In a few hours he would cross the town square, leading mourners beside the kist in which his mother lay.

Magnus sat down and pressed his back against a familiar flatness of granite. The wind edged around the rock, and he tried to listen, but he had too much anger and impatience. Many mourners would share the weight of grief with the family; many loved his mother and had watched her die with their silent sorrow. But they accepted it, as she herself had done, as his own family had done. Their acceptance made him rage, and he denounced God.

"Her death is not just!"

He wished for an echo to repeat his accusations.

"And if God is not just"—he pressed himself closer to the granite, trusting its support—"there is no God."

Magnus knew there would be no answer. Only the wind of the mountain offered comfort. From the frustration of unvented anger, rather than sorrow for his mother, his tears came and fell. He wondered if the world had been created as a test or joke.

To the southeast, over Corryhabbie Hill, the sun rose through a fine mist, making a brilliant hole in the lavender sky. Magnus saw the green Glen Fiddich forest, and to the east the River Fiddich winding through its pale limestone bed to its sharp turn west into Dufftown. Beauty on such a day only compounded his bitterness.

By the time Magnus Macpherson had come down the braes of Ben Rinnes, his life was in his own hands. He was separate from all those who accepted death on any terms but doing battle. He was tall for his age, and awkward with his sudden size. Sometimes when he moved, he moved farther than he expected, and there had been accidents. The worst had been his ma's favorite blue china pitcher. The moment he thought of it, it reminded him of his mother's blue dead eyes looking at him beyond her last, the pitcher crashing in pieces at his feet. Those eyes had held him with a silent urging for the living of his life.

Magnus' life had begun in the first months of the new century, the significance of which was not lost on the Reverend James Macpherson. As soon as he could wrest the bairn from the arms of his mother, he took him on the required "higher movement" right up on the roof. He walked with him seven times around the house sunwise. Then he gave him his first washing, careful to leave the right hand alone to ensure the child would not know poverty.

Magnus had grown up much like any other young Scottish boy. He was not an outstanding student; he had a difficult time learning what he did not wish to learn. His teachers at the Mortlach Senior Secondary School considered him bright but stubborn in his intellectual pursuits. It was as if he sensed from the beginning that his life would be long, and he had the time to wait and watch.

Father and son saw little of each other after Mrs. Macpherson died. Occasionally they would share a night on the brae together. Magnus learned about distilling whiskey under the careful eye of an expert. He also learned about a careful nose and tongue. For if the truth were known, the Reverend Mr. Macpherson gained his reputation with his care of the body as well as the soul. He used two vital skills: his praying extempore and his distilling exemplary.

The cleric was fortunate in his calling. Dufftown, his parish, was located where the River Fiddich and Dullen Water met, the most ideal confluence of pure lime water in the Highlands. Because of the water, some eighteen of the finest single malt whiskeys were distilled in the area. When blended with tasteless corn-grain spirits, these "malts" were what gave taste and body to what the world knows and loves as "Scotch."

In spite of being surrounded by the finest malts in great variety, the Reverend James Macpherson preferred his own product, which he called "The Creation." He also preferred not to pay tax to some foreign (Edinburgh or London) government.

On a brae south of Dufftown, the cleric had discovered, by falling into it, a cave having no other entrance. A burn of good lime water flowed through it, which served his needs perfectly. Although the place was always cold and windy, both father and son would work up a sweat on the first night hauling up their supplies. When they reached the entrance to the cave, invisible by day as well as by night, the Reverend Mr. Macpherson would take off the layers of heather laid there. Then together they would lift the planking across the entrance, climb down the ladder, return the planking, and begin The Creation.

On the first night, they would anchor the sacks of barley in the burn to allow the grain to soak for a few days. When the hard starch of the grain was softened, they would return and lay it out on the rocky floor of the cave to let it germinate. Over the next week to ten days the Reverend Mr. Macpherson would spread and turn the swollen barley each night, allowing Magnus to catch up on his sleep. The germinated barley gave him what was called a perfect "malt."

The next step was mashing, for which Magnus was needed. To stop further germination beyond its perfection, the malt was scooped up and put in a peat-fired kiln. This gave the malt a distinctive peaty taste. Then they transferred the dried malted barley to a forty-gallon cauldron to boil in the pure lime waters from the burn for several hours. This brew was the mash. When the boiling was done, he and Magnus drained the liquid, and poured it into a fermenting vat. Then they added the barm, or yeast, to the worts. The magic of the ferment began.

Those who disapproved of the Reverend Mr. Macpherson's nocturnal occupation accused the good cleric of receiving the barm from the fairies, as an advance on their share of the final product. The Reverend Mr. Macpherson did nothing to dispel the rumor, being certain of its merchandising value. The barm was vital: what actually happened in fermenting was that yeast, put into the vat with a careful introduction, proceeded to mix socially with the worts, or sugar-infused liquid. Having gained such a familiarity, the yeast then proceeded to eat the worts as fast as it could ingest them. The yeast then would excrete the most valuable essence of The Creation, tasty alcohol. A truth which Magnus enjoyed was that what the world loves and drinks as whiskey is nothing more than quality distilled yeast shit.

Fermenting took about two days. The next step took the greatest skill and care: the distilling.

They judged the ferment by the size of the snowballs of bloated barm floating on the top. Under the cauldron, a peat fire was built to a careful heat. Together father and son lifted a large pot with a tube coming out of its side to the top of the cauldron, making a tight fit. Working quickly, they connected the tube to a worm of copper coil, which ran down through a barrel of cold water and came out at the bottom through a spigot.

When the first distillation known as low wine was complete, and Magnus had transferred it to the saving cauldron, they picked up a branch from a rowan tree, each hit the cauldron with it twice for luck, and shook hands. Then the Reverend Mr. Macpherson ran the low wine into the boiling cauldron once again, and the final step began.

The first parts of the distillate were oily and were known as foreshots. But then the bead of the liquor would clear and begin to flow.

On one such night, when Magnus was fourteen, the liquor was of a superior quality, and the Reverend Mr. Macpherson broke out in song, singing one of his favorite Easter hymns, which season it was. When the verses were finished, Magnus, moving with a bucket of water to cool the coil barrel, asked his father a question that had troubled him for years.

"Pa, when you preach against the drinking, standing there in the pulpit where you store the good whiskey you make, you're preaching against your own self, are you not?"

"Magnus, hear me now." He propped the pitcher under the spigot and sat down next to it. Then he looked at his son.

"There are the laws of God and the laws of man, and neither are written in the books. Written-down laws change with time and geography. God's law and Man's law don't change. In the end they're both the same. They're both about the wanting. And the wanting never changes."

"But God can have whatever He wants, can't He, Pa?" Magnus asked.

His father gave a great sigh and tasted the liquor from the spigot.

"Not since the curiosity got to Him and He decided to make human beings. The irony of it: all God wants is good, and He went and dreamed us up. It was perverse, to say the least of it." He shook his head with compassion.

"Maybe He was bored."

The Reverend Mr. Macpherson let out a laugh which roiled the smoke from the peat fire lingering above him.

"He must have been. He must have been, like His son Jesus at the wedding at Cana must have been bored. He summoned up His miraculous powers for the very first time and changed water into whiskey."

"Was it not wine, Pa?"

"Remember what I told you about geography. If Jesus had lived in Scotland, it would have been whiskey. And that's all I do, is imitate our Lord Jesus, trying as best I can to satisfy the laws of God and man. I see them clearly, not in the church canons or the nation's statutes, but in the wanting . . . and that's the true secret."

"What is the true secret, Pa?"

The Reverend Mr. Macpherson stood up and came to look at the level of the fire.

"Hear me now, Magnus. If you know the wanting, and can give to it, you will be rewarded greatly."

Magnus looked at his father, who was staring into the fire as if he saw God and the devil together.

"Rewarded with what, Pa?"

"Power. . . . Give to the wanting. Give God goodness whenever you can. It's all He wants. And with humans, great bouncing balls of unmitigated fire! The wanting of humans is infinite. And for him who can give to it, the price will be paid gladly." The Reverend Mr. Macpherson turned from the fire and looked into his son's face for a moment. Then he went back and sat beside the spigot.

As he cooled down the fire, Magnus wondered for the first and last time, "Why do people have the wanting?" Then he dismissed the question. It was beside the point and only God's concern . . . maybe. The wanting was there. Then a new thought occurred to Magnus: "Always be sure they have the wanting for what you can give them."

The Reverend Mr. Macpherson corked the final cask, let the tailings run off, and together they damped the fire. As they walked slowly home, pleased with their night's work, the Reverend James Macpherson said, "You were born with the first month of the new century. It's your century, son. And it's not me nor anyone that's giving it to you, not even God. It's you who's going to take it. But it won't be here, son. This century's place is America. And when you get there, don't be poor like we've been. Gi'e to the wanting. Be rich and be an American."

From that moment, Magnus knew where he was going and spent the rest of his childhood waiting to get there. He had to go to war first, as if it were a ceremony of growing up and going away. Near Bapaume, in France, soon after he was eighteen, Magnus joined the Gordon Highlanders of the 51st Highland Division of the British Third Army. He arrived at the front on the twentieth of March 1918, in a drizzle and a thick fog.

At five o'clock the next morning, six thousand German guns opened fire simultaneously along a forty-five-mile front from the Sensée River to the Oise. The bombardment went on for four and one-half hours.

Magnus had little time to talk with the other men. One asked how old he was, shook his head, and whistled at the answer. Another asked his home, nodded, and said to himself, "Glasgow."

They checked their bayonets. At 9:30 they heard their machine guns. At 9:40 they saw the green flares make a muck of the red sky, and before they saw the yellow of the gas mixing in with it, they smelled the stench of mustard, and the cry for gas masks went up and down the line.

The Germans were there. Not ten feet away, black figures, making no noise, came out of the mottled fog with the bizarre suddenness of a theatrical cue. One plunged over the parapet and jammed his thigh down on Magnus' bayonet. The German fell sitting, with the blade cutting deep into his groin and lodging in bone. The force of his fall flipped Magnus' rifle in his arms and pulled him down on top of the German, who was thrashing like an animal nailed to a board. Magnus got to his feet, yanked at his rifle, but the bayonet was too firmly lodged. The German was kicking violently. He felt someone behind him, pulled the trigger, and blew his bayonet free in time to pivot and jam the rifle butt through the glass of another gas mask. He heard the skull crack. He then shot three other Germans, but not before one of them put a bayonet into Magnus' left arm. He heard the cry to fall back. For a moment there were no more Germans, but the second wave would be coming. He looked around. He saw the man from Glasgow sitting up against the revetment timbers, sinking in mud, blood pouring from a wound in his right side. Magnus reached down for the man and tried to pull him up. But the man swung at him.

"Don't be noble wi' me, chiel. You're alone, and don't forget it." He smiled and died with the exertion.

The war was eight months from armistice when Magnus joined it. On the eleventh hour of the eleventh day of the eleventh month of 1918, it ended in an exhausted silence broken by the exhalation of a few cheers. Magnus spent that Christmas in Cologne, giving his holiday rations away to hungry children and losing his virginity for the price of a chocolate bar to a young girl he met outside the cathedral.

Within a week he was in London, where he was treated like a hero by the cheering crowds, as were the thousands of other troops pouring through to be mustered out and returned home. Magnus sat alone in Green Park trying to understand the number "ten million" and to conceive of that number of men dying in a war. He thought of the man from Glasgow, over and over again, dying in the trench, saying, "You're alone, and don't forget it."

Then he was mustered out and traveled north by train to see his family. He arrived unannounced at Dufftown station, a year older, no longer a stranger to the world or the century, but as he walked the mile from the station, he knew he was a stranger in his own town.

He stayed in Dufftown only long enough for his father to arrange for him to ship out as a seaman's apprentice on a clipper from Spey Bay carrying whiskey to Nassau. It was not the whole way to America, but it would be close enough for Magnus to work his way for the rest of his passage. The clippers were no longer going directly to the United States, because the Americans, God Himself knew why, had decided to go dry.

Magnus left Dufftown on one of those days when the light seemed to slant through prisms and an expectation of rainbows came as a fine rain passed eastward under the westward sun. Kath, Kristin, and the Reverend Mr. Macpherson saw him to the station and said goodbye with a silent holding.

Within a week Magnus was violently seasick, trying to be a deckhand to a cargo of twelve thousand cases of the Glenlivet. That same week, in America, the Eighteenth Amendment was ratified.

All the major distillers of the United States began to focus on Nassau, its perfect harbor, its warehousing facilities, and its sleepy frontier-of-the-Empire law enforcement. Itinerant sailors arrived who owned crafts of questionable seaworthiness, advertised themselves as ready for charter. Members of American gangs were sent to the island by their organizations to prepare the supply of product for the illegal market. Prohibition brought profit to paradise.

By the time Magnus arrived, the bootlegging activities in Nassau had reached nervous levels of activity. The thirst in which the new citizens of Nassau believed with blind avarice began to take hold in the United States. The parched cry from the American mainland could be heard loud and clear, and a marketplace was already established: an area of ocean outside the three-mile limit running between Cape May, New Jersey, and Montauk Point. It was called Rum Row.

The historical bootlegger was one who sold whiskey to the Indians on the frontier, carrying the liquor in a flask in his boot. On his first day in Nassau in the spring of 1919, Magnus saw bootleggers who did not bear the slightest resemblance to that image. Bootlegging had become an all-inclusive term referring to anyone involved in the process of getting illegal liquor to those devoted hordes who wanted it.

On Bay Street Magnus saw the sweating suppliers in their soaked-through linen suits hustling from ships to wharf, stockpiling cases and barrels, arranging for them to be hauled to warehouses. He saw the entrepreneurs who had sent whiskey stocks to Nassau and were sitting on their investments, haggling for the price of whiskey to go their way. He saw the lines of schooners, ketches, yawls, and luggers with their crews waiting to be hired for a run to the mainland. And he saw men who wore hats down low on their faces, in broad-lapelled and strangely patterned suits and pointed shoes, moving through all the conversations, saying little, occasionally recognizing someone with a hard nod, and never talking business on the sidewalk.

Under the hot, wet tropical sun, the native blacks moved among the sponge, fish, and produce markets. They carried impossible loads on top of their heads from the ships, from the farms, and from the warehouses. Magnus always remembered the smell in Bay Street of the special sweat that rose in the presence of fast money. That day was the first time he saw a bluidy Englishman sweat, and he realized that they did not mop their brows because the gesture would have been considered a weakness in the intensity of haggling.

Magnus came ashore carrying a canvas bag with one change of clothes in it, a brief kit, and his kilt, dirk, and sporran in case of a special occasion. He had enough money to last him three days if he stayed in a hotel, or a week if he did not. On his first walk up and down Bay Street he looked for what jobs might be open to him. All the noise and hurry was oppressive to him after his weeks at sea. People ran into him without as much as a "Sorry." As he moved into the street, he barely avoided being run over by the donkey-drawn drays hauling their twenty-five-case loads of liquor to the warehouses. A black policeman yelled at him for interfering with traffic.

He soon left Bay Street and wandered behind it up the hill away from the wharves. There he found a different town, one of stately palm trees, banana trees, lemon, lime, and coconut. There were languid white houses with jalousied windows behind stone walls with bougainvilleas and hibiscus blooming in burning combinations of color. He glimpsed parasols and long white dresses on porches. In one backyard there was a delicate china tea service with a green tapestried cozy keeping it hot for the steaming afternoon. A woman came out and saw him gazing at the tea service. She hesitated, looking at him with apprehension. He stared for a moment, wondering if he would ever belong in such a fragile, gracious scene.

For the first two days Magnus looked around. The first two nights he slept on the beach to the west of town, using his kilt as a cover and washing himself in the sea. He learned that jobs were numerous, but to get anything better than stevedoring took a good record of employment. He also learned that anything to know of the bootlegging world was heard over the bar at the Lucerne Hotel on Frederick Street. On the third night, at the bar, Magnus found his first job and took his first professional step into the liquor business.

The Lucerne was a three-story wooden structure with wide porches, galleries, gardens, and a row of palm trees around it. Other hotels in the town might have been considered, relatively speaking, more opulent. But the Lucerne had an atmosphere conducive to bootleggers, and became their hangout.

When Magnus walked into the bar, carrying his canvas bag with him, he found it dark and noisy. The haggling had moved in from Bay Street, card games were played at three tables, and in a corner, a dice game with loud yelling at every point progressed.

"Don't fiddle the dice, you bastid."

"O.K., four-flusher, match that."

"Match what, beard-jammer? Looks like cockleberries to me."

"How about something on the side, cellar-smeller?"

"Stop the chin music; play the African golf."

The dice were thrown, followed by cheers and groans. A sailor grabbed the dice.

"They're eggs!" meaning that the center, like a yolk, had dropped to one side, influencing their fall.

A fist was thrown and everyone grabbed his money. With practiced dexterity the bartender cleared the bar of anything breakable and ducked. Magnus stayed clear of the fight, but saw that the money on the floor had included thousand-dollar bills.

Someone threw a chair, and as if it were her cue, a little gray-haired lady in her sixties appeared at the door. She took a bottle proffered by the bartender, walked over to the confusion, and smashed the bottle on a table. As quickly, the fighting stopped, and the little lady said, holding the jagged bottle neck in front of her, "Now, you gentlemen know if this continues I'll have to ask Tommy to close the bar."

"Yeah, Mother" was muttered throughout the room.

"And I'll expect whoever had the pleasure of throwing that chair to pay for it."

Everyone looked at the guilty party, a man in a silk brocade vest with mossy teeth.

"Yeah, Mother," he said, and headed to the bar. The little lady smiled her sweetest smile and walked back out the door, leaving the bottle neck on the table. Money was returned to the floor and the suspected dice were replaced. Enthusiasm was again voiced, the anger repressed for another time, and the game went on. Tommy appeared again, and with the same adroitness repositioned the bottles. He received twenty dollars from the moss-mouthed gentleman, glided over to Magnus, and in a hard cockney asked if he might like a drink.

"Ello, mate. A li-le sompn?"

Magnus could not afford a lager, but did not wish anyone to know it. Part of Tommy's talent was to know right away.

"Would you be havin any malt whiskey?"

"Ah, a Eyelander, for sure. Tike a peek." He opened a locked cabinet behind the bar and displayed a collection of twenty-three pure Scottish malts with pride. "What's yer preference? You're new, so I'll mike the first on the ouse, as an hinvestment."

Magnus made his choice and Tommy poured.

"Lookin fer work?"

Magnus nodded. Tommy looked him over, taking in his size, then smiled, and moved down the bar, saying, "Drink yer broth."

Magnus was glad to, but determined to make the malt last the evening. He turned to the room and saw men trying to relax their desperation, greed, and anticipation. He watched them, until he felt someone looking him over.

At thirty years of age, Grace Lithgoe described herself as "a woman with a past that was nobody's business." She was tall, thin, and had a knowing smile. One eye was just off center to the inside, not enough to be cross-eyed, but enough to make a close look from her seem to burn as a warning. Magnus saw the warning and disregarded it. He noticed instead her lush-complexioned skin, black hair, and a deep dimple on one side of her face.

She had traveled the world, and came to Nassau representing the great Scottish distillers Haig and McTavish. Her job was to see that their whiskey was safely stored, then sailed to market and sold for the best price. Her pleasure was men, and her interest in Magnus was immediate.

Most of the men in Nassau were wary of a woman who was smart and ambitious. She played poker with anyone ready to lose, and not even the sharpies who came over from the mainland got away with cheating her. When she wanted something, she usually baited the right trap to get it. And she could be pungent bait if she chose. That night she chose Magnus Macpherson.

Grace was sitting at a table with Bill McCoy. McCoy, who would give his name to the language as "the real McCoy" and get little in return, was a tall man with a big voice and a bigger laugh.

With him were George Murphy, McCoy's supplier, Frenchy Rivet, his cook on board, and Loren Lathrop, the U.S. consul in the Bahamas. No business was discussed at the table in order not to compromise Loren Lathrop's position. As the United States' representative in Nassau, Lathrop watched a great many men legally preparing to break the law of his country. Some of these men, like McCoy, were his friends, and men to be admired.

Magnus met the look Grace was giving him until Tommy came up behind him.

"This ere is Mr. Erter, and e as a problem."

Magnus turned to see a man with a mean face and a withered arm, who said, "I've got fifteen hundred cases of gin on a wharf to get loaded on a schooner by dawn, or I lose my deal. You interested?"

Mr. Herter was an American, a charterer, one of the numerous middlemen who matched a boat to a specific delivery.

"I'm interested, if you're payin'."

"It's nigger work and I can't find any of them. Came up at the last minute, ya see—"

"And yer in a hurry . . ." Magnus said.

He watched the man's forehead rise in surprise, and the sneer harden.

"I'll give ya four dollars an hour. It's usually three, but it's late."

"Late it is, so make it eight dollars an hour and you've got a stevedore."

"Eight? You must be jagged."

"I'm sober enough to know I'll be saving you about a hundred times what you pay me for the night. Oh, and you'll have to be paying Tommy for my drink."

If Magnus had not been so big, he might have felt a bomber from Mr. Herter's good arm. But he was big, and his mathematics were sound, so after a dyspeptic moment of staring, Mr. Herter flipped a coin on the mahogany bar and said, "Come on. You Scots are worse than Jews."

"We're trying to be."

Mr. Herter headed for the door.

Tommy was smiling broadly. "Ere, tike is money, hit's yours."

"No. I like you owing me one."

As he walked out, Magnus glanced at Grace Lithgoe. She had heard it all. He was glad.

Magnus spent the rest of the night moving cases from a wharf, up a gangplank and down into the hold of a schooner. He stacked them tight against the bulwarks under the careful and unfriendly eyes of the captain. The work was hard, and after the first few hours, Magnus' back began to pain him where the cases lay on it, and his legs turned thick and wobbly. But a half-hour before the sun hit the topsail of the schooner, Magnus watched Mr. Herter flip off forty-eight dollars cash from a large roll, using the fingers of his one good hand. Magnus sat on the wharf as the crew of the schooner cast off. Heavy in the water, she sailed westward around Hog's Island, the reef a half-mile off the shore.

"Hey, you."

He knew who it was. He turned and wiped sweat down his chest to his stomach.

"Me?"

"Yes, you." Grace walked over to him. He did not wipe his hand on his pants, but let it hang, dripping.

"You're up early . . . or late," Magnus said.

"It took longer than I thought to clean those guys at poker." She was very close to him, and with no modesty looked his body over. "You ever been on a boat?"

"How do you think I got here, walkin on the waters?"

The sun appeared over Hog's Island. Neither of them took notice.

"If you can keep your smart mouth shut and give a listen, I might have a better job for you. A friend of mine has a boat, and he's looking for a supercargo."

"Who's yer friend?"

"McCoy."

"A good friend to have."

"You know anything about sailing?"

"Just not to put any of the body's liquids into the wind."

Grace guffawed. "You do have a smart mouth. You think you could learn anything?"

Magnus looked at her cocked eyes and knew there were two questions for which she was looking for an answer. He reached out his wet hand, put it on her shoulder, feeling the quiver there, and answered both of them.

"I'm a gleg learner."

"You'll have to tell me what the hell that means sometime."

"I'll be glad to show you what the hell, anytime you want."

She smiled, but only said, "I'll tell McCoy you'll be around at two this afternoon."

"I'll be there. What do I owe you for this, then?"

Grace looked him over again, slowly.

"I'll think of something special." She turned and walked on down Bay Street.

Magnus went back to the Lucerne Hotel. The gray-haired lady

who had entered the melee the night before was sitting at the front desk.

"Good morning," she said, her clear blue eyes glinting hospitality. "Welcome to the Lucerne."

"Thank you, madam. I was wondering if I might have a bath."

"Of course you can, if you'll register. My name is Mrs. Sweeting."

"And mine's Macpherson, and may I say, you were elegant last night in the bar."

"Oh. Thank you, Mr. Macpherson. Did you think so? Well."

She leaned forward with a smile of conspiracy. "You've guessed my secret: elegance. Please don't tell a soul."

Magnus and Mrs. Sweeting became good friends. He took up residence at the Lucerne in a small back room she rented to him by the month. He did her many favors of delivering and receiving, and paid attention to her elegance, which endeared him to her.

He met McCoy that afternoon aboard the *Marshall*. McCoy had come in a week before with another ship, the *Arethusa*, and was playing with the idea of being a shipping tycoon rather than a sailor.

"I'm straight with my crews. This is gangster booze we're moving off Atlantic City. They aren't the friendliest people to deal with, but their money's good, and they offer protection from the Coast Guard. I pay my supercargoes one hundred dollars a month, and a hundred-dollar bonus when you get back to Nassau. You're going to have to start loading in now, and you'll sail at midnight. You want it?"

"I'm not much of a sailor."

McCoy nodded, appreciating the honesty.

"You only have to hang on. I can see you can lift a ham or two."

A "ham" was a pyramid of bottles, each wrapped in corrugated paper, stacked 3-2-1, and sewed up in burlap with double sail twine. McCoy's supplier, George Murphy, had invented the packaging, having realized the distillers' cases took up too much room in the holds of rum-running ships.

"I'm with you, Mr. McCoy."

"And since you were ace with me, I'll be ace with you. I don't know this crew. I know they can sail the *Marshall*, but . . . just watch out for yourself."

"I will."

"I'll be coming up from Miami on a train to meet you with one of the boys from their 'syndicate' as soon as I get the *Arethusa* under sail."

He turned to look at his prize, freshly painted white, with new rigging, sails, topmasts, and a raking bowsprit, which would allow her to set a flying jib. Magnus saw her, too, and wished he were going aboard the *Arethusa* rather than the *Marshall*. But this was too big a chance to be choosy. He wanted to get on board anything which would float close to America.

He started loading hams aboard the *Marshall* right away. He had to hurry before they sailed out of the harbor in the light of a near-full moon.

While he was working, Grace Lithgoe came by to see McCoy on business. She met Magnus on the gangplank.

"So," she said.

"So. We sail at midnight. I won't have an opportunity to express my thanks."

They were both quiet for a moment, looking at each other.

"You can owe me," she said, almost as a whisper.

"I don't like debts."

She smiled and said carefully, so no one else could hear, "Don't worry about it. . . . I'll get my pounds of flesh."

Then she saw McCoy.

"Bill, what's this balloon juice I hear about you only wanting a thousand of my Haig? I know damn well you're taking two thousand of that Dewar's banana oil. You're going to ruin yourself selling stagnant bilge like that. . . ."

She walked head-on into McCoy's bear hug and laugh, and they haggled at the top of their lungs for the *Marshall* to carry at least five hundred more cases of Haig's perfection. Magnus watched the slim flanks under her long black skirt, and the tight muscles around her pelvic cradle. Her breasts were firm and high and she arched her neck as she went about convincing McCoy. Magnus wanted her that moment, more than he'd ever wanted a woman before. With a regret for not being able to satisfy his debt that instant, even though the suggested collateral was ready, he went back to the work of loading hams.

McCoy was right; the crew of the *Marshall* were a silent bunch. For the first three days, Magnus did not feel like talking. As they passed off Cape Hatteras, he got his stomach back and noticed that the crew's silence had a reason: from the captain down to the deckhands, all were helping themselves to the cargo.

Silent drunks are often mean drunks; when Magnus mentioned something about the situation to the captain, he was told to shut up or be lashed to the mast for the rest of the trip. Magnus realized he was the only sober man on board, and the only one who knew nothing about sailing. He was amazed that even with the amount of liquor they consumed, they kept the *Marshall* well trimmed and under sail. But as the cook got drunker, they ate less. Luckily, the weather was good and they made fine progress before a southwesterly breeze.

They reached their destination off Atlantic City in less than twelve days. While finding their place on Rum Row to meet the contact boats, the captain, mate, and crew decided to avail themselves of a particular brothel on shore. Magnus learned of their decision only when he came up from clearing the cargo from the bulwarks, readying the hams for unloading. As he appeared on deck he saw the last of the crew slipping over the side into a skiff for the short row into the beach. The row was very short, for while Magnus had been below, the captain had brought the *Marshall* close enough to shore to see the boardwalk. He also neglected to bring in any sail before he left the ship.

"You're welcome to come with us," he yelled up to Magnus. "No room in the boat, but you can hang on to the gunwale."

A blather of levity followed from the crew.

"I think I'll stay here. My chances are better for not sinkin."

They left Magnus alone on the two-masted schooner in full sail, with 2,700 cases of illicit booze in the hold.

He was lucky; he had good weather and a lot of water. The first thing he had to do was get out of sight of Atlantic City, so he ran to the wheel and tried to get the feel of the rudder under him. He became adept at ducking the boom as it came across and back again, deflecting a wind which Magnus was too busy to worry about.

When he was out of sight of land, Magnus concerned himself with keeping a course, filling the sails, and gaining a sense of the wind's direction. Then he lashed the wheel and hurried to the bow to bring in the jib sails, which were in a confusion from all the luffing. When the wind changed, he rushed aft to the wheel, ducked the boom, and felt the force of the rudder turning against her course, forcing the schooner back off-wind.

He plotted his course with the compass and ship's clock, going southeast for a quarter-hour, then bringing her around and heading back northwest for a quarter of an hour. However, this navigation did not allow for drift, wind, or current. By sunset the *Marshall* was not only considerably north-northwest of where McCoy had hoped to meet it, but was out of the area where the gang had paid for its Coast Guard protection. When Magnus again brought her around to a northwest tack, he saw the USS *Seneca,* a Coast Guard cutter, about three hundred yards off his port bow and closing fast. He was startled enough to forget about the boom and was knocked senseless on the deck.

The next thing he remembered was being yanked off a cot by two Coast Guardsmen and hustled off the *Seneca* down the gangplank to a waiting paddy wagon. The back of his head hurt badly. He could not touch it because he had wrist manacles on. He knew he was in New York because the paddy wagon had "NYPD" on its side. As the grilled-windowed doors were slammed shut, he caught a glimpse of the *Marshall,* tied up behind the *Seneca.* She was covered with police, who were carrying out hams like ants moving their eggs to safety.

The paddy wagon was filled with other prisoners, but it was too dark to see any faces. They smelled of cheap perfume, sweat, and urine. Magnus could not breathe, and lost consciousness. He barely remembered staggering up endless metal stairs, hearing clanging gates and locks opening, iron bars closing behind him. He was thrown into a cell and fell on the floor as the last lock rattled into silence. He felt hands going through his pockets and tried to struggle against them. He vomited where he lay, heard guttural whispers, and felt a kick in his stomach. He felt like throwing up again, but knew he better not, and almost passed out with the effort. He lay quietly on the floor, realizing he had arrived in America.

A day later, Magnus was awakened choking on smelling salts. A short man with lines of fatigue around his eyes held a pencil flashlight, examining him.

"There we are, nice dilation. He'll be fine to start rotting away in here." The man laughed apologetically, then shook his head at his own despair with the place.

"You hear me all right?"

Magnus nodded and grimaced at the pain it caused his head.

"What d'ya got there? Bad head?" He prodded until he hit the sore spot.

"Ah, a little concussion . . . no fracture, or you wouldn't be feeling as good as you do." Again he laughed at his own sad humor.

"Well, I'll tell you, they won't let me X-ray you, so I'd just sit here and take it easy. Eat as much as you can keep down. They're coming right in to question you, so save your strength. I'll tell 'em about the concussion. . . . How old are you?"

"Twenty."

"You're a juvenile, get your lawyer to—"

The guard interrupted.

"Come on, Doc, stop with the law practice. They're all the same breed of bug. Can they get at him for questioning?"

The doctor looked down at Magnus. He laughed and said, "The baying of the hounds is near." The laugh stifled itself, he closed his eyes, shook his head, picked up his medicine bag, and moved out of the cell.

"He's got a concussion. If you shove him around, he'll heave all over you."

The guards handled Magnus with care, leading him out of the cell and to a small dark room off the cellblock. The four men in the room questioned him until he could not talk straight. They asked about who owned the boat, who sold the liquor to the captain, who was supposed to buy it, and what he knew about syndicates, Arnold Rothstein, the Unione Siciliane, where the boat was bound to meet its contact boats, and after the sale of liquor, was it going to Bermuda, Bimini, Nova Scotia, Nassau, where?

Magnus could honestly claim ignorance to most of these questions; to others, he played dumb. He did not mention McCoy by name. When confronted by the registered ownership of the *Marshall,* he offered nothing except that he was a supercargo concerned with loading and unloading. He kept repeating this until his speech slurred and they allowed him to return to his cell.

There were bunk beds, but because of his head Magnus preferred to sit on the floor up against the wall. His cellmate was a tall, emaciated Greek who spent the days picking his nose. At night, he would reach around his top bunk and rub balls of mucus into the bottom of his mattress just above Magnus' bunk. He spoke no English; Magnus was glad.

For three days Magnus sat on the floor and tried to understand what had happened. He was marched in a long row to a mess hall. He sat, staring at his plate, eating automatically, looking around the huge room. He tried to distinguish faces, but they all seemed alike. He wondered what a mirror would show him, if his own face were included. ". . . all the same breed of bug." He would march back to his cell, the stench of the toilet there making him want to vomit anything he had succeeded in eating. Then they would lead him off to be questioned by Coast Guard officers, by treasury agents, asking the same questions: the syndicates, destinations, McCoy, Unione Siciliane, buyers, Rothstein.

Back in his cell, he thought about the choices he had made, of leaving Dufftown, leaving Scotland. He could have stayed. What a luxury of choice that was, the richness of staying, yet the greater richness of going.

He looked around his cell. The choices he'd made since going on the *Marshall* had landed him in a place where choice was wrung out like oil from a haddock on a crofter's board. God, he thought, is this the place I'm to be?

No. There's always a choice. I choose to survive, God damn me for it if He will. I'll not be a bug, not here in America. How in bluidy hell do I get out of here?

It was night when they came for him again. By then he had examined the lock on his cell, learned the guard's routine, located three potential hiding places in the cell for utensils he was planning to steal from the mess hall. When they led him down the cellblock, he kept track of the number of steps, noticing the positions of guards and checkpoints, which windows were free of bars on the ground floor through which he might get free with a hostage.

But they took him past the room where he was usually questioned, past the final checkpoint, and then there were no more bars. The guards left him in a room with an avuncular police officer who gave him a kindly stare and asked, "Magnus Macpherson?"

Magnus nodded.

"You got twelve hours to get out of the United States. But let me give you some advice: only take one."

"And how am I to do that?"

The police officer nodded in return and said, "There's a gentleman outside waiting to see you."

"What gentleman?"

"I believe you'll notice his car."

The officer called for the guards, who took Magnus to the front door and held it open for him. Magnus had a momentary temptation to run, but decided on a more dignified exit. He nodded to the guards and walked down the steps as if he knew exactly what was happening to him. Immediately he saw the car.

The officer had been right; the car could not be missed. It was a long black Packard with spoke wheels and enormous white balloon tires. The chrome of its headlamps and grille gleamed from a streetlight, and the leather straps holding the spare tire and bootbox on the back shone from saddle soap and polish. When he reached the sidewalk, Magnus stopped, unsure of how to approach such opulence. A man opened the door of the back seat and gestured to come over.

Three men sat on the back seat. Magnus stepped in and the door slammed shut behind him.

"Mr. Macpherson, sorry, but you'll have to sit on the floor."

Magnus did so, stretching his legs across the car, leaning up against the door. The car began to move immediately.

"My name is Arnold Rothstein," said the man in the center, "and I appreciate you dummying up the last three days. You took it in the neck and did yourself proud."

To Magnus, Rothstein was extraordinarily elegant, his clothes fitting perfectly, his tie the richest silk, his cufflinks diamonds, and his hands immaculate, the nails shining. He never smiled. Magnus thought it was because the man trusted the words he spoke without needing a facial expression for emphasis or moderation.

"I'm sure Mr. McCoy appreciates it, too," Rothstein said.

Magnus was startled to hear the name. One of the other men said, "You bet he does," and chuckled.

"I have a favor to ask you," Rothstein continued.

Magnus smiled. "I have a feeling I owe you one."

Rothstein dismissed the owing with a flick of his hand, and nodded to the man on his left, who gave Magnus a small carpetbag. Magnus took it and held it in his arms.

"I want you to give that to Mr. McCoy for me."

"Am I to be seeing Mr. McCoy, then?"

"Soon. I only trust someone with the kind of money in that keister for a short time. Mr. McCoy said you could be trusted. We're taking you to Long Island to meet a contact boat unloading Mr. McCoy's schooner. You'll go out on it with the payment. Agreed?"

Magnus nodded; then the three men on the seat began talking in low tones to each other. The name he had been asked about in the prison over and over again was Rothstein. He looked at the man's perfect haircut, the resplendent shine on the shoes. There was more than a visible splendor. There was a power Magnus could feel which excited him. Rothstein could open prisons. He could afford trust. He could glide through the streets in a car a king would covet. Magnus tried to look up over the windowsills to see where the car was going.

Arnold Rothstein glanced down and without any warning tone said, "You got a hundred and fifty G's and a cannon in your lap. Keep your eye on those. The scenery's 1 . . . ." He stopped before saying "lousy" and said, "boring" instead.

Magnus took his advice and sat patiently on the floor of the car. He was amazed with the change in his luck from prison to a limousine. This place America. The extremes of possibility seemed very wide. The limousine drove silently through towns, then farms, finally to a beach, and stopped.

"Good, the contact boat's on the beach. Max, take a look at her. I'll get five more. They'll make anything the Coast Guard has look like can openers."

The man called Max got out of the already opened door. Rothstein looked down on the floor.

"All set, Macpherson?"

Magnus moved to get out, but Rothstein held on to his shoulder and said quietly, "The cannon in the bag. When you get out deep, you'd be doing someone a favor if you sank it."

The gun had been used by Umberto Anastasio, one of Rothstein's many "soldiers," to kill someone named Joe Turino. Anastasio was now in jail facing the death sentence.

Magnus nodded, got out, and without looking back, walked across the dark sand to where a five-ton truck was being loaded with hams.

Max, whistling softly through his teeth, was walking around the contact boat. She was sixty feet long with flush decks, driven by two 450-hp Liberty engines which made thirty-five knots light and twenty-five loaded. It had 1¼-inch-thick bulletproof glass around its cabin, watertight bulkheads, and dumping hatches on the bottom in case the cargo had to be jettisoned.

Max nodded, turned, and went back across the beach. Magnus saw the lights of the limousine go on after it had turned back toward New York City.

As the contact boat roared out through the darkness to find the *Arethusa,* Magnus opened the bag he carried, took the gun, which was wrapped in a silk handkerchief, and held it. He felt the weight off it, then tucked it, still wrapped, carefully in his belt. To waste such a thing was against his Scottish instinct.

He turned to see the lights of New York City sinking in the distance and smiled, wondering which lights from those New York towers would be his. There was no longer any doubt in his mind where his place was. The only question was how soon he could get back there.

2

The *Marshall*'s capture had led to the issuing of a federal arrest warrant with McCoy's name on it. McCoy knew if he were apprehended it would mean several years in a federal penitentiary. He became more cautious. Rather than hiring a crew of sailors hanging around Nassau, he hired Gloucester fishermen. Having proven his trustworthiness by staying with the *Marshall*, Magnus was given a permanent job.

But McCoy did not have control of the marketplace. His buyers were becoming the large, increasingly dangerous syndicates and gangs who bought whole cargoes of hooch on consignment. As McCoy became more dependent on them, he became increasingly wary.

Crime was becoming a business, a loose confederation of diverse talent which, because of a sudden influx of capital due to the cornering of liquor, needed room to expand. A national thirst could not be stopped; it could only be quenched. Liquor was money; money was power to the gangs. If lives could not be bought, they were ended.

McCoy and Magnus both were aware of the increased risks. Each for his own reasons wanted to keep the *Arethusa* sailing clear, but doing so became increasingly difficult. McCoy's reputation was established; "right off McCoy's boat" and "the real McCoy" were used and misused to guarantee quality. Therefore the vanity of the various criminal groups demanded they be supplied by McCoy himself, and the *Arethusa* could carry only five thousand cases at a time.

In spite of the dangers, Magnus spent an idyllic four years on Rum

Row. Each month in fair weather and almost every six weeks in foul, the crew of the *Arethusa* would stow a load of liquor below, weigh anchor, and leave Nassau headed for the Row. The profits were enormous. George Murphy paid Grace Lithgoe $10 per case of Haig's Pinch-Bottle Scotch. McCoy bought it from Murphy for $19 per case. On the Row, McCoy would sell it over the side for $40 per case. From that point on, the liquor was no longer an interest of McCoy's nor was it Scotch. It was cut with water and grain alcohol and mixed to various ratios, usually around one hundred drinks from a single bottle, and sold in a speakeasy for fifty cents a shot. On a ship from Glasgow, five thousand cases of Scotch was worth $50,000. When McCoy bought his cargo from Murphy, he paid $95,000. Over the side on Rum Row, McCoy sold his cargo to the bootleggers for $250,000, which gave him a profit of about $130,000 a run. Each bottle, cut to a hundred drinks in the speaks, was worth $50, making a case worth $600. Therefore, the final market value of McCoy's five thousand cases of Haig Pinch was $3,000,000.

McCoy knew that with so much money moving over his ship, he had to have a happy crew. He paid them well, made sure Frenchy Rivet fed them royally, and let his regulars carry some liquor on board to sell on the Row for their own profit.

In fair weather there would be breakfast of biscuits, ham, eggs, and coffee on the cabin hatch. Any man's birthday or any holiday was cause for a celebration. On the Row, fresh food was supplied by McCoy's brother, Ben, who would arrive on the first contact boat. Also, in fair weather, there would be Grace.

She came aboard soon after McCoy had lost the *Marshall*, and with it the thousand cases of Haig she had talked him into carrying. Her official reason for her trip was to see that the whiskey for which she was responsible was sold first and best, making up for the previous loss to the drinkers of Haig's products. Her real reasons were to get out of Nassau, have a few laughs with McCoy, and Magnus.

She was the first person on board to carry a gun, which she hung above her bunk in McCoy's cabin. When Magnus carried her bag in to her, he saw it in its holster. She turned around, discovered him looking at the gun, and said, "Don't worry."

"You know how to use that thing?"

"I use it anyway it gives me pleasure."

Without taking his eyes off her, Magnus closed the door and bolted it.

"It's time I started settling my debt to you."

She nodded slowly, running her cocked eyes over his body.
"You have a smart mouth. It's a mean mouth, too." She walked
over and put her finger on his lips and moved them back and forth.
"Just look at how it goes across here, mean, mean as all hell . . .
Ow!"

Reaching out for her, Magnus bit two of her fingers and held on as
she tried to pull away.

"Damn you, let go of my . . ." He let go when his mouth was on
top of hers. She hit him with her other hand. He grabbed her fist and
held it; his tongue sank between her lips. Their hands traded inti-
macies. He grabbed her and lifted her backward to the wall. She
pulled her skirt up and did away with some lace. Holding her with
one hand, pressing her to the wall, he freed himself with the other
hand and entered her as she wrapped her legs around him. She
pulled and struggled up his body for a better position. He lifted her
higher and carried her to her bunk. A grimace of joy pulsed on her
face. Her eyes opened at the last to watch him; he reached his own
conclusion rigid, driving, and then silent.

They held each other as the sounds of the *Arethusa's* loading
again became audible to them. When she felt his muscles begin to
shift, she held him in her for a few moments longer, then gave a
sweet "Oh" as he left her. He put his clothing back together, and
they smiled at each other, the relationship's immediate future defined
with no questions needed but one. Magnus asked it.

"What about McCoy?"

She pulled up and leaned on an elbow and smiled lovingly.

"Nobody owns me. He knows it . . . and so do you," she said.

"I don't want to own you. But my debt is a large one and I've only
just begun to pay it."

He left her lying there, smiling, her long thin legs stretched out on
the cot, her skirt still up around her waist.

Magnus heard her warning, but it did little good. He would never
admit to loving Grace Lithgoe, but he felt a terrible craving. He had
a difficult time on the anchor watch those nights when Grace and
McCoy shared the cabin. The phantom pictures of their pleasures
made him rage aloud to himself and curse into the wind.

In the daytime he did his work and punished himself for hating
McCoy the night before. The daytime was never so bad; all over his
schooner, McCoy was laughing, telling stories of the Row, and teaching Magnus about sailing and navigation. Grace smiled at him without any hesitance, getting on with the crew as if she were one of

them. Then in the night she would come and join Magnus in his watch and make love there, he under her to protect her from the hard deck. Or, if McCoy was at the helm, they would go to the cabin.

As time passed, Magnus reached a passion where having her was not enough. He wanted more and knew there was no more. But knowing was useless, and Magnus let her possession of him spread dangerously through his mind and into the future.

"I wonder about you, you know," he said one night after he had known Grace a year.

She stretched the length of the bunk and rolled her shoulders up against the wall of the cabin.

"What do you wonder, you hard-mouthed bull?" She kissed him and flicked his lips with her tongue.

"I wonder what's to become of you."

"Don't waste your time. I don't."

"Don't you want to find a place for yourself, then?"

"I find it when I wake up in the morning."

"But I mean . . . Don't you want a home?"

"Well, hell, no I don't. It's too much baggage, and the lighter you travel, the more you see. I carry my home with me just like a snail. Except it's not on my back, it's right in here." She took one of his hands and put it on the breast over her heart.

"You'll end up alone, then."

"You bet! . . . Just like everybody else."

"No . . ."

"You don't think so?"

"I think friends, lovers . . . wives, husbands . . . children . . ."

"Baked bilge! Friends come and go, lovers burn out faster than gunpowder. Wives and husbands die off. Children get away from you as soon as they can. They're all insulation. We're alone, Magnus. You're alone and I'm alone." She smiled sadly at him, and reached out to touch his hair.

Magnus held Grace Lithgoe closer, as if the gesture could disprove her theory.

"You're not alone right now, if you notice, and I plan to know you for a time."

She looked at him, and kissed him gently on the cheek.

"I know you do, you lovely, lovely man." She traced his lips with her fingers and kissed him again for the thought. Then she said, "But I'll tell you something: one day, either you or I are going to walk off this boat and we'll never see each other again. And if you think it's going to be any different, your head's a bag of bull wool."

Magnus never believed her. He expected always to have the sudden ache in his chest when he saw her on the wharf coming aboard for a trip to the Row. He wanted to feel the heat and urging in his groin forever when he thought of her pliant body. Magnus was young, and Grace was right.

McCoy knew what was going on. He had too many other things to worry about besides whom his passenger was enjoying. He had no sense of possession of her and was glad she could keep herself entertained when he was busy, as well as keeping a member of his crew as contented as Magnus was. He liked Magnus, for his care with bottles and bookkeeping, and for the energy his intense watching suggested. McCoy felt much like an older brother, teaching him the intricacies not only of sailing but also of getting through life with as graceful a passage as possible.

"Lying is more trouble than murder. One lie always leads to another, and before you know it you're living by them. Same with secrets. Can't stand 'em. You start hiding things, gets to be a habit worse than any joy powder there is. Then you start having secrets from yourself. You know how bad it gets? These gangsters, they're so crabbed into secrets they bull you telling their name."

Magnus wondered if he should talk of Grace, but decided there was no secret. McCoy went on.

"You know what I like to do? I like to go up to those guys and say, 'Hey, I'm Bill McCoy, I'm a bootlegger, what d'you do?' I'll tell you what they do, they go back under a rock. You know what I'd like to say to them? 'Hey, you live that way and you better hang crepe on your nose, 'cause your brain's dead.'"

He shook his head and joined Magnus laughing. He looked up to see the sails of the *Arethusa* fill, and then around at the sea.

"It's the big trouble with living on land: too many places to hide secrets. They're all over the walls. And the law will find them every time. All right, bring her around, bring in the jib sheets, and we'll see if we can sell some hooch."

When they reached their position on Rum Row, the hard work began. A few independent sales were made in the daytime. An occasional pleasure boat would appear, or a couple of fishermen would row over to the schooner for a few cases. Most of the selling, however, took place at night, when the pros arrived. Contact boats pulled up, men yelled the brands they wanted, and the loading began. Sometimes as many as fifteen were loaded at a time. Magnus would start running hams to the various boats, calling a tally to McCoy. If the boatmen were known, they were invited aboard and Frenchy would feed them as the loading went on. High up the mainmast on the cross-trees a sailor would watch the horizon with night glasses to warn of a Coast Guard approach.

When a contact boat was loaded, money was passed to Magnus or thrown on deck to McCoy, rolls of one-thousand or five-thousand-dollar bills held together with rubber bands. No one ever tried to shortchange McCoy, because his business was too important. But as time passed, the trips became more dangerous. Independent gang-sters known as "go-through guys" began staging pirate raids. They had speedboats powered with stolen Pierce-Arrow automobile en-gines which could be mounted below the water line, giving maximum quiet. The contact-boat sailors carried no weapons, to be clear of the law if they were caught. The go-through guys did, Thompsons and ice picks. Sometimes they would band together, hijack a rum-runner, unload its cargo, and murder its crew. For this reason, Grace Lithgoe convinced McCoy to arm his schooner, refusing to ship her product with him unless he did. McCoy brought a Lewis machine gun to be mounted on his cabin, and two Thompsons to be wrapped conven-iently in furled sails. He gave each of his crew a .44 and told them all to stand clear of each other when any craft came near, to avoid a surprise. McCoy hated it, but he knew it had to be done.

In the summer of 1923, a gangster named Frankie Yale decided he wanted a load of "the real McCoy." Hard pressure was exerted in Nassau and the *Arethusa* sailed with a full load, bound for "Broad-way and Forty-second Street," just outside New York harbor.

Grace was aboard for the run, and came to Magnus on the for-ward deck during his watch the first night out of Nassau. Magnus was waiting for her, for he'd spent some of the money he'd saved and bought her a present.

They lay on the bow, using his kilt as a blanket. The night had a proper moon, and after they made love, Magnus reached over to his pants, searched a pocket, and pulled out a ring.

"Now, don't be thinking I'm going to ask anything of you, but I have a present for you. I don't even care if you wear it or not, but I saw it, and I wanted to give it to you. If you don't like it—"

"Stop apologizing and let me have it."

"I didn't think till now about it fittin' your finger."

He looked at Grace. Her mouth was open, and for the first time since he had known her, she had nothing to say.

"Yes, weel, to hell with it, I thought you—"

"Gimme that goddamn ring."

She grabbed it. It was a gold band with tiny pieces of lapis lazuli in a mosaic of a dragon. It fit her thumb. A sob came from her throat.

Magnus laughed. "You like it, then."

"Hell, I can't even see it out here. Nobody's ever given me a ring before. And look at me. Look at me! I haven't cried since I lost the ball I played jacks with. It isn't the goddamn ring, either. It isn't even you, you lovely, lovely man. You just hit me in the face with a god-damn symbol. Watch out for the symbols, Magnus, they'll get you every time." She rolled over close to him and let herself cry for a few moments.

"What are you trying to do to me?" she said quietly.

"Just give you a present."

She sat up to look at his eyes in the moonlight. She shook her head, then looked away and tried to sound hard again. "I don't have anything to give you back . . . Nothing."

"Sure you do."

"What?"

"All the nights like this you're going to give me, and days in the cabin . . . The nights and the days are all I need; the rest of your time you can do what you like."

She turned back and smiled at him, then tried to see the ring in the moonlight. "You make me feel things, Magnus, that I don't want to feel. I'll give you your days and nights, but don't go buying any more presents. . . . Now, where the hell am I going to wear this thing?"

She decided to let it dangle on a gold chain around her neck. At breakfast, McCoy asked her where it came from. She told him she took it from a nose she bit off when it got into her business without an invitation.

They arrived on the Row, and the contact boats arrived soon after. None of the crew of the *Arethusa* trusted the gangsters who came out to the boat wearing their pointy-pointy shoes and flared-lapeled suits, with fedoras pulled down over their faces, supposedly to make them look tough. But nobody on the *Arethusa* laughed; all they wanted to do was unload and get back to Nassau.

Magnus worked hard on the consignment. There was no relief, no jokes, and only one payment at the end of it. For two nights Magnus worked. The gangsters did not help him at all, just ordering him to move faster, as if he were their servant. He held on to his temper, saying nothing, while the entire crew of the *Arethusa* stood on deck watching every move on the contact boats, each one with his .44 stuck under his shirt. Grace had hers in a spring-steel garter belt.

By the end of the second night, Magnus was exhausted. He picked up the last hams and carried them over to the contact boat, where three gangsters waited, bored and uncomfortable. As Magnus moved to the back of the boat, a swell tipped it and one of the gangsters was thrown against him. He dropped the hams in order to catch the gangster and keep him from going overboard.

The man turned around and looked at Magnus. He had a round face already going to fat in his early twenties. When he spoke, his mouth and eyes made him look like a raging swine.

"You clumsy grease-picker . . ." He reached between his lapels for his shoulder holster, but saw Magnus was unarmed. Magnus never carried McCoy's gun, claiming it would cause more harm than it could prevent. In this case he was right. The gangster merely gut-slugged him and turned to walk away. But Magnus, being tired, picked up a bottle from one of the hams, smashed it over the man's head, lifted him up and threw him overboard.

His two colleagues were so startled, they simply watched as their friend broke surface and started bellowing: "Drop him! Drop the son of a bitch!"

They turned toward Magnus, who ignored them and climbed back aboard the *Arethusa*. When one of the gangsters reached for his gun, he heard Grace yelling: "I'll blow off anything you got in that suit, and I don't mean just your arms."

The two dry gangsters looked up to see the two Thompsons and a couple of .44's.

"Fish him out and duck out of here," McCoy yelled down from behind the Lewis machine gun. "He asked for the swim, so he's got no complaint."

As they pulled their colleague out of the water, he gave them hell for not having killed Magnus. As soon as he was aboard, he turned to the *Arethusa*.

"Where are you? Yeah, there you are, I see you. What's your name? Come on, what's your name?"

Magnus looked silently down at the man, and thought of an angry pig.

"I find out who you are. I don't forget you. You remember me because I'm coming after you with this, grease-picker."

He held up an ice pick at arm's length, and for a moment looked like an absurd reproduction of the Statue of Liberty visible behind him. Then the contact boat started and he lost his balance again. As the boat pulled off, the gangster screamed, "I find you, grease-picker, I find you."

That was how Magnus met Umberto Anastasio. To the rest of the crew the incident was just one more sign that the Row was dying, and Magnus himself soon forgot the incident. In fact, for a long time the only thing Magnus remembered about that summer was that he met Mary Fleming.

She came in a black-hulled speedboat which caught and reflected the sun of the Indian-summer morning. The *Arethusa* had returned from Nassau, and McCoy had put off from Long Island with an unconsigned cargo. The sales had gone briskly; there were a lot of familiar faces with old stories, which were a welcome relief after the gangsters' silence.

The black speedboat came skimming over the water at full throttle and hove to neatly. What Magnus saw was a surprising combination. Piloting the boat was a stunning young girl of about nineteen, with flaming red bobbed hair, wearing a scandalous new Annette Kellerman one-piece bathing suit which covered only half of her million freckles. Beside her sat a placid three-year-old child.

"Hello! Is this McCoy's ship?"

Magnus was involved with the freckles but answered the question. "It is."

"That's the nines! I want twenty cases of your best champagne. I really do want the best."

"I'm sure of that."

She turned to check Magnus' expression, concerned at having said something to which someone not of her world might take offense. She saw the hard mouth and the dark eyes and was held by them. Then, noticing a trace of a smile, she laughed her relief. Magnus went below. She stood leaning against the gunwale until she felt someone watching her. It was Grace Lithgoe. They smiled at each other, but with very different smiles.

When Magnus returned, carrying a load of hams, the girl was chatting with McCoy, laughing at his questions as to which gang she worked for, and would she put in a good word for him.

But the conversation between them stopped when Magnus climbed down into her boat. He stacked the hams, then turned and caught her staring at him. She laughed nervously, then looked away toward land, trying to change an unspoken subject.

"Well, this'll show him."

"Who?"

"My brother. He's such a cuckoo. Said I couldn't get champagne for my party. Well!"

"This'll surely show him."

"I'll say. It's the only thing he'll drink, he's so scared of the Irish curse."

Each time Magnus brought a load of hams down into the speedboat, they talked about what a grand night it was for a party. With a growing sense of the fact that the twenty cases were almost aboard, they tried to find a way to say what they were really thinking but it was hard, particularly with McCoy, Grace, and most of the crew enjoying their tension.

Finally the forty hams were stacked and covered with canvas. Magnus turned and looked at the girl, determined he would stand there until something was said by one or the other of them.

She held out money.

"Thanks for loading for me. You're a peach."

He reached out and took her hand; he did not let go.

"It goes with the price. . . . Where do you live, then?"

"In Southampton. . . . It's too bad you're stuck on this ship."

He knew why she said it, but wanted her to say more.

"Why?"

"You know why. You could come to the party."

They looked at each other and it was too much for them. He let go of her hand, and she turned away.

"But it's a long swim. Why don't you listen for it? You'll probably hear it out here. . . . Where are you from?"

"I'm a Scot. And whose wee child is that, and please don't tell me it's yours."

"No, no, he's my sister's. I brought him along because the Coast Guard would never think a girl in a suit like this with a baby was running bootleg champagne, would they?"

They smiled. Then there was no more to say, and she watched him climb back aboard the *Arethusa*.

She started the motor but before she rammed the accelerator down, she called up to him with a confident persistence, "I wish you could make it tonight."

He did, wearing his kilt, dirk, and sporran, with a dinner jacket McCoy had at the bottom of a footlocker, a white shirt, an old green bow tie that Frenchy Rivet boiled in black ink and pressed on the galley stove, and a pair of knee-high socks that Grace had with her.

McCoy took the *Arethusa* in as close to the beach as possible, and Magnus went over the side into the skiff. The crew gave him a rousing cheer, and just before he pushed off, Grace called to him. She took the chain from around her neck and let the ring fall into the sea. Then she smiled and blew him a kiss. By the time he reached shore, Magnus understood.

When he got to the beach, he heard the party. His entrance was a sensation as he stood in his kilt looking through the several hundred people for the bobbed red hair. When she saw him, her eyes widened, and then set with certainty. She walked across the room to him, took his hand, and led him to the dance floor. They danced three dances before they bothered with finding out each other's names.

3

. . . people you didn't want to know said
"Yes, we have no bananas," and it seemed
only a question of a few years before the
older people would step aside and let the
world be run by those who saw things as
they were.

—F. Scott Fitzgerald

The first Flemings had come to America in the 1840's to escape the potato famine in Ireland. They were industrious and managed to scrape together enough money to buy some farmland on Long Island. They did not begin to amass their fortune until one of their sons, Richard Fleming, went on Sherman's March to the Sea through Georgia, and knew rich farmland when he saw it. When the Civil War ended, he obtained a carpetbag and retraced the general's march, buying the scorched earth at rock-bottom prices.

In ten years the value of his real estate had quadrupled, and he began trading up. By the time he was thirty-five, he was a millionaire. He sold out at his price and brought his money, along with his considerable charm, back to New York, where he began to look for a good Irish Catholic girl to found his dynasty.

Within six months he met one who was about to become a nun. With God's help, she decided that her true vocation was to be the mother of Richard Fleming's children. As she flourished in maternity, Richard flourished in real estate. By the time he died in 1917 at the age of seventy-four, there was a considerable fortune to be divided among his seven children and the thirty-five grandchildren.

One of the sons, Joseph Fleming (and he insisted on Joseph, never "Joe"), had convinced the old man that the stock market was a place to make money. He had bought himself a seat on the New York Exchange and had made his own fortune. In recent years Fleming and Co. had handled most of the family investments and had done well by them. Everyone respected Joseph, at least to his face. He was successful with their money, and with the money from other rich Irish Catholics, the Murrays, the McDonnells, and from the west, some MacKays.

Joseph Fleming also assumed the responsibilities of the Fleming family's moral health. He would admonish his brothers and sisters and their children about their behavior in long letters referred to behind his back as "Joe's Papal Bulls."

Mary's mother, Ilene Fleming, was the perfect match for such a man. She was a snob. She wished her husband did not spend so much time at Fleming and Co., working. She would have preferred Joseph to care for the stable and race the horses at Saratoga, which was pleasant and one of the few places she could mingle with real society without the stigma of being an Irish Catholic. She hated the grand Protestants who looked down on the lace-curtain Irish, and confessed each week before taking her Communion that she delighted at the thought they would eventually rot in hell for their false religion. In the meantime she did what she could to secure her family's social position and busied herself raising her six daughters and one son.

By the time of the party, three of the daughters had married correctly, to rich Catholics, and two were pregnant. They were all present, along with two dozen cousins and a majority of Mary's aunts and uncles, the night Magnus entered in a kilt. Four of Joseph's siblings were living in the thirty-acre Fleming compound in enormous houses built for each family. They worshiped together in the chapel built at one end of the compound, and those Flemings who did not live there came to visit often, particularly when there was a party, and especially if the party might get on the society page of the New York *Times*. For the Flemings were in Southampton because they knew they would not be accepted in Newport or East Hampton. They were there because Judge O'Brien and the Murrays had come before them and had made it possible for the Irish to join the Southampton Beach Club. They were there because, with relative social impunity, they could be Catholics together.

Mary had succeeded in living through nineteen years of internecine struggle without making a single serious enemy in the family. She was much beloved, and seemed crowned, for her red hair was unique in the entire family. But no one loved Mary more than her only brother, Junius, known to all as "Juny." He was an archetypal example of "flaming youth," with a penchant for driving his Stutz Bearcat across his aunts' and uncles' lawns and crashing it into trees.

This came less from alcoholic indulgence than from youthful ex-
uberance. He was, after all, rich, good-looking in a patent-leather
way, and apparently very intelligent. He did well at Portsmouth Priory, and went to Yale, instead of the Jesuit Georgetown University.
This upset his father, but not his mother who was quite aware of who
went to Yale and who went to Georgetown.

Junius Fleming was two years older than Magnus and regarded
Mary's guest with two-faced superiority, friendly when they met, then
laughing with the family afterward. Magnus distrusted him from the
first second he laid eyes on his slick hair, tricky eyes, and mocking
mouth.

At dawn after the party, Mary showed Magnus the whole compound. The family had been courteously tolerant of Magnus at the
party. Between dances, Mary had introduced him to cousins, aunts,
and sisters. They all had been pleasant, but Magnus had felt the
looks and rolling eyes when his back had been turned. Mrs. Fleming,
Mary's mother, had asked whether he knew Lord somebody, and
seemed disappointed when he did not. Mr. Fleming looked over
Magnus' head and took little notice of him. Magnus smiled, gave up
trying to remember names, and did not care about their laughter. He
wanted Mary; and he told her so at dawn as they strolled over the
money-greened lawns to the boathouse.

"But, Magnus, I'm only nineteen."

"And I'm twenty-three, so if you take an average, we're both
twenty-one."

"But I've only known you one day, *less* than one day."

"And we've both been living our lives, nineteen and twenty-three
years, just waiting to meet each other. And now we've done it and
there's no point in wasting any *more* time, is there?"

She laughed then, a sound Magnus thought to be like bubbling
honey.

"What's the matter with me? I can't think of a single reason. . . .
You're a terror, Magnus Macpherson."

"I just know what I don't want."

"What you *don't* want?"

"I don't want another day of life without you."

They were standing under a four-hundred-year-old tree near the
boathouse. She turned to him and felt the certainty of his conviction.

"You scare me, Magnus. I . . . ." She laughed. "I just want to go
run across that lawn and scream!"

"You're not scared of me, Mary Fleming. You're scared of yourself loving, and you already love me."

She looked at him, trembled, then went ahead and screamed, holding on to both his hands. "How do you know that?"

He held her close against him and said quietly, "Because I have a feeling of love I couldn't be having alone."

They kissed each other, a long, gentle, ecstatic kiss. Then Magnus looked into her half-closed eyes. "Mary, I have little money. . . ."

"Money doesn't matter," she said.

"That's true . . . when you have it. But I'm going to have money. A lot of money. I want you to know that, and to know I'm not looking for anything around here but you."

"*Please* don't worry. I could live with you on twenty-five dollars a week. But, Magnus . . ."

She looked away over the clear horizon of the bright dawn with another purpose.

". . . you're not a Catholic."

So the struggle began. Had it been Mary alone, they would have married as soon as Magnus returned on his next and last trip aboard the *Arethusa*. But Mary was a Fleming and a Roman Catholic. Magnus was taking on more than a strong-willed, easily loved nineteen-year-old girl.

They barely spoke again that morning as Mary drove her black speedboat out toward the *Arethusa*, towing the skiff. They clasped hands, tightly. Holding on to each other helped smooth the differences between them. After he kissed her good-bye and reached for the rope ladder, he said to her, "I am going to marry you, Mary Fleming. But it's you I'll marry, not your family or your church. I'll be back in a month, and I ache already with the missing of you."

For Mary it was a busy month planning the logistics of a frontal attack on several family bastions. Luckily her relatives had all seen Magnus, liked him as a curiosity, appreciated his good looks and humor about wearing a skirt. But few were prepared to take him seriously as a mate for their own Mary. As her intention spread through the compound, there were reactions of shock and delight that Uncle Joe might have a black Protestant in his own family.

At first Joseph Fleming would not discuss the subject with his daughter. When the matter was brought up, and Mary brought it up every day, he would look loftily above her and shift the conversation to some Protestant horror such as their casual communion or the murder of fetuses. Mary finally confronted him in his study.

"Father,"—no one had ever used anything more familiar—"I think the best way we can settle this is to allow Magnus to stay in the rooms above the boathouse when he comes back. That way, we can all get to know him better, and you'll see what a fine person he is."

Joseph Fleming raised his eyes to a beveled edge of oak paneling as he spoke.

"My dear, I realize that I must accept the fact that this 'person' exists. Therefore, I do."

"Thank you, Father, he certainly does."

"Yes. And you must accept the fact that if I see that person anywhere in the Fleming compound, I'll notify whatever authority I must to have him deported as an illegal alien."

Joseph Fleming never raised his voice. He let his eye wander down from the molding to make sure his daughter received his words with respectful shock.

She did not. Her face revealed nothing, nor did her words.

"May God forgive you, Father." She crossed herself and left the study. She walked straight to the family chapel and stayed there for a day and a night without meals.

This totally alarmed her family who remembered that when Mary was twelve she had stopped eating for almost a week when she discovered a married sister kissing a man who was not her husband. Mary's fast had not been a conscious ploy, but an emotional trauma. It resulted in Joseph Fleming's having the distasteful task of not only disciplining one daughter for moral deviation, but of calling in an "alienist," which was the name applied to psychologists by a suspicious public. The doctor succeeded where the priests had failed, a fact which severely upset her father, who did not call the alienist again on the several occasions when Mary stopped talking or eating. Instead, prayers were said, and God was praised, for each time Mary "recovered her senses." But this time, as the hours of Mary's self-denial in the chapel passed, Joseph Fleming became increasingly alarmed.

Mary's mother filled the time with cables to an Edinburgh detective firm, instructing them to find out everything about a family called Macpherson in a place called Dufftown.

Juny Fleming simply waited for the crisis to reach a degree of tension and exhaustion where moral positions could be bullied and swayed.

"Father, let him come."

"I'll not have your sister marrying—"

"No, of course not. But let him come. Mary will be very happy. Then give him, say, ten thousand dollars to go. Mary will be very sad for a while. But it will be the bootlegger who causes her unhappiness, not you."

Joseph Fleming looked at his son, and nodded with approval. Then he went to the chapel, where he saw Mary slumped down at the Communion rail in front of the altar under the Crucifix. He knelt down beside her and crossed himself. Mary slowly turned to see who it was.

"Hello, Father."

"Mary, your young man is welcome to stay in the boathouse when he returns."

Her eyes opened wide, and tears flooded them.

"Oh, Father," and she fell as she tried to move over to hug him. Joseph Fleming stooped down and helped his daughter to stand.

"Father, dear Father, He heard my prayers! St. Anthony heard my prayers! Bless you, thank you, thank you . . ."

They walked arm in arm back to the house, and by the time Mary had eaten two bowls of chowder, she was laughing and planning how to make the boathouse more comfortable. She did not notice the looks exchanged by her father and brother.

Four days later, Magnus returned.

He had said good-bye to Mrs. Sweeting and Tommy at the Lucerne, and had put everything he owned in his canvas bag. Grace did not make the run this time. She had walked off the *Arethusa* in Nassau with a crooked smile at Magnus, and had not looked back. The trip north to the Row had not been fast enough for him. McCoy rowed him in to the beach. They shook hands in the dark and said good-bye.

"Thanks, Mr. McCoy, for all you've taught me."

"Good night, Magnus! You knew it all. I just taught you to recognize it."

They stood awkwardly for a moment, not knowing how to say good-bye.

"I'll keep an eye out for you on the Row. I'm sure I'll be needing a bit of the real McCoy now and then."

McCoy looked seaward, out toward the *Arethusa*, a rolling shadow on the fan of moonlight.

"You better look quick. It won't last much longer. . . ." He shook his head once, as if accepting fate's lousy chances, and added,

"Good luck, Magnus. Marry her if you can, and if not, kidnap her, steal a ship, and sail away to real happiness."

"I'll do it."

Magnus helped get the skiff out through the surf. He watched as McCoy rowed out to the *Arethusa,* got aboard, and sailed into the dark.

Magnus slept a few hours under his kilt. At dawn he got up, made himself look as presentable as possible, walked down the beach ànd into the Fleming compound.

He lived in the boathouse for almost a month without making any overt move concerning Mary. While she grew certain of her love for him, he won over members of the family, particularly the women, who admired his quiet looks and, in spite of themselves, enjoyed the stories of Rum Row. Someone found him a set of bagpipes, and before long most of Mary's cousins were doing eight-some reels. He could sail with the best of them, and the boat on which he was captain or crew usually won the yacht-club races.

Magnus had no delusions about who his real adversaries were: Mary's father and her brother, Juny. He knew Mrs. Fleming would never accept him, but she could not stop the wedding if the two men agreed to it. Juny seemed friendly and offered to teach Magnus tennis, but both of them knew it was a time of mutual observation. On the court, Juny was amusing, jovial, and bitchy with family gossip, telling Magnus stories about many of his kin. Magnus knew this was meant to disarm, and was doubly careful.

After a month Magnus took a train to New York City and bought a plain gold band at Tiffany & Company with some of what he'd saved on the Row. That night he officially proposed to Mary and said she didn't have to answer until after he spoke with her father and brother the next day. She answered anyway.

"Yes! Yes, yes, yes, yes, and what Father and Junius say makes no difference. Magnus, don't let them scare you off. I'll go with you no matter what they say."

"I know you will, and I love you the more for it. But I think we both want them at the wedding. I want brother Juny to be watching, and I want Mr. Fleming to *give* you away . . . to me."

The next day there was to be a family polo match, and Magnus asked to speak with Juny and Mr. Fleming just before it. Juny was the best player, and Magnus depended upon him to pressure the meeting to a conclusion.

The three men met in Mr. Fleming's paneled study. There were oil paintings of some of the Flemings' horses and numerous trophies on the highly polished antique surfaces around the room.

Juny came in wearing his polo whites, carrying two mallets. He and his father had sherry, Magnus did not.

"I don't believe it's a surprise to either of you that I want Mary for my bride. I'm asking you, Mr. Fleming, for your permission, as I'm aware of the love and respect she has for you."

Mr. Fleming sipped his sherry and as usual looked just above Magnus' head. Magnus went on.

"I've also gained a respect for the Flemings, and for their faith. It is not my faith . . ."

Joseph Fleming's eyes dropped and looked directly at Magnus for a moment.

". . . but I promise you both I would always respect Mary's faith, and that should there be children . . ."

Mr. Fleming turned his head away quickly.

". . . I would agree to their being educated in Roman Catholic schools, at least until they were old enough to choose for themselves. Mary and I discussed this—"

Mr. Fleming turned quickly and interrupted. "Mr. Macpherson"—he had always called Magnus this, never using his Christian name—"may I ask what *is* your faith?"

"It is something I have no words for."

"I see. Do you have a faith?"

"In many things."

"Is God one of them?"

"Mr. Fleming, with respect, sir, I came to ask about Mary. Our faith, our beliefs, are different, I do not deny it. But your God, or anyone's—I canna but believe whoever He is would look on Mary and me with kindness."

"You are blasphemous, sir!" The sherry in Mr. Fleming's hand was shaking, so he put it down.

"No, sir. It cannot be blasphemy, for I have a deep faith in what I just said."

Magnus kept his eyes on Mr. Fleming, but caught a flicker of a smile from Juny. Mr. Fleming looked at Magnus; then his eyes returned to the ceiling.

"Mr. Macpherson, theology is beside the point. You've asked my permission to marry my daughter. My answer is no. My only curiosity about you is that you had the audacity to ask it in the first place.

Did you really think you could jump off your rum boat and take advantage of my daughter so easily?"

"I've taken no advantage, sir, I—"

"You have! You—"

"Excuse me, Father, I don't think . . ."

Juny smiled winningly at his father, at Magnus, then back at his father.

"No, Mr. Macpherson. Arguing would be a waste of time, and there is a polo match. So let us settle this as quickly as possible. I wish you to leave, but I wish you to leave discreetly; that is, I do not wish Mary to know of our terms. You must think up some reason or other which she will believe, and I'm prepared to offer you five thousand dollars for your . . . creativity."

Magnus watched Mr. Fleming as he reached for his sherry. He looked over at Juny, who was concentrating on moving a mallet head over the toe of one of his riding boots. Magnus knew that his father's suggestion was no surprise to his son. He suddenly sensed the irony; he was again in America, and money was being dropped in his lap.

"With respect, sir, but it seems a niggling sum."

Both Juny and Mr. Fleming looked up at Magnus, quickly looked at each other, then went back to their activity with sherry and the boot.

"Ten, then."

"Ten thousand dollars?"

"Ten thousand dollars, Mr. Macpherson, and we would hope you might leave, say, a week from today."

"'We would hope'?" Magnus looked at Juny, who glanced at him, smiled at the fact of it, and shrugged. Magnus smiled back, stood up, and began to pace around the room.

"Weel, it's very generous, very generous indeed, I must say. But you're asking a great deal. You're asking me to lie to the woman I love. You're asking me to break her heart, for I believe she loves me as much as I love her. You're asking me to cover up the pain your money's to cause her. And you're asking me to take *your* lie on my back, for this offer of yours is the foulest lie of all."

They were both watching him now, and they were both angry. Magnus saw they were, and went on. "It seems you're asking a great deal. I canna but believe it's worth . . . fifty thousand dollars."

Juny was up out of his chair, grabbing his mallets as if to swing.

"You son-of-a-bitch whore!"

"Silence!" Mr. Fleming stopped Juny, and began scratching across a checkbook. He tore the check out and threw it on the floor in front of Magnus.

"Here is your price. Don't think it indicates your worth, only our love for Mary."

Magnus stooped down and picked it up, read it, then asked "With respect, sir, may I be borrowing your pen there?"

He did not wait for Mr. Fleming to offer it, but took it and quickly wrote on the back of the check: "Pay to the order of Mary Fleming Macpherson," signed his name, and held it up for them to see.

"Now, *gentlemen,* you see there's no way I can cash this check. But I'll keep it, for I canna but think Mary would find it interesting reading, that her father and brother would try to destroy her happiness for such a price. I'm certain if she knew it, she'd leave this house forever and wouldn't care to spit on your graves, which would be what you deserve."

The two Flemings looked at each other.

"Give me back that check," Mr. Fleming said. "It's no good, I'll stop payment . . ."

Magnus laughed. "It was never good as money. It's a document, sir, of your deceit. And if you want your daughter to know about it, you'll just try to stop our wedding."

Juny gave an exasperated laugh.

"My God, Magnus, what do you want?"

"I have what I want; I have Mary. You made a mistake thinking you have anything I want. As to your money, you're paupers if you're trying to buy me."

"Mr. Macpherson, you—"

"With respect, Mr. Fleming, from this time on I'd like you to call me Magnus. It would make Máry happy. It will also make her happy for you both to greet her at the polo match with words of congratulations, and as for a date, my birthday is three months away and I canna think of a better way to celebrate it than by marrying your daughter."

"I'd rather die first!" Mr. Fleming slammed the sherry glass down and cracked it.

"Then die! For by God I'll show this check to every house in the compound, then I'll send it to the New York *Times* society editor, who seems to worry 'The Family' so much. And Mary and I will be gone in twenty-four hours, if the whole Fleming family isn't gabbling this afternoon with the news of Mary's wedding by the final round."

"Chukka," Juny corrected.

"So you add blackmail to your list of talents." Mr. Fleming's skin tightened across his face.

"Mr. Fleming, don't dare make moral judgments to me. You just put a price on your daughter's happiness. How could you offer less than everything? . . . Make your choice, either you'll be at the wedding or you won't. As to me marrying your daughter, that's a choice you don't have, and as a matter of fact, you never did."

He turned and looked at Juny, who was smiling at him. Magnus smiled back, knowing Juny's pleasant expression was one he could never trust, that Juny used it to disarm and to cover his own rage, which, if he showed it, would only add to his loss. And Juny could not bear losing.

"Magnus, there's something you should know. Mary is a very sensitive . . . fragile girl. She's perfectly healthy, but she's had some, well, you might say she's a little moody in the head. . . . She stopped eating once, almost starved because her sister . . ." Juny was still smiling.

"Junius, be quiet!" Joseph Fleming roared at his son. "My daughter is quite good enough for this—"

"Father, she starved herself, she stopped talking—"

"My daughter is perfectly—"

Magnus interrupted. "It won't work, Juny. Trying to tell me something's wrong with Mary would only make you a swine, so don't do it."

Magnus left the room. Father and son stayed in the study for an hour and a half, causing a delay in the polo match. Finally they both arrived at the field. Juny played brilliantly, wearing out three mounts and scoring seven goals. By the end of the match many of Mary's relatives had come to Magnus and offered congratulations. One of Mary's aunts even cried, but neither Mr. nor Mrs. Fleming said a word to Magnus, and he carefully avoided them. Magnus had won, and he never believed in pouring salt into a wound.

Mary was in a state of joy unlike any she had ever known. When she asked Magnus for every detail of his meeting, he constructed a scene which gave Juny and Mr. Fleming much credit for patience and understanding. She, in turn, thanked her brother and father for their kindness, gratitude which each of them shrugged off silently.

The three months before the wedding were hectic for everyone. In spite of not having discovered anything bad in her investigations about Magnus' past, Mrs. Fleming was far from pleased with the match. Magnus' family were so ordinary—no titles, no lineage, no money, no reputation, except as good honest folk. Nevertheless, Ilene Fleming was determined to give her daughter a perfect wedding.

They decided on a small informal ceremony with only the immediate family in the chapel at the compound. Magnus was, after all, a bootlegger and a Protestant who said he was not going to convert. The reception, though, would be another matter. Fifteen hundred guests would come on a special train from Grand Central. Meyer Davis and his orchestra would play, a new yellow-and-white-striped tent would be filled with three thousand gardenias and heated in the January cold by one hundred special braziers. The caterers were hired, and Mary's dress, by Chanel, was being sailed over from Paris with a fitter along with a new cloche hat by Reboux, and shoes, and jewelry. The wedding presents arrived and were displayed first in the "music room" (so named for the Victrola in one corner), and when it was filled, the overflow went into Mr. Fleming's study, which did not please him. Nothing, in fact, about the whole affair pleased him, and he became particularly irritated with his wife's growing enthusiasm.

Magnus had only two things to do: buy a wedding outfit and find a pig farm. One day he went into New York to see if he could afford a plain dark suit at DePinna's. Several Fleming cousins had suggested it as *the* place to buy one. That night Magnus also managed to meet with Arnold Rothstein.

Rothstein's office was Broadway itself. His limousine would pull up at Forty-ninth Street at ten P.M. He would get out and start walking down the Great White Way to Forty-second Street. The limousine followed close behind him, as he usually carried about two hundred thousand dollars in thousand-dollar bills. As he walked, he collected and took bets. The two men following in the limousine carried enough hardware to blast open a section of sidewalk.

Magnus waited at Forty-eighth Street. He saw Rothstein walking slowly down the street, elegantly dressed against the wind in a homburg and chesterfield overcoat. Magnus let him pass by, then said his name quietly.

"Mr. Rothstein."

Rothstein stopped, and immediately the two men in the car were out on the street, the driver holding a handgun, the other a sawed-off shotgun. Only then did Rothstein turn around and look at Magnus.

"I don't think I know you."

Magnus talked quietly but fast.

"My name's Macpherson. You got me out of jail once, I delivered some money to McCoy and took care of a forty-four."

Rothstein nodded and looked at the men in the street, who returned to the limousine. Then he turned and indicated to Magnus he should walk along with him.

"Don't come up behind me. They're supposed to gun anything that stops me moving. What can I do for you, Mr. Macpherson? You have a bet?"

"Not right now. But I plan to have one, and I'd like to place it with you."

"My pleasure. What's the bet?"

"That I can produce three hundred gallons of 190-proof alky a day."

Rothstein glanced over at Magnus and kept walking.

"That's a bad bet. I'd say you can do it."

"So would I. So forget the bet. I'll need to sell it to someone."

"You have a still?"

"I mean to build one."

"Three hundred gallons a day. That'll take some money."

"I mean to get it, but don't worry, not from you."

"You don't understand. Loans is . . . are my business. Maybe we could work out something."

"What kind of interest do you charge, Mr. Rothstein?"

"My usual is twenty-five percent per month until the principal is paid back. Then ten percent of the profits for my investment."

"Weel, you see, that's pretty high for me, and besides, I have no collateral."

"Sure you do, Mr. Macpherson, it's walking along here beside me." Rothstein gestured with a gray-gloved hand directly at Magnus' throat.

A man in front of them called Rothstein's name, hurried over, and slipped him something without a word. Without looking at it, Rothstein put it in his pocket, and again glanced over at Magnus.

"I just put two and two together and came up with the *Daily News:* Macpherson, Fleming, marriage. I take it you can get your own capital."

"I can."

"What you're asking me for is a buyer."

"Yes."

"I'm not in the bootlegging racket anymore. I just invest. But I owe you a favor for sinking that heater, so walk along with me down to Forty-third Street."

In the next three blocks Rothstein met seven men, talked to few of them, laughed as he paid out to one. Three policemen walked by, scrupulously examining the sidewalk for litter. At Forty-third Street a man was standing on the corner, waiting with a smile. He was a little older than Magnus, and dressed in a more conservative fashion than most gangsters. However, his shoulders were heavily padded and he shifted from one pointed-toe shoe to the other.

"Evening, Mr. Rothstein," the gangster said.

"Hello, Frank, come over here. Meet Mr. Macpherson. He's going to run a still, and I thought you should meet him. Macpherson, this is Frank Costello. He and I have a little business venture."

The smile was gone from Costello's face, replaced by suspicious analysis. There was no sign of greeting, just examination, as the three of them moved down Broadway at Rothstein's pace. Magnus was in the middle and didn't want to be. He glanced at Costello once, then looked straight ahead.

"I trust him, Frank."

"If A.R. trusts you, I trust you. What ya got?"

Magnus explained the situation, and Costello gave him a piece of paper with a phone number written on it.

"Memorize it, then eat it. When ya got something, call the number. If anyone other than you calls it, you got a problem."

Magnus nodded and put the piece of paper in his pants pocket. Rothstein looked across at both of them.

"Good seeing you, Macpherson. We're even, right?"

"Even. I'll be saying good night to you both."

"And send me an invitation. I promise not to come."

Magnus slowed his pace, and the two men continued on ahead of him, starting to talk as soon as they were out of earshot.

On the train ride back to Southampton, Magnus wondered if fear were part of the price of power. If it were, perhaps such a price was too high. He decided to find out. The first step to power from his perspective was money; therefore he had to find a pig farm.

While ashore in Nassau, Magnus had added to his father's knowledge of distilling and had developed the technical know-how to run the kind of still he had just described to Rothstein. One-hundred-ninety-proof alcohol, or "alky," was much in demand as the basis for most fake hooch sold as drinks or in bottles. Almost pure alcohol, it could be mixed with just about anything, cut to just about nothing, and still have the desired effect on a drinker. The bartenders would state categorically that "the whiskey in this bottle is the real McCoy," and be telling the truth. However, the whiskey at best made up only about five percent of what was in the bottle.

By listening to McCoy and his supplier, George Murphy, at the Lucerne bar, Magnus had decided on alky. Murphy had given him the name of a contractor in Garden City, Long Island, who would help him build a still for a fee and not a percentage. But it was up to Magnus to find a good location.

Dumping large amounts of mash in the ocean or a river would lead to a still's speedy discovery, as Treasury agents were trained to looked for such residue. Magnus knew from Scotland, however, that used mash was a prize feed for fattening hogs, and the steady smoke from a still fire would be accepted as a necessity for curing pork in a smokehouse. Therefore, a pig farm solved two major problems.

Clyde Wilkenson raised hogs outside Kingston, Long Island, about a fifteen-mile drive from the Fleming compound. He was a friendly red-faced man who always had something in his mouth to chew: gum, hay, tobacco, nuts, or his tongue. With an eye to making money he tried to buy land for another farm near Quogue, thinking the catchy phrase "Quogue's Hogs" would make him rich. The local citizens, however, had expressed a huffy prejudice against anything porcine. Therefore, he was open to Magnus' idea as long as he would get something for nothing. A week before the wedding, Magnus shook hands with Mr. Wilkenson and promised a deposit and the start of construction in exactly three weeks.

By the dawn of his wedding day, Magnus had just about everything he needed. He did not want to wait anymore. He opened his sporran, which contained the last of his cash, a few hundred dollars, and the .44 he got from Rothstein, still wrapped in the silk handkerchief. He laughed to himself as he put on his kilt, thinking of the financial cliff he had built for himself.

He and Mary were leaving after the reception for a night at the Plaza in New York. The next day they were sailing on a cruise to Bermuda. They would drive into the city in Mary's brand-new Ballot coupé. Magnus was aware that all the gifts were for Mary, and that he was considered as being "along for the ride." But what people thought did not bother him. He knew he would be on his own soon enough, and was proud he had taken nothing from the Flemings, not even their offer to sail his family over for the wedding.

He crossed the frozen lawn, passing the huge tent, which was straining at its bindings against the wind, and walked into Joseph Fleming's house. No one was awake; the family dogs no longer barked at him. He climbed the stairs, careful to skip the third one, which creaked, walked along the upstairs hall, silently turned the knob of Mary's door, and walked in.

Mary was standing in front of her full-length mirror, holding her wedding dress up to her naked body. She gasped when she saw Magnus, but then smiled, trying to cover herself with the dress as he closed the door and crossed over to her.

"Magnus, you're not supposed to see me today until—"

He did not let her finish, but took her in his arms, one hand gently moving through an arc from her shoulder to the base of her spine. Mary let the dress be held by their bodies, and put her arms around him. When the kiss ended, she whispered, "Magnus, I'm so happy, what are you doing here, I love you. . . ."

"I was invited to this great enormous wedding . . ."

"I don't think I can last the day. I'm about to burst. Magnus, we're getting married today! Oh! It's your birthday. Your present's down . . . You know what I'll give you?"

"I'll just hike up me kilt."

"Don't you dare! After all this time, I'm not giving in now. No! Don't let go. Just whisper to me. I can hear you better this way. What are you doing here?"

"I've come to marry you."

"That's not until after lunch. How'm I ever going to eat—"

"No. I've come to marry you now. Just us here, without all the prayin', and family and hoopla. That's all fine, but I want us going through all that knowing it's us that's done it, just us, with no need of any of that."

He felt her body change, so that it did not fit against him any longer. She reached for her dress, and when she pulled back, Magnus saw her frown. He took the ring from a pocket and put it on her finger. Mary stared at it.

"Don't worry, darlin' Mary, we're married now, and—"

Her head snapped up. "No."

She took the ring off hurriedly and held it out for him to take back.

"Mary, I didn't mean for you to wear it. I'll be givin' it to Juny for the ceremony. But I wanted us—"

"Magnus, here, take it, please."

He took it from her, and she looked up at him.

"Oh, Magnus, I love you so much. But I can't be married to you here. I can't."

"Mary, it's just for us, knowing—"

"No, Magnus, marriage is a blessing of God. I can't be married without that. You see, don't you? I want so much for our happiness to be blessed . . . so much."

He looked at her, then smiled and forgot to whisper.

"Weel, I don't think we've shut Him out of the room. Don't you think He might be blessing us right here?"

"Shshsh, please, Magnus, it's more than that, and part of my marrying you *is* my family. We're all part of it together, and they're a part of us, and don't you see, it's not a separate thing, it's all of us. . . ."

"Mary, Mary you canna believe they'll ever let me into the club."

"They *are*. Yes! That's what this marriage is. I'm joining with you in the life God's given me, and you're joining with me and everything that *is* me. And God must bless us. . . ."

"After lunch. . . ."

She nodded quickly and smiled with love that Magnus could not deny. He put the ring back in his pocket.

"Weel, I'll go put on my nice new suit now." He turned and went to the door.

"Magnus . . ."

"Dunna worry, darlin' Mary, I love you with all the life in me, and I'm tellin' you, standin' there all outside that white dress . . ."

Mary giggled and looked down at herself.

". . . that in my eyes, and I'm sure in *one* of God's, I'm married to ya *now*. But I'll wait for you until after lunch, and you better be there on time, or God'll go cross-eyed."

"Magnus!" and she crossed herself, the dress falling half off, causing her to give a short yell. She then covered her mouth with the other hand. The dress fell down, to veil only her feet with modesty.

Magnus stood at the door. Mary stood with one hand over her mouth, the other trying to decide which area of her beauty to cover and reaching no conclusion.

"Did I tell you, sweet Mary, that red's my favorite color?"

"Get out please!" she gasped, not moving for fear she would be somehow more naked.

The wedding ceremony flowed with spiritual fastidiousness. Joseph Fleming gave Mary away with a silent anger. Juny was all charm and ease, pretending at the altar to have lost the ring Magnus had given him. Magnus had wanted Bill McCoy to be his best man, but McCoy had turned him down because of his indictment, much to the Flemings' relief. Magnus went through the ceremony saying what he was supposed to say, kneeling when Mary knelt, but failing to cross himself as everyone else did.

Father Fulton Sheen, a young priest Joe Fleming had taken to, officiated. As part of his benediction, he included a prayer that ended, "Let them know that they are *one,* made one in the love of Jesus Christ, bound as one by the Holy Spirit, married as one by Thy power, which is beyond our understanding, but which we witness in the daily miracle of the universe. Just as there is the light from a single star, so Magnus and Mary are joined."

Magnus saw that Mary was looking at him with the weight of God's entire universe on her shoulders, placed and balanced there by her faith and family. Magnus had a sudden sense of her responsibility and knew he could never share it. For a second he had an urge to walk out. Mary's look held him there, next to her, but made him wonder.

The reception was a spectacle of both precision and confusion. The caterers were resplendently arrayed and organized like an occupying army, with their rounds of French champagne, courtesy of McCoy. But the special train arrived a half-hour late, and motoring all the guests from the station to the compound was an exasperating madness. Then a corner of the tent gave way to the wind, causing havoc at one of the bars until the canvas was tethered. In spite of the braziers, the women kept their fur coats on most of the time.

Magnus waltzed nicely with Mary and contributed a full share to the picture required of a beautiful couple. He then danced a silent dance with Mrs. Fleming, she not looking at him once, but smiling bravely to her friends around the dance floor.

When the panicked edge of the reception had been liquored down to a low roar of enjoyment, Magnus went looking for Juny. He found his best man at a dark corner table in a deep and earnest discussion with a striking blond. She wore a silver-fox coat, a black turban, and a large wedding ring which could not be missed.

"Ah, the man of the hour. There you are, Magnus. May I introduce Mrs. Wellington Banning . . . my brother-in-law, Mr. Macpherson."

"I'm so happy, congratulations, I must go, Juny, please, so nice, I'll be seeing you, Juny."

Juny rose and they watched her go.

"Poor lady. You know who she is? She's a Browne from Chestnut Hill. Married an old rubber sock, rich as Rockefeller, but he lives on looseners." He laughed at his own joke.

"Looseners?"

"Prunes! Morning, noon, and night. Can you imagine that Sheba in a house full of prune pits? Oh, boy, she's a lulu, full of pep, and no matter how hard she tries, for fashion's sake, she can't get rid of those bosoms, on which I'd like to tap-dance barefoot!"

Juny did a fast soft-shoe to the ever-flowing music.

"Juny, can we talk a little business?"

"Sure we can, Magnus. You know, you're a nifty guy. Let's go find a drink and put it where the flies can't get it."

He put an arm around Magnus.

"Let's talk first."

"O.K. What's on your mind?"

"I want to borrow fifty thousand dollars from you."

Juny blinked twice and sat down in his chair, the false camaraderie sobered off his face.

"Oh?"

Magnus sat down across from him.

"Yes. I want to go into business."

"Can I ask what kind of business?"

"The distilling business."

Juny laughed out loud.

"Oh, Magnus, how darb, how really *darb*." By the end of the sentence the laughter had turned murderous. Magnus began talking very fast.

"I can make you a damn fine offer; I'll pay you ten percent interest every month I keep the principal, and I'll give you a hundred percent return on your investment when I pay it back."

"Ten percent a month? That's one-twenty a year."

"I'll pay you back before that."

"Have you talked to my father about this?"

"No. He's six feet above contradiction, and I figure you're just like me in wanting to make a little money of your own."

He had touched a place of great sensitivity to Juny, and Juny hated him worse than ever for it.

"You lounge leach, you're not worth fifty cents."

Magnus was ready for insults and paid no attention to them.

"I'll put up some collateral."

"Collateral? You?" Juny looked around, wishing for a drink. "You better snow again, I've lost your drift." He laughed automatically and then gave it up. "You're a ponce, Macpherson, living off a rich woman, and all of us know it. And she'll know it sooner—"

"I've made you an honest proposition, Juny. I'm not interested in your opinions of me, just in your money. Do you want a deal that I guarantee in six months will make you a hundred thousand dollars' profit of your own?"

Juny looked up at Magnus and saw money. He wanted it.

"What's your collateral?"

"A certain check your father wrote once."

An hour later, through a blizzard of rice, Mary and Magnus drove off to the Plaza in her new car. Magnus insisted that she drive, for he would have the Flemings see him only as a passenger in any car they bought. On the road he and Mary laughed and talked about the reception, about her pregnant sister who kept her stomach swathed in her mink coat, about Juny getting a little too drunk and causing a slight scene by clutching at Mrs. Wellington Banning. Mary was talking, as well as driving, a little too fast; Magnus laid his hand gently on her leg. She jumped.

"Magnus. What are you doing?"

"Nervous?"

"What? . . . About what? . . . No. Yes. Of *course* I'm nervous!" She laughed. "I feel like driving off the road into that field and never even getting to the Plaza."

"That'd be fine with me, then. We could just slip into the back seat and—"

"Magnus!" She glanced over at him; then, for the first time on the drive, she became quiet. She gripped the steering wheel hard, but a smile remained on her face.

"Magnus, I don't know what . . . to do."

"You'll surprise yourself."

"I'll keep my eyes closed the whole time."

"I doubt it, darlin' Mary."

Again she was quiet. Then she said, "My sisters told me lots of things, but none of it sounded . . . like you."

"It probably didn't sound like us."

"It didn't. Elizabeth told me that Harry . . . *growled*. Do you do anything like that?" She smiled, still nervous. Magnus took her into his arms and kissed her. The car swerved, and Mary pulled over to the side of the road. At first she held onto the steering wheel as he kissed her. Then she wrapped her arms around him and kissed him longingly. Then she whispered, "Magnus . . . touch me."

He lifted her skirt above her knees and slowly, gently stroked her thighs. Mary shuddered and began to breathe through her mouth as Magnus kissed her ear, her neck. Her legs parted slightly.

"Oh . . ." Mary said. She looked at Magnus and smiled. "Get me to the Plaza. Will you drive, please? . . . Fast?"

Without a word, Magnus got out and hurried around to the driver's side. Mary slid across the seat, but not so far that she would not lean against his shoulder and put an arm around him.

As the car sped toward Manhattan, Mary quietly watched the road, smiling to herself. Magnus asked, "Still nervous?"

She shook her head and kissed his neck. "No."

"Is there anything you want me to tell you?"

"I don't want to know anything. I want it to happen and I want to be as amazed as I was back there on the road. . . . The only thing I know is that I want to be naked with you so much, it must be a sin."

Magnus glanced quickly at her, but she was smiling. He drove even faster.

After they registered at the Plaza, Magnus saw that Mary was blushing intensely as they followed the two bellhops to the elevator.

"What's the matter, darlin Mary?"

"They know!" she whispered desperately.

Magnus smiled. "Not for sure."

"Everyone in the lobby knows!"

"Just think how envious they are."

She nudged him in the ribs and tried not to laugh in the elevator.

The bellboys explained light switches, laid out luggage, pointed out the flowers and champagne, which were obvious. Then, after receiving tips, they retreated out of the suite.

Without preamble or hesitance, Magnus and Mary undressed. When they both were naked, Mary looked at Magnus as exposed and vulnerable as she had looked that morning when her wedding dress had fallen away. Then she took a quick breath as her eyes fell over his body. Any trace of apprehension dissolved into desire. She took a step toward him, hesitated, and her eyes widened. At the same moment she crossed herself quickly and began to sob.

"Mary . . ." Magnus moved toward her, but she put out a hand.

"It's all right. I don't know *how* to feel like this. Laughing . . . crying, isn't enough. Oh, God, Magnus, do everything to me now."

She fell on him. Then, as they kissed each other, she clutched his arms, his back, his buttocks. Erratically, she jammed her pelvis into him. He picked her up and carried her to the bed.

He did everything to her as she wished; as they were changing positions, she unexpectedly reached her relief. She collapsed in a stunned astonishment. Without any hesitation, Magnus made certain that her sensation would happen again, and it did. She cried the second time, and laughed a high-pitched, airy groan the third as she watched Magnus, fascinated. They both relaxed into the positions in which they would fall asleep. The only words were from Mary.

"No wonder . . ." she said, smiled at Magnus, and went to sleep. He watched her for a time, a strand of red hair falling over her eyes, her freckles barely visible without the summer sun. She shuddered once, involuntarily, as she went deeper into sleep. Magnus wondered if she were blaming herself in her sleep for the sex she had enjoyed. He knew that he had felt a distance from her as they made love. He had been overly aware of her curiosity and had remained at an observer's distance. He felt that she, on the other hand, had become lost in her discovery, and at the same time had to protect what she had found from being touched and spoiled by the rest of what she was.

Magnus brushed the hair off her forehead, hoping she would wake up. There seemed so much to say. Mary didn't move, and soon Magnus fell asleep.

The next morning, after the banks opened, as Mary was getting dressed, Magnus met Juny for coffee in the Oak Room. Juny was in a foul mood, with a rotten hangover. He exchanged fifty thousand dollars in cash for the check of the same amount. Magnus mailed deposits to the Garden City contractor and Clyde Wilkenson, and two hours later was on board the cruise ship.

Two weeks later he returned in time to supervise construction of the still on Mr. Wilkenson's pig farm, and three weeks after that he produced his first batch of alky. He called the number Costello had given him, and four hours later a truck arrived with Costello's representative, two gangsters, and two loaders. The representative said nothing until he tasted the product. It was good alky and he made Magnus a solid offer. The first batch was loaded on the truck. The two gangsters remained to protect the place from either the law or hijackers. They would be relieved by others, so there would be guards around the clock. Costello's syndicate would supply Magnus sugar, yeast, and five-gallon tin containers at cost plus ten percent. Any bribes to local officials, "granny fees," or police on the road, "grease spots," would be split fifty-fifty. Every five days a truck would come to pick up the alky and Magnus would be paid the agreed price in cash. There was no contract, not even a handshake. The deal was as certain as the desire to live. As Magnus watched the truck drive off Wilkenson's farm to the Acaponick Road, he figured he would gross one hundred thousand dollars every thirty-two days.

The technology of bootleg hooch was rapidly advancing. Magnus had built a mushroom steam still. The alky produced was based on sugar, which cut down the time of fermenting a yeast-bloated mash from five or six days to seventy-two hours. Another advantage was that the amount of alcohol distilled from a sugar mash was double that from an equal measure of grain mash. Sugar-mash fermentation time could be further reduced to forty-eight hours by the use of a "kicker" or "tickler." The chemical name of this additive was urea, used elsewhere as fertilizer, in plastics and resins, and to increase the flow of urine in man or beast. It would seem a questionable substance to include in a liquid meant for human consumption, but the indiscriminating yeast seemed to regard it as a culinary delicacy, and gobbled up the sugar mash with an even more efficient gluttony.

Steam was used to cut down on the time of distillation. It was piped straight into the mash, heating it to its own temperature, and carrying off with it the vapors for distilling. For this a boiler was needed to build up a constant supply of high pressure steam. To heat the boiler, Magnus decided on gasoline burners. All of the workings were housed in what looked like an addition to Mr. Wilkenson's barn. The mushroom still, because of its height, had a silo built for it with an entrance filled with corn for the pigs. There was also a false room which Wilkenson hung with hams and bacon to be smoked as a by-product of the alky.

Magnus had worked hard and spent his money well. He had found three so-called "chemists" who knew enough about distilling not to get blown up. To make his profit, Magnus had to keep the still working twenty-four hours a day. He divided the day into four shifts, taking one six-hour period himself. He was tired and knew he could not keep a shift himself and worry about supplies and schedules as well. As soon as he could, he went looking for a blind overseer who would be able to work in the dark. Gasoline burners could be masked efficiently, but a light used to read gauges, seen through an open door, an unguarded window, even through the cracks between boards of a shed, were a beacon to Treasury agents driving by or flying overhead. Rather than take a chance on such mistakes, Magnus decided to find someone who did not need light, who could learn the complex routine of the still by memorizing space, feeling valves and heat, tasting and smelling the product, and reading the pressure gauges, hydrometer, and thermometer in special gauge faces by touch.

Through local charities Magnus met numerous blind men whom he considered for the job. He picked a man named Mathew Fowler, mainly because he had been sighted once and lost his vision several years before in a factory accident. His previous experience meant it would be easier for Magnus to explain the mechanism of the still. Fowler had, in the years since the accident, learned Braille, which meant he was willing to try things and had not given up on his life. He also had a wife, and they had gone ahead and had a baby girl, even after his accident, which meant he had hope and determination. When Magnus told him about the job, and how much he would pay for it, Mathew Fowler held out his arms searching for his wife, and when she walked into them, they both wept openly.

Magnus guaranteed all his workers legal insurance, life insurance, and as much future employment as he, a bootlegger, could guarantee. He trained them himself, making sure they understood his own particular style with the alky. He took a great deal of extra time with Mathew Fowler. He sat through the nights at the still, watching him. He taught him to move carefully from the mash vats to the sugar supply, back to the still, checking water levels in the condenser, reading boiler pressure, gasoline pressure, temperature, and proof level with the hydrometer. Fowler would taste, smell, feel, and listen for any change in the bubbling, hissing, and dripping. Magnus shook Fowler's hand one night and left him on his own. He went back to the Fleming house, where he and Mary were living, and tried to sleep. He waited all night for the phone to ring and Wilkenson to tell him the still had burned down or blown up. But it did not ring, and when dawn came and he knew Fowler's shift was over, Magnus fell into a sleep that lasted twelve hours.

When he woke up, he saw Mary sitting in a chair by the window, looking out, leaning her head on one hand, legs stretched out and propped on the radiator. She was wearing a skirt and blouse, with a sweater against the early-spring breezes. She slowly pulled at strands of hair over her ears as she stared out at the sea.

Magnus watched her for a moment. It had been a hard time for Mary. When he told her about his plan for the still on a pink beach in Bermuda, she had been shocked. She begged him not to get involved, to leave bootlegging behind, and to get an honest job. She knew her uncles, cousins, or even her father would surely help him find something else. Magnus had told her that using her family in any way would be the most dishonest choice he could make. The truth was he was a bootlegger; he had never given her a reason to think anything different.

Mary had planned to return from their honeymoon and find an apartment in New York City. The whole family was there, and it was such an exciting season. Cal Coolidge was cleaning out the corruption of Teapot Dome and making America safe for business, and for Fleming and Co. The hemlines had gone down. There was a great rush to the color jade, which Mary considered one of her best colors. The theater season was dazzling. Eubie Blake was playing jazz, and George Gershwin had performed his *Rhapsody in Blue* for the first time. But Mary had not taken part in the season of 1924 because she knew her family and her friends would be talking about her bootlegger husband. So she stayed in Southampton with him, spending a great deal of time alone as Magnus put his still together. Magnus knew Mary was ashamed, but would never admit it, even to herself. He also knew he was about to make it up to her.

"Good morning, darlin Mary."

The chair creaked as she turned to look at him.

"It's almost evening." She smiled, but did not move.

"Come here to bed with me."

She got up and came to the bed. She did not undress, but lay down with him, hugging him. Magnus felt the habit of it, not the wish. He held her quietly for a while, then whispered in her ear.

"I know, darlin' Mary, I know."

"What?"

"How hard it's been for you."

She squeezed him and snuggled her mouth up to his ear and whispered back.

"It's been hard for both of us. You're really exhausted, I hope you know. Has the blind man worked out?"

"Yes. It'll be different now. I can put the three other men on two eight-hour shifts, with one of them relieving the others, and all I'll have to do is relieve Fowler when he wants. . . . But he's so damn happy working, I doubt if I'll have to."

"Good. I don't like sleeping alone, even in my own room. Oh, Magnus, talk to me, whisper me things."

"What things?"

"I don't know, whatever you'd whisper to a lover in an empty house." She kissed him and pressed one leg along his thigh.

"Weel, how about, 'Darlin Mary, how'd ya like to live in a house of your own?' "

She stopped breathing for a moment, then whispered, "What do you mean?"

"I was just whispering to my lover in an empty house. Then I'd go on to say, 'Over there in my pants is thirty thousand dollars in cash, which should be enough to put a down payment on any house in East Hampton you might want.' "

She sat up and looked at Magnus.

"East Hampton?" She did not whisper.

"Shshsh. Whisper."

But she would not.

"What about East Hampton? What house?"

"I'm talking about our own house, living in our own house."

"East Hampton?"

"Or Amagansett, or Quogue, or anywhere you like. I only said East Hampton because it's closer to Wilkenson's . . . and I imagine your family would approve, as it's even grander than Southampton, and the people over there won't hate us because I'm a black Protestant." He laughed, alone, which he noticed and stopped.

"Magnus, we don't have to leave here. If we want a separate house, Father said he'd build—"

"Darlin Mary, do you think I'm stayin' in any house of yer father's one second longer than I have to? You dinna think we'd be stayin' here forever?"

"Not here, in the house, but, well, nearby."

"East Hampton is ten miles down the road."

"It might as well be Timbuktu."

"That's in yer mind, and yer family put it there because they need it."

"Need what?"

"They're snobs. They need the distance because they're scared. You needn't be afraid, Mary. We canna be afraid, or we'll never get out of here, or anywhere."

"I don't want to get out of here. Scared of what?"

"Of other snobs. There's always a bigger snob. And we do want to get out of here, Mary, so we can find our life, whatever it is, without three hundred Flemings around telling us how it should be. And you can thank God we can get out before they all start arriving like some great migration in May—"

"Stop it."

She got up off the bed and went to the window. Magnus looked at her for a moment, then stood up and walked over for his pants. He put them on, took the money over to Mary, and put it on top of the radiator so she could see it. She closed her eyes, shook her head, and turned back to the window.

"I know it means nothing to ya, but canna you think what it means to me, Mary?"

She turned to him quickly, the words blurted out too fast for care, and tumbled further by the emotion gripping her throat, causing tears.

"You *don't* know, you don't know, what anything means, what it is here that you insult, and hate, my family, *my* family, and what is it you're doing, you're just trying to take me away from them, tearing me off, tearing me away from my life, from them. *I am* my family, you know that, you have to know that, you've seen me here, with them, always. . . ."

"Mary, I know damn well you're a Fleming, but do you know who in all the world Mary is?"

"I, I . . ."

"Well, I do, and I fell in love with her and married her, and she's who I want to live with, not with one of those Flemings who flock out to Southampton every summer."

"I don't want to live alone in East . . . No, I don't mean alone, I mean—"

"Yes, you do, Mary. You just can't imagine yourself as a person without this bluidy family. What is it? Is it being surrounded by people all the time who tell you what a great thing it is to be a Fleming? And they should know, shouldn't they, saying it to their mirrors as well as to you? Is it that you think you're all so special in some way?"

"Yes! We are; I'm proud of my family."

"Fine! I'm proud of mine, too. Mine go back for generations of clergy and whiskey smugglers. Every family goes back to something or other. No one arrived on the earth rich. Your family goes back to farmers, and be proud of that. They've had money a wee while, but darlin Mary, don't think that changes anyone's genes. You Flemings aren't breeding special-blessed Catholics. Your people haven't been bothered with worry, that's all. Nothing interferes with your polo matches and yacht races and cocktails. It's all swank and posh and hotsy-totsy."

Mary stared at him.

"Magnus, you hate me."

"Don't be daft. I love *you,* not your family and its snobbery and fear. I love you, Mary, the woman who comes across the water on her own to buy hooch. I love the woman who says to hell with all of it and walks over the dance floor to get a man whose name she doesn't know, and can decide in a day she's going to marry him. You would have chopped the whole compound into kindling to do it. That's the woman I love. You were going to leave here to marry me. Why can't you leave now?"

"Because now I don't need to. We don't."

"I do. We do."

"I don't want to!"

"Then you don't have to."

He turned and walked to the door.

"Yes, I do. I have to, if you go."

He was back, grabbing her shoulders so tightly she could not breathe for a moment. He did not speak right away. His rage was so great she was afraid and focused on the small scar under his left eye, fascinated as it changed color to a dark purple.

"Mary, never come with me because of your religion. Never! Obligation kills love. Don't bind us with your duty . . . or we'll be living in a hell."

She blinked and looked up from the scar. He had not yelled, or shaken her, or hurt her. But Mary was frightened. She was frightened of his fierce determination to have his own way, and of her unknown and uncharted life with him. Tears came to her eyes, and by a curious refraction, she seemed to glimpse through Magnus the crucifix that hung on the wall above their bed. Her mouth opened and she thanked God silently, then said with determination, "I love you, Magnus."

She undressed and got into bed. They made love purposefully.

In three weeks they bought a large house on the beach in East Hampton, and Mary spent the rest of the summer furnishing it. In October Magnus paid Juny back with the agreed hundred percent interest. That fall, Mary spent more time in New York, seeing her family, going to the theater, and shopping. The stigma of having a bootlegger husband softened. She contributed time as a surrogate penance with the Guild of the Infant Savior, a fashionable Roman Catholic charity created to "give sanctuary to destitute young girls facing motherhood alone." It was an apropos choice of charity; she told Magnus on Christmas morning that he was to be a father.

In March, the still blew up.

4

There's only one solution, dear.
Let's calmly disappear.
Let's fly away
And find a land that's warm and tropic;
Where prohibition's not the topic
All the live long day.

—COLE PORTER

The call came at 3:30 A.M., not from Wilkenson, but from one of the gangsters on guard. His partner was badly burned, the still was destroyed, Fowler was dead, the local police had arrived, and the feds would be there soon. The gangster hung up.

Magnus put the phone down. He'd had the call before, in recurring nightmares, but this time it was real and the blind man was dead. Of all the people involved with the still, Mathew Fowler was the only one Magnus liked. The rest, including himself, were in it for money; Fowler was in it to be alive. Magnus bent over on the bed clenching his body.

There was no time for mourning; his nightmares had alerted him to the potential dangers. He woke Mary, explained what had happened as he got dressed, and told her to pack what she could in fifteen minutes. He made two phone calls, went to the back porch, pried up some floorboards, and pulled out the cash he had hidden there. He packed most in his canvas bag, keeping ten thousand dollars in his pocket.

When he got to the car, Mary was sitting there staring straight ahead. Her bags were in the truck. They did not speak as Magnus drove to Mrs. Fowler's house in the village of Promised Land.

The woman, in her late thirties, with short hair pressed to one side by the sleep Magnus had interrupted, stood behind the screen door in an old faded robe. She knew who they were, knew what had happened. Her first words were, "Won't you come in?"

They went in, but did not sit down. Mary became very conscious of the fur coat she was wearing and wanted to take it off. Mrs. Fowler sat down and let her tears flow. She made no sound or movement, but her tears fell steadily, making spots on her robe.

Magnus started to sit in a worn armchair with crocheted antimacassars, then realized it was Mathew Fowler's favorite and moved awkwardly away. He looked at Mrs. Fowler and saw what her life was going to be. He blamed himself for it, thinking he'd been so clever to hire a blind man. He looked from the ravaged face of the woman to the empty chair and wished he could share the pain.

"It's all right, Mr. Macpherson, sit down. It's better than looking at it empty."

"I don't know what happened, Mrs. Fowler. I thought more of your husband than I did most men in the world. I won't dare ask you to forgive me. But you can be sure—"

"Hold on, Mr. Macpherson, you got it wrong. You did something for him that . . . well, listen here, we had the happiest year of our lives, that's all. You let him be a new man, bless you for that. He was dying when you come around; he was fighting, but he was dying. After he started on the job, oh my, oh my . . ."

She put her head on the back of her chair and laughed.

"We'd come home in the mornings after I'd pick him up, and he'd chase me all over the house, breaking furniture, trying to get at me . . . we laughed, oh my . . . how we laughed. You gave us that, Mr. Macpherson. . . . You want some java?"

"We have to leave. The police will be here, and you might think on what—"

A two-year-old girl appeared at a door and stared at them. Her mother went and picked her up.

"Iris, what are you doing awake?"

Mrs. Fowler held the little girl in her arms without any display of emotion. Then she turned to Magnus.

"There's something you should know so you won't go blaming yourself. When Mat got hurt at the factory, his eyes pained him a lot. They gave him morphine, and he got hopped on it. He tried real hard to get off it, and he did by the time he started working for you. But a month ago, one of your jigger men at the still started giving him joy powder. Mat told me last week. . . ."

Magnus and Mrs. Fowler realized there was no more to say. They both understood what had happened; there was no blame between them. Magnus put the money from his pocket on a table and said, "You'll hear from me every month."

He reached out for Mary's hand, and they walked out of the house. In the car they clung to each other silently; then he pulled away, feeling guilty at having so much life in his arms. They drove to Montauk Point. A motor launch was waiting, which took them to Block Island. At dawn they met a seaplane, which flew to Quebec and landed on the St. Lawrence River, in time for Magnus and Mary to check into a suite at the Château Frontenac and to have a late breakfast. Mary called her mother about the house and the car. She had two suitcases of clothes and a fur coat. Magnus had only what he was wearing, and in the canvas bag, seven-hundred-thirty-six-thousand dollars in cash.

Mary felt they had lost everything, but Magnus was hopeful. When he'd arrived in America, he'd had considerably less. To Mary, Canada was cold, with snow and ice everywhere, and farther away from the Fleming compound than Timbuktu. She could not reach out for them, call and make herself heard. Magnus, on the other hand, did not mind the cold. He saw the ice glittering like a treasure waiting to be taken: Canada had no prohibition.

They spent their first day in Quebec trying to discover how they might belong in that strange place. Mary located a real-estate agent, an obstetrician, and a church. Magnus deposited his money in the Quebec branches of Canada's six largest banks, and was asked to lunch by an officer of each. By the time Mary returned to their suite, she had seen two houses and would see four the next day. Magnus had spoken to six distillery owners on the phone and arranged to visit three of them.

That night they ate a quiet meal in the suite. Mary avoided looking at him, and when he caught her eye, she smiled only to escape.

"Mary, you can go back anytime you want, for as long as you want."

She didn't look up as she spoke.

"Are you giving me some kind of permission?"

"It's not permission. I understand how you feel about being here."

"Magnus, I've wondered about something today. I'm tired, all this happened too fast. But . . . why Quebec? I understand about getting out of the country, but why not Montreal, or Toronto? Why way up here?"

"There's a distillery twenty-five miles up the St. Lawrence at Neuville I think I can buy."

"You knew that before today?"

"Nothing certain. I've been talking with the owner on the phone."

"But you were thinking of it. Why didn't you tell me?"

"There was nothing to tell. He's agreed to nothing."

"Magnus, you were thinking about buying a distillery. That means you were thinking about coming to Canada. If this hadn't happened and the man had agreed to sell you this distillery, what would you have done? It seems as if the still blowing up saved you a lot of trouble."

Magnus put his silverware down.

"Mary, there was nothing definite to tell you. It was one choice of many. I've been doing a lot of business, trying to find different ways to expand. I've been looking into warehouse receipts in Pittsburgh, and buying and selling bond in Kentucky. And I'm not the only one talking to Mr. Brisbane. There's some brothers up here named Bronfman who're—"

"Who is Mr. Brisbane? What brothers?"

"He owns the distillery I'm after. Mary, what I'm trying to tell you is, there *wasn't* anything to tell you. I'm in a business; you couldn't have thought I was just sitting around counting my money. What happened this morning forced a choice. We had to come here. . . . And you won't have to feel ashamed of me up here, for what I'm doing is lawful."

"Ashamed? How could you think . . . ? I was frightened for you, either getting blown up like Mr. Fowler or being put in jail. I have a right to know what you're deciding about our life. Don't confuse me with all the names and terms of your business, storing them up for months and then shoveling them at me, hoping I'll be overwhelmed, and *eat my dinner* like a good girl!"

She dropped her silver on her plate and pushed it away. A wine-glass overturned and they both watched the blot spread over the tablecloth.

"I'm sorry, Magnus, I'm so tired. . . . I don't know where I am. I thought for a minute I didn't know who you were. I feel like I'm lost, and . . . Oh, dear God, am I going to have my baby in this freezing place?"

She put one hand across her eyes. The other lay in her lap. Just before she began to sob, Magnus thought he saw something in Mary he had not ever seen, intangible, spilling over like the wine in so small a quantity, but spreading, staining the tablecloth to its edges. Magnus took her in his arms, and felt her tears on his neck, her arms clinging to him, her hands grasping at the cloth of his coat. The sobs quieted, and she shook her head, angry at herself.

"I'm not going to be this way. We're together, all three of us, and that's what's important, not where we are or why." She smiled at Magnus. "I'm going to love Quebec, . . . but not tonight."

They laughed quietly together.

"Take us to bed, Magnus, we're so tired. . . ."

In the bedroom, he helped her undress and slip into the flannel robe he had bought for her that day; the size allowed for the expansion of her belly. She fell asleep as he lay next to her, stroking her hair back over her ears.

He would tell her what he could. He would tell her the names of people in his business, and any plans he might have which involved her. But there were going to be plans she could not know, and people she would not want to know. For although distilling was legal in Canada, the market was still the United States. The buyers there were the same gangsters. By making the jump to Canada and owning distilleries, Magnus' importance to those buyers would be greater, and inversely, so would be the danger. The profits, however, justified the risks. Magnus figured if he could buy the distillery in Neuville, ship his whiskey to Windsor, Ontario, and sell it across the river to the bootleggers in Detroit, he could be a millionaire in a year.

In spite of not having slept since the phone call that morning, he was not tired. Suddenly in the dark Mary touched him in a desperate passion. He met her desperation with his exhilaration. They made love for a wordless time and sank deep into sleep in each other's arms.

Canada had already tried prohibition, and gave up on it just as the United States went dry. So exasperated was the Canadian government with enforcement that when their prohibition ended, control on the manufacture and merchandising of liquor was minimal and they resented American efforts to curtail the flow of liquor across what would be called "the longest unguarded border between two civilized nations." Canada simply refused to spend money upholding a law which their national experience had just proven absurd. Therefore, the Canadian government was unconcerned about the foreign destination of the liquor produced in its dominion.

Magnus was not the only one to take fast advantage of the situation. The Bronfman brothers, sons of Russian Jewish immigrants, had already built a distillery in LaSalle, near Montreal, and set up the Distillers' Corporation, Limited, to operate it. Magnus heard that none of the five brothers knew a thing about distilling, but two of them, Samuel and Albert, were learning and were also looking for other distilleries to buy. Magnus knew he had to move fast to secure Brisbane's distillery in Neuville. He did, leaving the Bronfmans to buy another in Waterloo called the Joseph Seagram Distillery.

The day Magnus closed his deal, he drove Mary down to Neuville in their new Buick touring car to show her the plant. They made a handsome picture of a prosperous and pregnant couple. Magnus was enormously proud of owning things, and particularly, a distillery. His father, and his father before him, had never even held a deed to their own home, which had been provided by the Church of Scotland. Ownership became an appetite to Magnus, and would soon be a craving.

He took great pleasure in showing Mary through the distillery in the company of his foreman and his manager, explaining what mash was, why limestone water was so important, what a condenser is for, and what happens when whiskey ages in a barrel. He let her taste the product at the try-box, and told her all about the days with his father making The Creation. They walked down the row of pneumatic malt bins, which sprouted grain like a pressure cooker with almost as perfect plumules as the Reverend Mr. Macpherson would grow by instinct on the floor of his cave.

"Mary, can you think of a name for our first product?"

"If it's a boy, I want him named after you."

"No, no, the whiskey, the whiskey."

"How about 'Mother's Milk'?"

"You're outrageous."

He explained that the distillery housed plants which produced a Canadian whiskey and a rye whiskey. There were four maturing warehouses, and a bottling unit capable of packaging two thousand cases a day.

"Two thousand cases a day? Magnus, can you sell all that?"

"Mary, in six months I'll sell ten times that much. Brisbane made vile whiskey, and he didn't believe in advertising."

"Who'll buy it? Do people drink that much?"

"They do, and more. There's no end to the wanting. We have a standing contract with the Canadian government for twelve hundred cases a day. I'll make such whiskey that they'll beg me for all they can get."

"That's so much, Magnus. I had no idea. . . . Why wouldn't you sell it all to the government, if they want it?"

Magnus looked at Mary and smiled. They'd had such a nice day;

he didn't want it to be spoiled. But he had promised to try to tell her about his business.

"There's a better market. . . ."

He watched as her curiosity was displaced by a quick look of fear. She took a step back and turned around.

"Magnus, can we go, please?"

They drove back to Quebec in silence until Mary asked, "Magnus, do you have to sell to the bootleggers?"

"It'd be stupid not to."

"It would be honest, . . . legal."

"Mary, prohibition's the thing that's dishonest. It's a lie; with time, it'll be thrown out. Why should I respect it when no one else does?"

"It's the law, Magnus, you're taking advantage of it."

"Yes, I am. It's the nature of business to take advantage of an opportunity. But I'll be breaking no law in Canada or the States, even the one that's a lie."

Mary shook her head violently.

"Magnus, you know what you're doing. People use your whiskey to steal, to corrupt . . . people will be murdered for your whiskey." She was having trouble controlling her voice. "How can we live, how can we have a family, knowing it's all based on that? . . ."

"Mary, if I didn't sell one bottle of whiskey into the States, there'd be just as much stealing and corruption, and just as many people would be murdered. If I don't sell my whiskey, the Bronfmans or Hiram Walker will sell more of theirs. As long as there's prohibition, there'll be enough whiskey for stealing and murder, no matter what I do. But it isn't the whiskey causing it. It's greed; people will always be killing each other for that." He smiled quickly over at her, hoping he'd turned the conversation. He wanted so much for her to be happy with him but Mary continued to look straight ahead out of the windshield.

"I love you, Magnus, but I . . . I *hate* this whiskey business! Dear God, what can I do to convince you to stop it? You must be a brilliant businessman. You could succeed in banking, railroads . . ."

"There's nothing else I can do so well right now."

She glanced over at him, then turned back to the road.

"Magnus, is it me?"

"I don't know what you mean, but I'm sure I'd say no."

"I mean that because my family has a lot of money, you might feel that you have to—"

Magnus interrupted.

"Your family has nothing to do with anything I do."

Quietly Mary contradicted him.

"Yes they do. Juny gave you the money to start."

Magnus nearly drove off the road, which scared them both.

"Magnus, be careful."

"How did you know that?"

"Juny told me. He was angry when we left Southampton and said he'd never have lent you the money if it had meant I would have to leave."

"Did he tell you anything else?"

She glanced over at him, worried. "No, just that you'd paid him back. I asked about that. . . ."

Magnus looked at her quickly again and was sure Juny had said nothing about the check. Just like Juny to take credit for the loan and not mention the collateral.

"Are you sure, Magnus? Would you be so . . . consumed with all this if it weren't for me and my family?"

"My life didn't start when I met the Flemings, Mary. Before that, I was poor wanting to be rich. Now I'm going to be; that's all that's happened. Being poor meant no more to me than being rich does to you: we were both born to it. I knew I wanted to change. My family owned nothing except our clothes. I went to school as a charity student, and I knew it every day. We ate regular, but not much, and there's damned little variety in oatmeal and cabbage. But we were as happy as the Flemings. . . ."

He looked over at Mary, who remained silent. Magnus went on.

"I just knew from the beginning I wasn't going to live my life poor. And by God, I'm not. I left home to get rich. It's a better way to go through life, Mary, and the richer you are, the better it can be. I came to America to get rich. And I'll tell you something else: you *have* to be rich in America. If you don't get rich, America doesn't work."

"You don't know what money can do. My being rich is already making you—"

"Damnation, Mary! My mother *died* of being poor. She had consumption, and we hadn't the money for doctors, or medicine, or sending her to a climate where she'd be helped. All we had was prayers!"

Magnus wanted to make sure his disgust had not been taken personally. He pulled the car over to the shoulder and reached over to take Mary's hand.

"If there's something wrong with me or the world, Mary, you don't have to take it all on as your fault."

Without looking up she said, "There must be something I could do to convince you."

"Like starving yourself?"

Startled, Mary stared at him. "How did you know that? . . . No."

"Juny mentioned it once. Why did you do it, then?"

"I didn't want to eat if my sister was betraying her marriage. I just couldn't eat knowing she was doing what she was doing. Why did Juny tell you?"

"What was she doing? Breaking the rules of the Fleming compound? It isn't any more perfect in there than it is out here, Mary. And you can't make it that way."

Mary watched a car go by in the opposite direction.

"I know, but I don't want to make it any worse. . . . I'm so surprised Juny told you about that." She leaned against him as she continued. "It was just . . . impossible for me to go on eating, or anything else, as long as I knew there was something so terribly wrong in my family. . . . It seems foolish now, but I understand why I did it."

"What happened to your sister?"

"She's still married."

"Is she happy?"

"Happier than if she'd had to leave the compound."

Magnus glanced quickly at Mary. She caught the look and pulled away from him. "Happiness isn't the most important thing in the world, Magnus."

"What is, Mary, the rules of the compound? And are you planning to build a new one for our family, all bound together with Roman Catholic laws for perfection?"

Icily Mary said, "My children will be Catholics."

"Weel, I hope they'll manage to be human beings as well."

"Don't ridicule me. Stop it. Stop it right now! You don't understand. You were separated from your own family, Magnus. You've always been alone. You like it. I don't want my children to be like that. You just go on and sell your whiskey to whoever you want. I will *not* let it affect my family. You can find your own happiness. Do you think you can find it that way, Magnus? Do you?"

He turned away and started the car up. Before he drove out onto the road, he said, "I'm going to be rich, Mary, happiness or no.

That's certain." He put the car in gear. "But any chance of me being happy will take you loving me."

They drove for a long time before Mary reached over and took one of Magnus' hands from the steering wheel to hold it.

"I can't help it, Magnus, what you do is wrong to me. When we got married, it never occurred to me that this is what you'd do. I suppose I was naive. I thought . . . No, I didn't think anything. I pray God I keep loving you as much as I do, and that you keep loving me. I fear the whiskey will wash something away between us, and I'm scared of any distance from you. Without you, I'd be alone, completely alone . . . and I couldn't stand it."

Before he could stop himself, Magnus said, "Not for long," and took her hand and put it on her stomach.

Mary looked over at him and smiled. "I know." She looked down and put both hands over his. "I know."

Magnus took his hand away slowly, indicating he needed it to steer. But he was uncomfortable with what he had done. He had distracted Mary with their child from knowing how often his whiskey business would take him away from her, from knowing how imperfect the world was, and that she was, after all, like anyone else, alone. He wanted to tell her he didn't like being alone either, but he was afraid to display any weakness. He wanted to explain how she'd been protected by her family, to tell her about the check her father and brother had offered, to clarify the blinding guilts imposed by her church. But even as he took breath to begin, Magnus knew her faith was more important to her than any truth; she would never believe him, tainted with the world as he was. They drove back to Quebec in silence.

Magnus renamed the business, incorporating as Macpherson Distilleries, Limited. The title implied the plural, and as he traveled up the St. Lawrence to Montreal, then on to Toronto and along the Great Lakes Ontario and Erie, Magnus looked for other distilleries to buy. He had been assured by the bankers in Quebec his credit was good. What Magnus did not know was that those bankers, who were French-Canadians and anxious to keep business in their French province, trusted him only because he had married a Fleming. Their assumption was that Magnus was as good a risk as the venerable investment-banking firm.

As he continued to expand his market, he focused on Detroit as the best route to the States. The Detroit River, which runs thirty-one miles north and south between Lake Erie and Lake Huron, failed miserably in separating wet Canada from thirsty America by its mile-and-a-half width. A fast speedboat could cross this boundary, at forty miles an hour, in four minutes. Over the previous decade, the city of Detroit had filled with immigrants to take jobs in the automobile factories. Its population swelled to one and a half million, the fourth largest in the United States. The immigrants, mostly from Europe, regarded alcoholic beverages as part of their culture, if not their souls. Fifteen thousand "blind pigs," or illicit taverns, did business in the Detroit area: one for every hundred men, women, and children. Straight liquor was so easily procured that the usual cutting or needling was unnecessary.

Early in 1925, Magnus walked down the more than ninety wharves on the Windsor side of the Detroit River. These wharves, built specifically for liquor shipping, handled 85 percent of all illicit liquor entering the United States. However, as far as liquor and crime were concerned, Detroit was considered a suburb of Chicago, 250 miles away. Chicago was becoming Al Capone's town, and with the help of his friend Johnny Torrio, he was buying it with Canadian liquor.

In the early twenties Torrio, Capone, and the Unione Siciliane ran the South Side of the city, while an Irishman named O'Bannion ran the North Side. An uneasy truce existed between the two, respecting the "Avenue of Blood," Madison Street.

But the tension grew, and finally members of the North Side shot down Johnny Torrio. Glad to be alive, Torrio decided to take a rest in Naples, leaving Capone in charge of the Chicago empire. Capone's personal annual income rose to a tax-free five million dollars. He was thirty years old and had recently been infected with the syphilis that would eventually kill him. Magnus knew that if he wished to market his liquor through Detroit, he would have to contact the so-called Purple Gang, who were under contract to supply Capone with Canadian liquor. On a pier on the Windsor side of the Detroit River, Magnus watched speedboats move hooch back and forth as if they were on a private pond. One of the speedboats came up to the pier. Five men were in the boat, two manning it, two holding sawed-off shotguns below the gunwales. The fifth was a short Jew in a rumpled suit, with a cigarette stuck to his bottom lip. His round wire-rimmed glasses encircled eyes that held a constant expression of apprehension.

"You Macpherson?" he called in a high phlegmatic voice.

Magnus nodded as the man got out of the boat, followed by the two guards carrying the shotguns. Simultaneously a covered truck drove onto the pier and backed up to the speedboat. The two other men started to load cases of whiskey handed down by the truck drivers.

"Name's Weiss. Heard tell you got some hooch to sell."

"*I* don't. But I know of a little Canadian company that buys from me. They might have some."

"Um. Got a name, this little company?"

"Yes. Acme, Limited."

"No."

"No what?"

"Is it incorporated yet?"

"It will be soon."

"Don't call it Acme. Bronfman calls his bootleg company Atlas. Too confusing. Now, talk turkey. How much and how soon?"

"Tell Bronfman to change the name of *his* company. I like Acme; it has a ring to it."

Weiss looked at Magnus, his mouth grimacing around the cigarette.

"There'll be mix-ups. You'll lose some whiskey."

"Weel, you and I will see that doesn't happen."

Weiss held the grimace and watched Magnus through a cloud of smoke. Then he sighed, and his shoulders hunched down.

"How much and how soon?"

"Five thousand cases a week as soon as you say, and ten thousand a week as soon as you want."

Weiss's doubt squeezed his entire face in on itself.

"You sure?"

"I'm sure."

"You got balls in your brains, Macpherson. We'll take your five thou; I'll let you know about the ten. You got a warehouse here?"

"I'm open to suggestion."

"We got one, down on Thirty-five."

"What're your rates?"

"Competitive."

"I'll find my own warehouse, then."

"What? Why?"

"Why not? Unless you give me a deal for doing business with you, I'll look around."

Shaking his head, Weiss reached for his cigarette butt, which was burning his lips. He ground it out on the pier, felt in his suit for a pack of Camels to replace it. The pack was empty, and he threw it in the water.

"I couldn't be so lucky that you smoked humps, could I?"

"No."

"Never been that lucky." He looked off at the boat loading. "Keep an eye on the guy in the purple porkpie. He smokes his humps half-way down; I used to live on half-smoked dinchers in Cicero."

One of the men with a shotgun had a cigarette up to his mouth, holding it from underneath with four fingers and a thumb. Weiss turned back to Magnus.

"Macpherson, we'd *like* it. Just think of it that way, we'd just like it if you, uh, 'Acme' used our warehouse."

"I'm sure you would. And I'd like to use it, if your rates are lower than anyone else's. But, Weiss, let me tell you, and anyone else that needs to hear, I'm in this to make money, just like you people are. I'll take no threats. If there are going to be threats, I'll be happy to walk away and make less money with somebody else."

Weiss took in a deep breath, looked to heaven, and shook his head. Then he let go with a long sad sigh and asked the sky, "Why me? I'm a bookkeeper, and I have to tell the facts of life to the goy ganef. . . . Macpherson, um, no threats, all right? No threats. I'm not even going to bother you with the truth. Macpherson, you're in business with us. You walk away from it, and I'll tell the world, you won't *ever* deal with anyone else. Facts, just facts, no threats. And you use *our* warehouse."

"What are your rates?" Magnus said quietly.

Weiss's eyes opened so wide they eclipsed the glasses. His lips bunched up, and his face looked like it was muffling a small blast in-side his head. Magnus met this with his calm curiosity about rates. Weiss turned and walked quickly over to the guard with the cigarette, grabbed it out of his hand, and said, "Don't you know these things'll kill you, putz?" and walked back to Magnus, puffing hard.

"I'm not going to haggle with you, Macpherson."

"Ah, come on, haggle, Weiss. If you're the bookkeeper I think you are, you enjoy it."

This surprised Weiss, and he started laughing when he was sucking smoke in. The coughing left him breathless for a while. But then they haggled, Magnus quoting the rates of every other warehouse in Windsor, Weiss coming back with trucking costs from one warehouse to another, both of them reaching a conclusion and enjoying themselves thoroughly. Magnus agreed to use Weiss's warehouse, but at a decent price.

"Tell me something, Macpherson. How come you're down here yourself? Bronfman wouldn't be seen dead around here. He sends his people to deal."

"I like to haggle; besides, I can't think of any 'people' I'd dare put up against the likes of you besides myself. And why shouldn't I enjoy myself? On this side of the river, there ain't a law I'm breaking."

"You're a lucky man." Weiss ground the cigarette butt out on the pier. He saw the speedboat was loaded and the truck was about to drive away. "Be seeing you, Macpherson." He went to the boat, got in, and bummed another cigarette from the gangster in the purple hat.

Magnus got to know Ted Weiss well on his weekly trips to Windsor. He learned that Weiss was on loan to the Purple Gang from Capone's organization to look after the books and keep track of the deals with the Canadian liquor suppliers. He was born and raised in Cicero, Illinois. He learned early that a Jew in Cicero had to be smart before tough to stay alive. If not, he would have to kill someone, for which Weiss had no talent.

Ted Weiss was reticent to a point of invisibility; he did not like being pointed out by anyone. He was trying to earn a living and to stay alive. He knew that people who were pointed out got more than attention pointed at them. He was at a distinct disadvantage because he could not kill just to be killing. He had been urged to try it, and failed, thereby suffering a certain lack of respect.

He had no ambition for fame or infamy. As a release from the pressure of the accuracy of his bookkeeping, what he really liked to do was play gin rummy and cheat. He and Magnus began a ritual weekly game among the stacked cases of Macpherson whiskey relabeled for export as "Log Cabin." They both accepted that cheating was a part of the game, and so was getting caught. In the middle of one tense game, Magnus received word he was about to become a father. Ted Weiss helped him find a seaplane to pick him up on the pier outside and fly him back to Quebec.

Magnus Macpherson II was born on April 2, 1925, at 4:30 A.M. at the Hôtel Dieu in Quebec, the oldest hospital in North America. He weighed nine pounds and seven ounces, and came into the world bellowing. Mary had a long and difficult labor, but was ecstatic with the birth of a son. She laughed and told Magnus all her plans. She had prayed hard that it would be a boy and had already determined how to offer up her thanks. She planned to become active in the hospital's auxiliary, open up her new home on Richelieu Street in the "upper" city to fund-raising for the Eskimo missions of the diocese. Magnus listened, delighted with her joy, transfixed by his son, who Mary insisted would be named after him. He found it difficult to go home at night, and much more, to travel south to Windsor. But he had to go. He therefore did not see that the excitement Mary felt for her future was often interrupted by long periods of depression.

Her mother, father, and Juny flew up while she was still in the hospital. They did not stay in the house on Richelieu Street, preferring a suite at the Château Frontenac. Magnus managed to be out of town on business for their visit. Their grandson met the Flemings as he had met the world, bellowing. Mary showed him off for three days while the Flemings were in the city, but when they left, she became so despondent as to cause her doctors concern.

Magnus was called; he returned to Quebec immediately. When he went into Mary's room at the hospital, a priest was sitting by her bed. The priest rose, and without any greeting, Mary automatically introduced them.

"Father Montier, this is my husband, Magnus Macpherson." She did not look at either of them; rather she smoothed a crease in her sheet with her fingers.

To Magnus, the priest looked about thirty, yet there was a dark exhaustion about his eyes which made him seem older. Magnus went over to the bed.

"Darlin Mary, the doctors tell me you're doing fine, but they can't make you believe them." He smiled as he kissed her. She glanced at him briefly, then went back to the crease in her sheet.

"I know what they think," Mary said in a monotone.

"Do you, now? And is Father Montier here to listen to your diagnosis or a terrible confession?"

He looked at the priest, who smiled slightly.

"Don't let him fool you," Mary said. "He's a doctor, a psychiatrist. He works at St. Bridget's Asylum, but they let him come up here to see me." She smiled at the priest, still without looking at Magnus. "They all think I'm having what they call postpartum depression, isn't that right, Father Montier?"

"That's what they say." His voice was grated, even though he spoke softly. He coughed at the end of his sentence.

Magnus felt an intruder in their Catholic intimacy, and wondered how a psychiatrist fit into the game.

"Well then, darlin Mary, it'll pass then, won't it, and you'll be coming home with your son, and we'll all go for sleigh rides and everyone'll see us coming down the street, the sleigh bells jangling their ears off, and they'll say, 'Oh, Lord, here come *all* those mad Macphersons.'"

Mary looked at him sharply, saw the glint and the dare in his eye, and couldn't help laughing. Magnus joined her and hugged her as she said, "They'd be right, too." But soon her laughter stopped and Magnus saw she was staring out of the window.

"It's still cold, isn't it?"

"It's almost spring, Mary."

She looked back at the crease of the sheet.

"Bishop Roulieu came to see me this morning, Magnus, just before Mother and Father left. He said . . ." She began to cry. "He said that men of science call this 'depression' because they have no other word for it, and they have to call it something. But he said he thought it could be a 'holy silence,' part of a struggle for grace I have to fight, that I might be a special child of God, chosen to confront certain tasks. . . ."

She looked up at him with hope and expectation of his understanding, but he could only look back, and finally turn away to hide his anger. In turning, he glared directly into the face of the priest.

A nurse came in, carrying Magnus II, who was howling for his dinner. As was the hospital custom, the men were asked to leave the room. Father Montier wondered if he might call again, and Mary barely nodded.

As the two of them went to the door, Mary asked, "When do they go away to school, twelve, isn't it?" She shook her head as she gave her breast to the child.

Outside, Magnus turned to the priest and said angrily, "What do you think of your good bishop's prescription, Father?"

"What you or I think doesn't matter. Your wife seems convinced—"

"I'd as soon horsewhip him."

Father Montier smiled. "It wouldn't accomplish what you wanted. In our faith, it'd be martyrdom; the good bishop would be delighted."

Magnus looked at him a moment. "What can I do about Mary?" He felt a need to trust him.

"I don't think it's postpartum. When she gets home, keep an eye on her. She'll need someone to lean on. Her sense of being cut off seems—"

"She can't lean on me. She won't."

Father Montier watched Magnus, then nodded and said, "Then hopefully she'll find what she needs. But I'd watch her search carefully. Good-bye, Mr. Macpherson."

Magnus watched the priest walk quickly down the hall, wondering what Mary could possibly find. Then he heard a joyous cry through the door, followed by the nurse's laughter. The sound made him happy almost to tears; the relief he felt was bone-deep.

He went back into the room, and Mary put out a hand to him as she held the child to her breast with the other. "To hell with the rules," Magnus said. "I need to hear that mother's whoop again."

"Your son, it seems, bites." She laughed happily and kissed Magnus gladly when he leaned down to her. He sat on the bed, and they talked for hours of their growing family, of his new aging warehouse, and the expansion of the bottling plant. She seemed delighted, and when he spoke of their house on Richelieu Street, Mary corrected him and said it was "our *home* on Richelieu Street."

When they finally left the hospital, Magnus Macpherson II was five weeks old. Mary was excited about getting home, and once there, settled into the routine of motherhood with alacrity. A nursery had been prepared in a room next to their bedroom. For the first several months Mary kept the baby's crib next to their bed.

They hired a nurse, a cook, and a nursemaid. Magnus felt odd with all the strangers, but Mary was used to them and knew the attitude that they could respect. Over the next month Mary appeared to flourish, gaining her way into a Quebec society which soon adored her, for she was a Fleming from Long Island, gave perfect dinner parties, and started to work hard for the church. Her dresses were ravishing, and she appeared to be a perfect mother. Before the snow melted, she and a group of other young mothers took their children to the toboggan slide built on Dufferin Terrace. Mary and her baby would shriek with delight as the toboggans descended the slope three abreast.

During those months, however, her friends never saw Mary close the door after a party and turn around already in tears. They did not question the two- or three-day "sniffles" which kept her in bed. She was, after all, a young mother, from Long Island and not used to Quebec's severe cold. They did not know she lay in her bed, not eating, not talking. In a few days she would be up and about, having a lunch for the Reverend Sisters of the Order of Charity, attended by Bishop Roulieu, or going to Montreal to a fashion show at Eaton's. She even took French lessons with her husband two nights a week. Her friends were thrilled, as she seemed to be, the day Mary Fleming Macpherson told them she was pregnant again.

That night, Magnus drove in from the Neuville distillery at ten o'clock after flying up from Windsor. The French nanny who had replaced the nurse to look after Magnus II was a wise old woman who informed Magnus that "Madam is in 'the gray room,'" her euphemism for Mary's depressed condition.

Magnus had spoken to Mary on the phone from Windsor. She had told him the news, had been laughing and excited when he promised to get home that night. But now, the gray room. Magnus felt the familiar despair at her depression. He decided to try to fight it, and collected every candle in the house.

When he went into their room, it was dark. Magnus closed the door and lit a candle.

"Mary?" There was no answer, no movement. He could see her in bed, her eyes reflecting the single pinpoint of light. He dripped wax from the candle and stuck it on a table, then lit others and spread them around the room as he talked.

"Mary, darlin Mary, I'm so happy to see you, but I do want to see you. No more gray room tonight. We have too much to talk about. You're going to have our second child! Mary, can you tell yet what kind it will be?"

She turned in the bed and looked to the other side of the room. Magnus went there and spread more candles before her.

"And I have a few pieces of news, for in my sad attempt to keep up with you, I can tell you that Macpherson Distilleries will soon be two distilleries. I've convinced a poor sod to sell out to me. In Guelph. They call it 'god-awful Guelph.' But the distillery's a good one."

Mary did not move. Magnus lit the last candle.

"And in honor of your forthcoming occasion, it might relieve you to know that as of this moment the future child's father is worth two million, and I promise another million for every child you give . . ."

He watched Mary, who blinked several times and then began to cry. Magnus went right to the bed and took hold of her shoulders firmly.

"Mary, no. There's no need . . ."

She cringed. "Don't hurt me."

The shock of her fear hurt him before he could consider its irrationality.

"I'll *never* hurt you. Never! You know that. . . . It's you that's doing it, Mary. If somebody else were doing this to you, I'd kill them. But how can I stop you from doing it to yourself? What makes you do it, Mary? Why are you crying?"

"I . . . don't know. I really don't. I want to be so happy; I can't be, and I *hate* myself for being . . . this way. Magnus, the candles, the candles . . ." She put her arms around him and leaned against his chest. "They're beautiful, aren't they?"

They sat together on the bed for a long time, Magnus gently rocking her back and forth. She finished crying and was quiet for a while.

"What can we do, Mary?" Magnus asked.

"I don't know."

"Mary, if you want to go back home, I want you to go. I'll join you when prohibition is over. Don't mistake me, my darlin Mary. I love you and our son and now our whatever-it's-to-be. But we'll take a vacation from each other if it'll—"

"No. We're one, Magnus."

"We're not one if it does you damage, Mary."

She pulled back from him so she could look at him.

"Yes, we are."

"No!" He sensed the massiveness of her faith crashing over him, and his only defense against it was anger.

"Yes we are, my dear, dear Magnus. And if I've been chosen to go through this—"

"Chosen? You've been talking to that damned bishop. Mary, no God would choose you for madness."

The word was said; the silence which followed it was like a needle in Magnus' brain.

Mary said calmly, "I'm not mad. I've been given a task, Magnus; I have to work through it. If the final result is madness, then I've failed. What I hope and pray for—and if you want to help me the most, my dear Magnus, you'll pray for me, too—is that I'm going to come through this with a greater understanding of my life and my God."

Magnus stood up and walked across the room. He balled a piece of soft wax in his fingers and dropped it back in the well under a candle's flame.

"Mary, I'll buy every candle in Canada and make the cathedral blaze with them. I'll roll around praying on the floor if it will do you good."

"Just one candle. Just one real prayer."

Magnus turned to her and saw she was barely smiling. He was conscious of a slow panic of hopelessness.

"No, no, no. Mary, you're working yourself into a place you can't get out of. I know what you're driving at with your 'one candle, one real prayer.' You're thinking you're responsible for my soul, that until it's saved and I'm praying, God's going to hold you with this great sadness, that until your marriage is perfectly Catholic, you have to suffer for it. And you can't leave me, for that's a sin. You think you're caught here in God's trap, Mary, and somewhere in your mind, I'm the steel grip that's holding you."

"It's not a trap. It's my life's struggle to grace."

"You heard that from the bishop, and I won't accept it. Mary, I'd pray if I thought you'd believe it, but I'll get on my knees to *you* and beg *you* to go to your home, with the child . . . with our children, and get out of this cave that the priests are pushing you into."

Mary crossed herself slowly as she said like a prayer, "This is my home. You are my husband. God is with us."

"Christ, Mary!" he cried. "Stop hiding behind your damned faith! You're cutting us to bits."

She turned away and said nothing.

Magnus sat down in a chair, exhausted, worse than defeated. Tears of frustration and sadness came to his eyes. He waited for Mary to turn back to him, but she didn't. After an hour of silence, they both fell asleep. The candles burned all night, leaving melted wax and small burns on flat surfaces.

Months went by, and during her pregnancy Mary's moods moved through frightening extremes of both activity and despondency. In May of 1926, a girl was born, with Mary's red hair. She was named Eleanor.

That same month Magnus' quota to Ted Weiss went up to 25,000 cases per week, the second distillery in Guelph began producing at full capacity, and Magnus was forced to travel, leaving Mary alone more than he wished. Each evening at six he spoke to her on the phone. When she was in "the gray room" and unavailable, he tried to change his plans and return to Quebec. He began to realize the strain was draining him. At the same time, his success was supplying him with an excitement that sustained him through his eighteen-hour days.

By 1926 Macpherson Distilleries was a presence in the North American liquor scene. Magnus was looked on as a comer, audacious enough to outbid the Bronfmans for a distillery, but subtle and smart enough to feel no compunction to outdo them. He was content to let them have their time in the sun, and its resulting heat. Magnus was more interested in consolidating his own business and in finding the best way to prepare for his return to the United States. By that time, anyone knowledgeable about the liquor business was making plans for the end of prohibition.

Magnus entertained his American guests in a suite at the Château Frontenac that he used as an office. It was expensive, but Magnus learned quickly that lunch with a view of the St. Lawrence amidst rich office space counted for much in the eyes of liquor men. He told Mary he could save himself a lot of trouble just by framing a hundred-thousand-dollar bill and putting it on his office wall.

In Windsor, he made up for the expense. His office was a dusty room on a wharf. It had a table, two chairs, and an overhead lamp, used mainly for weekly gin rummy games. One cardboard file case contained the corporate records of Acme, Limited, and would, in a fire, surely burn. One solid-steel file case contained a few bottles of The Glenlivet malt whiskey to refresh the gin-rummy players. Magnus never tried to fool anyone, much less himself; he considered his own product a far second to the great malts of the Glen Rinne.

Louis Rosenstiel was one of the whiskey men who came to Magnus' office in Windsor. In his mid-thirties, he talked fast, dropped names, implied power, and laughed out loud. Magnus recognized the bluster, but was comfortable with Rosenstiel, as he sensed an energy similar to his own.

During prohibition, a legal liquor business in the United States existed, but it did not involve the actual liquid. In 1920, when distillers could not dispose of sixty-eight million gallons of whiskey before the Volstead Act took effect, the government agreed to put the liquor into warehouses under bond, and to give the owners warehouse receipts for the amount involved. In theory, the receipts would be realized sometime in the future from the eventual sale of the whiskey for "medicinal purposes."

Most people in 1920 believed that warehouse receipts were good only for the bottom of bird cages. A measure of Louis Rosenstiel's foresight was that in that year he started a brokerage business for dealing in warehouse receipts. He made enough profit to buy into a moribund company which owned a rusting old distillery and four warehouses filled with government-bonded rye whiskey in a small town in Pennsylvania called Schenley.

By the time he met Magnus, Louis Rosenstiel was the biggest whiskey dealer in the United States. He was averaging gross annual sales of six million dollars in warehouse receipts, distilleries, and supplies. He had just come down from Montreal, where he invested in the Bronfmans' company.

He seemed to enjoy Magnus' company and talked volubly.

"Oh, yeah, and I'll tell you something for sure: Sam Bronfman's the only one to talk to in Montreal. The other brothers are getting pushed out. Very comfortably, mind you, but Sam, he'll run things there. I heard the other day he got so damn mad at his brother he threw a phone at him. But it was attached too close and bounced back and crowned Mr. Sam on the noggin. He had a bump that was a beaut."

Magnus nodded and smiled, saying little.

"Macpherson, I like you." Magnus could think of no reason. "Let's do some business."

Magnus put his glass down. "Good. I want to buy a hundred thousand worth of your warehouse receipts now, with options for another batch every three months for two years . . . at the same price."

The offer was outrageous; no one would grant options at current prices. The market was going up every day as prohibition weakened. But Magnus' suggestion did not cause Rosenstiel a moment's hesitation. "You got it, and in exchange I'll buy twenty percent of Macpherson Distilleries, Limited, at your price."

"No."

"No? What do you mean, no?"

"Macpherson's isn't for sale."

"Everything's for sale, Macpherson, right down to the short hairs. What we're trying to find is the price."

"I want the options, and I'll pay money for them."

"But it's not enough, get me? Why don't you find out what *I* want?"

"Why don't you just tell me?"

"You don't like to talk much, do you?"

"Not when it might fog a good blend."

Rosenstiel studied Magnus over a flat smile.

"How's this, Macpherson? I've got a warehouse five miles up the Detroit River. I'll give you the options if you'll sell me twenty thousand cases and ship them to my warehouse each time you exercise one of them."

Magnus watched Rosenstiel for any sign that there was something dubious about the warehouse. He saw nothing, but he sensed a greed about Louis Rosenstiel which was as indiscriminate as that of a jackal.

"I'm not sure I can do that. I have something of an exclusive contract for my exports."

"No exports. I'm just building up my stock, that's all. When prohibition dies, I want that warehouse busting at the seams. How about it, Macpherson?"

Magnus hesitated. Something about the deal kept him quiet, staring at Rosenstiel. Perhaps it was the warehouse. And why would he want cases for stock instead of barrels? But Magnus could not see that it was his business, and Rosenstiel did not quiver a finger in the time Magnus imposed. Usually a long silence brought out some nervous movement indicating that something was wrong.

"Done. You'll have your cases, Mr. Rosenstiel, as soon as I get your papers."

"Call me 'Louie.' You'll have 'em before you piss what we just drank."

The papers, warehouse receipts, and payment for 25,000 cases of Macpherson's whiskey were in Quebec in five days. Magnus admired such efficiency. Making such a deal gratified a kind of lust in Magnus. He shipped the liquor to Rosenstiel's warehouse in another five days, along with his first payment of a hundred thousand dollars for the warehouse receipts.

Ten days later, Magnus was in his office at Windsor waiting for Ted Weiss, shuffling a deck of cards in preparation.

The door was kicked open. Three men came in fast. Two grabbed him as the cards flew into the air; the third man stood in front of him with a Colt .45. Magnus knew from Weiss it was a gun carried mainly to kill.

"You're taking a trip, Macpherson."

"Long or short?"

"Depends."

Magnus saw the gun in the air coming down on the back of his head. The next thing he remembered was coming back to consciousness on the floor of a covered truck, the vibrations of its motor roaring the cold metal into his head. The first thing he saw was the

.45, held by the man who had used it. His head hurt, and he raised an arm to touch it.

"Stay right there. Don't move. I don't care if it hurts."

The truck drove on for about an hour longer. Magnus heard the amount of traffic around them increase. He tried to figure a way out, but the gun never wavered. The man who held it was a professional, the back of the truck was stacked with liquor, and behind the cases, the doors were solid and probably bolted.

The truck turned several sharp corners, then stopped. The back was opened, a stack of cases was loaded down, and Magnus was hustled out into an alley by the two men who had grabbed him. The gunman followed. Magnus spotted a sign near the door they entered. It said "Deliveries. Hawthorne Hotel."

He was dragged up two flights of stairs, then into a room. He was trying to keep on top of what was going on, but his head was bothering him and his vision blurred occasionally. He kept thinking about Ted Weiss. Why hadn't Weiss warned him?

The two men dropped his arms. He stood in front of a desk, behind which sat Al Capone. Magnus was dizzy and stood with his legs apart in order not to fall.

"Macpherson, didn't Weiss tell you, you don't deal with nobody else over the border but me?"

Magnus watched the wet cigar slither between Capone's lips.

"You paid for that, and I've respected it," he said.

Capone jumped up and came around the desk. Just before he hit him, Magnus saw a raw animal madness on his face, his lips curling up over his teeth, the eyes looking for a kill. Magnus fell to the floor. Capone kicked him in the balls.

"Don't lie to me, you goddamn stinking . . . what the fuck you call a Scotch guy? Come on, you guys. I'm a wop; what do you call a Scotch guy? I'll tell you what you call a Scotch guy who lies to me. You call him 'dead.'" The men in the room chuckled at their boss's sense of humor.

Capone went around to the desk, opened a drawer, and put a bottle where Magnus could see it was Macpherson's whiskey, not relabeled for export.

"We hijacked a shipment of booze coming in for Bugs Moran and Hymie Weiss on the North Side. How come it had a thousand cases of your stuff, Macpherson?"

Magnus knew right away where it had come from. His first reaction was anger at Rosenstiel, but he realized he had little time for such extravagant emotion. He had to talk fast, and he was having a hard time getting his breath.

"I sold some cases to a man who wanted stock. He put it in a warehouse to keep until the end of—"

"You dumb fucker. I'll call you a dumb fucker because what else can I call a dumb Scotch guy? Did you sell to Rosie Rosenstiel?"

Magnus saved breath and nodded. Capone sat down at his desk. "That's what I said; you're a dumb fucker. You trusted a kike. I don't like kikes. They're all together, think they're blood brothers 'cause they get their cocks cut up."

He was showboating, and his boys let him have what he wanted. It gave Magnus time to breathe.

"Macpherson, you got the wrong friends and the wrong enemies. I been told you threw a friend of mine in the drink." He started to laugh, a deep, gutty laugh that came up in grunts. "Yeah, listen to this, you guys, this dumb fucker threw Albert Anastasia in the drink. Umberto had enough iron on him to sink him like a goddamn anchor." The men looked at Magnus with incredulity. In the middle of all the laughter, Capone suddenly stood up and yelled at Magnus, "He wants you dead, dumb fucker."

In the silence that followed, Magnus tried to remember the gangster and the night about which Capone was obviously talking.

"I don't know who you mean."

"Well, dumb fucker, you learn. Fast. You don't sell to kikes anymore, and you don't dunk Umberto in the water. Get him out of here."

Magnus was jerked up from the floor and carried down the stairs. He stayed jackknifed as much as he could, as his testicles were still painful. He was thrown into the back of the truck. The same man got in with him, holding the .45. The doors of the truck were closed, and Magnus kept track of the sounds of the bolts. There were two on the right side. The truck was empty except for him, the gangster, and the .45.

For the first hour Magnus expected to be shot at any turn in the road. Then he realized they would probably take him back to Detroit, even to Canada, and kill him there. His strength came back, and he waited, ready for some chance to get at the .45.

As the truck hummed north, Magnus tried to figure out who Albert Anastasia was. If he was the gangster he threw overboard on Rum Row, how did he find out Magnus' name? Then he knew:

McCoy. The Coast Guard had finally caught up with McCoy. Magnus sent him money to help cover his legal expenses, and a good lawyer had succeeded in getting him a short sentence. But McCoy loved to tell stories. If Anastasia wanted to know the name of a member of the *Arethusa*'s crew, an inmate could ask McCoy an innocent question about the name of his supercargo.

Just as Magnus figured this out, the truck swerved. Magnus sprang in the second the gunman looked around. Shots were fired outside, the truck skidded, and Magnus and the gangster were thrown against the side. Magnus was on top and took advantage of it. He jammed his knee into the gangster's side and heard ribs snap as the truck crashed into something and stopped. There was another shot outside. Magnus had a grip on the gunman's hand that held the .45. He pinned the man's other arm down and with his free fist beat as hard as he could on the man's windpipe. As the man lost consciousness, Magnus grabbed the gun.

Outside, everything was quiet except for a motor running. Magnus laid the gangster's body out and got behind it, ready to shoot whoever opened the doors. He heard a voice calling: "We got five choppers out here, so come out of there easy when the door opens."

It was Ted Weiss.

"Weiss? I'm alone in here."

The two bolts were thrown and the doors opened. Weiss peered in, a cigarette stabbed in his lips.

"Step on it, Macpherson. Drag him out."

Magnus got out of the truck. Weiss and he dumped the gangster, and Weiss got in the truck to see if it would run. It did. Magnus saw on the side of the road the bodies of the two men who had been driving the truck. A sawed-off shotgun lay beside them.

"Come on."

Magnus jumped into the cab as Ted Weiss moved it out on the highway, grinding gears as fast as he could.

They drove in silence for fifteen minutes. Magnus looked over once or twice, and saw Weiss's face squeezing itself into contortions around his cigarette.

"Check under the seat, should be a sprayer." Magnus took the sawed-off twelve-gauge in his lap.

"If somebody comes up the side, tries to butcher us, I'll lay down on the wheel, you lay across my back, stay below the window until they're beside us, then poke up and make a sieve."

Magnus broke open the gun to make sure it was loaded.

"You're late for gin rummy, Weiss, but I'm glad to see you anyway."

"Enjoy Chi?"

"Not much. Did you know about my trip?"

"Heard about it, too late to wish bon voyage. They told me to take the day off. . . . Some day off. Heard you sold to Rosie Rosenstiel, and you was about to get too full of holes to skin."

"You hear a lot."

"A Jew in Cicero's gotta have the best clothesline in town to eat his matzo-ball in peace. Why didn't you tell me about Rosenstiel?"

"It was none of your business. He said he was putting my liquor in a warehouse—"

" 'To wait for prohibition to end.' O.K. Here's a brainstorm. Suppose Rosenstiel's in thick with Meyer Lansky, a top boy back east, on things like phony medicinal permits for bonded liquor. Suppose Lansky has a connection to Hymie Weiss—no relation of mine—and Bugs Moran of the North Side Gang. And suppose it's agreed up and down and crossways for that warehouse of Rosenstiel's to get knocked over every once in a while by some North Side troops. And suppose Rosenstiel collects insurance on the theft."

"Is that what goes on?"

"All rumor, speculation, and lies. But I heard it on the clothesline, and you learn more from that than college."

Magnus sat silently, figuring out how he could repay Louis Rosenstiel. But there were still too many unanswered questions.

"I was believing you didn't kill people, Weiss."

Ted Weiss glanced quickly over, unfolding his face behind his glasses.

"So tonight I lost my cherry."

"Why?"

"Hadda save my future. Can't last much longer doing this. They're all killing each other, and Al ain't exactly a Jew lover."

"I heard."

"So, figured it's better for me if you're alive and vice versa, 'cause somebody's gotta teach you how to play gin rummy. . . . And with your luck, Macpherson, you're going places I want to go."

"You call this lucky?"

"You're alive. Anyone else'd been pork about ten miles further down the road from where I picked you up. You can bet on it; you're a lucky son of a bitch. Just stay that way for another half-hour till I get us to the river. Figure that's what we got before some bootlegger spots my little hijacking act back there and phones Capone. He'll be mad in fourteen languages, and he's only got fifty cards in his deck."

They reached Detroit, and Weiss drove through the city on back streets and alleys, avoiding traffic and checking his rearview mirror. They were five blocks from the waterfront when Ted said calmly, "They're here. Try to get off both shots. Hope you can swim." He lay down flat on the steering wheel so he was barely able to peer through the windshield. He did not speed up.

Magnus lay across his back with the shotgun just below the driver's window and waited. He could see the headlights reflecting into the cab, then the car pulling up beside the truck.

"Now."

Magnus jerked up, aimed, fired. He felt his right arm break. He fired again. He saw a face blown away, the body lurch half out the car window. The truck jerked ahead, Weiss jamming the accelerator.

"Get off me."

Magnus pushed himself back to his side of the cab. Blood was pouring down his right arm. He hadn't seen the car, but apparently he had hit it. Weiss was swerving the truck to keep the car behind them. There were more gunshots.

"Don't worry, the back is armored. You catch one?"

"Seems so."

"Hang on."

Magnus braced himself with his foot against the dashboard. He took off his belt and looped it around his arm, pulling it as tight as it would go. He looked up as Ted Weiss skidded around a corner, crashed through a barrier, and drove full speed down the length of a pier. The car was close behind, and someone in it opened up with a Thompson. Ted Weiss never hesitated. He kept the accelerator down all the way off the end of the pier. Magnus watched the water come to meet them. As soon as the truck settled, he opened his door. Weiss grabbed him.

"Sit tight. It'll take a minute to sink. Let 'em shoot their rocks off, think we're dead. When the water's up to the windows, the doors'll open easy. Lemme see that."

Magnus felt an intense pain as Ted Weiss tightened the belt. He noticed the water had reached his knees. Then suddenly it seemed to cover him, and he lost consciousness.

A man he had never seen before was looking down at him. He felt nauseous, and the pain in his arm was agonizing.

"You haven't seen me, I haven't seen you," the man said as soon as Magnus opened his eyes. "Get to a hospital and say you had an industrial accident, a crate fell on it. The bullets are out, but don't move that arm. It needs a cast."

Magnus realized he was lying on the gin-rummy table in his own office in Windsor. He turned his head, saw the well-dressed man buckling up a doctor's case.

"Can I stand up?"

"If you can't, lie there until you can." He picked up his case and was gone.

Magnus stood up, almost passed out cold again, then moved gingerly over to the file cabinet with the malt in it. He opened it, took a bottle, sat down, and swallowed deep. Water of life, water of life. He knew it was good for the bowels and wondered what it might do for rejoining bones.

The sun was low over Detroit to the west; he had been out all day. His shoes, shirt, and coat were in a damp pile in one corner of the room. His arm and shoulder were tightly taped, and he could see two pieces of window-molding acting as splints. The back of his head had a scab and a sharp pain, and his wounded balls felt like swollen balloons.

He took another swallow and choked, laughing. Weiss was right. He was a lucky son of a bitch. Then he stopped laughing and started hating Louis Rosenstiel.

Two months later, the warehouse that Rosenstiel owned five miles upriver burned to the ground. The blaze was spectacular and could be seen up and down the wharves of Detroit. The fire took place the night after Magnus had delivered and collected for twenty thousand cases and purchased his second $100,000 of warehouse receipts.

Regretfully, two days before the fire, Dominion Insurance of Canada had suddenly canceled their policy on the warehouse. A stockholder had informed them of its illegal aspects and threatened a corporate-mismanagement suit. When Rosenstiel, screaming mad, made arrangements to find the stockholder, he was informed a Mr. Norman of 1806 Chaplin Crescent in Toronto was to blame. Unfortunately, Mr. Norman did not exist, and Chaplin Crescent was a garbage pit. Whoever invented Mr. Norman had cost Louis Rosenstiel about two million legal dollars.

During that time, Magnus "laid dead," as Weiss advised him, letting his arm heal, allowing Al Capone to cool off until the gesture of the warehouse fire put Magnus back in his good graces.

Weiss kept doing what he always did. No one suspected he had anything to do with Magnus' return trip from Chicago. Magnus' survival was considered just luck; it was presumed that a North Side Gang's hijack had saved him. Magnus sent an executive from the Guelph distillery down to Windsor to keep track of the shipments. After Weiss let it get back to Capone that the Rosenstiel warehouse fire was a peace offering, Magnus went to Windsor himself. The gin rummy resumed, and there were jokes about Weiss parting the waters of the Detroit River and walking Magnus through. Ted Weiss didn't laugh much. He waited for the right time to retire from the Purple Gang and join Macpherson Distilleries, Limited.

He had no choice. Hymie Weiss, no relation, one of the leaders of the North Side Gang, shot up the Hawthorne Hotel with twenty choppers one day at high noon, but missed Capone. Capone concluded: "Enough is enough." He decided to clean out the North Siders, beginning with Hymie Weiss. Weiss was dispatched on October 11, 1926, across the street from the Holy Name Cathedral on State Street by two machine guns. No such elaborate end was planned for Ted Weiss, just a simple razor cut from ear to ear, for no other reason than Big Al did not like Jews named Weiss anymore.

The butcher was less than an artist and missed Weiss's carotid artery. The gash he cut poured a lot of blood on the floor of Magnus' office, where Weiss arrived nearly dead. Magnus held the wound closed with his hand and got him to a hospital.

Two days later, when Weiss came out of his sedation and saw Magnus at the foot of his hospital bed, he said, "Got any humps?"

Magnus had bought a pack, anticipating the request. He lit one and put it in Ted Weiss's mouth.

Weiss sucked in, looked at Magnus, and said, "O.K., Macpherson, we're even."

5

Everybody was at scratch now. Let's go—.
But it was not to be. Somebody
had blundered and the most expensive
orgy in history was over.

—F. Scott Fitzgerald

James Fleming Macpherson was born on October 15, 1928. He had been conceived on the last night Mary and Magnus made love to each other. Afterward, they shared the bed but did not share a sexual relationship. Magnus accepted the distance rather than taking a chance that his reaching to touch her would shatter the calm surface on which they continued to live their lives. He suppressed the grief and separation he felt, and worked harder and longer.

Six months after the birth of their third child, Mary divested one of the small servants' rooms of any comfort or distraction, furnishing it with a chair, table, single bed, and Bible. On the wall was a crucifix of an agonizing Christ, under which a votive candle burned on a small shelf. The room was painted gray as if to underline the concrete expression of the old reference to Mary's depression.

The first night Magnus was home after the room was completed, he noticed it, walking down the hall to the children's rooms. He entered, was at first appalled, then alarmed. After closing the door as if sealing up a contagion, he went downstairs to the sitting room.

Mary and the children were gathered in front of a fine fire, the baby in a crib, Mary holding her three-year-old daughter in her lap, and Magnus II, an independent four, playing with a set of toy trucks his father had given him. Mary looked up at Magnus as he came in, smiling.

"You'll be very proud of your daughter, Magnus. Listen. Go on, my darling WeeDee, for your father. . . ."

The little girl was embarrassed and looked around to see what her older brother was doing, then looked down at the floor and began to recite: " 'Hail Mary, full of grace, the Lord is with thee. Blessed are thou amongst women—' "

"Fa, watch me. Look at me," Magnus II interrupted, and, having gained everyone's attention, he crossed himself dramatically and ended the gesture with a snappy salute, very pleased with himself.

Magnus would have liked to laugh, but he was too wary of what was going on in his house. He expected to look in the crib and see his youngest, Jamie, clutching a rosary.

Mary scolded her eldest.

"Magnus, don't ever joke about such a thing. That's a sacred gesture."

The boy, chastised, sat down with his trucks, but sneaked an impish glance at his father. Magnus didn't smile, but he let his son know with the slightest nod that he did not condemn the gesture. Then he sat down on a settee across from Mary. She smiled at him again and quickly looked away, concerned with the baby. They had lost their ease with starting conversation; one or the other had to blunder into it and since Mary seemed contented with silence, Magnus was usually the one.

"Have you seen the papers today, Mary?"

"Yes."

"Did you see where the Yanks are yelling bluidy murder for the Canadians to shut the border to liquor, as if Canada can solve their problem. Silliest thing I ever heard. . . ."

"No, I didn't see that. . . . It's good to have you home, Magnus." She smiled, but couldn't keep it steady, as if reconsidering.

"I'm buying another distillery," Magnus said, with a slight edge of irritated insistence. "It's in Hamilton, newer than the others; no trouble getting it up to scratch."

Mary did not respond for a minute. Then she glanced into the fire and spoke quickly.

"I took WeeDee with me today to the hospital. She made a great hit with the nurses, didn't you, WeeDee?" The little girl looked at her father shyly, then down at her dress. Mary did not go on. The silence became excruciating.

Magnus II broke it. "Why is WeeDee called that? Her name's Eleanor, isn't it?"

Magnus and Mary looked at each other to see which of them would answer. Magnus started carefully.

"When your sister was a wee thing, she was like . . . a steady stream. It was a frightsome display, and I used to say, *'Again* she flows. Our lovely daughter flows like the River Dee, a wee Dee.' Occasionally she'd begin to cry, and your mother and I would look at one another and nod. 'WeeDee.' " He watched Mary to see if she would join him in the memory. She smiled but did not look at him.

"You mean pee-pee?" Magnus II asked enthusiastically. Magnus only had to nod before his son began to march around the room chanting, "WeeDee is a pee-pee, WeeDee is a pee-pee!" WeeDee herself climbed out of her mother's lap and yelled, "I am *not* a pee-pee. I'm not!" She began to cry. Mary went to her and spoke to Magnus II severely. The noise and crying startled the baby to wakefulness, and he, too, began to shriek. Magnus went to the crib, picked Jamie up, and tried to quiet him. But the child shrieked on and reached for his mother. Mary came over for him, trailing Wee-Dee, still crying.

The French nanny came in, and the children were taken off to bed with promises of stories. Mary started to go with them, but Magnus held her back. The nanny took the baby and left the parents in front of the fire.

"I should go help Madame," Mary said.

"She's all right. Stay with me awhile."

Mary came back and took her same seat. They both stared into the fire. Magnus took her hand, felt her wanting to go.

"You're enjoying your work at the hospital, then?"

She nodded. "It reminds me how lucky we are, how grateful we must be. . . . Cardinal Roulieu came by while I was there," she said as she stood and went to a small table across the room. "He brought me a gift, Magnus. Think of that. With all his new duties as a cardinal, he could still remember to bring me a little gift. . . . Here it is. It's his own personal copy of *The Dialogue* by St. Catherine of Siena." She opened it and started idly leafing through the pages.

Magnus watched her with a hopeless grief.

"I'm not surprised he remembered, Mary. It's a damned expensive book."

"No, it's not, it's . . ." She looked at him suspiciously. "What do you mean?"

"You helped raise thirty thousand dollars for his charities. It seems that's worth a secondhand book."

She stared at him for a moment, during which time Magnus hated what he'd said. He'd meant it pragmatically, to put the cardinal's gift into a perspective less awesome to Mary, but the mention of money sounded as if he were belittling her work.

"I'm sorry, Mary, I meant . . ."

She looked down at the book, and searched for a passage.

"I know what you meant, Magnus. I know what you think. . . . Here it is. In the fourteenth century, St. Catherine said that God had taught her '. . . to build in my soul a refuge in which I could dwell so peacefully that no storm or tribulation could ever disturb me.'" Mary nodded to herself, then closed the book.

Magnus felt the low panic of losing her, even though she was still there in the room.

"Is that how you feel, Mary?"

"Yes." She said it with certainty.

As a wall petrified between them, he stood up and said, "Leave me, Mary."

"What?"

"Go back to Southampton. Take the children with you. There's room down there in that compound for me at least to visit. But what you're building here is no 'refuge'; it's a prison. You'll go into that gray room upstairs and I'll never see you again. I'd rather have visiting privileges in Southampton."

She was surprised at his mention of the room, but she responded without hesitation. "Magnus, I will never leave you. We are one in the eyes of God, and I must care for my children. None of it may make any difference to you, but it does to me."

"Mary, can you say you still love me?"

"Yes." Again with certainty.

"Even though you hate everything I do?"

"Yes. Yes! I do love you!"

"And the children, what of them? I'm their father. . . ."

"Magnus, I love my children, and I love you. But what you do . . . infects all our lives. Magnus, please, understand me. I need a place, just a small room where I can go to pray, to feel at peace in the middle of all this . . . this . . ." The word didn't come. "I don't know what it is, Magnus, but I feel lost in it. I need a place that's . . . pure." She held the book in her arms close to her body. "I have to go say good night to the children." She left Magnus alone in the sitting room.

Magnus sat and drank for an hour before he could control his anger. The malt helped a little, but his anger only led to despair.

When he went up to their room, Mary was not there. She did not come to their bed that night.

Mary kept St. Catherine's book with her. She continued her work as a volunteer at the Hôtel Dieu hospital. In order to emulate St. Catherine, she insisted on being with the most hopeless victims of disease. Eventually she had the bed moved out of her small gray room, and at night slept on the floor.

Magnus did not know what to do. He had sworn to Mary and to himself that he would respect her religion. But he began to question his decision as Mary became more withdrawn, particularly his agreement to have his children raised as Roman Catholics.

Finally he called on the young priest he had met at the hospital when Magnus II was born. Father Montier had aged in the few years since Magnus had seen him, grown a beard, and apparently had given up combing his hair. He slumped in his chair in his office at St. Bridget's Asylum; his neck was bent so low as to seem deformed. They both could hear the muffled howling of the inmates.

"Your wife seems to have forced her reality to match her neurosis, 'the gray room,' sleeping alone on the floor." He shook his head. "I don't know what to tell you, Mr. Macpherson. What do you want me to tell you?"

Father Montier looked up only long enough to lean forward and bow his forehead down into his hands.

"Tell me what I can do to stop my wife from going mad."

Father Montier sighed without looking up.

"I doubt if you can do anything. And I'm not sure she's going mad. An excess of faith to an outsider seems insane, but . . . Macpherson, as a doctor, I say it's a neurosis. As a priest, I say it's faith. There's very little you can do about it, either way." The priest looked up. "The damage is done, as they say." He shook his head and let it bow back into his hands.

"What damage?" Magnus asked.

"When she was a child: parents, family, faith. There are problems she has which she has to find her way through. Faith may be one of her problems, but it's also something she can grasp."

The priest hesitated, staring at the hand he had used to gesture. Then he shook his head and for the first time met Magnus' eyes.

"Mr. Macpherson, I'm not a good one to talk to. I'll find you someone else. I'm in a state of doubt, with which I won't bore you."

"Father, I'll speak to no other than yourself. . . . I've envied people who had faith; it seemed a strength I didn't have. I don't envy them anymore, for it must be a terrible . . . devastation to lose it."

"Yes, Mr. Macpherson, but you have to remember, both the strength and the devastation *mean* that faith does exist."

"I'll hope you regain whatever it is you want, Father. But please, tell me what I can do for my wife."

Again the priest sighed, then was quiet.

"You can let her know you love her all the way to God or the Devil and back again."

"She knows that."

"I can't think of anything else."

Magnus stood up. "You mean I just stand there watching her get pneumonia, lying on the floor, letting my children see their mother go mad?"

"Do you love her that much?"

"I love her more."

"Then there's—"

"Don't *dare* tell me there's nothing—"

"What do you want, Mr. Macpherson? A pill for her to take every two hours? Listen to that howling out there. There is no pill for faith or madness or whatever your wife is going through. The only thing you and I can do is help her through it."

Magnus sat down again.

"Why does she have to go through it? Because of her goddamned church and family? If that's—"

"Because she's alive. Don't blame *anything*. And for God's sake"—the priest smiled—"and for your own, don't blame yourself."

"What will happen, Father?"

The priest closed his eyes. The fatigue of their struggle and his own overwhelmed him.

"Mr. Macpherson, I'm embarrassed to have to say this, but the only prognosis I can give you is that 'God only knows.' I'll keep an eye on her as much as she'll let me. I'll try to be her priest, not her doctor. I doubt if she'll see me any other way."

"Thank you, Father, I'd be grateful. . . . One last thing. Do you think, or does the Church think, that God is putting Mary through this because of me and my business?"

The priest's eyes opened, and a trace of amusement eased the pain in them. "No."

"I think you're laughing, Father."

"Your question is symptomatic of two things: creeping guilt and creeping faith. You'll probably want to be careful of both."

Magnus nodded, then left. He walked back to his office at the Château Frontenac, looking down over the St. Lawrence River. Magnus wished he had faith. Even as he wished for it, he sensed what a relief it would be to put the whole of Mary's enigma on God, to give over worry to faith, and to let Him have the triumph or the damnation. Magnus believed he would have done it if he could have believed God would take on the responsibility. But he didn't and he went back to his office feeling as hopeless as before.

Mary did see Father Montier, as a priest, but their meetings did not bring about any alteration in her life with Magnus. In spite of Magnus' love for her, his patience with the hours Mary spent in the gray room began to fray. During the expansion of Macpherson Distilleries, Limited, Ted Weiss took most of his anger. The bookkeeper had become indispensable to that expansion, and had a problem of his own: as he recovered from the slit throat, the doctors ordered him to give up smoking. To Weiss, withdrawal caused more suffering than the wound, and he went through it in a furious silence. After the first month he tried to distract himself and his boss by conceiving new marketing ideas and establishing a clothesline. He learned that the gangs were consolidating enforcement under Magnus' old friend Umberto Anastasia, who was rising fast in the world of crime.

Bootleg hooch was making the gangs rich and powerful, and they were poised for bigger things. Anastasia was a leader in a gang which specialized in union locals. The gang terrorized and killed, then took the unions over. They raked in kickbacks from the dues-paying members, and held up employers with extortion, lightly disguised as labor negotiations. Using this technique, Anastasia took control of the New York docks.

He had been invited to attend a clandestine meeting in Atlantic City of a number of gang leaders who planned to take over and organize crime, including Lucky Luciano, Meyer Lansky, Vito Genovese. The guest of honor was Johnny Torrio, Capone's old partner in Chicago, who had developed an economic philosophy for American crime.

"Since I been back from Italy, I been fiddling around on Wall Street. It's crookeder than any crap game I ever run. I hear them talking all the time about 'competition, the most important part of capitalism, it stimulates profit, it stimulates people to work and make money.' I say to them, that's all to the mustard, but they're going to have an opera on Wall Street that'll make stone weep. With our thing, competition is a waste. You waste money, you waste time, and you waste each other. Nobody needs to take from anyone else. This is the big end of what I got to say: there's more than enough for everyone. You don't believe me? Go home, look at a map of America. Stop thinking twenty blocks on some west side or other is the end of the world. You guys can divide up this whole country and die in your beds."

Anastasia was impressed with the philosophy; so was Juny Fleming. Juny dealt with Johnny Torrio on Wall Street and was smart enough to listen to Torrio, even though he never admitted his luncheon guest at Delmonico's was a Chicago gangster. Nevertheless, Torrio's advice convinced Juny that the competition on Wall Street was madness that summer of 1929. In the dog days of August, when the rest of the family were ensconced in Southampton, Juny stayed in town. He, too, looked at a map of America, and moved most of Fleming and Co.'s holdings from Wall Street to real estate.

When the Depression came, it had no effect on the thirst Magnus satisfied, except to increase it. On Black Tuesday, Magnus was also looking at a map of America; with Ted Weiss, he put pins in it to indicate distilleries he might buy.

His problem was not economic but political. The Canadian government, after a decade of intense manipulation on the part of the United States government, finally made it illegal for liquor manufactured in Canada to be exported to any country enforcing prohibition.

With a depression on his hands for which he was being given full credit, President Hoover decided that the success of prohibition was vital to his reelection campaign in 1932. He decided to make the Detroit River a test of his will against "the systematic war being carried on by international criminals."

When Magnus heard, he was enraged, shouting at Weiss: "If Mr. Hoover wants to get elected, he should promise every voter a bottle of Macpherson's whiskey on election day."

"Send a check to Franklin Roosevelt; he likes to drink," Weiss suggested.

"I think I will. It'll make old Joe Fleming madder than a knotted snake; he gave Al Smith a lot of money in hopes of being made an ambassador."

"So what do we do until the election?"

"What's going on at Windsor?"

"Picture this: about three hundred speedboats for sale dirt cheap, the Royal Canadian Mounted Police wall to wall all over our side of the river, and a couple of guys putting armor all over tugboats and planning to run across Lake Erie."

Magnus shook his head and looked out the window down the St. Lawrence.

"What's Capone doing?"

"Screaming. Can't buy his way through anymore, and the feds are after him for income-tax evasion. If they only knew."

"Do you know, Weiss?"

"A little."

"That's too much. If Capone remembers you can still talk about numbers, you'll need to take a care for yourself."

Weiss knew it. "Yeah."

"Weiss, where could we buy some German submarines?"

Magnus was surprised when Weiss sat down on the couch and laughed.

"What in the bluidy hell is so funny?"

"Great idea, run subs over from Europe right up the St. Lawrence, load them at the distillery at Neuville, then sink and take the hooch anyplace they want it."

"So what's wrong?"

"Didn't say—"

"There's always a price for your admiration. You say how well I've played a hand of gin just when you're going to cheat me blind."

"You learned that? Damn."

"So tell me what's wrong with submarines?"

Ted's face lost the smile and it folded in on itself again. He absent-mindedly reached in his coat for the package of cigarettes that was not there.

"You break laws now, and I don't care how well you break them, they'll be coming after you forever. You don't want to live that way. You got a chance at being rich, an important man, Macpherson. Even being respectable. You break the law, you'll never be that. You won't be able to buy out of a bad reputation. And listen, if they want, they'll change laws to get you."

Magnus nodded, and turned back to the view of the St. Lawrence. He remembered his father saying law was geographical, and McCoy telling him the importance of a solid reputation.

Magnus went through his desk pulling everything out until he found a map of Canada. He spread it out in front of them.

"In French class, my teacher reminded me of something. When the French lost the American continent, they held on to—there they are, thirty miles off Newfoundland—those two islands right there. We used to stop there on McCoy's boat on our way to Halifax."

"St. Pierre and . . . what's that, 'Mike-wall-on'?"

"Miquelon," Magnus said, giving it an exaggerated French furl. "But St. Pierre has the harbor."

"What about them?"

"They're French; they're as much French as Paris. And France doesn't prohibit the sale of liquid anything. We can export our stuff to St. Pierre legally, and then find a buyer. Those little islands are only five hundred miles from New York harbor."

"Wait a minute, Macpherson, are there warehouses? And the weather—does it freeze up or—?"

"I don't know. Let's get over there today and find out. I'll call for the seaplane."

"Today? Wait a minute, Macpherson—"

"No, not a second. I've just come up with this idea, but I know damn well Sam Bronfman's already there."

Sam Bronfman was very much there. The enormous production of his Distillers' Corporation, Seagram Limited, enabled him to supply the East Coast as well as Detroit and Chicago. And St. Pierre was a perfect location for exporting, legally or illegally.

Before prohibition in the United States began, the island of St. Pierre had a population of 2,500. The citizens spoke pure French, wore wooden shoes and zebra-striped jerseys, and barely managed to survive on the industry of cod fishing. They were a courteous people, hardworking, and they closed their few cafés where liquor was sold at eight P.M. sharp.

During prohibition, or what the local citizens called "La Fraude," some massive changes had taken place. Not only Bronfman and the Canadian distillers, but the European distributors had bought land and built enormous concrete warehouses. Freighters began to arrive from Canada and Europe, and every St. Pierrais was pressed into the service of off-loading.

"What do you think?" yelled Weiss over the noise of the seaplane's engine and vibration as they flew over the island. The fog had blown off, and they could see two freighters being worked in the harbor.

"I'm embarrassed."

"What for?"

"For not getting here sooner. When we land, I'll get off and find office space and warehousing—"

"Where?" His gesture pointed to the five-mile granite island, its town, where there were plenty of warehouses plainly visible, but all were newly constructed, and therefore controlled by the competitors.

"I'll find it. You get back to Quebec and move every barrel of stock you can over here. Let another man close out Windsor, you stay clear of that, get an export license for Acme, and find out everything about shipping out of Canada to St. Pierre. I'll find out about moving it south from here."

"How you going to do that?"

"I figure if I walk from one end of the quay down there to the other, I'll run into a familiar unfriendly face. . . . And you might call my wife. Tell her I'm liable to be here for a time." He turned away so Weiss could not see the pained look on his face.

Magnus met a friendly face on his first walk down the Quai de la Roncière. It was Samuel Bronfman himself. He was coming ashore from a fast motor launch. Magnus caught up with him in front of one of the larger warehouses and introduced himself.

"Ah, the avaricious Mr. Macpherson," said Mr. Sam, looking over the top of his glasses. He was a heavy man, but his corpulence seemed to Magnus to be charged with a slippery energy.

"None of that flattery, Mr. Bronfman. Next to you, my avarice is only a wee ambition."

Bronfman's business smile changed to a real one.

"Call me Sam. I hear you had some dealings with Louie Rosenstiel. Sad about that warehouse of his burning down."

"Yes. Sad. Call me Magnus."

They shook hands.

"What can I do for you, Magnus, and if you're looking for warehousing, I'm sorry to say that I can't give you a square inch, and I doubt if you'll find much more on the whole island." His biggest smile was saved for this unhappy bit of information.

"Well, Sam, why would I be looking for warehousing here? This town isn't large enough to drink much of my whiskey, especially after you've burned out their mouths with that stuff you sell. I'm just a tourist. But you could do me a favor and tell me where I can find a bed."

"You're a devoted tourist to come in on a seaplane." He indicated his binoculars. "Try the cafés, some of the fishermen have rooms. And while you're here, Magnus, you might think about this: how would you like to sell Macpherson Distilleries to me?"

Magnus stood looking at him, knowing well that Sam Bronfman could make a deal standing in the street.

"Are you making an offer, and if so, how much?"

"Sure I'm making an offer, of six and a quarter million. Think about it. You could relax the rest of your life." He started to turn toward his warehouse.

"Sam, that's quite an offer."

"Glad you like it." Bronfman began to walk away.

Magnus let him go for two more steps, then said, "I'll give you ten million for Seagram's. And you relax the rest of *your* life."

Bronfman turned back to Magnus, and watched him for a moment, pressing his lips together. Then he said, "I relaxed once. . . . Never been so bored before or since. Keep your money and I'll keep mine. Maybe we'll meet again. And I'm sorry about the warehousing." Sam Bronfman gave a final smile and moved across the quay to his warehouse.

"Hey, that you, Macpherson?"

Magnus turned and saw a man who seemed somehow familiar, but whose face had been badly disfigured by fire. His left eye looked through what seemed to be a hole punched in stretched skin tissue, and a section of his temple was pink and bald.

"Pretty, ain't I? Don't know me? Johnny. Johnny Gianni. No wonder; haven't seen you since your goddamn still blew up and made me into a whole new person."

He laughed, but only one side of his face moved.

Magnus recognized him then, and tried not to react.

"Are you up here working for Costello, then?"

"No, I'm up here for the sunbathing." Again the man laughed, a bitter, barking laugh which brought him the attention of passersby, and gave him his only shared social enjoyment, a revulsion of himself.

"I'd like you to tell Costello something for me."

"I told you, I don't work for Costello. He moved to slots, gambling. I'm with Longie Zwillman, and the only thing I want to do for you's pour acid in your eyes!"

He spoke with feral desperation. Magnus moved closer to him, watching his hands, careful they did not move to a pocket or inside his coat, careful no one could hear.

"Don't waste your time being angry with me or feeling sorry for yourself."

The gangster started to reach, but Magnus grabbed both his arms and held them down, squeezing hard enough to make them useless.

"Find out how I can be helping you. That'd be time well spent."

"How can you? Look at me, how could—?"

"You tell me. You find the doctors. Find what has to be done. If you have to go to Europe, I'll send you."

Magnus felt the man relax. He was looking at Magnus, the conflict of hate and hope contorting the portion of his face unaffected by scars.

"You don't mean that. . . ."

"Yes I do. Let me know. And tell Longie Zwillman I'll be ready for a buyer in two weeks."

The gangster nodded and started off down the quay. Magnus called out to him, "Wait a minute," and walked slowly over to him. "Which one of you was supplying the blind man, Fowler, with joy powder? Was it you?"

"Naw! Not me. It was . . . What's it to you, anyway? What difference does it make? He's dead! I'm the one that's alive with—"

"Was it you, Gianni?" Magnus said flatly.

The man's face contorted. He said, barely audibly, "Yeah. It was me."

He turned and hurried away.

That night Magnus stayed across the harbor on a narrow promontory called the Ile aux Chiens in a fisherman's house. He tried to sleep but was unsuccessful. For hours he lay in the dark, anticipating the next groan from the foghorn.

The usual missing he felt for his home was further depressed by his suspicion that he had no home, that what he missed was an image created by his own wishing. He thought of Weiss calling the house and telling Mary what had happened. In his mind he could hear the relief in her voice when she learned he would be away for a time. Perhaps his absence would help her; he hoped so. Perhaps she'd have more time to find what she was looking for, and then she could come back to him. The foghorn blew, and through his sleepless anxiety it seemed to say, "No-o-o-o. . . . No-o-o-o." He tried to cover his ears with his pillow, but it did little good. He wondered what would happen if she never came back to him, if her absence was final. He had not considered that possibility. As he lay in the darkness, he tried to think of a way to stop thinking. Abruptly he got out of bed, dressed, and went out of the fisherman's house.

Magnus walked for a half-hour out the Cap à l'Aigle road, wishing he had a bottle of malt. At the end of the road he saw the outlines of a large building. Actually, he smelled it before he saw it. Magnus had found his warehouse.

The Frigorifique had been used to freeze cod before La Fraude. After many scrubbings of disinfectant, it made a perfect warehouse. In two weeks Ted Weiss arrived with the first shipload of whiskey. Relabeled "Old Duff," the hooch was exported legally by Macpherson Distilleries, Limited, in Canada to Acme, Limited, on the French possession of St. Pierre. It was soon sold and exported to the United States through Longie Zwillman's Reinfeld Corporation.

The Reinfeld organization was named for the brothers who ran it. Originally they had been immigrants from Poland to Canada, and began their careers in the business with the Bronfmans. The Reinfelds moved to the United States at the start of prohibition, and under Longie Zwillman's protection they supplied at least 50 percent of all the hooch delivered between Boston and Philadelphia. Their operation had none of the glamor and excitement of the old Rum Row days. Freighters anchored safely outside the new twelve-mile limit and powerful syndicate contact boats made the runs. Cold, efficient, and deadly, the Reinfeld people paid cash in advance for the product, and Magnus was not bothered with nostalgia.

He spent more and more time on the island to oversee the movement of his goods. His French improved. He forgot the society parties in Quebec, and enjoyed the simplicity of life among the St. Pierrais.

He had not tried adultery, which seemed to him a belittling relief of sexual need. He believed Mary had her own torment; any betrayal on his part out of anger or frustration would only add to her struggle. He did not have time for an affair of any depth, nor did he have any ease with casual carnality. Magnus still loved his wife.

On one of the infrequent nights he stayed in his own home between trips to the distilleries and St. Pierre, Magnus lay alone in their bed. He found himself becoming frustrated, then angry. His usual rationalizing about the gray room had no effect. He got out of bed, went down the hall, and knocked on the door of the gray room.

"Mary, it's me."

There was a silence, during which Magnus' fury grew beyond control. She said quietly, "Magnus, I'm praying."

After turning the knob and finding it locked, he kicked the door open.

She was on her knees before the crucifix in a long brown flannel gown and turned to look at Magnus with surprise and irritation.

"Pray on, then, Mary. But I've come to sleep here with you."

Mary did not speak, but put her rosary on the Bible next to the chair and stood up, looking at him, vulnerable but noncommittal, waiting for whatever was going to happen. They looked at each other in the light from the single votive candle.

"Do you know what you're doing to yourself, Mary?"

"I know what I'm trying to do."

"Do you, now? Then do you know what you're doing to us? Because I've lost you, and I don't know who or what to fight to get you back, besides yourself. And I'm here to do it."

Mary went behind him and closed the door. His tone changed from its level of angry urgency, knowing at least they shared the same closed room.

"Mary, come back to us."

She looked away, her eyes filled with tears, and she shook her head, jerking it quickly.

"I know this causes you pain, Magnus, and I beg you to forgive me. But it's an act of my faith in—"

"I'll not forgive you! You have to know what it's doing, this 'act of faith.' Mary, living your own life is an act of faith. You're not a nun. You weren't meant to be, nor a saint either."

"I know that! I'm not trying to be either one, and please don't say that I am. I *am* living my life. This is my life, here in this room. I'm trying to find my God and learn—"

"But what of us? Do you leave us behind, your husband, your children, while you search around in the corners for—"

"Stop it! I haven't left the children, I haven't left you. . . . I am not a part of your life, Magnus. You know I'm not. You have your business; I have my prayers." The edge of accusation in her voice changed to distaste. "And if you came in here for sex, well all right, do whatever you want."

He grabbed her arms and held them hard. His rage urged violence, his love wanted only for her to reach out and touch his cheek.

"Don't dare blame this on me and my business. I'll be as much in your life as you'll let me. You've locked me out of it. And I want to know why." He was shaking her hard, and she began to cry. When he saw, he pulled her gently into his arms and held her, kissing her ear, her neck, her hair. The love he felt for her made him ache, and he hated himself for causing her pain.

"Mary, I love you so. . . ."

But she pushed herself away so violently she lost her balance.

"No! I don't want to cry." She wiped her eyes with her hand. "Not in front of you. I don't want to share even my grief. I'll share it later on my knees. Grief, Magnus." She slowly pointed her finger at him. Her voice came out all dull and hard. "Your life is covered with blood. Who'll pray for you, other than me? God forgive my weakness for telling you. What you do spills blood on the streets every night. I watch you hold my children in your bloody hands. I'm too weak and full of sin. My prayers for you go unanswered, and my faith doesn't even touch you."

Magnus felt nauseous. He was about to shout, "You're raving mad," but did not; he feared he was right. As she went on, Mary obsessively pressed the forefinger she had been pointing at him onto her forehead.

"Don't you see I was born for this? I was blessed with my loving family, to learn and feel love, real love . . . so that I could give all of it up." She almost started to cry again, but jabbed her head with her finger. "No! No! I had to give them up and put my faith up against your horrible bloody hunger. Do you understand, Magnus? I will suffer from my Lord, as you make Him suffer!"

Her eyes burned as she went to the crucifix, knelt down, and took up her rosary beads.

He stood silently, feeling his own volatility as well as hers.

"So *you'll* go on suffering because *I'm* making Him suffer. D'ya think your Roman Catholic God approves of such . . . blackmail?"

The word arched her spine. She jumped up, smashing at his face with her fists, grabbing his hair and pulling it as hard as she could.

"Bloody! . . . You are bloody!" she cried with each blow. Magnus protected his face. When she grabbed his hair, he pulled her into his arms. He kissed her neck as she beat on his back and kept kissing her until she began to cry and pulled him against her. She kissed his head several times, then cried out, "Lord! My God!" She arched her back, pulling away, but started moving her pelvis against him.

"Mary, my dear love, come back. . . ."

She hit him in the face as hard as she could. Without thinking, he slapped her back. Mary stared at him, the sweat from her struggle running down her cheeks. Then she closed her eyes and slowly arched her head back as far as her spine would allow. With one hand she jerked up her flannel gown, through the tight press of their groins.

Magnus looked at her as if she were a stranger.

"Oh, no . . . oh, no." Her eyes opened with his words as he backed her to a wall for support and let go of her. "You'll not make me your devil, Mary, any more than you have already. There's no blood on my hands except what you see there. You take my love and make yourself a martyr. God, woman, do you need that so much?"

Her eyes widened further, until she brought her hand up, and again she touched her forehead. Then she closed her eyes and began to move her lips in prayer.

Magnus watched for a moment, then left the room. He went back to their room, dressed and walked to his office. He never slept in the house again.

The next morning, Magnus went to the asylum and told Father Montier what had happened.

"I know now, Father, that I'm the cause of—"

"No! I told you before, don't blame—"

"I'm not blaming. But I *am* the object of whatever's happening. I'll gladly leave, separate, divorce her if it will help."

"If that happens, her failure, as she sees it, will be complete. If you want to help her, keep loving her."

"And give her an excuse to feel guilty for *my* sins."

"Mr. Macpherson, *she* has chosen to make her life hell. Why, I can't say. There's need in her for this conflict. She would have found it one way or another. As to her guilt . . ." The priest's face tensed as if he did not trust himself to speak. When he did, he chose his words carefully. "Guilt is a device of the Church. She grew up with it. Remember, we're required to confess our guilt before every communion; and from what I understand, her family was fervent in their devotions. Under pathological pressure, such a habitual emotional reaction could be forced out of proportion. We may never find the cause of her illness unless Mary wants us to. I wish you could pray. . . . I wish I could."

"What about our children?"

"You think they're in any danger?"

"No. I'm more concerned about the ideas she's filling their heads . . ."

Magnus stopped, realizing the awkwardness of telling his worry to a priest. But Father Montier nodded.

"There's room in their minds for more than one set of ideas. I think they're probably hungry for them. Take some time to give them yours. . . . For that advice I'm sure to be running in some circle of hell. . . . There'll be some confusion, but at least they'll have choices."

Magnus smiled and got up to leave. Father Montier did not return the smile, but looked at Magnus and said, "Can I ask you something?"

"Of course you can."

"Mary accused you pretty severely for the kind of life you live. Did it bother you, all those accusations about 'blood'?"

Magnus looked at him.

"Should it have? No. Not for a second. People do what they do because they choose it. The people Mary was talking about . . . chose to be just where they are. They take greater risks and get greater profits. That's their business. We all draw our own lines. And I've drawn mine on *this* side of any blood. . . . Do *you* think . . . ?"

"I didn't ask so I could judge; I was only curious how it affected you."

"It doesn't."

Two weeks after that conversation, in the summer of 1932, Franklin Delano Roosevelt flew for seven hours in a plane from Albany to Chicago to accept the Democratic party's nomination for President. Their campaign slogan was "A New Deal and a Pot of Beer for Everyone."

To thoroughly irritate Juny and Joe Fleming, Magnus had contributed fifteen thousand dollars to Roosevelt's primary campaign against Al Smith. When Roosevelt won the nomination, Magnus' contribution became an investment. He immediately wired another twenty thousand to the campaign with the message, "Urge change 'Pot of Beer' to 'Bottle of Whiskey,'" and pledged that before the campaign was over, he would send sixty-five thousand dollars more.

As soon as Mr. Roosevelt ended "Herbert Hoover's Depression," everyone would be able to buy a Ford and drive to buy a bottle of whiskey, and the new wet Congress would end "The Noble Experiment." Magnus knew that whoever had the most and best whiskey would make his fortune. Few distillers in the United States had stock. Magnus and the Bronfmans, however, had been setting aside stock in Canada. Louis Rosenstiel had bought up warehouse receipts for whatever whiskey was left in government warehouses, and bought distilleries with brands that he could market immediately. They had a head start.

But Magnus wanted more quality stock. Other distillers thought that after the chances the American people took during prohibition, they would drink anything legal and safe. Magnus believed the public's taste had become vastly sophisticated because of the constant testing in the speaks. A whiskey of superior quality would not only find a large market, but command a high price. He believed everyone wished to share somehow in the best things in life. A bottle of quality whiskey was one of the cheapest ways to do it.

6

"Promised, promised, promised, promised, promised,"
say the leaves across America. . . . And everywhere,
through the immortal dark, something moving in
the night, and something stirring in the hearts
of men. . . .

—THOMAS WOLFE

In 1932, using the persuasion of a native son, Magnus secured a guarantee of 56,000 barrels of single malt whiskey each month from fifteen distillers of the Glen Rinnes. After the American election, ratification of the constitutional amendment ending prohibition would take at least another twelve months. By then Magnus would have more than a million gallons of malt to combine with his aged stock in Canada and new grain alcohol. The fine taste of his new blend, he believed, would put him far ahead of his competitors. But he wanted more Scotch whiskey stock and all that was left in the world belonged to the Distillers Company, Limited, in England.

DCL was formed in 1877 with six Scottish distilleries. In the mid-twenties it was joined by John Haig and Co., Buchanan-Dewar, Ltd., and John Walker and Son, Ltd. By 1932 the company controlled twenty-six of the largest distilling companies in the British Isles. Each of these companies remained an entirely separate manufacturing and distributing entity, engaging in zealous rivalry among themselves far more intense than against any outside company.

The company found itself in the early thirties being courted with an ardor before unknown. DCL had aged whiskey, and Rosenstiel, Bronfman, and almost every other American distiller was trying to buy. But DCL planned to wait until the form of a beneficial plan became clearly visible. Magnus had such a plan, and late in the summer of 1932 he took his eldest son on a short vacation to New York City, not by coincidence at the same time Thomas Herd, the director of DCL, was visiting the city.

After a week of baseball, zoos, movies, and visits to the Statue of Liberty and as many museums as the child could stand, Magnus left his son at the Waldorf and had a meeting with Mr. Herd at the DCL offices. Magnus suggested a triangle. It would be formed by the British Isles, the North American continent, and, for no other reason than Weiss had told him that "wops love Scotch," Italy. DCL would send aged stock to Magnus in the United States. Some of the finished Macpherson product would be shipped to Italy, where Macpherson Distilleries and DCL would establish a distribution company together. Profits from Italian sales would flow back to the United States to Magnus, and to the British Isles to DCL, completing the triangle. The Italian distribution company would market DCL's products as well, as would Magnus' company in America, if DCL would allow him rights. Mr. Herd listened with great interest as Magnus explained his plan.

"Mr. Macpherson, we already have many distribution offers in the United States, as well as a very pleasant operation in Italy," Mr. Herd said after a moment of consideration.

"I'm aware of that. But I don't like pleasant operations. I like competition, don't you?"

Thomas Herd, who held the reins on twenty-six skittish distillers, smiled.

"I like your triangle, Macpherson."

"If it works in Italy, you might consider an octagon."

"An octagon?"

"And Spain, France, Germany, the Low Countries, and Scandinavia."

Mr. Herd looked at Magnus with a bemused tilt of his head.

"Shall we just say Europe?"

"Why limit ourselves, Mr. Herd?"

"You are suggesting a rather far-reaching commitment, Mr. Macpherson."

"There's no more local business. If we can't talk about the world, Mr. Herd, there's no point in talking."

The two men gazed at each other over the high polish of Mr. Herd's Sheraton desk.

Macpherson Distilleries, Limited, received options on five million gallons of DCL's aged whiskey. Magnus and Thomas Herd agreed to go on a trip to Italy as soon as prohibition ended. Herd also implied he would like to have Macpherson Distilleries distribute Haig and

Haig's products in the United States if Magnus could promptly set up a distribution organization.

After his meeting with Thomas Herd, Magnus returned to his suite at the Waldorf-Astoria in time to join Magnus II for lunch. The trip had been the boy's first time away from home, and he had been having a "wonderment time," as he wrote to his mother on a postcard. Mary had opposed the trip at first, but had given in when Magnus agreed to allow Magnus II to visit the Flemings in Southampton. She had arranged with Juny to fly the boy from Long Island back to Quebec in a private plane.

Juny arrived at the suite at the stroke of two, as arranged. Magnus II taunted his uncle immediately.

"How do you do, Uncle Juny? I've heard a lot about you. Should I believe it?"

Juny laughed. "Depends on who you heard it from. Well, Magnus, you're looking"—he looked Magnus up and down with a hooded smile, as if Magnus' tailoring were a stolen costume—"boomish." Juny was dressed in a seersucker suit, and a straw boater. He had taken to crinkling his forehead as a sign of studied casualness, like the men in cigarette commercials. Magnus still loathed him.

"As usual, Juny, you outlook yourself," which meant nothing, but which seemed to please Juny, who said, "We'll have a whale of a time meeting another member of the family. . . . Sorry you can't come out. Spiffy weekend, a clambake . . ."

"Sounds busy. I doubt if I'll be missed. One Magnus Macpherson is no doubt enough."

Magnus said it so Juny would note to which family the boy belonged. Juny merely smiled and said, "We heard from Mary the other day."

"I wish she was here. What did she say, Uncle Juny?"

"She misses her son a great deal. A great deal." He glanced at Magnus to make sure the exclusion was received. It was.

Their bags were loaded by the bellhops onto a wagon. They all went down to the street, where Juny's car was waiting. Magnus said to his son, "Keep up with the bags, Magnus, tell them which ones go in the car." The boy ran ahead with the bellhops.

As Juny watched the boy, he said offhandedly, "How does Mary keep it straight with two Magnuses in the house?"

Juny knew that one Magnus did not live in the house.

"She manages."

"We're a bit worried about her."

" 'We'?"

"Me and my family. We haven't seen her. She won't let us come up, even to see the two new children."

"Certainly the Flemings have enough children down here to keep you busy."

Juny smiled his nasty smile at Magnus.

"Why is it all you Protestants are so fascinated by the number of children we have? Does it upset you?"

"No, it seems a likely accomplishment if you put your mind to it. What is it that's worrying you about Mary?"

Juny quickly stepped in front of Magnus and, still smiling, said, "You've begun pushing her around. Watch your step, Macpherson. If you touch my sister against her wishes, I'll come find you and sag you bloody."

Magnus wanted to lay him out on the sidewalk, but did not because of his son. He was also humiliated that Mary had shared their troubles with her family.

"I've not pushed Mary, ever. She may have stumbled from pushing me away. . . . No. Those aren't Mary's words, they're yours. And it's not your business. But you *should* worry, you and your family. For it's you and your church that's made her deny who she is. That's what's hurting her."

"What are you trying to say, Magnus?"

"You know damn well. As to your grand threat, tell your family you're a hero for threatening me. But if you ever get courage to do it, I'll welcome it with a kiss of the fist on your eyeteeth. Now, shut up in front of your nephew."

Magnus II came running up and dragged them over to where the porters and chauffeur were loading baggage into Juny's new twelve-cylinder Hispano-Suiza sedanca-de-ville. He kissed his father goodbye and jumped happily into the backseat.

Magnus said quietly to Juny, "Nice car, Juny. Buy it yourself?"

"Someday you'll go down, Macpherson, and I'll be there to spit on you."

He started to get in the backseat, but Magnus grabbed his arm and pulled him back.

"Until then, Juny, how'd you like to make some more money? I need capital, between fifteen and twenty million. I can go to any investment banker in town to float stock, but I'll give Fleming and Co. first refusal, to keep it in the family."

Juny looked at Magnus with amazement. "How can you possibly dare ask, after what you—?"

"There's no memory in business except about money. As I remember, we made some. Think it over. There'll be a lot of velvet for you."

Magnus let go, and Juny dropped into the backseat. Magnus watched as the enormous car moved slowly away from the hotel and disappeared between buildings. He stood for a moment looking across the street at the desperate men watching the rich climb into their limousines. The rich were always around, and what a burden for the rest. Magnus looked down at his well-shined shoes and the crease of his pants. He was one of them.

He hailed a taxi and hurried to catch his train to Wilmington, Delaware. He had his whiskey stock; he would get his capital and his American distilleries. What he needed next was a chemist. As the train sped through the hobo jungles beside the tracks, Magnus thought he could have been out there, if it weren't for whiskey. Water of life.

Soon after his graduation from college, Dr. Joseph Heinrich Bromberg had established himself as a brilliant industrial chemist in Germany. He lived in Munich with his wife. During the late twenties, in opposition to the anti-Semitism and stormtroopers of the Nazi party, they had joined the Communist party. The Depression in 1929 brought Adolf Hitler to prominence, and in 1930 Dr. and Mrs. Bromberg were severely beaten and forced to watch the stormtroopers burn their home to the ground. When nothing was done by their government, the Brombergs left the country. They first stayed in London, where Dr. Bromberg was hired as a consultant to John Walker and Son, Ltd., by Sir Alexander Walker. Very quickly E. I. du Pont de Nemours & Company heard of Dr. Bromberg's availability and brought him and his wife to the United States.

Magnus heard of Dr. Bromberg from Sir Alexander Walker, a director of DCL. He wrote the chemist and received a cordial reply. Magnus hoped that it meant Dr. Bromberg was dissatisfied at Du Pont.

They met at a crowded Chinese restaurant and sat in a corner booth. Dr. Bromberg was a short, round man with a careful mustache and goatee. He spoke English meticulously. Before long, Magnus confirmed that the doctor was not content in Wilmington.

"You see, Mr. Macpherson, Du Pont is magnificent. But it is a chemical factory, and the chemists are factory workers. We are well-paid factory workers, but just the same . . . You understand me?"

"Tell me what you want, Dr. Bromberg."

The man smiled. "You know, scientists are considered to be above vanity. Science requires that no sign of the individual personality can appear in one's work. But may I be frank, Mr. Macpherson? Inside every white-coated chemist there is a movie star aching for the alchemy of fame."

"Are you a movie star, Dr. Bromberg?"

Amused, the chemist closed his eyes to formulate his answer.

"Let me put it this way. It does not have to be a movie. It can be a very small production." His eyes opened and he looked across at Magnus with gall. "But I would like to play the leading role."

"It must be difficult for you here in Wilmington to be in the chorus."

"Exactly, Mr. Macpherson. You understand."

"I do. At the moment we have as much scientific knowledge of whiskey as we do of mud. I want you to teach me everything there is, and then discover and invent more. I'll provide you with whatever you need . . . and you will definitely play the leading role."

"What would be the salary, Mr. Macpherson?"

"Dr. Bromberg, I prefer not to give you one."

"You prefer not . . . to give me one?"

"No. In the leading role, I need a real performer . . . an artist. No price should be put on an artist. What I propose is supplying you with an open checking account. Pay yourself what you think you deserve."

Dr. Bromberg sat motionless and astounded. Then he broke into a wide grin.

"Mr. Macpherson, you are a clever man. You offer, not what I want, not what I need, but what *I* think *I* deserve. You will make me write down on checks, for all the world to see, the price of my vanity. You understand me perhaps too well, but I think I will enjoy working for you."

The next day Magnus flew by seaplane to meet Ted Weiss on St. Pierre. Ted was waiting for him on the quay. As Magnus stepped out of the motor launch, Ted Weiss greeted him with a display of noisy affection and gave him a hug. Magnus thought Weiss had gone crazy until he felt a heavy weight slip into the inside pocket of his coat and knew it was a gun.

"What's that for?"

"Walk along the quay, just keep talking and smiling."

"What's the matter, Weiss?"

"Anastasia's on the island."

They walked, checking familiar corners and doorways, avoiding the eyes of strangers, and watching their hands instead. Finally they began to speak through their smiles.

"You're sure?"

"Sure."

"Did he see you?"

"Doesn't know me. He knows you."

"Is he here to see me?"

"Donno. Saw him when I came in this morning. Didn't ask him. Doubt if he's up here for the nightlife."

"Where is he? I want to see him."

"What?" Weiss began to laugh as an antidote to panic. "No. That's not what you want. What you want is to get back to the plane and get your ass out of here."

"Where is he?"

"He and two guys. *Two guys*, Macpherson."

"Where? How long has he been here?"

"A week, ten days, doing nothing. *Waiting*. Staying on that boat, coming in for dinner at the Café de l'Universe."

Magnus looked out into the harbor and saw a large motor yacht pulling gently at its anchor.

"He coulda seen you get out of the plane."

"He could have. So we'll be careful. But he could be up here for a lot of other reasons."

"So go!"

"I just came through New York, Weiss, with my son. I had to worry that every shadow had a killer in it. I've got some things to tell him. I want to settle this thing."

"You don't settle with Anastasia, except down to the bottom of a river. I know you got things to tell him. So put 'em in a letter."

"We'll see him tonight. Now, tell me what you're doing about buying me American distilleries."

"Distilleries? Macpherson, there's something you never learned about what comes first. Keeping a pulse comes first."

"What about the distilleries?"

"We got two, and telling him anything ain't gonna work."

"Which ones?"

142

"Colonel Burnside's in Kentucky, and the old one outside of Pittsburgh."

"That'll make Louie Rosenstiel happy, having us as neighbors. Are they firm?"

"As firm as money."

"Good. I'll close the deals this month."

"Dammit, what if you're dead, Macpherson?"

"Stuff me, put me on roller skates, and I'll close the deals this month. . . . Go find out where those three men sit when they have their supper."

That night, at sunset, a small launch went out to the motor yacht anchored in the harbor. It picked up three men and brought them into the Quai de la Roncière. The three men left the launch, walked down the quay to the harbor front Café de l'Universe.

They were ushered to their usual corner table by the owner. The café was a crumbling old wooden place with an uneven stone floor, a few leaded windows, and worn wooden furniture. On the walls a few pictures of Paris hung under sagging ancient beams. Fish was prepared over a burning fire. The bar was crowded until eight, when the café closed. The three men had made arrangements with the owner to come in just at that time, in order to dine alone. One of the three always wore an overcoat while he ate. It helped to conceal the shotgun he held up against the table with his knees.

Albert Anastasia sat with his back in the corner. When he ate his meal, one of the men joined him. Then the two of them had coffee while the third man quickly ate his food. No one approached the table except the owner, who brought the food and poured the wine.

As they were finishing their meal, there was a knock on the front door. One of the men at the table got up and went to the door. He looked out and yelled, "Closed. Closed." From the kitchen the owner translated: "Fermé. A demain." The knocking continued, irritating the man at the door, until he opened it. Before he could say anything, Magnus slipped in. The man shoved him against the wall and pulled a gun from a shoulder holster, while his partner in the overcoat cleared the shotgun in his lap. Both were ready to kill.

"What does he want?" Anastasia said from the corner.

Magnus said calmly to the man with the gun in his stomach, "Tell Anastasia my name is Magnus Macpherson. All I want to do is talk."

"Macpherson? Magnus Macpherson?" Anastasia asked. He had grown thick. His body seemed too large for his small head. His face had jowls and his small eyes seemed to have receded into his skull.

"Frisk him and bring him over."

Magnus was frisked quickly and thoroughly. Then he was ushered to the table with a gun in his back. Anastasia looked closely at him.

"Yeah. It's been some time, Macpherson. You come in here to die or to ruin my dessert?"

"Just to talk. You see I'm not carrying anything."

"You can die anyway."

"So can we all. For instance, the picture beside your head has a couple of holes behind it, one for a sprayer, one so my friend out there can hear if he should use it. Drilled them this afternoon."

Anastasia looked at his two men. Magnus talked too quickly for them to do anything stupid.

"Don't anyone move too fast. Here, allow me, I'll just tilt the frame here . . ."

Magnus moved slowly to the picture. He lifted it so that Anastasia could see the two barrels of a shotgun about ten inches from his head. There was another hole above them. Magnus took the picture down and leaned it against another table.

"Now he can see a wee bit."

Anastasia's man with the shotgun spoke urgently in Italian. Anastasia answered him angrily, then turned to Magnus.

"What's the problem?"

"I want to talk."

"So talk."

"I'd feel better, and so would my friend, if your protection was out of hearing."

Anastasia spoke to the two men in Italian. They got up and moved to a table across the room next to the fire. Magnus slowly sat down. Anastasia's expression never changed.

"What d'ya want to talk about?"

"About me staying alive."

"This ain't the way to do it."

"I know, but it's the only way I thought I could talk to you without dying first."

"Why would you think that?"

"I heard it from Al Capone. I also heard you like killing."

Anastasia started to get up and lunge at Magnus, but the twin barrels came right out of the wall and pressed against his head and he sat back down.

"I'm not talking to you, Macpherson."

"Then listen. And remember. Joe Turino. You shot him in 1920."

144

"That's twelve years ago. I can only count to ten."

"You used a forty-four. You gave it to Arnold Rothstein. He gave it to me."

"You?"

"By chance. I was supposed to sink it in the ocean. But I kept it . . . again by chance. I had no idea of it belonging to you. When I heard you were all for me dying, I wanted to know about you. I read about the Joe Turino case, and about the gun everyone was looking for. The dates were right. I wondered if I might have that gun. A friend of mine who knows something of fingerprints found two of yours on the barrel. You don't leave evidence anymore at your killings. The law can't get anything on you. But that gun could fry you."

"Fingerprints don't last so long."

"We took lots of pictures of them at the time. I put them with the gun in a safe-deposit box. The Division of Investigation in Washington gets the key to it if anything happens to me. . . . That's all I wanted to talk about. The best thing for you is for me to grow old."

Immediately the gun barrel disappeared back through the wall. Magnus got up and calmly rehung the picture, making sure it was straight. Then, without looking either right or left, he walked slowly to the front door. One of the men sitting at the table by the fire jumped up, but Anastasia shouted at him in Italian. As Magnus opened the door, the gangster bellowed, "Macpherson, I'll find a way, and I'll piss on your grave."

For the next two months Magnus spent most of his time in the United States, buying the two distilleries, incorporating, setting up distribution, and talking to advertising and marketing people. He sat down with the executives at Fleming and Co., including Juny and Joseph Fleming, and structured the capitalization of Macpherson Distilleries, Incorporated. Weiss began shipping liquor from the British Isles to Canada, warehousing it, with arrangements to move it into the United States as soon as the law allowed. Roosevelt was elected President on November 9, 1932, by a landslide. The Democrats were in total control of a wet Congress. By Thanksgiving, Ted Weiss and Dr. Bromberg were in Kentucky expanding the distillery in preparation for manufacture and blending. By Christmas, Macpherson Distilleries in Canada had amassed ten million gallons of aging whiskey in charred barrels ready for shipment to the Kentucky distillery. By the new year, Magnus had a string of distributors lined up from Maine to California. A million-dollar advertising campaign was launched, an unprecedented sum at the time.

Magnus was ready; he had seen to it that every element of Macpherson Distilleries was poised for its invasion of the United States. The company was incorporated in Delaware on January 2, 1933, which authorized capitalization of one million shares of common stock. The following day Fleming and Co. floated two hundred thousand shares at twelve dollars a share. By the close of the trading week, they were going for thirty dollars. Magnus had personally made close to five million dollars on paper. His first reaction was to call Quebec and share the good news with his family. But before the connection was put through, he told the operator to cancel the call; by that time, the distance separating him from his family was too great. It had little to do with geography or all the time he spent on business. That autumn, the family difficulties seemed to have intensified.

When Magnus II had returned from his visit with the Flemings, the previous summer, he noticed his mother began to care for him with an automatic efficiency. His feelings were hurt. Because he was the oldest, his mother had used to go to his room last at bedtime, after seeing Jamie and WeeDee, to sit on his bed and talk or tell him stories. But that fall she stopped in his room first, and for only a short time. She seemed more interested in getting her visit done so she could go on to the other children.

Magnus II already had an intense, selfish pride, and therefore did not complain. He was confident he could win his mother back. But as time went by, she seemed to steel herself against his expressions of affection. She was always racing around taking care of WeeDee, who was starting school and who seemed to need daily shopping trips for dresses, coats, and shiny pencil boxes. His mother also spent more and more time with Jamie, and even took him into that room of hers. Magnus II listened at the door once. All he heard was his mother praying. When he looked in the keyhole, he saw his mother on her knees, and Jamie sitting nearby under the candle sucking his thumb, holding onto the pillow that he dragged everywhere. Then his sister, WeeDee, came down the hall and saw him spying. He had to give her a dollar which he took out of his mother's purse, to keep her quiet.

Magnus II felt displaced from his mother's affection. He decided to write her a note. It said: "If you hate me, I'll go live with my Fa at the hotel." He slipped the paper under the door of her gray room, then ran and hid in the cellar until dinner.

His mother said nothing to him until he was in bed. She did not sit down, but stood across the room.

"I don't hate you, Magnus. I love you and pray for you every day. But you're no longer a little boy. You're growing up. You went away on a trip . . . with your father . . . a long trip. You stopped saying your prayers."

"Do you hate Fa? Is that the reason?"

"No, I don't hate anyone, Magnus. I have a great affection for your father, and for you."

"Then why can't he stay here with us?"

"He can. He chooses not to."

"Because you're always in that room!"

His outburst startled his mother, and she grasped her hands together in front of her and kneaded them hard as she glared at her son.

"I am *praying* in that room. You're old enough to understand that."

She continued to glare at the boy for a moment. Then her eyes dropped and she said, "You've grown up to be a Macpherson."

She turned and went out the door, closing it quietly behind her. She was wrong; Magnus II did not understand. He kicked off the bedcovers, ran and opened the door. His mother was about to go into WeeDee's room.

"Then I hate *you!*" He slammed the door shut, ran to the bed, and cried himself to sleep. His mother did not come back. He never cried again. The next night, when Mary went to Magnus II's door, she found it locked.

The next time Magnus returned to Quebec, he heard of the incident from WeeDee. She was an observant little girl and knew how to tantalize with information. She generally traded something she knew for something she wanted, and she was a hard bargainer. For a thorough report on the breakdown of the relationship between her mother and her older brother, WeeDee exacted a promise from her father that he would take her on his next long trip to New York.

That evening, before Magnus left the house, he told Mary that if she showed the slightest prejudice against any of the children, he would have them all come live with him. The two of them stood in the downstairs hallway. When they were together in the house, neither of them liked to commit themselves to the intimacy or the permanence of going into a room. Mary listened, rigidly nervous, but did not say a word. He asked her if she understood; she nodded. Magnus waited for her to say something. Moments passed. Finally he turned away and went out the door. Outside, he felt the cold air seep into him, and realized he was covered with sweat.

Christmas passed pleasantly, in spite of Magnus II remaining wary, watchful, and polite. Magnus was not able to be in town for the new year, as his presence was required for incorporation in Wilmington and New York. This satisfied Mary, who spent New Year's Eve with Jamie in the gray room. She told Father Montier a few days later that she held the little body sleeping in her arms for hours as she knelt before the crucifix. At the stroke of midnight, when the horns and bells sounded all over the city, she "felt the task of time" pass from her onto her little son. For her, it was a sublime moment. After she put Jamie in his own bed, she returned to her gray room, weeping and laughing, and gave thanks to God for her deliverance.

Father Montier was familiar with spiritual exhilaration. He saw too many people reach it, only to swing and fall to some opposite extreme. When Mary continued for a number of days at a level of frantic activity, Father Montier became concerned. He tried to reach Magnus, who was out of town. Ted Weiss took his number at St. Bridget's, but when Magnus returned the call, Father Montier was attending to his patients.

Mary went on with a glowing feverish joy, planning a big anniversary party, inviting everyone at the last minute, even calling Magnus in New York to make sure he would be there.

When Magnus received the call, so soon after he had decided against his own call, he was amazed. Her voice was as he remembered it as she ran over the green lawns to the boathouse in Southampton. She even giggled as she let him know she was sleeping in their bed. Magnus caught her excitement and was anxious to return to Quebec for the first time in years. He went directly to Tiffany's to buy her a present. The next day he caught the train. He would arrive just in time for the festivities.

Mary went to the beauty shop on the morning of the party. The hairdressers had not seen her since Jamie had been born. She had her hair cut and waved into the current style of a short bob. Then she and WeeDee went shopping for party dresses. By the time Magnus II arrived home from a school outing, the house was in an uproar. Unhappy at being left out of the preparations, he went up to his room and slammed the door.

He sat on his bed listening. He heard Jamie cry, then laugh. He heard the extra servants arrive, then the musicians. One of them started playing the piano. A glass broke. Magnus II smiled.

He got up and went to the door of his room. He opened it, saw no one was in the hall, and crept down to Jamie's room. He peered around the door and saw the nanny was occupied with polishing one of Jamie's shoes. Jamie was standing patiently, trying to balance on one foot. He saw Magnus II and smiled expectantly.

Magnus II went into the room. Jamie was wearing a suit with short pants and a necktie. Magnus II looked at him a moment, grabbed the tie, and tightened it around Jamie's neck. Jamie let out a piercing shriek, which brought the nanny running. Magnus II then ran down the hall to WeeDee's room.

He went in and closed the door quietly. WeeDee was at her vanity mirror. She saw him and turned. He put his finger to his lips for quiet and leaned on the door laughing. WeeDee heard Jamie's shrieks from down the hall and knew her older brother had caused them. She turned back to her mirror to finish trying to apply the lipstick with which she was playing.

"Magnus, why are you such a stinker?"

Magnus II stopped laughing. He went over to WeeDee and grabbed the lipstick out of her hand. WeeDee watched him and smiled. It made him furious, and he ran out of the room with her makeup, yelling, "What are you doing with this junk? You look stupid."

He almost ran into his mother, who was coming down the hall in a dressing gown. He escaped into his room and locked the door. When his mother knocked, he refused to answer.

"Magnus, let me in."

Still he said nothing.

"All right, you stay in there until you're ready to apologize to your brother and sister."

"No! No! I won't. Not to you either!" He threw the lipstick at the door.

"Then don't come to the party." His mother waited for a reply. When Magnus II said nothing, she went away. Then he had an idea.

WeeDee was the first to come downstairs in her new party dress. Her mother had washed off her attempt at makeup. She accepted the approbation of the staff graciously, and when the musicians played a short fanfare as she entered the living room, she gave a nice little curtsy.

The house looked resplendent. The crystal stones glittered, the rooms were filled with hothouse flowers. The sideboard was covered with food, and two bartenders were polishing champagne glasses. The nanny brought Jamie down, now completely recovered from his brother's attack and wanting nothing more than to slide across the polished floor in his new shoes.

Then Mary appeared at the top of the stairs. The servants hesitated as they saw the transformation of their mistress. WeeDee ran to the stairs and said, "Oh, Mummy, you look so beautiful."

Mary smiled and started down. The jade-green dress made her red hair appear as a luminous halo around her face. She wore deep red lipstick and mascara, the "Hollywood" makeup which was fashionable that season.

Halfway down the stairs, she hesitated.

"WeeDee, come on, let's go get your brother."

WeeDee ran up and took her mother's hand. Together they went back up the stairs and down the hall to Magnus II's room.

Mary knocked, and noticed the door was ajar. She pushed it open and said, "Magnus, may we come in?" Then she staggered so suddenly back into the hall, she almost knocked WeeDee over. Mary banged up against the opposite wall and stood staring into the room transfixed.

Magnus II had made a cross with wire and bed slats, and was spread-eagled on it against the wall above his bed. He had a small towel around his middle. There were large black smears under his eyes, and blood marks on his hands, feet, and side.

"Mary Fleming Macpherson, look at yourself! Have you forgotten me? A party? Why aren't you praying on your knees? Kneel down! Kneel down!" Then he laughed.

Mary did not move. WeeDee reached over and closed the door. She went to her mother and hugged her. "Mummy. It's all right. Mummy . . ."

At that moment Magnus came in the front door from the station. WeeDee and Mary could hear him. Still Mary did not move. Downstairs Magnus greeted his youngest. "Well, don't you look a proper one. Come here, Jamie. What's going on around here? It looks like a party. Where's the beautiful hostess? Where's my darlin Mary?"

WeeDee felt her mother shudder. A mask of a smile came on her face, and she started to go down the hall.

Magnus II opened his door, still laughing. Mary did not look back.

"Hey, it was a joke. Where are you going? Come back. It was a joke."

Mary continued down the stairs. Magnus II and WeeDee heard their father say, "There she is. . . . Oh, Mary, my darlin Mary, I can't breathe for seeing you looking like that."

Magnus II stared at his sister and said evenly, "If you tell him what happened, I'll kill you."

WeeDee believed him, but did not react. "Mummy will tell him" was all she said.

Magnus II smirked. "No she won't."

He went into his room, closed the door, and locked it.

The first guests arrived at the front door. Magnus knew as soon as she reached the bottom of the stairs that something was wrong, but Mary assured him she was fine, and welcomed her guests. They had no chance to talk.

When Magnus wondered where his namesake was, WeeDee said he was angry and did not want to come to the party. Magnus went up to his son's room, and they talked briefly. Magnus II, who had cleaned himself up, just told his father he felt left out of the family so much that he might as well be left out of the party. Magnus felt a familiar anger but did not wish anything to spoil the evening. He promised Magnus II to bring up some cake and ice cream after everyone had left, and they would have their own festivity.

The party was a great success. When the last guests left, Magnus found he and Mary were alone in the hallway. He gazed at her, already giving in to the hope that for some inexplicable reason Mary was the woman he thought he knew. He took Mary in his arms and said, "You're the loveliest person in this strange world, and I love you past adoring. Are you back with us, Mary?"

She tried to smile, and kissed him. "I want to go up and see the children."

"Yes, I promised Magnus ice cream and cake."

Mary nodded, reached out, and touched his cheek. "No matter what, they're all going to be Macphersons, you know." She smiled sadly, then turned and went upstairs.

Magnus and Magnus II were halfway through their ice cream when they heard Jamie begin to cry. They nearly finished before there was someone else's scream and something crashed.

In the hallway, they saw the nanny at Jamie's door covering her eyes. In the room, Jamie was cowering in the corner of his crib, screaming, staring at his mother lying on the floor. Mary had cut her left wrist lengthwise up the arm. In her right hand were the straight-edge razor and her rosary.

"Get your brother!" Magnus rushed to his wife and tried to stop the bleeding. Magnus II grabbed Jamie out of the crib and tried to hold him. But Jamie beat at him so hard, Magnus II let him go. The little boy ran out of the room. WeeDee appeared at the door and yelled at the nanny to call a doctor; the woman went immediately to get help. WeeDee went in to her father.

Magnus II was staring at the body on the floor. He looked at his sister as she knelt down and shook his head, warning her. She shook her head back at him, then tried to help her father.

When he saw Mary on the floor, Magnus knew there was nothing he could do. She had not cut herself in a way that she could be saved; she had done it to be certain. As he tried to make a tourni-quet, he remembered images of her white wedding dress falling away from her the morning of their wedding, of her coming across the dance floor to get him the first night they met, of the spilled wine spreading over the tablecloth on their first night in Quebec. He wondered what the first day without her would be like. She was not coming back; she was leaving them, and had been saying good-bye all through the evening. He wanted to say so much to her, but the hopelessness of their lives together was finally permanent.

He looked up and saw Magnus II shaking his head viciously at his sister.

"You two better get out of here."

"Father, can't I—?"

"No, WeeDee, go on."

"Yes, Fa. Come on, WeeDee," Magnus II commanded. He looked at his mother a moment, then fled.

A doctor ran in from down the street. He pronounced Mary dead. An ambulance arrived, the police, and reporters. In the confusion, they thought Jamie had run away until they found him in the gray room, balled up on the floor with his favorite pillow, sucking his thumb under the crucifix.

Before the funeral, Magnus moved the children out of the house and into the Château Frontenac. They all stayed close to one another, going out only when necessary. The Flemings arrived in Quebec en masse, and also stayed at the hotel. Magnus wanted no contact with them, as they were already accusing him of driving Mary to her death.

The children stayed strangely separate, except for meals. Because they were so confined, they were restless, and separately they tried to keep themselves occupied in their own rooms. But the tension grew. Jamie would not speak; Magnus often had to scold him severely to make him eat. Magnus himself felt numb to almost everything around him. He moved automatically from the suite to his office, making arrangements and accepting business condolences. He tried to plan beyond the funeral but found it impossible.

He tried to look after the children; he read to them, listened with them to the radio, and managed to get them out of the hotel at least once a day in a service elevator. But the winter was bitterly cold, and their walks were short ones. Jamie would begin to cry and they would have to hurry back to the hotel. They were all uncomfortable with their sudden intimacy.

At dinner the night before the funeral, WeeDee unexpectedly began to cry. Magnus thought that grief finally had broken through her characteristic emotional reticence, but WeeDee was reacting to fear.

"Please make him stop, Father."

She held her small hands up in front of her eyes.

Before Magnus could conjecture about whom she was talking, Magnus II blurted out, "I'm not doing a thing to you, so you shut up!"

"You stop looking at me. . . . Father, he stares at me whenever we have meals, whenever he sees me. . . ."

"I do not. You shut up, WeeDee! I'm warning you."

"Both of you be quiet," Magnus said as he looked from one to the other. They sat on either side of him at the table; Jamie sat opposite, looking down, eating nothing. Magnus glimpsed the enormity of being responsible for three motherless children; the complexity seemed overwhelming.

"Why are you staring at your sister, Magnus?" he asked, trying to remember if he had noticed it.

"He's trying to scare me," WeeDee sobbed.

"I am not! You shut up, WeeDee, or I'll . . ." His mouth worked itself into tight knots, and without warning he grabbed his dinner knife and threatened WeeDee with it.

Magnus jumped up and pulled the knife out of his son's hand, yanking him out of his chair in the process.

"What the hell's the matter with you?"

Magnus II looked up at his father, at first with fear, but quickly he turned vicious.

"Nothing! Nothing at all, Fa. My mother just committed suicide, that's all."

"And how does that make you different than the rest of us?"

The boy quickly looked at his sister, then back at his father. "Because I know why she did it!" he yelled.

WeeDee gasped.

Magnus started to shout him down. "No one can know why—"

"I do! I do! She did it because . . . of you, Fa! Because of you, because of you. . . ."

Magnus could not speak. He watched his son as if he were some kind of animal.

"She couldn't stand you, she moved out of your room, she hated what you did, she hated her life with you, but she couldn't get away. She did it on *your* wedding anniversary, *your* birthday. She killed herself to kill you inside her."

"Stop! Magnus, stop," WeeDee screamed. "I'll never tell."

Her brother turned on her and yelled at her, "There's nothing to tell; *this* is the truth! This is what happened. This is why she killed herself, WeeDee, because of *him*." Again he turned and pointed at his father.

They all heard a groan, then gagging. Jamie vomited on the plate in front of him. When he finished, he looked around at them, his brown eyes wide with fear. WeeDee went over to help him, but the boy shook off her arm, got up, and wordlessly went to his own room, shut the door, and locked it.

WeeDee ran to her father and hugged him around the waist. Magnus looked at his son and said, "You're wrong, Magnus. I can't explain why tonight, but I know you're wrong. . . . This isn't the time for us to accuse each other or frighten each other, no matter what we think. We have to get through tomorrow together. After that, we'll see where we are. . . ."

Magnus II's face calmed; he shrugged and turned to go to his own room. Without looking back he said, "Good night, WeeDee."

Magnus felt her shudder, then say, "G'night."

"WeeDee, why are you so frightened? What did he do?"

She pulled away quickly and shook her head. "Nothing. It's just that he's such a stinker sometimes." She tried to smile. "I'll go see about Jamie."

Magnus nodded as she hurried out of the room. Having accepted being alone for so long, he could not readjust to the bonds between himself and his children. As he waited in the sitting room for a bell-boy to clear away the dinner table, he wondered what bonds, if any, were left between him and them.

Magnus remembered the funeral as being both grotesque and stifling. He stood through it with his children beside him in the front pew. The other side of the church was filled with Flemings and all of Mary's friends from Quebec. By then, they blamed him for everything. His refusal to kneel or genuflect did not help the situation. He was there out of respect for Mary, not for her church or her God.

As he followed her casket down the aisle out of the cathedral, he saw Juny step out into the aisle.

"You're her killer, Macpherson! I'm going to destroy you! I swear here before God, I'll destroy you!"

Magnus did not stop, and other members of the Fleming family pulled Juny back into his pew and boxed him in.

At the back of the cathedral, Magnus saw Father Montier. It was he who had gone before the church hierarchy and convinced them that Mary should be allowed a Christian burial, which at first they were going to refuse, as she was a suicide. The priest had argued that Mary was not responsible for her death, that she had suffered severe mental aberration, and that her desire for death was motivated by wanting to be reunited with Christ rather than to escape the pain of life. As Magnus passed by, he took the priest's hand and shook it. Father Montier did not look at him as he spoke.

"I'm sorry. I failed."

"Don't blame yourself."

The priest looked up. Then Magnus went on.

Mary's body was taken by the Flemings back to Southampton to the cemetery of the Church of the Sacred Heart. Fulton Sheen, by then a professor of philosophy at Catholic University in Washington, D.C., conducted the burial. Magnus could not think of another place where she should be buried, and had suggested it. His gesture did nothing to placate the Flemings. Two days after the service, Magnus heard that Juny and Joseph Fleming were beginning legal action to take the children away from him.

Three days later, he and his children were on a ship bound for England. His two sisters, Kath and Kristin, met them at the docks. Magnus said good-bye to his children. They were sad to leave their father, but Magnus had prepared them with stories of life in Scotland, where they were to live with their two aunts until their father felt they were safe from Fleming interference. Magnus sailed back on the first ship bound for New York. He did not return to Canada.

Fleming and Co. tried to renege on its capitalization of Macpherson Distilleries, Incorporated. With the help of a major Wall Street legal firm and a young lawyer employed there, William Wallace Gibson, Magnus moved to another investment-banking house without any damage being done. The Flemings, however, did what they could by word of mouth.

A few months later, Magnus wrote his sister Kristin:

March 4, 1933

I went to Roosevelt's inauguration. Not a bad seat for a hundred thousand dollars. FDR gave the bankers hell, to prepare them for where they'll all be going. He said, "The money changers have fled from their high seats in the temple of our civilization. We may now restore that temple to the ancient truths." I could have told him there's only one "ancient truth": the wanting. But he'll learn. Now I'm ready to sell some whiskey. America is panting to buy. There was a great puling crowd at the Capitol, all of them clapping and praying for Roosevelt to save their hides. I was alone. Memory is pain you have to live with.

I met the President, and a lot of politicians, and an Irishman from Boston who thinks he knows a wee bit about whiskey. If he does, I'll find a use for him.

Love to the children. Try to tell them that I miss them. I hope they're behaving themselves. They'll be coming home soon.

June 2, 1971

"I would suggest—"

"No. No suggestions. Tell me what I have to do to be anointed an honest-to-God, flesh-of-*their*-flesh Macpherson. About a hundred and fifty million dollars is riding on it."

William Wallace Gibson, known as "Double," a nickname derived from his initials, sat behind a cluttered desk of legal briefs and watched Gus Fowler pacing the room as he spoke.

"I've been a closet Macpherson all my life," Gus said. "Now I have to get out . . . or those two are going to lock the door."

"They don't have the key, Gus."

"What's the key?"

"You don't have it, either. Magnus is the key. Where is he now?"

"He's the key to nothing, Double, you know that. Anything he writes, they can contest. And no court is going to admit an old man who can't talk and drools and . . . That son of a bitch Jamie knows Magnus' mind is as clear as, as . . ."

"Vodka." William Wallace Gibson smiled, and Gus scoffed.

"You won't let me get mad, will you?"

"Not on my time. Where is Magnus now?"

"Out in Connecticut at some plush nursing home. . . . Goddammit, it's like an elephant burial ground; WeeDee took him up there to die, Double. You know damn well she did, and don't tell me any different. You can love her all you want, but at Magnus' funeral that bitch goddess will turn to solid ice."

Gibson turned away and presented his profile supported by his hand, one finger pressed against his temple. He'd copied the pose years ago from FDR and used it often. Many believed William Wallace Gibson to be vain. But vanity had little to do with his appearance. He wore English suits, handmade shirts, and ever-gleaming shoes as a costume to impress judges, juries, trustees, politicians, and clients, all of whom he regarded as his audience.

Much of his practice had been gained through the influence of Magnus Macpherson, who discovered Gibson in the early thirties during his battle with Fleming and Co. Gibson was appointed counsel for Macpherson Distilleries, and his legal firm, Gibson, Potter, and Larkin, established soon after, was retained by the corporation. Since then Gibson had become a consultant to government, industry, unions, and football organizations. He had been urged to run for public office, to take over airline and steel companies, to head investigations of corruption, to buy a team. But William Wallace Gibson knew the place of power; in privacy, everything was possible.

"Gus, my affection for WeeDee is certain, but difficult to measure, even by me. I would suggest your speculation about us is futile." He turned to meet Gus's defiant look and penetrated it with a practiced disarming smile. "However, I can attest to the improbability of her ever turning into ice."

Gus was not mollified. "Double, you sure you can advise me on this?"

"Of course I can. Whether you take my advice or not is up to you. In the meantime, you're making a mistake about WeeDee. She is not attempting to take anything away from her father, nor is she waiting for him to die. Your assumptions about her are, as usual, emotional and in error." He paused to see if Gus would accept more. Gus was glaring at him, but remained silent, so Double continued.

"You should know by now that WeeDee is extremely . . . fastidious and expedient. She has become a superb businesswoman. When Magnus became ill, she knew as quickly as Jamie that M.I. had to appear invulnerable. With the cash reserve we've put aside to go into the Mexican oil business—what? a hundred and seventy million?—M.I. is a sitting duck for a takeover. Gus, WeeDee did exactly as *I* advised her. As to her actions with Magnus, she did exactly what the best doctors advised her. She is not greedy; she does not want revenge. She is compulsively efficient, and I believe she loves her father."

They both looked evenly across the crowded desk, knowing that if, for whatever reason, Gus was not included in the division of Magnus' estate, seventy-five million dollars would go to WeeDee.

"Gus, you've always jumped to conclusions. My interest here is obviously to see that Macpherson Industries keeps going. To me, you are vital to that progress. I believe you know that. As to WeeDee, my motives are antipodal to hers. If it were my choice, I would have her give up everything, her newspaper *and* M.I., and retire with me to the South Pacific."

"I wish you luck. I'd be glad to help with a fast abduction."

Gibson glanced at Gus for a moment, then laughed.

"It won't happen, but we enjoy the dance. . . ."

"So what do I do to become an official Macpherson?"

"First, I'll tell you what you don't do. Don't think the courts will help you at all. Paternity is a difficult case to prove anytime. But thirty years after birth, any consideration of legal claims is usually absurd, and generally involves dissolutes claiming movie stars as parents. Also, if Jamie and WeeDee chose to defend themselves, which they would have to do if you force the case into the courts, they would only have to enter the newspaper speculation, not to mention the medical reports, about your mother."

Gus stood up quickly and went back to the window. He betrayed nothing of what he was feeling.

"What else, Double?" he said quietly.

"Don't divide yourself anymore from WeeDee and Jamie. They are in power, legally in power. You are making whatever abyss there is between you deeper."

"They'd just as soon see me fall into it."

"I happen to know WeeDee has a genuine affection for you. Jamie . . . well, I doubt if Jamie is fond of anyone. But he is driven to succeed with M.I. And you are very much a part of that, which I believe he appreciates."

"That fucking Jesuit believes I'm a family curse for the evil Magnus has done. He can't let go of that."

"No, but you must."

"Me? *I* don't see myself as any curse, Double."

"I mean you must forget Jamie's position and stop letting it interfere with your judgment. Let him think whatever he wants. He is not the key."

"And neither is Magnus; he's out of it."

"Not until he's dead."

Gus stood above his chair, quiet for a second. Then he sat down.

"Let's have it, Double. I won't talk till you finish."

"I'm always grateful when we reach this point in our conversations." William Wallace Gibson smiled. Then he went on.

"As of this moment, you have no legal claim that *I* would care to defend on the estate of Magnus Macpherson. You cannot prove paternity; the courts would regard you only as a family interest and a company employee. The only way you can share in the estate, whether foundation or corporation, is for Magnus to give you your share, legally, before he dies. He can do this by an outright gift, or by adopting you. I believe you refused the latter."

Gus glared, and nodded.

"I would say that was a mistake . . ." Gus started to get up, so Gibson talked fast to keep him from interrupting. ". . . But that is beside the point. Now Magnus must include you, legally, before he dies, not just in his will, because Jamie and WeeDee could break that if they chose. Magnus must *give* you your one-third of the fatted calf."

He paused to see if Gus agreed thus far. Gus was nodding, so Gibson went on.

"In order to do that, Magnus must reach a state of legal health where he can reassume the control of his estate. You must expedite that recovery."

Gibson depended on Gus's being able to suppress his volubility for only so long. He prided himself on being able to guess that limit and to lead Gus to an inexorably fast conclusion.

"Oh, great, thanks a lot, Double. I'll just go touch him on the side, and, lo and behold, he'll pick up his bed and throw it at me! What the hell are you saying?"

"A stroke can be cured."

"That's not what they said at Columbia Presbyterian."

"I'd suggest finding a second opinion."

From the experience of their relationship, Gus sensed the change in pattern and knew Gibson was headed toward something.

"Where?"

"Portland, Oregon."

"Portland, Oregon? What the hell opinion could I get in Portland? The best doctors in the goddamn . . ."

Again Gus checked himself. "Why Portland?"

"The Good Samaritan Hospital has a stroke-rehabilitation unit there. I hear they're doing advanced work."

Gus was up and walking around the room, ignoring the view. Gibson watched him. He tried to guess what Gus's next question would be. He hoped it would not be the ordinary "how."

"Double, can I get him out of that nursing home legally without Jamie and WeeDee knowing until after the fact?"

Gibson smiled.

"As his son, you can. The burden of proof that you're not is as heavy as the burden of proof that you are. Let others assume that burden if they choose. By the time there is any resolution in the courts, Magnus, hopefully, will be recovered. Plan carefully."

"Double, you really think he is my father?"

William Wallace Gibson saw a touch of uncharacteristic want in Gus's look.

"Biologically, we'll never know. But, Gus, biology doesn't matter. Magnus wants you as his son. I would suggest taking the vernacular quite literally: '*You* better believe it.'"

Gus nodded, turned, and walked out of Gibson's office.

He flew to Portland that afternoon by commercial airline, stayed twenty-four hours, and returned. For the next five evenings he went by limousine out the Merritt Parkway to Alabaster House in Connecticut to visit Magnus Macpherson. He arrived consistently in time to be seen by the day shift before they left. The night shift was on when he departed. He slipped the security man on his father's floor a good tip for taking extra care of Magnus Macpherson's safety, "in case of a fire or something." He befriended Magnus' nurses, and on the third evening brought gifts for all of them—purses, umbrellas, scarves. He noticed that the two R.N.'s who were in charge of the shifts despised each other. The fifth night Gus made it worse by flirting with the one with acne scars. Then he went down the hall.

Magnus lay in a rage.

"I *hate* this place!" was the first note he wrote to Gus. The therapy received at Columbia Presbyterian allowed him to roll off his bed and drop into a wheelchair for the trip to the bathroom, there to struggle, lean, and squat, then return to the bed. His speech had improved; he could say a few words, but they seldom were the correct ones. The only noticeable deterioration was his temper; the nurses who fed him anticipated their duties with increasing trepidation.

Gus told Magnus nothing of his plans, passing the time explaining what was happening at M.I. and commenting on the fact that the entire liquor industry continued to wallow, except for the goddamn vodka people, and that Bing Crosby had invested in a tequila company.

"I mean, you can't get more respectable than that, Magnus. I can see him singing 'White Christmas' sipping a margarita now. Pretty soon boozemakers will all be legitimate . . . even me."

Magnus smiled on the good side of his face, but then it soured. He stared at Gus, then said, "Pi . . . Ri . . . Pine . . ." shook his head in frustration, and signaled for the writing pad. Gus held it for him.

"Get me out of here," he wrote.

"I am." In the silence that followed, Magnus' bad side contracted from his foot to his armpit. He had felt these contractions more and more recently.

"When?" Magnus scrawled on the pad.

"Forty-eight hours."

"WeeDee will be here," Magnus wrote furiously.

"Shit!"

Magnus watched him. He hated dependence.

"Then we'll do it in twenty-four hours, tomorrow night."

Their eyes locked. Magnus nodded.

"Just don't act any different tomorrow. Be your usual irascible, impossible self."

Magnus smiled, then slowly began to laugh. The laugh was no longer the falsetto groan he forced out in Paris, but it still was a bizarre noise, something between a whinny and an asthmatic sigh. When he heard himself, Magnus let himself laugh even more. He enjoyed the change of the sound, no matter how ridiculous. He would be getting out of Alabaster House. He remembered laughing the day in Paris when Gus came and told him he wasn't going to die. Now the boy was getting him out, and giving him possibilities again. He would never have believed Gus Fowler would be the one, the only one on whom he would depend. Gus *was* his son; there was survival between them.

The next evening at the regular time, Gus's limousine drove through the gate of Alabaster House and parked outside the front entrance. Gus went in, followed by two men. He gave the nurse with acne scars a small bunch of flowers and introduced the two men as colleagues who had come to pay respects to Mr. Macpherson. The nurse, embarrassed to desperate blushes, kept her eyes on the flowers and ignored the visitors. On their way down the hall, the three of them passed the security man, who snapped off a little salute.

A half-hour later, the evening shift came on. In the nurses' station the staff went over the patient list. The nurse had placed her bouquet of flowers in a glass, and was delighted when one of the other nurses asked where they came from.

One of the men who was presumably visiting Mr. Macpherson walked down the hall. When the elevator arrived he took out a sprocket key that fit the elevator controls and turned it so the doors remained open.

At that moment the other visitor pushed Mr. Macpherson past the nurses' station in his wheelchair. Gus followed and pulled out a legal document folded in blue paper and put it on the desk.

"This absolves Alabaster House. I'm taking Mr. Macpherson, and it is entirely my responsibility."

He turned and followed the wheelchair to the elevator. The head nurse reached for the document and knocked the glass with the flowers on the floor.

Gus had almost reached the elevator when the hospital's security man appeared, all confusion, but reaching to unsnap his service revolver.

"Hold it! Hold it! What's up here, what's up? You can't. . . . Is that Mr. Macpherson? You can't—"

"*Balls!*" It was Magnus. The word reverberated out of the elevator. The security man, startled, queried, "What say?"

Magnus was delighted to have another opportunity; it was the first time he produced a word which was exactly what he wanted to say: "BALLS!"

"Take your hand away from your gun," the man at the elevator controls said. He was now wearing dark glasses, and the guard could see the bulk of a shoulder holster. He put both hands high in the air.

"You're not supposed to be doing this," he said, then felt foolish.

Gus walked up to him and pulled his arms down. He looked at the old man reassuringly.

"He's my father."

Then Gus turned and went into the elevator. The doors closed immediately. There were no further problems. At the front entrance, the two men lifted the wheelchair into the limousine and locked it into the special clamps.

When they had passed through the gate, Gus looked at Magnus and smiled.

By the time the director of Alabaster House was able to reach Jamie Macpherson in Manhattan, the private jet carrying Magnus and Gus was over Nebraska. By the time WeeDee arrived in New York the next day, Magnus was in the stroke-rehabilitation unit in Portland, struggling with the help of two therapists to crawl on all fours to regain a sense of balance. He was tired from the flight, and there was pain up and down his bad side, but he kept at it, muttering each time he fell down, ". . . balls . . . balls . . ."

At the same time, a phone rang in the chairman's office of Fleming and Co.

Juny coughed and picked it up. He had not been feeling well; the doctors had suggested that his pacemaker needed to be replaced. He came to the office every day promptly at 8:30 and sat behind his desk as rigidly as if he were astride a polo pony. But habits seemed ritualistic to Juny, and empty.

"Yes?"

"Mr. Fleming, John Gianni. I just got word that Magnus Macpherson was flown to Portland last night. He's entered a stroke-rehabilitation unit there. I thought you'd want to know, sir."

John Gianni was the son of Johnny Gianni, Longie Zwillman's trusted soldier. The son had gone to Georgetown Law School with Juny Fleming's third son and was calling from Nassau, where he specialized in international investment banking. Besides his impressive and immediate access to such useful information as Magnus Macpherson's whereabouts, Gianni had access to certain financial resources which he was anxious to place in legitimate enterprises.

"Thank you, Mr. Gianni. I appreciate the information."

"They're going to keep him alive as long as they can, maybe even bring him back to bolster company morale."

"So it seems." Juny felt his stomach churn with adrenaline and prepared for the jump from his heart which caused him pain.

"I'm afraid we can't wait, Mr. Fleming. . . . Can you, sir?"

Juny Fleming breathed deeply several times before he answered with his usual decisive tone, "No. Perhaps you could fly up next week and we'll discuss the matter."

"I'll be there tomorrow."

"If you're here in time, I'll take you to lunch at my club."

"Thank you, sir. I will be."

Juny hung up the phone. He did not want to take someone like Gianni to his club. It was distasteful, but it might disarm the young man. Besides, no one at the club would take notice. They had not taken notice for several years. Respect, yes, but not the kind of attention to which Juny was accustomed.

"God*damn* you, Magnus Macpherson," he said aloud. Juny knew he talked to himself. He did not care. "If you won't die, I'll bury you anyway."

II
The Wanting
1933–1950

. . . corruption
Never has been compulsory . . .
—ROBINSON JEFFERS

7

This generation has a rendezvous with destiny.
—FDR

"What's your opinion, Weiss?"

Magnus stood with Ted Weiss in the middle of the ninety-fifth floor of the new Empire State Building. Weiss did not answer, but walked over to the wall where the radiator was recessed, a space-saving idea that Weiss liked. He looked out of one of the windows and ran a finger along the edge of it, which was set flush with the outer wall.

"Pretty swanky."

Magnus walked over to the window. The view was to the south and east.

"You can see the whole world from up here."

"Macpherson, *you* could see the whole world from the cellar. You got it in your head. You know what's really out there? Brooklyn."

"But farther out . . . Look at it, Weiss, enjoy it."

"Don't like it up here. Someone comes up after us, there's only one way to go: up. And then what? Don't want to end up like King Kong."

"That monkey's making this place the most famous building in the world; that's where Macpherson Distilleries should be. And who'll be coming up after us, anyway?"

"You're making a pile in the liquor business. Somebody's gonna be coming up after you the rest of your life."

Magnus knew Weiss was getting to something, nailing down Magnus' expansiveness. He was also pulling at his upper lip with his teeth, which he had taken to doing since he gave up smoking.

"All right, Weiss, you'll be glad to know that from the other side of the building all I saw was New Jersey."

Weiss glanced up. "Too bad. You shoulda seen more."

"What the hell do you want me to see, Weiss?"

"This country! And *that's all!* You have this holy vision of selling Macpherson's whiskey to the whole damn world."

"That's because we only have the whole world to work with."

"No you don't!" Magnus watched their transparent reflections in the window. "You don't have the world, Macpherson, and I don't care how much shmeer you put up in Europe, you'll waste it. Outside these forty-eight, you'll waste anything you shag after."

"What makes you so sure, Weiss?"

"You know how much scrap metal the Canadians are exporting to Japan? The Japs are saying it's for earthquake repair, but they've already invaded China. And the Germans just made Hitler their dictator, and he's beating up Jews and trying to take over Austria. And Stalin in Russia! Macpherson, they'll be chewing up the world in five years. You see what I mean when you get over there." Weiss turned and walked away from the window. "So where do we play gin up here on the ninety-fifth floor?"

Magnus stayed at the window, seeing Brooklyn. Weiss's view put a confinement on his vision. He did not like it, but it made uncomfortable, irritating sense.

"It isn't enough, Weiss."

"What?"

"Just America. There are markets—"

"It'll take five years to set up any international market. You have a firm base here. I'm telling you, if you cross the Atlantic, you'll lose it."

"It's *there*, Weiss. Wiley Post just flew around the whole damn world. We have to go after the world, or people will remember we didn't."

"People won't remember, just you. You got a dangerous urge to use *all* your good ideas at the same time. If people remember anything about 1933, it won't be the World's Fair, or Jean Harlow, or the Lindbergh baby. It'll be the end of prohibition. Look ahead, Macpherson. There's gonna be a war, whether we're in it or not. The time to go for the world is after that. Right now, you got your own war against Bronfman, Rosenstiel . . . not to mention the Syndicate. . . . You come out good in that one, that's what people are gonna remember."

At that moment the elevator doors opened and the leasing agents for the building appeared, discreetly smiling.

"You want this place, Macpherson?" Weiss said quietly. Magnus turned back to the window so only Ted could hear.

"Yes. Haggle them down. The building's still half-empty, King Kong or no. And get an option on two more floors. We'll need the space to make war on America. But I'm going to England, and Italy."

"They say Rome is beautiful this time of year. Mussolini's black shirts march at night, and the Pope offers blessings during the day." Ted Weiss walked over to the leasing agents and began his negotiations. "What happens when the elevator operators strike or there's a power failure? You supply people up here with parachutes, or what?" The agents, having heard the joke many times before, laughed too hard and oozed assurance.

Magnus caught the elevator and rode down, changing cars at the seventy-eighth floor.

"Make war on America." Had he said that? As he walked out of the front entrance into the hot August day, he smiled to himself. The weapons and the rewards were the same: money.

His car waited for him at the curb. His next meeting was only ten blocks away; he signaled to his driver he would walk.

August had been sweltering, but Magnus hadn't minded. He was glad to be out of the cold of Quebec. The memory made him shudder slightly; it had been eight months since Mary died. It was not long enough; he had been restless, traveling between New York, Washington, and his new distilleries, glad for the excuse not to have to stay in one place too long. The next day he would be sailing for Europe on more business, and to bring his children back to America. He shuddered again and hurried on.

Magnus abruptly noticed three men were walking along with him. Their suits were expensive, but were tailored to allow for shoulder holsters.

"Mr. Macpherson, you know you're not gonna be hurt, or it would have happened already." Magnus glanced at the other men; they were all together.

"What's it take three of you to do, then?"

"Pickup and delivery."

One of the men was holding a hat in front of him.

"For whom?" Magnus asked, hoping Anastasia had not gone completely crazy.

"You'll see."

Another man went ahead and opened the door of a black Packard waiting at the curb. When he turned, Magnus noticed his face for the first time. It had changed from the burn-scarred mask Magnus remembered from the quay at St. Pierre. They said nothing, exchanging only a quick look of recognition.

The ride was short; no one said anything. Magnus was taken to the Hotel Claridge to offices on the seventh floor, located just behind the huge sign for Camel cigarettes that blew smoke rings out over Times Square. As they got out of the elevator, Magnus saw the sign for the Reinfeld Corporation and realized he had been abducted by Abner "Longie" Zwillman.

Zwillman had begun his career in the early twenties driving trucks for various bootleg gangs, until he impressed his bosses, Meyer Lansky and Bugsy Siegel, enough to start his own organization. He did so, running the protection for the Reinfeld Corporation which supplied the East and Midwest with booze from Canada. The operation was a huge and well-run organization. Zwillman made millions, invested in movies, real estate, and hotels. He did it all and stayed out of the papers, becoming one of the major organizers of the syndicate.

Zwillman smiled at Magnus, then told the five other men in the room, "Get out."

Magnus noticed they were both about the same age.

"I hear you don't like people around when you talk, Macpherson." Zwillman looked amused.

"Don't believe everything you hear."

Zwillman chuckled. "Anastasia doesn't *tell*. But it gets around. Everything gets around. . . . I hear you're going to Europe tomorrow."

"I'd planned on it. Am I going to make it?"

Zwillman came around his desk. "Of course you are. Of course, here, sit down, have a seat. Do you like cigars? Here, take some, Cuban, a friend of mine brought them up from Havana." Magnus declined the cigars but took a seat. "I know you, Macpherson. We met nine, ten years ago. You had a still out near Kingston on Long Island. I was the guy came out and tested your alky for Frankie Costello, set up the guards and delivery. You were the only guy never tried to water your stuff."

Magnus did not remember him.

"You've come up in the world, Zwillman."

"So've you, Macpherson. Now we're up here together, I'm hoping we can renew the acquaintance."

"The last time I got picked up like this, Capone almost fogged me."

"The pisk. Please. Don't worry. I'm truly sorry for the way you came here, but I had to see you before you left town."

"Sounds urgent."

"As urgent as money."

They looked at each other, not smiling, trying to see the other's notches, notches that could be weaknesses, something to grip. Magnus sensed that Zwillman was smarter than the other gangsters he had met. He had vision, personal confidence and carefully hidden power. And he could kill if he had to.

"Let's hear about this urgency, then, Zwillman. But let me say, and there's no offense intended, we're not together except in this room."

Without a pause Zwillman waved away the problem. "I take no offense, Macpherson. I only want to talk business, legitimate, legal, clean as an angel's ass. All I want to do is arrange for a company I'm starting to distribute your whiskey. That's all." He shrugged his shoulders, holding his hands palms up in front of him as if living could not be simpler.

"The Reinfeld syndicate's going out of business?"

"Yeah. Terrible what they do to you in Washington, changing laws like that. All our talent would be thrown out on the streets. So we're going to start a company to help them out. This country can't afford to waste talent like ours. These people know everything about getting liquor into the bars, into the clubs, and making sure the owners sell it. In fact, I don't know of another organization that can guarantee sales like this one can."

"What's the name of your company, Zwillman?"

"It's not mine. My name won't be on it or near it. My investment's fronted, so you won't have to worry. We're calling it Brown-Vintners."

"Is this part of Johnny Torrio's business?"

They looked at each other. The only sound in the room was an intermittent noise like a suppressed belch as the cigarette sign pumped out its smoke rings.

"You know a lot, Macpherson. No. Johnny Papa's company is Prendergast-Davies. They're gonna cover the eastern seaboard. We're going inland to the Middle West."

"Zwillman, do you know how many distributors I have lined up already?"

"I got a good idea."

"I'll tell you: seventy-five in Manhattan, a thousand all over the country. You tell me why I want another distributor."

"You need us. You won't be able to move a bottle from your distilleries without us. Your salesmen won't be able to unload it on the retailers. Without us, all you'll have is the best whiskey made . . . a lot of it." He saw Magnus put his hands on the arms of the chair, ready to stand up again. Zwillman stood up first and walked around the desk. "Macpherson, don't make me say any more. I'm a businessman. I'm starting a legal distribution company that can serve you well. And this company's gonna last. You know ninety-five percent of those other guys'll be finished in a year or two, I can promise you that."

"You can't make promises, Zwillman. Too many of you have a habit of dying early."

Longie Zwillman stood next to his desk, looking down at Magnus. The smoke machine kept its rhythm.

"I *can* make the promise. Nobody needs to get killed anymore. There's divisions, organizations all over the country, Macpherson, everywhere *you* want to sell whiskey."

Magnus already knew about the syndicate. He even knew Lucky Luciano and Meyer Lansky were in Havana that day negotiating with the new regime for gambling rights on the island. It was his business to know such things; he also knew he had to accept reality and let syndicate-controlled distributors sell his whiskey.

"I'll do business with any legal distributor who can deliver my whiskey." Magnus stood up so that he looked evenly at Zwillman. "But just between us, I don't like doing business with you."

Longie did not stop smiling. "So don't like. But I'll tell ya, everybody in this country's going to be doing business with us, Macpherson. Think of yourself as a pioneer."

Magnus went to the door and waited for it to be opened by the men outside. After a moment he turned back to Zwillman, who was still smiling and had something more to say.

"Macpherson, I think you got something on Anastasia. If you didn't, you'd be dead. You're a lucky person; I'm glad for you. . . . It's interesting, though; if I ever need to get Umberto, all I need is for something to happen to you. . . . Interesting." He leaned over his desk, pushed a button, and the door behind Magnus opened.

"Zwillman, if you have problems with Anastasia, believe me, don't depend on me to solve them."

Magnus turned and walked out. Only one man came with him, the man with the new face. Magnus finally remembered his name. Johnny Gianni. He hardly looked at Magnus on the way down in the elevator, but out on the street when they were alone, the man turned to Magnus and said quietly, "Thanks for the face."

"It looks good."

"Not bad. I can get laid. Look, I owe you a favor."

"Stay alive, Johnny. I'm going to need it."

Two cars drove up, thumped over the curb, and straddled the sidewalk. Eight men piled out, including Ted Weiss. Gianni let everyone see his hands were empty. Weiss came over to Magnus. No one pulled a gun, but bystanders ran and ducked up and down Forty-fourth Street.

"You all right, Macpherson?"

"Get back in the cars and get out of here."

"What're you—?"

"Get out of here. I'm fine."

Weiss gestured with his head, and all the men returned to the two cars.

"How'd you know, Weiss?"

"You didn't show for your meeting. They called. Got this feeling and pulled in the clothesline. . . . *Longie Zwillman?* Jesus, Macpherson. You starting a social club?" He got into one of the cars, backed into the street, and drove away. Magnus turned back to the front entrance of the Hotel Claridge. The man with the new face exchanged a look with him, then went inside. Through the revolving door, Magnus saw at least six gun barrels glint in the light.

After letting Zwillman's men see he was alone, Magnus turned and strolled down Forty-fourth Street, across Times Square to the Astor Hotel. A speak on the second floor had stocked malt through prohibition. At that moment, Magnus needed some water of life.

The speak was crowded, and Magnus was lucky; they had a bottle of Highland Park malt. He poured in a little Poland water to release the flavor, and sipped away at the hard fact which Zwillman had pointed out: with the syndicate, there is no life insurance. You cover yourself with Anastasia, you open yourself to Zwillman. The only way to protect yourself was to stay useful.

"Hiya. Mind if I join you?"

Blond curls. The color looked real, but the curls were so lacquered they seemed brittle. Her blue eyes were barely visible through crusts of coal-black mascara; she wore lipstick that screamed *red!* And, most unfortunately, she chewed gum. She might have been seventeen, or she might have been forty-two. But under the make-up veneer, Magnus recognized a genuinely sensuous woman.

"I wouldn't mind a bit."

"Oh. Thanks . . . How was your day?" Her voice was all powder and fog.

Magnus looked at her, hearing a routine and refusing it.

"Would you like a drink?"

"Oh. Thanks. You bet. How was your day?"

"What would you like?"

"I'll have what you're having. Thanks."

Magnus spoke to the bartender, then turned back to her. She looked at him and smiled. Magnus smiled back. She took her purse.

"Do you have any smokes?"

"I don't smoke."

"Oh. Neither do I. I just like to hold them sometimes. Where are you from? You talk kind of funny."

"Scotland."

"Ooohhh, Scotland. . . ." She tried to be interested, but wasn't. Her drink arrived, and she put her hand around it. "How was your day?" she said to the glass.

"Why don't you tell me about yours?"

She turned to Magnus with the dignity of a duchess. Her voice went down to a bleak intimacy.

"Don't make me tired. You know what my day was like. I'm in business. If you're not buying, say so, and don't waste my time. Because that's what I'm selling."

It was the most honest, self-aware statement Magnus had heard in months.

She started to take a drink, remembered her gum, hesitated, then with a royal gesture removed it from her mouth, reached gracefully over and dropped the wad in Magnus' malt. She took a swallow of her own, gasped, and started coughing.

Magnus took a ten out of his wallet for the barman, and a hundred for her. She was choking deeply. Finally she was able to hack out: "What do people in Scotland drink, anyway? Belladonna?"

"Put a little water in it. You'll learn to like it." She saw the hundred on the bar next to her purse and looked up at Magnus apprehensively. He got down from his seat.

"I can't stay, but your time's worth more than I or any man can afford. I hope you'll let me buy your drink."

She picked up the hundred and put it down her dress. Her nose and chin lifted to imperious angles.

"Go diddle yourself, Scotsman. I'm a garbage can and I know it."

He stared at her for a moment before leaving. Her eyes were clear of self-pity or self-deception. He heard her ask for a champagne cocktail as he went out the door. On the street, crossing Times Square, he had an intense urge, something between lust and compassion, to go back and ask her to come with him to Europe. Then he glanced at the cigarette sign, the smoke rings pumping out of its flat, happy face. Behind it, Longie Zwillman was arranging for the sale of Macpherson's whiskey.

"Some sign." A drunk was lying up against the statue of George M. Cohan. Magnus nodded. The drunk laughed and said, "Problem is, this ain't no place for smoky halos. Listen, friend, you look like a philosopher. I'm a philosopher, too. You think you might give me ten dollars? My sister, a nun, is collecting money to feed the lepers of the Bronx."

Magnus took out his wallet. "I only have a twenty."

"I see. Well, would you consider . . . ?"

Magnus gave it to him. It came too easy for the drunk. Even he felt a twinge of guilt as he pocketed the bill.

"I'll pay you back."

"No, it's for the philosophy . . . and the lepers of the Bronx."

They looked at each other, then both started laughing. The drunk got up and said, "I have to go tell my sister. She'll be tickled pink."

Later that night, the woman Magnus had met at the Astor Bar put the hundred-dollar bill he had given her into an envelope. She labeled it "California, here I come," taped it behind her mirror, and went to sleep.

The next morning, Magnus went aboard the ship for England. He discovered his stateroom was just down the passageway from one occupied by the man he had met at Roosevelt's inauguration, Joseph Kennedy, the Irishman from Boston who thought he knew something about whiskey.

Magnus found an engraved calling card from Kennedy waiting on his desk. On it was written: "We met at the coronation. You had some ideas about whiskey. Come drink some of mine, at 7."

For three days Magnus enjoyed Kennedy's company, slowly becoming aware that Kennedy was courting him. Magnus watched, kept up his part in the act, and waited.

"Magnus, what's your interest in Distillers Company, Limited?"

Kennedy peered at him across the card table. They were playing gin rummy in the lounge. It was three A.M., actually four, as they had just crossed a mid-Atlantic time zone.

Magnus was aware he had been allowed to win. "Whiskey. What's yours?"

"The same." Joe Kennedy put his cards down. "I've been working with DCL for some time. I'm already the U.S. agent for Dewar's, and Gordon's gin."

"Congratulations."

"It isn't enough."

"You want Haig."

"Exactly."

Magnus put his cards down and rested the palms of his hands on the table. "It seems the game's over. You want me to give up Haig."

"I would be grateful."

"How grateful?"

"Eternally," he said flatly.

"That's a long time. I'm thinking the Haig franchise will be worth millions to whoever has it over the next ten years."

"My gratitude will be expressed as needs arise, Magnus. Anyone in the liquor business has more needs than most. Whatever the value of the Haig franchise will be damn small compared to what you'll make in the next four years, or the next eight years, depending on Mr. Roosevelt's longevity."

Magnus reached for his cards, stacked them, and flipped them onto the table. "I've enjoyed the game, but I think I'll go to bed while I'm still ahead."

"Just a minute, Magnus. I want Haig. What do you want for it?"

Magnus let Kennedy sit a moment. Haig was the smallest part of his interests with DCL. He was more interested in the international plans, and getting whiskey stock. Kennedy knew about debts and the paying of them. He could be helpful for a long time, but some instinct told Magnus that Kennedy would use and forget anyone who did not fight him. Magnus had fought him. It was time to make a deal.

"I don't need your gratitude, Joe. What I want is your friendship."

Kennedy sat motionless. Then he leaned forward and extended a hand.

"Magnus Macpherson, you're a son of a bitch. You almost got me mad." He took a swallow of brandy. "Have you ever thought of getting into politics, Magnus?"

"You flatter me."

"I don't flatter."

"I like the liquor business."

Kennedy swirled the cognac in his snifter.

"That's just how you make your money. It's what you do with it that gets in your blood."

Kennedy pulled apart his black tie and loosened his wing collar from its stud. "Only two things get in your blood: politics and the motion-picture business."

Magnus gave him a quick glance, as Kennedy's excursion into motion pictures was fairly notorious for the money he made and the women he knew.

"Which do you prefer?"

"Politics. More power. More *real* power. Out in Hollywood they have the showy kind of power, yelling at waiters, firing directors, hiring starlets. But they're pants pressers out there, making all that money. If you want to enjoy yourself, Magnus, put a little money in the movies."

"I'll give it some thought. As for politics, I'm a Scot and a bootlegger, so I doubt if there's a future for me."

They stood up to leave the lounge, throwing their dinner jackets over a shoulder.

"Magnus, you're more American than America."

In London, Magnus relieved Distillers Company, Limited, of its commitment to him, and Joe Kennedy was given the United States rights to sell Haig and Haig.

Thomas Herd, the director of DCL, expressed relief to Magnus for his diplomatic withdrawal.

"I'm glad you gave Haig to Kennedy. If you hadn't, we might have given it to him in spite of our agreement."

They were boarding the Ala Littoria trimotor with a young DCL executive for their trip to Rome.

Magnus sat in the seat across the aisle from her. "I know that. It would be hard for you to resist him when he already had two other brands, not to mention the President's attention. It worked out to all our advantages."

"Good!" Herd yelled over the motor's starting. Magnus was

impressed that Herd showed not the slightest interest in what Magnus' advantages might be.

The aerodrome at Croydon, twelve miles out of London, was nothing more than a solid square of turf, allowing a plane to take off in any direction. The vibration and bouncing across the field did not seem to disturb Thomas Herd, who piped, "What do you know about Italy?"

"I hear Italians get thirsty like everyone else. That's all."

"What about Mussolini?"

"From his pictures I'd say he likes to strut."

The trimotor lumbered off the ground with a final lunge and rose swiftly over the English countryside.

"The fellow likes two things, I hear." Thomas Herd continued to yell above a necessary volume. "Closing saloons and war." Several people in front of them glanced around, and Herd lowered his voice. "Neither are good omens for us. Also, I hear he's envious of Mr. Hitler."

The plane made stops at Paris, Milan, and Venice before Rome. At Venice it was delayed for an hour and a half. No one was told why; they were ordered to stay aboard the plane in preparation for immediate takeoff. Herd was irritated, as he had arranged for them to attend a very important nobleman's palace for a dinner party for which they had brought ten cases of Magnus' whiskey. The delay would make them all late.

Finally another plane landed. It was painted solid black, with only one marking on the wing and fuselage: a swastika. A party of seven men, three in black officers' uniforms, got off, talking animatedly, and boarded the trimotor. Magnus and Thomas Herd glanced at each other as the German party seated itself. The Italian crew were excessively attentive; outside, Magnus could see the three officers remaining at attention. One of the Germans stood up and spoke in Italian, then English, apologizing to the other passengers for the inconvenience. A few hours later, they landed at Littorio Airport outside Rome.

When the trimotor taxied to its place, the young DCL executive, Peter Crichton-Stuart, tapped Magnus on the arm and pointed outside. On the tarmac were two limousines and an eight-member motorcycle escort. The German stood and requested first in Italian and then in English that everyone remain seated until his party left the plane. The four men went quickly down the aisle to the exit, marched to the cars, and the motorcade moved quickly and silently away.

"I'll be blast," Crichton-Stuart said. "Look at the pendants." Each of the limousines had a diplomatic flag flying from its left-front fender. "That's the papal insignia."

After an hour clearing customs, they reached the Hotel Majestic. Herd had Peter deliver the whiskey directly to the palace of their hosts and explain the reason for their being late. Magnus would have preferred to soak in a tub, but Herd said this evening was the only way to get whiskey started in Italy. Once introduced *gratis* to the aristocracy, it would drain down to the public, who would pay for it. So Magnus fought himself into studs and a boiled shirt and went with Thomas Herd to the palace of the Prince and Princess Lamborelli.

When they arrived, they ascended a magnificent staircase, where their host welcomed them elaborately and thanked them profusely for the kind gift, which they indicated was being served to all the guests. The princess took Magnus' arm and led him into the grand salon.

About a hundred people were there, apparently waiting. Magnus spotted Fascist armbands on the dinner jackets of many of the men. When he explained to his hostess why he and Thomas Herd were late, she laughed and told him in a delicate English that something mysterious had taken place at the Vatican and many of her other guests had just arrived. She introduced Magnus to a group of people and was called away.

He turned and looked around the room. No one seemed to mind the late hour except himself. Peter Crichton-Stuart finally arrived and joined Magnus. Before they could speak to each other, there was a commotion at the entrance to the grand salon. Through the crowd Magnus saw a flash of scarlet and heard a burst of applause. The guests cleared a path, still clapping, and Magnus could see Prince Lamborelli leading two cardinals and two of the German men who had been on their plane to the end of the room. Behind them a large group of men wearing swastikas on their arms mixed into the crowd.

"Oh, the gentry have arrived," Peter said, smiling at Magnus. Thomas Herd joined them as the guests of honor collected and the applause reached a crescendo.

"Who are they?" Magnus asked Peter.

"The cardinal on the left is Pacelli, Vatican secretary of state. I don't know the other. I think the German is von Papen, Hitler's vice-chancellor. The other is his translator. It looks as though they brought the entire German embassy."

Prince Lamborelli raised his hand for quiet and began to speak in Italian. Both Magnus and Thomas Herd leaned toward Peter.

"He's saying Pacelli has some good news, but first Cardinal O'Connell, Boston, I believe . . . wants to propose a toast, something about his being decorated again by Mussolini." The American cardinal was looking around for a glass. A servant arrived with a trayful of Macpherson's whiskey. The prince beamed at Magnus and Herd.

Then Cardinal O'Connell lifted his glass. "We have been honored once again by your glorious leader." A polite applause spattered over the room. The cardinal acknowledged it with several little bows, then went on. "We have said it before, and we shall say it as long as we have breath to do so: Mussolini is a genius! He has been given to Italy by God to help this nation continue her rapid ascent toward a most glorious destiny. 'Duce'!"

A chorus began, repeating "Duce," the men in the room flinging up their hands, praising their leader. When quiet came, all eyes turned to Cardinal Pacelli, who smiled at the room with genuine kindness before beginning to speak. Peter Crichton-Stuart translated word for word, as Pacelli, the complete diplomat, allowed time:

"I suppose I should be very formal, but His Excellency the vice-chancellor and I have been so formal for many months." The crowd laughed. Pacelli turned to their host. "Your Highness, may I tell Vice-Chancellor von Papen that he is among friends and that we can drop our formality?"

The room answered the question with a chorus of *"Si! Precisamente!"* and more applause. Magnus noticed Princess Lamborelli laughing proudly, her jewelry shimmering in the candlelight. Then Cardinal Pacelli's expression became serious, and there was a silence. When he spoke again, the only other sound was translation.

"In an hour, the rest of the world will hear what we will share here as friends. I would like His Excellency to announce our news to you."

Von Papen began to speak in German. His aide translated to the room, and Peter translated for Magnus and Thomas. Von Papen knew his audience. Before speaking, he crossed himself.

"Tonight, Cardinal Pacelli and I have finalized a concordat between the Holy Father, Pope Pius XI, and His Excellency the chancellor, Adolf Hitler."

The room erupted into a cheering, yelling mass. Arms were raised in the Nazi salute, and the crowd began chanting, *"Sieg Heil! Sieg Heil!"* Magnus saw that von Papen had taken out a paper to read. When he could make himself heard, he spoke again.

"I have a statement that will be released in Berlin with the announcement of the concordat. . . . 'This concordat is an agreement of truth and purity. The future will be ours. The one true Church will nurture the further creation of the one pure race of men. Pure faith will run through the pure blood of our peoples, and together we shall find the glory of God and the glory of mankind.'" As the vice-chancellor went on, Magnus saw Pacelli look at the speaker, surprised and not pleased. "'Faith in God must be restored; will to conquer must be restored. Faith and confidence are one when used for the purifying of God's . . . and *man's* glory!'"

During the uneasy silence which followed, von Papen put the paper back in his pocket. He knew the proclamation had caused a certain resentment with the predominantly Italian gathering, and continued quickly. "I have also been authorized to announce at this time that His Excellency the chancellor has begun his preparation to become a member of the Holy Church."

Prince Lamborelli politely clapped his hands. Then an arm shot up. *"Sieg Heil!"* Others joined the chant. The Italians tried to overcome the cries with their applause. Someone started singing the *Te Deum,* and Cardinal Pacelli stepped forward and joined the singing. But still the arms jabbed upward, and *"Sieg Heils"* and "Duces" pierced the music.

In an attempt at conciliation, von Papen raised his glass of whiskey in the gesture of a toast. But before he could drink, Magnus moved over to him and grabbed the glass out of his hand.

"Drink your damn toasts, but not with my whiskey!" He poured the whiskey into a vase of lilies and put the glass down. His hand was shaking with rage.

An immediate uproar followed. The Germans in the salon moved up to protect von Papen. Magnus heard explanations being shouted around him: *"Americano. Americano."* As he moved through the room, he was spat on, and finally shoved. He reached the door and continued down the staircase. Behind him, he heard a group of men yelling Italian invectives at him. He did not look back. When he reached the front entrance, where a liveried servant opened the door for him, he realized Herd and Crichton-Stuart had left with him. They walked into the street together.

"Thanks for the company."

Thomas Herd took out his handkerchief and wiped something off his sleeve. "The conversation had degenerated frightfully. Needed some air."

They listened to the noise of the party from the windows on the floor above them, aware they would not be selling much whiskey in Italy for the moment.

"As usual, Pacelli wins out again," Peter said as he watched the glowing windows.

"At singing the chants, yes. But Hitler's playing the organ." Thomas Herd was looking up and down the street for their car. "Come on, it looks as though we'll have to walk it. Let's get back and get some sleep."

"Mr. Herd, I'd suggest we change and pack. It's quite likely we'll be put on the first plane out of Italy," said Peter.

He was right. Within the hour, a contingent of blackshirts picked them up and took them back to the airport.

When they were finally airborne, Thomas Herd saw Magnus smiling.

"What could you possibly find amusing, Macpherson?"

Magnus yelled back, "Kennedy. He said I should look into politics. When he hears about this, he'll urge me to become a Republican."

Three days later, Magnus was waiting at Paddington station for the arrival of the Royal Scotsman. He had not slept well for the previous two nights, thinking about seeing his children again. Mary had said once that Magnus made strangers of his family in order to leave them. He hadn't reacted at the time, but during the last few days he'd thought of little else.

Perhaps he'd left them too much alone; perhaps if he had stayed closer, Mary would be alive.

He had agonized over that idea. He remembered the advice he and Father Montier had given each other: ". . . don't blame yourself." Magnus did, however, and thought he always would.

He heard the train approaching, and a dull white light pierced the fog. Would his children be strangers to him? Magnus remembered he himself had begun to grow away from his home by the time he was nine. His mother had accepted his leaving, although she said nothing. When his father died, Magnus had been on a trip to Rum Row and only learned the news several weeks after the funeral. He remembered that he had been relieved he didn't have to go.

As the engine pounded by him, Magnus saw his children looking out of a compartment window. His sister Kristin stood behind them, smiling and waving. He tried to see their expressions. Magnus II looked arrogant, WeeDee agitated and wary, and Jamie frightened. He was a stranger to them, the person who controlled their lives, provided for them, and probably the person who killed their mother. Magnus felt a quick panic, but the accusations he saw in their looks turned him to a defensive anger.

During their stay in Scotland, the children had experienced their grief in different ways. Magnus II had never ceased trying to convince WeeDee by reason, repetition, and simple terror that his performance the night of their mother's death had nothing to do with what she'd done. The result of this continued assault, in the end at least, convinced him of his own innocence, and Magnus II began to hate his father and assume the responsibility of revenging his mother.

Her mother's death, coupled with her brother's intimidation, left WeeDee in emotional shock. She deeply missed her mother, but was terrified the suicide had somehow been her fault. She needed her father; she thought he, too, had been hurt badly by what had happened. But she knew that if she talked to Magnus, her brother would punish her in some way. Therefore, she couldn't say anything at all.

As they stepped off the train, Magnus hugged them. Very little was said, Magnus II offering a glib "Hello, Fa," and WeeDee an apparently genuine, "I'm so glad to see you." Little Jamie was silent and distracted.

On the drive to their hotel, Kristin made up for the children's silence by telling Magnus how they had fared in the Highlands. She seemed quite pleased by her decision to go to America to look after "my brother's brood." Kristin was twenty-eight at the time, and tired of the confining life of a small-town spinster. The children's coming had been a great excitement. Magnus' request for her to consider America was nearly overwhelming. She would be mistress of the house at East Hampton, a home the three children had never known.

When the youngsters had gone to unpack, leaving them alone in the hotel room, Kristin said, "Magnus, you have three strange children, and I love them dearly. They already think I'm amusing, and if I'm not mistaken, they'll soon regard me as magician and bosom friend."

"How do you mean 'strange'?" Magnus trusted his sister's perceptions better than his own.

"I'm not sure I can be answering 'how' or 'why,' but strange they are. At first I thought it had to do with your Mary's death . . ." Magnus heard the possessive and almost objected to its use, but he didn't interrupt. ". . . Then I began to think there was more. . . ."

"More what?"

"More . . . I don't know. I get the feeling they play because they know they're supposed to. I'm talking about young Magnus and WeeDee. Jamie plays, but always alone." She frowned, as if there were more to say, but she didn't know how to say it.

"And?" Magnus prodded.

"Your Jamie had nightmares, great screaming wakers, when he first arrived. I slept him close by so I was always near to hold him and sing him back to sleep. . . . I asked him once or twice what the dreams were, and at first he wouldn't tell me. But one night he did. . . . Magnus, he saw it all. Your Mary turned away from his crib to . . . do what she did, but there was a mirror on the wall and he saw her. . . . His nightmare was the razor going up her arm."

Magnus and Kristin sat for a moment looking at each other. She did not shrink from the image and waited attentively for a response. Magnus stood up and went to a window which overlooked Hyde Park.

"Does he still have the dream?"

"No, not for the last weeks. I called the doctor and he said to give the bairn time, so I did. Jamie began to trust me, I think, and slept better."

"And he's not doing it anymore? Waking up screaming like that?"

"No, but, Magnus, your Mary talked to him."

"What? In the dream?"

"No, before she . . . died."

Magnus came back to his chair and sat down.

"Tell me."

"I asked Jamie no questions, so what I know is scanty. That night, from what I'm able to puzzle out, his mother came in to Jamie as she always did, and knelt down beside his crib to hear his prayers. After he'd finished, he looked up and saw his mother crying. She said, 'I can't leave you here. Do you want to come with Mommy?' "

"Good Christ!"

"That's when he wakes up shrieking, when he dreams of her saying that, then cutting her arm."

"Does he understand what she meant?"

"Somewhere he does. He said that she looked at him a long time and shook her head. Of course he wanted to go wherever his mother went."

"She's still here! She's boring a hole into the boy's soul! . . . That poor woman, driven to that by her damnable God!"

"Quiet, Magnus, the children will hear."

He paused and walked across the room.

"What about the other children? Did Mary manage to . . . ?"

"I don't think so, and I think wee Jamie is already on his way to forgetting. Time is doing its good works on them, so let them, and Mary, be . . . for your own sake, as much as theirs."

"We bury the dead, Kristin, but never their living. She wasn't 'my' Mary; she never was. But she was 'their' Mary, their mother, and she's all over their minds, whether you and I see it or not. Now I know what they mean by haunting."

On board ship they had a relatively happy time, although Jamie was painfully shy and spoke to no one. WeeDee, on a dare from Magnus II, drank a glass of Macpherson's whiskey, became drunk, then ill, but convincingly explained it away as *mal de mer*. On the last day, Magnus II and a nine-year-old girl were discovered in a lifeboat, both with their pants down. He tried to avoid his father's thrashing by explaining that it was just normal curiosity, but Magnus did not listen. When it was over, the boy looked at Magnus and threatened, "Someday I'm going to beat you back!"

Magnus nodded and said, "When that day comes, we'll have ourselves a time."

8

> . . . meet every day's troubles as they come. What
> terrible decisions will have to be made! . . . and
> sometimes they'll be wrong.
>
> —FDR

In the thirties, the distilling business became the liquor industry;
power was concentrated in the top five companies and one of them
was Macpherson Distilleries. From his headquarters in the Empire
State Building, Magnus ran the most streamlined company in the
business. Sam Bronfman had the best-selling whiskey in Seagram's 7
Crown; Louis Rosenstiel had the most volume of sales and the most
profits. But what Macpherson's had was a lean efficiency from production to distribution. They could get the liquor to the drinkers
faster than anyone else.

The Macpherson products themselves were of a quality so superior as to make Macpherson's drinkers not only enthusiastic, but
dedicated. Macpherson's Prestige was a straight bourbon whiskey
which gave a rich mellow burn. Macpherson's Old Dufftown was a
blend of whiskeys and neutral spirits which was easy on the tongue
and a mere "kiss to the throat." But the whiskey which gave the company its real power in the industry was Macpherson's Century, with
its special flavor of the great Dufftown malts. Century was an instant
success and stayed a top seller for the entire decade.

Taxation on liquor had been one of the major incentives to state
legislatures to vote for the Repeal Amendment. Originally, they
believed liquor taxes would relieve the general tax burden. The new
liquor-tax dollars, however, were spent just like old tax dollars: fast.
So the search for more tax dollars persisted, and taxes on liquor were
steadily increased.

One of the trickiest schemes the federal government concocted was an idea that retroactive taxes could be paid on the illegal liquor that came into the United States during prohibition. Secretary of the Treasury Henry Morgenthau, Jr., decided that Canadian distillers owed sixty million dollars in excise tax and customs duties. How Mr. Morgenthau came up with this particular figure was unknown, but he drew up a bill to prohibit whiskey imports from Canada until the claim was settled.

The concept was a subtle kind of federal blackmail. Such a bill was almost certainly unconstitutional, but whoever fought it would be admitting responsibility for smuggling, and other illegal activity during prohibition. The bill was rather obviously aimed at the Bronfmans and Seagram's. But it threatened Magnus, too.

With the help of Macpherson's friends, William Wallace Gibson went to Washington and enlisted the State Department's aid, since Secretary of State Cordell Hull ranked the secretary of the treasury. Mr. Hull negotiated a settlement between the Canadian distillers and the U.S. government of three million dollars—five percent of Mr. Morgenthau's original demand. Admitting nothing, the Canadian distillers paid it: Seagram's, $1.5 million, and Macpherson's $750,000, the rest by other distillers. The price was small for legitimacy, or, more important, to avoid illegitimacy in the eyes of the federal government.

In the thirties, the syndicate became, as Meyer Lansky said, "as big as U.S. Steel." In the liquor industry, the syndicate's influence grew in wholesaling. The Thompson submachine gun was replaced by the baseball bat. When a wholesaler's truck filled with whiskey rolled up to a retail liquor store, four thugs would enter the premises carrying bats. The thugs had no need to hide their weapons; they would claim they were on their way to some "athletic occasion." They would tell the retailer that he had "the wonderful opportunity" to purchase fifty cases of the chosen whiskey, which they happened to have in the truck. If the retailer were smart, he would clap his hands with joy at the opportunity, and pay the wholesaler his price. If he were inexperienced, he might explain he had too much whiskey or another brand from another distributor. Batting practice would then begin, and soon, no one was amazed when the liquor-store owner needed not only fifty cases of the chosen whiskey, but a hundred and fifty cases, and a mop.

In the face of such techniques, retailers had little choice but to sign exclusive agreements with one wholesaler or another who could guarantee protection against "Louisville Sluggers," as the thugs were called. In this way, territories were carved out by wholesalers much as they had been in the old days. Small wholesalers without connections were shut out of the business and went belly-up, as Longie Zwillman had promised Magnus. If there were disagreements as to territory, they were settled by the syndicate. The wholesalers, by acquisition and control of territory, became vital to the liquor industry. For two years Magnus worked seven days a week. He arrived in the offices of Macpherson Distilleries every morning at 6:30. During the week he lived in a suite of rooms in the Hotel Astor on Times Square. The hotel was close to his office, convenient to restaurants, and if necessary, he could put on a quick spread for two hundred retailers.

Because of his connection through Kennedy with the Roosevelt administration, Magnus also spent a good deal of time in Washington working to oppose legislation inimical to the industry. His record of success there helped when he went to three banks and put together a loan of twelve million dollars to build the most advanced distillery in the world. Designed by Dr. Bromberg, it was located outside Baltimore and began bottling Century in 1935. He bought three more distilleries, paying more than their actual worth because each of them had produced a brand of whiskey with a reputation. This accelerated the pace of his continuous trips from distilleries to retailers' meetings to Washington and back again. Macpherson Distilleries was one of the first to purchase a corporate aircraft, and after the first few flights, Magnus' stomach adjusted.

On weekends Magnus went to East Hampton, but he would bring work with him and rarely spent time with his children, who, after a brief greeting, quickly retreated to their separate silences. With relief Magnus would turn to his papers and wait impatiently for the time to pass so he could go back to the station. His sister Kristin had the house well in hand, and the only one to display obvious resentment was his elder son.

"Fa, why do you come out here?" Magnus II said with a guileless smile. It was early spring, warm enough to sit on the porch. WeeDee was playing a privately vicious game of croquet on the lawn, knocking balls down to the sand as she triumphed over herself. Magnus was studying proposed fair-trade legislation. His son sat down on a white wicker chair across from him.

Magnus looked at the boy and tried hard not to see what was obviously there—a resemblance, even at that early age, to Mary, and even more to the boy's Uncle Juny. The corners of his mouth and eyes were snide and glib. There was fraudulence in the tone of the question.

"I come out here to see my family."

" 'See'? You mean to look at us?" Magnus II laughed disarmingly, as if sharing the joke with his father.

Magnus smiled. "There are times when you three are something more to watch than a cage of monkeys at the zoo."

Magnus II laughed enough to make the wicker of his chair creak. Then he quickly leaned forward and asked, "But you don't think about this as your home, do you?" He kept smiling and watched his father struggle for an answer.

Magnus started excuses, then stopped. He knew his son didn't care about them; he was after something else.

"No. It's not my home. I wish it were. But I can't be here enough to make it my home. . . . I hope you think of it as yours."

"Oh, it's *my* home, Fa. You bet it's *my* home." He looked away, the innocent smile compressed into the tight thin lips of dominance. He saw his sister thwack a croquet ball and run happily to the next wicket.

"WeeDee! Come here!"

She stopped in midstride, then let the mallet drop and ran up to the porch. As she came, Magnus II glanced briefly at his father to make sure he noticed the response to his command.

WeeDee smiled at her father, but then lowered her eyes and concentrated on a spot equidistant between her brother and her father, so as not to be looking at either.

"Tell Fa what you called me."

She looked quickly at him, surprised he would bring it up. Then she snickered and said, "I called him, well, because he's Magnus the Second, he writes his name 'Magnus II' or 'Magnus Two.' So I thought, 'Magnus Too,' t-o-o, and then . . ." She checked her brother to make sure he wanted her to continue. "I called him 'Magnus Also.' "

As Magnus II turned quickly to check his father's reaction, Wee-Dee took three quick steps away from her brother and said, "And then he made me promise never to say it again."

Magnus II snapped a look at her. When he was sure she was not going to continue, he shifted in his chair and said, "You know, Fa, you never call me by my name. I've kept track since we came back from Scotland. Not once have you ever called me 'Magnus.' Why is that, Fa?" He was smiling again, but the maliciousness was now open.

"I hadn't noticed it. But you and I, we know who we are, don't we? Perhaps there's no need for names."

"I think there is, Fa, and I'd like you to call me 'Magnus' when you're here."

Magnus II stared at his father without affection, without contempt, without any expression, leaving his father to guess at his emotion.

"Come on, WeeDee, I'll show you how to really play croquet." Magnus II stood up from the cracking wicker chair and walked off the porch onto the lawn.

WeeDee tried to see how her father had been affected; she saw he had been, but could not, as no one could, read his reaction. She snickered and put her hand over her mouth and then whispered across the porch to her father, "Isn't he a big bozo?" But instead of jumping in his lap with a hug, she shrugged and hurried to join her brother.

She, too, knew whose home it was. That was why she did not tell her father that Magnus II had taken her down to a deserted part of the beach with a bottle of whiskey and had opened it, pinned her down, pulled down her panties, and forced the neck of the bottle into her rectum until she swore never, ever to call him "Magnus Also" again. She hadn't told her brother that enough whiskey flowed into her and stayed there just long enough to give her a wonderful funny feeling. Since then, she had tried it on her own several times, carefully using an enema bag. Surely if anyone ever found out about it, they would be terribly shocked.

Magnus watched his two children play croquet. His son was already knowledgeable about how to use cruelty, at ten years of age. And WeeDee was all secrets behind her laughter and red hair. Thank God she didn't look like her mother, so as to be a living reproach to him. No, WeeDee looked like him, in spite of her hair; she had the same dark eyes, the same hidden smiles. He wondered if he would ever be allowed to know them.

His sister Kristin and his youngest, Jamie, appeared at the far end of the lawn. Kristin had not only adjusted to her new life in America, living in a big house, and being the surrogate mother of three; she was happier than she had ever been in her life. That day she was showing Jamie how to turn cartwheels. Finally tired of explaining, she did one herself, her bloomered legs arcing the air under a tangle of colors. Magnus II and WeeDee cheered. Jamie, intensely inspired, tried again. He managed to flip over, but fell on his back, knocking the wind out of himself. Kristin picked him up and walked over to the porch, praising him vigorously for his efforts. Jamie did not see his father until he and his aunt were directly in front of him. Jamie looked up, startled, then immediately down at his feet, and did not move.

"Oh, Magnus, there you are. Did you notice your youngest son's grand efforts? He's bound to be a fine gymnast."

"No I won't, Aunt Kristin." He turned to look up at his aunt, not unkindly. "But thank you." He walked into the house.

"A lovely boy, Magnus. As kind as a saint, well-behaved, mannerly."

"I hardly see him when I'm here."

"You're hardly here."

She sat down in a wicker chair and straightened out her skirts and scarves. Kristin had always had thin blood, and was susceptible to drafts. Her scarves had taken on greater lengths since her crossing of the Atlantic, and blossomed into fantastically matched hues. The natives of East Hampton who liked her had renamed her "Aunt Spinnaker." Kristin had never been dubbed with a nickname before and adored it.

"I'll not say all that business about children needing a father. Your children are as different as any three rocks in a field, and they're just as self-contained. I can't say if they need a father . . . or a mother. I get along with them without being either. I love them, and we all seem to survive. Magnus, I'm going to smoke." From her bloomers she took out a small cigar, bit off the end, and spat it a good healthy distance off the porch. Then she struck a huge kitchen match, and puffed the end of the cigar to a bright ember.

"I never do this when the children are about. I have no doubt they know. They know everything."

Magnus looked at the house where Jamie had disappeared, then at his other two children playing on the lawn, before he said, "I know little about them; I feel a connection, but it's the intimacy one has . . . with an enemy. The four of us are more guarded with each other than we are with strangers."

Kristin could not disagree. She took a puff on her cigar. "The children are doing well. Magnus is quite the master. WeeDee's learning to play the piano quite capably. But Jamie's a special one. There's already a direction to him; he reads everything. He has an intelligence you can well be proud of." A capricious glint came to her face.

"But what of you, Magnus? They're your own. Do you miss them, being away so much?"

The moment she asked, he knew the answer, but he hesitated admitting it. He did wonder about his children and what would become of them. He would give them the best of everything, open doors for them, protect them, provide them with choices he never had. But as to missing them? Didn't she really mean did he love them? Was there really no time, was he really too busy, or did he simply not love his children the way he was supposed to?

"I'll not lie to you, Kristin. When I'm here, I regret not knowing them. But when I'm away and busy with my life, I think little of them."

"I'm sad for you, Magnus." With a well-practiced flick of the forefinger Kristin sent the burning end of her cigar shooting like a comet onto the lawn. She wrapped the good end carefully in a silk handkerchief and redeposited the package in her bloomer band.

"Don't be sad for me, Kristin. It's a loss I don't know. I never really had these children. I was always a visitor in their home. . . . Families are intended to end one way or another, anyway. Look at the Flemings. They're scared to be alone, and they're scared to die, and none of their children can stop either one from happening."

There was a crack of a mallet on a ball. WeeDee raised her head triumphantly as Magnus II's ball went zipping toward the sand. Magnus II smiled at his sister, then swung his mallet over his head and hit her ball out of sight. As he walked away, he yanked wicket after wicket out of the grass. WeeDee watched him for a minute before running off in the opposite direction, toward the deserted part of the beach.

"That boy doesn't like to lose," Kristin said.

"Just like his uncle. I don't want them going to Southampton, Kristin. I have no doubt the Flemings will try to get them over there. But I forbid it. Is that clear?"

Kristin did not answer for a moment. "Whoops!" she said finally. "Is that how you talk to your executives, then? You sound as mean and nasty as old man MacDougall who used to spit at us if we said good morning. Remember him? He'd see us coming and start collecting the saliva he'd been saving for the occasion."

She made Magnus laugh and forget the emphasis of his command, which was necessary, since Kristin had already allowed the children to visit the Fleming compound that spring. And Magnus was right: Magnus II and his Uncle Juny had become immediate friends.

In 1935 the value of the Macpherson stock rose from thirty to forty-one, making Magnus' 420,000 shares worth $17,220,000. In 1937 he split the stock, and set up trusts for his children. He paid himself $105,000 per year, and Ted Weiss a hundred thousand even; the five thousand dollars were to let Weiss know who was boss and to guarantee that no matter what happened, Magnus would always have money for gin rummy that Weiss didn't have.

"The trouble with you, Macpherson, is that you don't know how to play. I don't mean cards; I mean fun. I think I'll arrange a few lessons for you."

Rain was falling outside the Empire State Building, and the wind suggested late-season sleet. They were drinking malt in the boardroom and playing gin.

"The trouble with fun is it takes too much time. Find me some kind of pill to take instead."

Weiss chuckled. "It'll get you, you know. You can't stay young without playing, and the way you're going, you'll be old before you learn how."

"I don't notice you 'playing' much."

"Hell, I go to the fights, hockey games, take a girl to tea. You don't even see girls."

"Tea!"

"I like tea."

They laughed and dealt the cards. But Magnus felt uncomfortable.

"Weiss, when I sell a case of whiskey to a new outlet, be it desert or ice floe, and I know Louie Rosenstiel and Sam Bronfman are burning or freezing their asses just behind me . . . to me, that's play."

"Gin."

"You distracted me. Let's see your goddamn cards."

"You need fun. You get mold in the brain without it. Didn't you used to be a sailor? Why don't you get a yacht? I know a guy in Florida . . ."

The *Arethusa*. Magnus had not thought about it for years. As Weiss dealt a new hand, Magnus remembered his easy balance on deck, the clear invitation of 360 degrees of horizon, the lightness of his life on board the ship. When he picked up his cards, he was still seeing the view of the deck from the mainmast, with the southerly wind on his back suddenly filling the sails and snapping a cover over the sky. And Grace Lithgoe was in the cockpit waiting.

"You better have some fun now," said Weiss, interrupting the reverie. " 'Cause when the war starts, you ain't gonna have time."

"Maybe I will. You're still sure about a war, Weiss?"

"Gotta be. You know, we're lucky to be in America. No master race here, just greed. If a Hitler shows up, he won't go into politics; he'll go into business and *buy* the goddamn world."

"What'll you do when the war starts, Weiss?"

"Dunno. But the sooner the better, so I won't be too old to fight back a little. I never had a chance to do that in Cicero. This time, I'll go looking for Hitler."

"Gin."

Weiss didn't object. He threw his cards down without counting and looked out of the window, frustrated.

"O.K., Weiss, I'll go have some fun as fast as I can, because when the war comes, I doubt if I'll see much of you around here. Tell your friends in Florida to send some pictures of yachts. And set up a trip to California. I've wanted to look into the wineries out there. I'll call Joe Kennedy in Washington and let him know I'm going. Maybe he'll know some 'girls.'" He said the word as if it were a foreign language. The idea of being with a woman exhilarated him. Then he thought of Mary, and the whole idea soured.

"Weiss, I'm too old for 'girls'; I don't have time."

"So go for business, but go. And Macpherson . . . you can always find time for girls."

9

Oh whistle while you work,
   (whistle)
Oh whistle while you whistle while you whistle
while you work.

              —WALT DISNEY'S *Snow White*

The first thing Magnus did was go to a good tailor. He bought a town house on East Sixty-fifth Street and hired a prestigious firm to decorate it. He called the woman who wanted him to invest in a Broadway play and agreed to attend a backers' audition. Next he called a fellow who had asked him to be on a committee for the Museum of Modern Art. He bought land in Chile for the future construction of a distillery. Business continued being fun. Finally, with ten pieces of handsewn leather luggage from Abercrombie and Fitch, he boarded the *Twentieth Century Limited.*

Weiss saw him off. A photographer was at Grand Central to take his pictures for an afternoon paper. Zwillman's man with the new face, Johnny Gianni, was also there. As Weiss and Magnus were talking, he slipped up to them and gave Magnus a small package.

"From Mr. Zwillman. A card inside." And Gianni disappeared down the long red carpet. Magnus opened the package to find a locket containing what looked like one platinum-blond hair. The engraved card read:

Heard you were going to Hollywood. This is a special good-luck charm for there.

              Regards,
              Zwillman

Weiss saw the locket and looked disgusted.
"What the hell is it, Weiss?"

"His girlfriend, Jean Harlow. Had her appendix out. Zwillman managed to get her pubic hairs, sells them to his buddies for five hundred bucks a hair. Consider it one of Longie's more tasteful gifts."

In sixteen hours Magnus was in Chicago, where he transferred to the Dearborn Station and climbed aboard the *Super Chief*. Forty hours later he was in Los Angeles' Union Station. A limousine was waiting for him, courtesy of Paramount Pictures, a company Joe Kennedy had reorganized a few years before. The car sped Magnus down Sunset Boulevard to the Garden of Allah.

Apparently the management was expecting him. He was given a choice "villa" beside the swimming pool. In the living room he found flowers from Paramount, a selection of liquor from one "Benjamin" Siegal, and several invitations to parties.

As he stood in the middle of the room, the phone began to ring. Ignoring it, he went into the bedroom, looked through three suitcases until he found the bathing suit he had bought for the trip, and undressed.

As he picked up the bathing suit to put it on, he glimpsed his own reflection in the full-length mirror of the bathroom door. He hadn't taken notice of himself for years. His stomach was still flat, the ribs above it rippling the skin, and his legs were thin, the muscles long and efficient. The hair of his groin was iron-black, feathering up his stomach in a straight line to his navel and fanning out from there, but his cock and balls looked like a lifeless white growth. He raised his eyes to his face. Still handsome, with only a few deep wrinkles, particularly the one between his eyes. He lifted his eyebrows to make it disappear. He took note of his scars, the small one under his left eye, the bullet hole on his right arm from the night he and Weiss got away from Capone, the bayonet wound from the war, the old marks on his leg from school soccer.

"Trevor!" The screen door opened and slammed shut, and a woman came across the living room. "Trevor, Jack's having a party and . . ." Magnus tried to get the bathing suit on but couldn't find a leg hole. Then she was there, blond curls under a yachting cap, blue eyes quickly covered with sunglasses.

"You're not Trevor!" The voice was still powder and fog. She wore white flannel slacks and a blue blazer with gold buttons.

He gave up trying to put his suit on and simply draped it as casually as possible in front of him.

"That's right; I'm not Trevor."

"You sure aren't. He came up to my waist. What happened to him?" She didn't remember Magnus, but she seemed content to stay and chat.

"I'm afraid I . . ."

"Oh. Of course not. You just got his room. You better fumigate it. Little prick probably went down to Tijuana for another load of the clap." She dismissed the memory of Trevor with regal disdain and continued to stand in the doorway, looking Magnus over from head to toe. The look caused a certain life to pulse through his groin, and with only the slightest movement Magnus held the bathing suit a bit farther out in front of him.

"You want to come to a party?" she asked, to keep the conversation alive.

"I'd like that, after a swim. Want to have a swim?"

There was only a slight shift in her voice as she decided.

"Sure. They'll be drinking for days." She moved to a chest of drawers. "Trevor kept a bunch of bathing suits in here in case some twelve-year-old wandered into his rotten clutches." She opened a bottom drawer, and there indeed was a pile of suits.

"*Voilà*, as they say in Paris, France," and she began to undress. Magnus watched, holding his bathing suit in front of him. She was naked in a moment and turned to Magnus as she was about to put a leg into her suit.

"Well, are we going swimming or not?"

He let go of his suit. "No, not just yet."

She looked down at him and smiled with appreciation. Then she looked up and said, "I'm expensive."

"I know that, but I have credit," and he went over to her, put his hands on her breasts, and spread his fingers over them. They were wide, the nipples already hard. Her eyes closed halfway, and she let her head fall back slowly. Her hair was longer than it had been in New York, the curls loose and soft as they fell on her neck. She took a deep breath, raising her breasts tighter into his hands.

"What do you mean 'credit'?" She was smiling, taking the sudden pinch of her nipple with a shudder, but not touching him in return.

"You know what credit is. The banks love you, the stores love you, everyone loves you." He let one hand slide down her stomach to caress a thigh. "Either that or you've made a payment in advance," he said as he leaned forward and kissed her ear. Still she did not touch him. He moved his hand from thigh to thigh and, as easily, entered her with first his thumb, then his fingers. She groaned and said, "I don't give or take credit."

"What do you give?"

"Nothing, till I get."

"Do you want me to stop and write a check?"

"Cash . . . but don't stop. Cash, oh . . ."

She began to roll her hips around, then opened her eyes and looked at Magnus.

"Two hundred, all right?"

Magnus moved closer to her, put his other hand on her neck, and kissed her mouth. Then, as they both gasped for satisfaction, he said, "Two hundred's too little. As I told you once, you're worth more than any man can afford."

Magnus felt her go rigid.

"What? What'd you say? Let go of me, you son of a bitch!" She tried to back away but couldn't with one of Magnus' hands on the back of her neck and the other between her legs.

"What's the matter, then?"

"You snuck up on me."

"I'd say the reverse was true."

"No . . . Get your fingers out of there. . . . I don't like sneaks. I remember you now. . . . What are you doing?"

"I remember you, too."

"Let go of me."

"Why?"

"Because I don't know you."

"How can you remember me, then?"

"I remember I don't like you. . . . What are you doing? . . . Stop it."

"I'm the one who doesn't know you." Magnus drew her toward him, fitting himself firmly into her.

"You can't just *do* that." She took a halfhearted swing at his face, but the arm collapsed around his neck and she held on. "For Christ's sake, we're *standing up* in the middle of the room! Oh!"

"You prefer a wall or a bed?"

"Bed . . . bed . . . oh. You bastard. Who are you anyway?"

He lifted her and took her to the bed.

"You tell me who you are first."

"I'll tell you later. Come on. Come on."

He fell on top of her. They heard the screen door slam again, and this time a male voice called, "Trevor!" A portly man with a short clipped mustache appeared at the bedroom door with a pitcher of something and announced, "You're not Trevor."

"No," Magnus agreed, "neither one of us." He did not pause, nor did she. But their guest recognized her, and continued with an exasperated explanation. "Oh, Evelyn, it's you. Well, someone stole my wheelbarrow and I have no other way to get over to Jack's party, so I better wait here and go with you. I'll just go into the other room and wait with my pitcher. There was a goldfish in it this morning, and I didn't think they could live in gin." The gentleman left the room, stirring his pitcher, finally leaving Evelyn and Magnus to finish what they were doing.

"Happy to see me again?" she asked.

Magnus paused. "More than you know."

"Oh, yeah? Why don't you tell me?"

"It's been a long time."

"Oh . . . Well, you didn't forget a thing."

"I'm going to be here a few weeks, and I'd like to see you. I've been told that Hollywood is inside out and that I may need a guide."

"So take a Gray Line tour. . . . What'd you say your name was?"

"Magnus. And yours is Evelyn."

"Yeah. Evelyn Lorraine. This agent came up with it, says it had more class than 'Georgine Blor,' which is my real one. Says I gotta look class and sound class; that's what the hicks want, so that's what the studios want. So, I wear clothes like I just got off a yacht."

"You're an actress?"

Evelyn Lorraine looked at Magnus and stood up. She put her hands on her small firm hips and said, "I'm getting better paid, and better off, but I don't forget my heritage. And don't you forget it, either, Mag . . . what?"

"Magnus, Macpherson."

"Magnus Macpherson? . . . Whiskey?"

"Yes."

A glint came into her eyes; she sauntered back to the bed, a smile of certainty on her lips.

"Well, well, Magnus, the price of guides just went up!"

"Are you two ready in there?" shouted the man in the living room, having come to the bottom of his pitcher. "Jack drinks all his gin first, so we won't get any if we're late."

The trip to the party was not a long one; Jack's villa was five doors down. The three of them entered, to find quite a selection of Hollywood's most famous drinkers. Evelyn's friend found out soon after arriving that his wheelbarrow had been sunk in the deep end of the hotel's pool.

This information was received with compassion by the guests, who shifted to the pool for a serious look. Because of her yachting outfit, Evelyn was obviously the only one to give advice on deep-water salvage, and Magnus found himself left between two young women who began stripping down to their underwear in preparation for a plunge.

Evelyn continued directing rescue missions until someone picked her up and threw her in. Magnus, the only one dressed properly for the occasion, found himself the only one not pushed, shoved, or jumping into the pool. Finally his host, deciding everyone should be wet, sent him sprawling into the water, where he surfaced amidst a bunch of naked women, and wondered if he were satisfying Weiss's definition of fun.

Evelyn Lorraine accept the role of Magnus' guide around town. As such she was incomparable, for she knew everyone. She was publicly considered an actress, although no one had seen her act. In fact, she never had. But such considerations didn't matter, not to the moviemakers or to Evelyn Lorraine. What she had was "sides," a face that photographed beautifully from any angle. She also had an outrageous personality, a sense of humor, and a body which was described in studio casting sheets as "soft statuesque." Besides all that, she adored sex. Whether all these attributes would add up to celluloid magnetism, no one knew. But Evelyn had been in Hollywood long enough to know that garbage cans made good movie stars. All she needed was a chance.

Harry Cohn of Columbia had promised her one; so had Jack Warner. Mr. Mayer at MGM had even paid for tap-dance lessons at the MGM studio school. She had gone to all of the right parties, given freely of herself to anyone who might be helpful, but no one had delivered on the promises.

Magnus made no promises. He just kept giving her things. During the five weeks he stayed at the Garden of Allah, he presented her with a charge account at Bullock's-Wilshire, a star sapphire, and a Ford convertible. In return, she was his roommate, chauffeur, and diplomatic buffer, putting off the number of people who wanted to see Magnus, whom Magnus did not want to see.

Benjamin "Bugsy" Siegal was one of them. He had murdered about twenty-five people by 1937 and the syndicate sent him to run the relatively virgin territory of the West, where the heat was less intensive. He was welcomed with brio by the studios, which was surprising only to those who did not know the movie establishment was paying millions of dollars in extortion to the syndicate-controlled International Alliance of Theatrical Stage Employees as a guarantee against profit-devouring strikes.

Magnus, who felt he already had too many connections with the syndicate, didn't want any more, and tried to avoid meeting Siegal. But even after Magnus turned down his numerous party invitations, Siegal persisted, arriving at the Garden of Allah at six one morning unannounced. The door to Magnus' villa burst open, and before Magnus or Evelyn was fully awake, Bugsy and two of his men were in the bedroom. Siegal was dressed in loud tweed and wore a binocular case around his neck.

"'Morning, Evelyn. 'Morning, Magnus. I'm Ben Siegal." He looked for the effect his name would have on them.

Evelyn, with a sheet pulled up over her, sat up in bed like a queen. "We've met," she said, all ice.

"I remember." He turned to Magnus. "I'm on my way to Santa Anita to watch the morning workouts. You comin'?" It was not an invitation.

"I know little about horses." Magnus knew he was going whether he wanted to or not.

"I'll teach you everything you need to know, Magnus. Come on. You'll enjoy yourself."

"I'll get dressed, then."

"Fine. We'll wait in the other room."

Magnus and Evelyn only exchanged looks as he put on his clothes. She knew she wasn't going because she hadn't been asked. But she pointed to a drawer where she had been keeping her things. Magnus opened it and saw stuck between the lace and silk a pearl-handled .22-caliber "ladies'" revolver. Magnus smiled and picked it up, grateful for the caring, but with not the slightest intention of taking it with him.

Unfortunately, one of Siegal's thugs peered around the door at that moment. He pulled his own gun and was ready to use it as he called his boss. Siegal came to the door as Magnus put the revolver down on the dresser.

Siegal watched, then said, "What's that, Magnus?"

"It's a joke." He stood and watched Siegal's face go mean with suspicion, then break into a pleasant smile and Siegal said, "You don't have to worry. We only kill each other."

Magnus nodded, put on a suit coat, and without looking again at Evelyn walked out of the villa.

They did not go to the racetrack. They drove north to a ranch in Newhall owned by a star of Republic westerns. On the drive, Magnus did most of the listening as Siegal dropped names of the stars he knew, the plush house he had rented, his membership in the Hillcrest Country Club, and numerous other claims to social prominence. "Class, that's the only thing that counts in life. Without class and style, a man's a bum, he might as well be dead."

Magnus knew that Bugsy Siegal killed by puncturing his victims with an icepick in order to allow the air of the stomach to escape so the body would not float when dumped in water. But he didn't know what Siegal wanted from him.

"I've heard a lot about you, Magnus. Hear you're a superb businessman." Magnus did not respond. They had driven past a ranchhouse and proceeded through several miles of desert. Finally they reached a hill of granite boulders, where two other cars were parked and eight men waited.

"I want to ask your advice about some things, Magnus, that's why I brung . . . brought you out here. Advice. That's all." Magnus remembered how Rothstein corrected his English.

"I can guarantee my whiskey," Magnus said. "But not my advice. Of course, you have to pay for the whiskey."

Siegal smirked; then they got out of the car. He went over and greeted everyone, talked a moment, then came back for Magnus.

"Come on, we'll take a little walk." Dust rose with each step, settled on their clothes, and mixed with their sweat to make a fine layer of grit. They walked for about two hundred yards. Magnus saw the cars driven off and a man appear with a movie camera.

"Longie tells me you're the smartest of the bunch, Magnus. That's why I wanted to talk to you. You stay on top of your companies."

A man called across the field, "Ready, Mr. Siegal?"

"Yeah, ready! Watch this, Magnus." He lifted his binoculars and leveled them on the pile of granite boulders. Magnus turned in that direction just in time to see them disintegrate, the explosion staggering both him and Siegal, whose hat was blown off.

"Yeah! Gorgeous!" Siegal shouted. "Yeah! Yeah!" Everyone hurried back to the place where the boulders had been reduced to gravel, smoke and dust rising above them in the air.

"What do you think of that, Magnus?"

"What was it?"

"It's called 'Atomite.' Better than dynamite, more compact. A friend of mine developed it. It'll blow hell out of anything you got."

"What do you plan to blow hell out of?"

Siegal glanced at him, a self-important smile on his face. "I leave that to my partner, Mussolini."

"Oh," Magnus said, and started walking back to where the cars had been reconvened. Siegal hurried to catch up with him and gave the answer to the question Magnus did not ask.

"See, I let Mussolini hear about this stuff, and he came in with me. He put up chicken feed, forty grand, but that's just a drop in the bucket if he decides to buy. I'm talking about twenty, twenty-five million in the long run, if there's a war. Nice deal, don't you think?"

"Is that the advice you brought me out here for?" Magnus asked.

"No, but what do you think of it? As a business venture. It seems to me a businessman has to find new places to make money. That's all I'm doing. That's why I wanted to talk to you. You're a businessman. You and I have some things in common, we both made a lot of money off hooch. You can go on with it, but it doesn't make enough dough for us. We're going to make our money in gambling, see, legal gambling."

Siegal didn't look to see how Magnus reacted; he was too deeply involved with his own ideas.

"I been financing a gambling ship offa Santa Monica, the *Rex*. Cost six hundred grand to float her. Worth every cent. Every day we clear about ten grand. We'd make ten times that if the boat was bigger and it was on dry land. So I'm going to build a hotel somewhere in Nevada, a real classy hotel with everything, elegant, real elegant."

Magnus was sure that Siegal could see his elegant hotel in front of them in the dust. The gangster turned from his vision and looked at Magnus. It was a look that convinced Magnus that Bugsy Siegal was not only crazy but smart, which made him dangerous.

"I'm going to build that hotel, Magnus. It'll cost a million and a half, recoverable in six months. I'll show you the figures. I want to hear what you think. If you like it, I want you to come in with us."

Siegal smiled briefly, then turned to the knot of men to congratulate them. Magnus knew this also was no invitation. He knew that Siegal thought Macpherson's Distilleries had made a lot of money because of the syndicate, and he was right. But to the syndicate, any money made through them was considered reserves on which a member could call. Magnus had no intention of agreeing with the theory, but he did not know how to reject the offer without offending Siegal or the syndicate.

At that moment one of the thugs called attention to a car approaching at top speed, creating a geyser of dust as it cut through the desert. There was a moment of tension, then Siegal recognized the black Cadillac. The moment it pulled up, the driver handed Siegal what seemed to be a telegram. Siegal read it and without a word jumped into the Cadillac, which sped back through the sand, leaving everyone else standing around the explosion site with little to discuss. The thugs eventually figured they should drive Magnus back to the Garden of Allah.

When he walked into his villa, he found Evelyn with all her belongings stuffed into the hotel's pillowcases. She tried to be angry to cover the fact that her nerves were strung out all over the room.

"We bought every other goddamn thing but suitcases!"

"Where were you going?"

"I was getting the hell out of here, let me tell you. A friend of mine went out to Santa Anita and called saying you and the Bug weren't there. I figured you were dead, and I didn't want to get stuck with the hotel bill."

"Thanks for the good thought."

"Don't ever look to me for good thoughts. If you're going to die or get killed on me, I don't want to be around. I've been around too many people dying, and I swear to God it rubs off. So don't look to me for the big cry. What happens to you ain't my business. What happens to *me* is my business, and goddamn, what happened? Are you going to make me stand here shaking all day?"

She ran over to him and kissed him. He told her everything there was to tell, but it was not until the next morning they understood Bugsy Siegal's sudden disappearance. Then the papers were filled with it: Zwillman's girlfriend, Jean Harlow, was dying of uremic poisoning. Her mother, a recent convert to Christian Science, had refused to allow doctors to see her. The actress's condition became so serious that the mother had been convinced by certain "friends of Miss Harlow" to change her mind, but by the time the actress reached Good Samaritan Hospital, she was in critical condition. That afternoon, Longie Zwillman arrived in Los Angeles by plane, and by one of those strange coincidences was given the villa next to Magnus and Evelyn. That night, Jean Harlow died.

Longie was desolated. The night of her death he became physically ill. At about three o'clock he started vomiting uncontrollably.

Siegal sent over his personal doctor, who by mistake knocked on Magnus' door. Magnus did not want to see Zwillman; his policy was not to see any member of the syndicate unless he was forced to a confrontation. He simply sent the doctor next door, and he tried to get back to sleep. But soon after, he and Evelyn were awakened by someone pounding on their front door. It was Longie himself.

"You gonna let me come in, or what?" Through the screen door Magnus could see that Zwillman looked desperate and sick. His eyes were wet and his face was white. He was dressed in a silk bathrobe over an undershirt with short socks and shoes. Magnus flipped up the hook of the screen, and Zwillman came in. He was alone, which was unusual.

"You got that locket I gave you?" His hair was messed up and falling over one side of his face. Magnus nodded.

"It's in the other room."

"Gimme it." Magnus went into the bedroom, signaled Evelyn to stay where she was, and found the locket with his cufflinks. When he went back into the living room, he saw Zwillman lying on the couch. Magnus walked over and dangled the locket in front of him. Zwillman grabbed it and put it in his pocket. He sat up, saying, "Aw, God . . . aw, God . . . aw, God. . . . You got a drink?" Magnus went to the bar and poured a tumbler half-full of Century. Zwillman drank it down.

"Thanks, Macpherson . . . I'm going crazy. There's nothing I can *do!* She's gone. I can't buy a buncha life and cram it back into her. Jesus, I can do anything, buy anybody, kill anybody, do anything. She's dead. That's it." He held up the locket and watched it turn. "You ever love someone who died, Macpherson?"

"Yes."

"How'd you get through it?"

"Just like you, with a lot of pain."

"Any way around it?"

"None that I know of, except forgetting."

"That'd be killing her twice. . . . Listen, I'm going to be sick again." Zwillman stood up unsteadily. Magnus helped him to the front door just in time. When he had finished, Zwillman came back in and sat again on the couch.

"Thanks. . . . Thanks. I feel better. The doc gave me a shot of something." He sat quietly and blinked at Magnus. "You doin' all right out here?"

Magnus nodded. "Fine. I'm sure you know how well."

"What's that mean?"

"Mr. Siegal's Nevada real estate."

"Bugsy's hotel? We know about that. What's it got to do with you?"

"He invited me to be a partner."

Zwillman's look became a glare. He didn't move for a few moments; then he stood up.

"As of now, you're uninvited. He has enough partners." He turned and walked to the door, hesitated, and turned back to Magnus.

"Will you come to her funeral? I'd appreciate it."

"I don't like funerals."

Magnus heard Evelyn come out of the room behind him. "I'd like to go. Jean was nice to me a couple of times." Magnus turned to look at her. She had on an elegant peignoir which she had not been wearing in bed, and had piled her hair on top of her head.

Zwillman was staring as if a vision had appeared.

"Thank you, I appreciate it." He didn't want to know who she was or if she were real, as it would interrupt the vision he wanted to have of her. Zwillman, holding the screen door, nodded his gratitude almost as a bow; then he left, letting the screen door slam.

Evelyn turned to meet Magnus' look. They stood watching each other. She knew what she was doing and offered no excuses. He respected her for it. At the same time, he felt the neat twin knots of jealousy and loss tighten.

As it turned out, Evelyn did not know exactly what she was doing; the results, however, were the same. The funeral was announced as being private, but in those days little was private in Hollywood. Evelyn's future began with a series of mistaken looks. As the coffin passed by, Zwillman turned away and caught sight of Evelyn, in black, looking like a Madonna. He stared at her for some kind of relief. Harry Cohn followed his look, as did Louis B. Mayer, who recognized Evelyn from the MGM school. Both men had a certain diplomatic flair and figured it would be a good thing to do a favor for Longie Zwillman. Within twenty-four hours Evelyn had been contacted by both studios to do a screen test. She decided to visit MGM first because Louis Mayer said he had Harlow's next picture ready to go, and if Evelyn's test turned out well, he might make her the star. The test was made the next day with Clark Gable; Mr. Mayer screened it that evening, and had his lawyers draw contracts that night. Then, through channels every studio had to contact organized crime, he let Mr. Zwillman know he was perfectly willing to make

Miss Evelyn Lorraine a star if he, Mr. Zwillman, were willing to pay for it. MGM could hardly afford the expense of a major motion picture starring an unknown.

When Zwillman received this message the next morning, he was packing to go back to New Jersey. At first he was confused, as he did not know who Miss Evelyn Lorraine was, having never been introduced to the vision that soothed his grief. Then some of his people told him she was the woman living next door with Macpherson. After figuring out exactly what had happened, Zwillman decided to deliver Mayer's message in person.

"Can I come in?"

Evelyn was pacing the floor, waiting for the phone to ring. She jumped when she heard Zwillman's voice.

"Oh, sure, come on in, Mr. Zwillman."

"Thanks, Miss Lorraine." She was surprised to hear her name. He gazed at her for a moment, then shook his head.

"Are we alone?"

Evelyn knew that this man was the reason everything was happening to her. She didn't know exactly how, and she didn't care. She just wanted it all to keep going that way.

"We sure are." She smiled what started to be a tantalizing offer, but then remembered the gravity of his grief and turned it to a look of brave compassion. Zwillman caught the adjustment, and for the first time in a number of days he laughed.

"You're good, Miss Lorraine, you're real good. And if it was a week ago, you and me woulda connected. . . . But now, well, you know how it is. Her dying makes that kind of thing poison for me." He looked at Evelyn with careful appreciation. "I'm really sorry, though. You're a very beautiful woman."

Evelyn, seeing her future dissolving, said gently, "We both know how it is; we're both up against dying. A good face dies as fast as you guys do. You have to think you're never going to die to be a dreamer."

She was looking out the front door.

"Like Macpherson does?" Zwillman said, interpreting the glance.

"Yeah." She shrugged, sure that her dream at least was lost.

"Keep him dreaming, Miss Lorraine. Macpherson can afford it, believe me. He can afford anything you want . . . even financing a movie."

"Why would he want to do that, Mr. Zwillman?"

"Because Louie Mayer ain't gonna produce your movie unless someone else pays for it. He thought I might, but I ain't."

They stood in the middle of the room. The conversation was over. They both knew the whole story. There was nothing left to do but end the conversation, which, being realists, they did succinctly.

"Good luck, Miss Lorraine."

"Thanks, Mr. Zwillman."

Evelyn was relieved after he left, because she didn't have to wait for the phone to ring anymore. All she had to do was the one thing at which she excelled: make a man want to give her what she wanted. She packed up her things, again in pillowcases, and left the Garden of Allah in her Ford convertible.

Magnus discovered her note, which read:

Thanks for everything you gave me. In return, I'm giving you a chance to get clear of me. What I need now is something I don't want to use you for. If you find me, I probably will, because it's everything I want. So take your chances.

Georgine Blor

It took him fourteen hours to locate her. By that time, he had already found out what was going on, had had a preliminary meeting with Mr. Mayer at the Culver City studio, and had called William Wallace Gibson to get on a plane and fly to Los Angeles to handle the deal. When he drove up to the bungalow at the San Ysidro Ranch south of Santa Barbara, Evelyn was sitting on the porch in a simple cotton dress, reading a book. As Magnus got out of his car she looked up and smiled. She had not doubted for a moment that he would come, and offered no spurious surprise.

"Where ya been?"

"Seeing Mr. Mayer."

She had not expected that.

"Yeah? What for?"

"To make it impossible for you to use me."

Never again would he see Evelyn Lorraine's mouth drop open. She stood on the porch, her fists on her hips, speechless. But before she could bluster into profanity, which was her way of expressing gratitude, Magnus told her, "And don't go being grateful. The day either one of us owes the other one damn thing, that's the day you and I will be finished. You better pack. You're expected back at the studio."

"I didn't unpack, you son of a bitch."

"Please. No gratitude. I expect to make a million dollars off you."

"You bastard, I'm going to make you so much money, you'll give up liquor and become a fuckin' monk."

"Don't make that much; monks are always grateful for something."

"Come in here; I'll give you something a monk sure as hell would be grateful for. . . . Magnus, you're taking a big chance giving me what I want."

"Why?"

"Because I want a lot, and I'll know where to come to ask for it."

"You can always ask; I can always refuse."

She smiled out over the green lawn and the trellised flowers. "Damn."

"What is it, then?"

"I wish I'd known you 'once upon a time,' like some goddamn fairy story. 'Once upon a time, Magnus met Georgine and . . .' What do you think would have happened?"

He went up behind her and put his arms around her waist. She leaned her head back on his shoulder.

" 'Once upon a time' is too long ago for us. We're damned lucky having now."

She turned and kissed him.

They spent a few hours in the bungalow. Then Magnus followed her back to Los Angeles in his car and waved as he turned off for Sunset Boulevard. Evelyn drove on to Culver City and Metro-Goldwyn-Mayer. In the next three years, she made six films back-to-back. Magnus made one and a half million on the first of them, after which Louis Mayer didn't want any more of his money. Evelyn Lorraine was a star, a combination of "funny, tough, and majestic," which made her easy to cast in anything from Russian royal palaces to colorful nineteenth-century gutters. Her beauty had the necessary catalytic reaction on celluloid, and she became wealthy, adored, and worst of all, famous.

Magnus and Evelyn kept their devoted but unobligated friendship very much alive during the years before the war. Their time together was hectic and often strained, necessitating a great deal of plane travel between coasts and a long-distance phone bill which irritatingly became a regular item on Walter Winchell's broadcasts. Evelyn was far from monogamous; the vicissitudes of her career and role necessitated numerous liaisons. Magnus was monogamous, but not out of principle. He lacked time, and he lacked interest, until the day when Iris Fowler appeared.

10

You must have been a beautiful baby,
'Cause, baby, look at you now.
—JOHNNY MERCER AND HARRY WARREN

"Is that you, Mr. Macpherson?" His voice over the phone reverberated with intense purpose.

"Yes, Mr. President."

"I appreciated your telegram offering to help. Mr. Hopkins told you what we have in mind for you?"

"He did. I'm flying down to Washington tonight, and will start immediately."

"Good. The secretary of war mentioned just today that industrial alcohol is vital if we have a war."

In October 1941 France had fallen, the German invasion of Russia began and Japan had invaded southern Indochina. Without any doubt, there was a war. The only question was how and when it would involve the United States.

" 'If,' Mr. President? I'm coming down there for a war."

"I know that!" Roosevelt snapped. "You just get down here, Magnus, and get us that alcohol. You can be sure I know we're going to need it."

"Yes. Mr. Pres—" The phone clicked, and Magnus hung up. He looked out of the window of his office. Indian summer. That night, a play in which he had invested was opening. His tailor was due in an hour, and his chief of marketing was coming to report on a new line of Macpherson gin.

He took out a deck of cards and rang for Weiss. He told Mrs. Styles, his secretary, to cancel the tailor, the marketing executive, and his seats for the play.

When Weiss saw the cards, he groaned, "Oy vey."

"What's the matter? Cards. A little gin."

"A little gin my ass, Macpherson. We haven't played a *little* gin in years. Every time we play gin now, it means more work for me, and some big idea from you."

"You can have the deal."

"You firing me or what? I don't want charity. We'll cut to deal. What's the matter?"

They cut; Magnus dealt.

"I'm going to Washington to work for Roosevelt."

Weiss nodded. "We convert to ethyl alcohol?"

"Right now."

"That fast, huh?" Weiss was looking for more information.

"Yes."

Weiss nodded and looked into his gin hand. Then he threw his cards down on Magnus' desk and said quietly, "It's about time!"

"Yes, it is."

"Tried to enlist today. Went to the Canadian RAF."

"Are they taking you?"

Weiss looked at Magnus hopelessly. "Told them I was twenty-nine, knew a lot about machines. They told me I was forty-seven and had flat feet. . . . I'm only forty-*three*, for Christ's sake, and what do they care about flat feet if I'm flying a Spitfire!" He tried to keep it funny, but he couldn't. He picked up his cards, but was too agitated to study them. "I sit here feeling Hitler peeling the skin off my back. Where can I go to fight that animal? I don't have a country to go to that'll let me fight him."

Magnus had been through some bad times with Weiss, but he had never seen him this disturbed.

"You'll be fighting soon, Weiss. But I doubt if anyone will let you fly a Spitfire to Berlin to cut out his black heart."

"No. . . ." Weiss shook his head. "What's this Washington thing? You need a second job? Roosevelt's paying you a lot?"

"One dollar a year."

Weiss looked to heaven. "For a dollar a year, he gets to tell Rosenstiel and Bronfman what to do. You ever tried to train panthers, Macpherson? I can see you now, holding your cards with the only finger you got left, propping them up against your nose."

"We'll play a little gin when the war's over."

Weiss's face folded in on itself. He hurried back to his own office. Magnus told Mrs. Styles to reach Evelyn Lorraine at MGM. He had planned to fly out to see her on the weekend, but he would have to cancel the trip. He told her to reach his children at their various boarding schools as well.

"Yes, sir. And, Mr. Macpherson, a young lady is here to see you, a Miss Fowler, Iris Fowler."

"Who is she?"

"I don't know, sir. She says you knew her father. He worked for you on Long Island. I told her you didn't have any business interests there that I knew of, but she—"

"Bring her in. Right away."

"Yes, sir."

Iris Fowler. It wasn't the wife; her name was something else.

His secretary ushered in a young girl who wore a white blouse, a full skirt, and brown-and-white saddle shoes. She wore a little lipstick but no other makeup, and her soft honey hair fell to her shoulders in a simple pageboy. Her eyes, open wide at the size and view of the office, were a pale, pale blue.

"Mr. Macpherson, this is Miss Fowler."

"Thank you, Mrs. Styles."

As the secretary left the room, Iris walked over to Magnus with a certain hesitancy about both how she was dressed and the intervening furniture.

"Hello, Mr. Macpherson. I hope I'm not bothering you."

"Not at all, Iris."

She seemed surprised to hear him say her name, then looked down and smiled, obviously pleased.

"I wasn't sure I should just . . . barge in like this, but I was upstairs, and I've wanted to meet you for such a long time. . . . Well, I didn't really 'barge' in, did I?" She laughed, and Magnus joined her. "I don't think even a tank could barge in here."

He could barely remember the night he and Mary had gone to tell Mrs. Fowler that her husband had been killed when the still blew up. When this girl—well, young woman, really—had crept into the room, looking at him with those same pale blue eyes, she had been only two or three. Now she must be . . . well, at least twenty.

"Sit down, Iris. I'm glad you came by. I wish you'd given me some warning, I'd have bought you a fancy lunch."

"Oh, no, I wouldn't bother you. You've been so . . . kind. I did want to meet you, though. I was so curious because, well, *I* feel like I've known you all my life. And . . ." When she started to laugh, she hunched up her shoulders and wrinkled her nose at the same time. ". . . Every time I saw your picture in the paper when you were in Washington or with"—a deep breath of awe—"Evelyn Lorraine! Well, golly, I just felt like I knew you, and . . . I was very proud, I guess."

"That's a surprise. I didn't know anyone was proud of me."

"Well *I* was." She smiled and looked down at her shoes, suddenly embarrassed. "If I'd known I was going to meet you today, I'd have worn something else."

"Such as what?"

"Oh, I don't know." She hunched her shoulders and laughed at herself. "Probably something very fancy, but very dignified, to impress you that I turned out all right."

No, thought Magnus, she's more grownup; she must be twenty-two.

"It seems you turned out just fine. Your mother must be very proud."

Her smile melted into embarrassment, and for a moment Magnus saw the eyes of the child looking at him from the doorway years before.

"Mom died. I wrote to Mr. Gibson about the checks. I thought he would have told you."

"He should have. I'm sorry about your mother."

"Oh that's O.K. She'd been sick a long time." Iris became filled with facts to cover the hurt she obviously still felt. "Mom had a heart block, the Adams-Stokes syndrome: it damaged the impulse fibers that keep the heart beating, and her heart just . . . stopped." Tears had come to her eyes. "Oh, for gosh sakes." She grabbed for her purse. "I'm sorry, Mr. Macpherson."

"That's all right, but could I ask you a great favor?"

"Oh, of course. Golly, I figure I owe you at least one great favor."

"Would you tell me how you happened to be here today, and while you're doing it, would you call me Magnus?"

"I'll . . . I'll try"—she flicked a glance at him—"Magnus."

He relaxed in his chair, pleased just to be looking at her.

"When I graduated from high school, I wanted to go to college, but Mom got sick, and my grades could have been better, so I went to secretarial school. Now I'm studying real estate. As soon as I get my license, I'll get a job and you can have Mr. Gibson stop sending the checks. . . . That's why I was here, one of the girls at the school's getting married and a bunch of us decided to give her a shower at the top of the Empire State Building. When I was up there,

I thought why not see Mr. Mac-. . . . well, you *were* Mr. Macpherson then. . . . Now you're Magnus."

She sat smiling at him, no longer hesitant. Her hands were folded neatly in her lap.

"How old are you, Iris?"

"Nineteen."

The phone rang. Magnus stood up and went to his desk.

"Yes?" She didn't look nineteen. She looked like a mature woman.

"Mr. Macpherson, Miss Lorraine is on the line."

"Oh. Put her on. . . . Iris, excuse me."

"Do you want me to leave?"

"No! Certainly not. I'll only be a minute. . . . Hello, Evelyn?" At the sound of the name, Iris' eyes opened again in wonder. She looked away to indicate she would not listen, but she did, even though she did not hear what Evelyn said: "Magnus, don't tell me you're not coming out here."

"All right. How's the picture going?"

"You're *not* coming?"

"Do you like William Powell, or is he—?"

"If you don't come out here this weekend, I'm going to take William Powell to Catalina and have him sixteen times on the beach."

"How old is William Powell?"

Magnus looked at Iris. She saw the look, caught it, and returned a smile.

"Magnus, what the hell's going on? You sound like you're in bed with somebody, which I couldn't care less about, but just don't talk to me like you're on the moon."

Magnus was looking at Iris. He turned away quickly.

"Evelyn, I'm sorry, but the President just called and I have to go to Washington tonight. It has to do with converting the industry to munitions manufacture, and it can't wait."

"Magnus, are we getting into this goddamn war, for Christ's sake?"

"It looks like it."

"Shit! I look lousy in khaki and I hate tap-dancing to marches. You know they sent me a script last week called *Berlin Blues,* about this vaudeville team that smuggles out secrets—"

"Evelyn, I'm in a meeting. I'll call you again, but I wanted to let you know about the weekend."

There was a short silence. "Magnus, go to hell or Washington, or wherever, I'm going to Catalina and ruin William Powell."

"Have fun."

"Prick."

She hung up. Magnus smiled as he put the phone down. Then he looked across the office at Iris Fowler. Her mouth was open wide.

"*President* Roosevelt?"

Magnus nodded. Nineteen. Almost twenty-one. And twenty-one was only twenty years younger than he was. The way she looked at him made him feel like showing off, like throwing the caber, like balancing five hams on each arm. He was forty-one, but that was just a date on a piece of paper. He felt thirty-five, even younger, thirty-one, and ten years made no difference at all. She was innocent and inexperienced, and so open and vulnerable he could not imagine how she had progressed through the world for nineteen years.

"Iris . . ."

"Yes?"

"I'm wondering about something." He had not felt shy for twenty years.

She caught his nervousness, and for the first time in their conversation blushed.

"Wondering about what . . . Magnus?"

That time his name sounded almost right.

"I'm wondering if you'd take on a very hard job, right now, leave your school, and come to Washington as my assistant. How's your shorthand?"

He knew it was rash, outrageous, mad, but he felt exhilarated by the possibility.

"I was second in my class, but I was first in typing speed."

"Good. This job depends on your being able to move quickly at a moment's notice. I have to go down to Washington tonight. My plane leaves at ten-thirty. Can you make it? Tomorrow you're going to have to find me a house down there."

"A house . . ." She stood up and started for the door. Her look of wonder became weighted with actuality.

"Iris?"

She turned too quickly and lost her balance. Then she started to hunch up her shoulders to laugh, but the thought of her new responsibilities stopped her.

"Yes?"

"Can you make it?"

"If I can't make this, I'll never be able to make anything in my whole life." And she went out quickly.

The President had appointed Magnus to head the distilling-industry section of the Office of Production Management. The purpose of the OPM was to convert American industry from peacetime manufacturing to what was euphemistically called the "nation's defense." The liquor industry's conversion was to be from manufacturing whiskey to making ethyl alcohol. Sixty gallons of ethyl alcohol were required to make the smokeless powder needed to fire a single round from a sixteen-inch naval gun. For defense purposes, Roosevelt wanted fifty million gallons. Government funds would be used to convert (and expand) existing facilities which the owners would be allowed to retain after the war. The distillers who were currently overstocked, paying high storage fees, and losing a lot of their whiskey to evaporation, were glad to help their country in time of need.

The heads of seven major companies went to Washington to agree on their separate shares of the government market. Magnus called the meeting at Roosevelt's request two days after he arrived in Washington.

For the first time, a group of distillers had agreed to agree. Still reeling from a federal tax increase and the announcement by several states that they were considering their own manufacture and distribution of liquor, all the distillers realized their desperate need for some good public relations. If the country needed smokeless power, the liquor industry would provide it.

The meeting was held in a large conference room overlooking the White House in the Old Executive Office Building. Louis Rosenstiel arrived in a limousine filled with lawyers, accountants, and charts. He was in fine spirits, for he knew Schenley had the largest production capacity in the industry, at fifty-three million gallons per year. He would therefore secure the lion's share of the new war business.

"Well, well, Macpherson," he roared as he came into the room. "I hope we get through this meeting before the building burns down, don't you, heh?" Rosenstiel had never forgotten the loss of the warehouse on the Detroit River. He was smiling, but Magnus knew Rosenstiel would smile in a slaughterhouse.

The other heads of the industry arrived, including Sam Bronfman, and took their places around the table, and Magnus called the meeting to order.

"Gentlemen, it's time to begin."

The opening went smoothly; the contracts with the government were signed, the quotas for each distillery established. Then Magnus introduced a little business of his own.

"Gentlemen, before we adjourn, Dr. Bromberg, the head of our research department, has a few words he would like to say to you."

Dr. Bromberg rose to his full five feet of height, happy to be the center of attention.

"I am pleased to be here, not only to make the announcement to which Mr. Macpherson refers, but to espouse an ideal which will serve our industry. I suggest that we consider a pooling of research to enable the industry to benefit from advances in technology. It is even more important we do it now, with the war. . . ."

Magnus saw Louis Rosenstiel signal one of his aides and whisper hurriedly to him. The aide responded, and Rosenstiel listened again with the care of a coiled snake, as Bromberg continued.

"Mr. Macpherson has given me permission, as the first step in sharing such information, to announce our development of a technique which will speed the process of fermentation from days or hours to minutes. The technique, we call flash conversion—"

"Wait a minute." Rosenstiel was on his feet. "I don't want to hear any more of this." The rest of his entourage rose as well. "For your information, Mr. Brom . . . What's your name?"

"Bromberg."

"*Joseph* Bromberg." There was an accusation in Rosenstiel's telling the man his own name.

"Yes." Bromberg smiled, delighted Rosenstiel knew it.

"Umhmm. Well, for your information, Mr. Joseph Bromberg, we already know about flash conversion. You see, a lot of us don't believe in pooling technology, or pooling anything else. We work best on our own, discovering what we can and using it as we please." He was hurling the phrases like knives at Bromberg, who looked nervously at Magnus. Rosenstiel's entourage stood behind him, an opera chorus ready to exit.

"You see, Mr. Joseph Bromberg, we're going to war to preserve our right to do just that. We aren't going to share ideas *or* profits. That's *socialism*, Mr. Joseph Bromberg, the joining of the *masses*. And there isn't one member of a mass in this room. Every one of us is as separate as an enemy; that's why it works."

"Mr. Rosenstiel!" Bromberg interrupted forcefully. "It's *Doctor* Joseph Bromberg. No one is forcing you to give or take information; it's being offered. There's a war to be fought; this process will help win it."

Rosenstiel looked at Dr. Bromberg. "I won't forget *you, Doctor* Bromberg." He turned disgustedly to Magnus and said, "Macpherson, where do you pick up these burlyque tenors?" He did not wait for an answer, but moved directly out of the room, followed by his staff.

The room had soured. Briefcases were snapped shut. Dr. Bromberg, angry, embarrassed, was about to turn away when Mr. Sam spoke.

"Thank you, Dr. Bromberg, for the offer. And to you, Mr. Chairman. It's appreciated . . . now that the self-appointed commander-in-chief has led his troops from the field." There was laughter, and Bromberg bowed slightly in Bronfman's direction.

"We've been doing some work on flash conversion at Seagram's, too," Mr. Sam continued. "But we aren't interested in sharing until it's patented. That's just business, and business never stops for war. Rosenstiel knows this. That's why he's a good businessman . . . in spite of being a schmuck. . . . Is this meeting adjourned?"

Magnus stood and said, "It is, if you give the stenographer a translation of 'schmuck' for the benefit of the goyim in the trade."

Mr. Sam laughed. "What is this 'goyim,' Magnus? Is Ted Weiss teaching you Yiddish?"

"Just so I can order in a deli."

"Give him my regards. And watch out for Louie. He's a dirty fighter. He comes after you when you're down."

"What can I do about it, Sam?"

"Don't ever go down." He smiled and walked out, just as Iris Fowler appeared at the door. No one paid attention to her; there was a great deal of commotion as the different distillers moved out of the room.

"What are you doing here, Iris?" Magnus said when they were alone.

"I just had to tell you, Mr. Macpherson. I found the house!"

"Magnus."

She laughed. "It's hard to call you that in here. But you have to pay for it tonight or it'll go to a general. Real estate's crazy here. Come on, we have to hurry!" She took his arm and led him out of the building to a waiting limousine. Magnus was very aware of her hand through his arm. He wondered if she were, too, or just excited at having succeeded with her assignment. Then he forgot about her reasons and enjoyed her hand.

The house was one of an old, restored brick row in Georgetown.

Iris showed him around the three floors and tried to point out with a flashlight how lovely the small plot of garden was in the back. There was a narrow garage, above which was a small apartment with a Pullman kitchen and bath.

"Do you like it?" she said, standing under the slanted ceiling of the garage apartment.

"As much as you do," he said, catching her enthusiasm.

"I *knew* you would."

"And this is yours, Iris, I'll need you to be here. You'll work in the house, taking calls, and getting me early coffee. I'll probably dictate when I get home at night, so it's convenient for you to be—"

She clapped her hands once and looked up to the beams that supported the roof. For a guilty moment Magnus thought she was reacting to what could be mistaken for a proposition. But then she looked at him with tears in her eyes.

"I've been wanting you to say that all day."

Magnus tried to see if she were implying more, if she had the slightest awareness where such proximity could lead. But he saw no more in her face than what she said: she was happy to have a new place to live.

She hurried him to the limousine and they drove to the real-estate office on Wisconsin Avenue. The broker explained he had to stay open late; business was very brisk. Magnus gave him a sizable deposit and told him his lawyer would call tomorrow. Then he and Iris started back to the Shoreham.

"Wait! We haven't eaten."

Magnus had forgotten about it. "That's good, Iris. You have to remind me to eat, too. Part of your job. Where do you want to go?"

"Back to our house . . . *your* house . . . well, I live there sort of, so it's our house; I can say that, can't I?"

"I don't see why not," Magnus said carefully.

"We'll stop at a place I saw and buy some hamburgers *à la grecque,* a bottle of milk, and a candle. You'll love it."

They became friends that night. Hamburger *à la grecque* was a feta-cheese burger with chopped-up Greek olives and lots of onions. Magnus had not had a hamburger or a glass of milk for a long time; both business and Evelyn Lorraine led him to fancier fare.

They sat in the kitchen and planned the house, what furniture to buy, where to put the phones, what colors to paint the rooms. Iris took notes and made suggestions. After supper she told him a little about growing up and how she and her mother had managed to survive. After her father's death, they had moved to Queens to a small apartment.

She hunched up her shoulders and laughed. "Magnus"—it sounded so easy—"you've made everything happen in my life. I remember Mommy opening the letter every month with the check in it, and thanking God right there at the mailbox. I'll tell you something: she trusted you more than God. She could depend on you; God, well, she said she never could tell what He was up to. . . . And now you've done . . . this."

In the next six weeks, the house was furnished, and their residence in separate quarters began. The massive amount of work at the OPM required Magnus to be in the office from seven in the morning to almost eight every night. Iris made sure he had a good breakfast, and she had a hot supper ready whenever he came home. She insisted on preparing it herself, letting the cook and maid go home early. As Magnus ate, she sat with her notes, giving him messages from Macpherson Distilleries and taking down his replies.

Neither of them had time to think much about their situation. Each evening Magnus was increasingly aware of how much he looked forward to getting back to Thirty-fifth Street. Iris had a house with a man in it for the first time in her life, and she did not stop to wonder whether the man was a substitute father, a fantasy, a friend, or employer. She just knew how happy she felt, how exciting it was to take messages from all over the country and even the White House. And each evening, she looked forward to Magnus coming home.

One Sunday, December 7, Magnus and Iris were going to see the Redskins play the Philadelphia Eagles at Griffith Stadium, with William Wallace Gibson, who had a box on the fifty-yard line. Magnus seldom took a day off, but had promised Gibson he would go. That morning he came down to breakfast to find a note from Iris saying that she had a sore throat and was going to stay in her room so he wouldn't catch it.

Magnus was relieved; he would much rather stay home and read. He called Double Gibson and used Iris' excuse as his own. Then he fixed an enormous breakfast, making two tries at scrambling eggs. Balancing the tray carefully, he went to the garage and climbed the steps to Iris' room.

"Miss Fowler?" There was a pause on the other side of her door.

"What? Oh. . . . Yes?"

"Room service."

"Room service? But I'm, I have a—"

" 'Starve a cold, feed a sore throat,' I've always heard. I made *you* breakfast for once."

"Oh, Magnus, I already made myself breakfast."

He suddenly felt silly and old, standing outside a nineteen-year-old girl's room holding a breakfast tray like a corsage.

"Oh. Fine, Iris. I just wanted to make sure you were fed," he said, all responsibility and business. He started back down the steps.

Her door opened, and she said, "If you have some coffee, I'd like some more." He turned around slowly and looked up at her. She was probably being polite, he thought. The look on her face was questioning, and he didn't want to give any answers, but she smiled as if a great truth had been revealed.

"This is the first time I've ever seen you without a necktie." He was wearing an open shirt and sweater. "You look so . . . fresh."

He noticed she was wearing a soft white flannel nightgown. Her honey-colored hair was parted and tied to each side with two pieces of dark blue yarn, which made her eyes seem a paler blue than usual.

"Coffee?"

"Yes, please."

He went up the stairs and into her room. He had never seen it until that morning. They both stood as Magnus looked around. It was all white and blue. The armchair had crewelwork violets and white piping, the hooked rug concentric circles of white and blue. Magnus saw Iris shiver.

"You'd better get into bed."

"Yes."

She pulled the covers up to her chin. They were both conscious of a tension as he put the tray down on a table.

"Coffee?"

"Please."

"It's milk, no sugar, isn't it?"

"That's right."

He prepared the cup, stirred it, and took it over to the bed. Iris watched him as he stood by the bed and handed it to her. Slowly she drew an arm from under the covers and reached out. Just as she touched the cup, she shivered and said, "Oh, Magnus," deep in her throat.

The cup spilled as Magnus put it on the floor; the coffee spread over first a blue, then a white, then a blue circle.

At that moment, half a world away, battle stations were being sounded on the ships of the Japanese armada 270 miles northeast of the Hawaiian Islands. Pilots and technical crews ran out to the 190 Mitsubishi fighters to prepare for takeoff. The ships were pitching deeply in the sea swells. Within the hour the planes were lined up on the flight decks ready for takeoff.

"Magnus."

"Yes?"

"What's going to happen to us?"

"We're going to love each other."

"How?"

"Like this."

"What is 'this'?"

"We'll have to take some time finding out."

He pulled her closer to him, and as they kissed, she slowly hooked her ankle around the back of his knee. She had been a virgin, but had given it up with a rush of release. They had made love three times in an hour. The second time she discovered her own pleasures and was happy they gave such obvious delight to Magnus. They lay quietly together until Iris said, "Magnus?"

It was one o'clock. They were still in bed.

"Yes?"

"Tell me about your children."

They talked for hours. America's war began. They ate cold scrambled eggs, cold toast, drank cold coffee, not wanting to leave the musky tight embrace of the blue-and-white room above the garage. Their instincts were correct, for when they came out at dusk, they found a different, deathly world. The phones were ringing in the house; a military courier had been waiting on the front porch for two hours with new quotas from the Department of War. Magnus and Iris listened to the radio as he put on a tie and coat. At the front door he kissed her and said, "Do I look old again?"

"I know exactly how old you are."

"I don't know when I'll be back."

"I'll be here."

He kissed her again, then hurried down the steps in search of a ride to the Old Executive Office Building.

Iris closed the door and leaned against it for a long time, letting the day settle in her. She thought she had experienced more in that last twelve hours than she had in all her nineteen years. She wanted to run, sing, fly. She had started a new life with a man who loved her and needed her to help him with his company and now the war. The phone began to ring.

". . . And those three children," she said slowly, and hurried from the door to answer the phone.

Magnus had told her what he knew of his children, which even Iris could see was a limited perception of them. She wondered what they would think of her; she was closer to their ages than she was to their father's. She also wondered what was causing them to behave as they were.

Magnus II was attending his third prep school, having been expelled from the first two. A letter from the headmaster of his current school warned Magnus that a similar dismissal was imminent. The cause was not scholarship; Magnus II managed to secure a place on the honor list at each of the schools he attended, but in addition to his studies he used his intelligence to intimidate the masters and manipulate his peers. He seemed to have "natural leadership potential," but used it for a variety of unsavory ends.

At one school he managed to recruit six other boys to break the honor code by cheating on a history exam. When caught, Magnus II admitted his role with no remorse, stating that the honor system was used by the school for its own convenience and that honesty was looked on as weakness in the rest of the world, where skill at cheating and lying were necessities. The school should teach how to avoid being caught.

The next school threw him out, not only for smoking but also for running a sales organization throughout the school to distribute, at a vast profit, a wide choice of cigarettes. He was currently at St. David's School in Connecticut, where the headmaster hinted in a series of letters to his father that Magnus was aiding his classmates in "skipping off" at night to a local whorehouse. The headmaster implied that Magnus II was not only arranging such matters, but was also collecting a healthy commission both from the boys and from the prostitutes.

The headmaster obviously hoped Magnus would take his son out of St. David's, but there were some facts he didn't tell Magnus. One was, in spite of having a lovely wife and four children, he enjoyed fondling an occasional student on the couch in his office. Magnus II had confirmed this predilection by offering himself as bait. Once he confirmed the lust, Magnus II offered to supply the headmaster with his pleasure from the student body for a price. The headmaster, righteously appalled, refused, but Magnus II produced a wire recording of their liaison. When the headmaster furiously unwound the spool, Magnus II told him it would cost at least five hundred dollars to replace it and one thousand dollars to secure the original. The money had been paid, the original recording destroyed. But the headmaster still wished to be rid of Magnus Macpherson II.

Unfortunately, Magnus disappointed him by insisting that discipline was part of the school's responsibility to its students and their parents. Whatever punishment his son deserved, his son should get. The idea of removing the boy before the end of the school year would be harmful to his education. However, if the headmaster believed himself incapable of handling the situation, another school for the boy's senior year would be found. That would make a different school for each year of Magnus II's high-school education. The headmaster agreed to this suggestion and sweated out another thousand dollars to Magnus II before the end of the school year, for the boy had kept a copy of the incriminating recording.

WeeDee had been enrolled at the fashionable Ethel Walker School, where she immediately established a reputation for wild social behavior coupled with a precise and careful obedience to school rules. She, too, had a natural intelligence, but it did not lend itself to the memorization of facts. Her popularity with her classmates was great, based on her willingness to perform the outrageous. She painted shoes on her feet and went to meals barefoot; she wore a large falsie in only one side of her bra. She edited a short-lived clandestine paper called "School Scandals," and sang risqué songs to her own accompaniment. No one had the faintest idea that WeeDee broke one rule regularly, for which she risked immediate expulsion. When she reached the low point of the depression that came on her for no reason she could understand, WeeDee always managed to "take a stroll" into the woods around the school. She kept a bottle of Macpherson's Century in a hollow tree there. At the age of fifteen, WeeDee was a lush.

Jamie had entered Portsmouth Priory, the socially correct school for Roman Catholic boys. When Kristin had introduced the idea the previous summer, Magnus had forbidden it and arranged for his younger son to attend Choate. But Jamie had, even at the age of thirteen, a quiet will of his own. At the beginning of the school year he left East Hampton and took a bus to Portsmouth Priory in Rhode Island. When he arrived, he called his father person-to-person, told him where he was and that he would appreciate his father sending a check for the tuition. His father furiously commanded Jamie to return to East Hampton. Jamie said calmly that if his father took him out of Portsmouth Priory, he would run away from any other school to which he was sent. If his father refused to pay for his tuition, he would ask his Uncle Juny for the money. Before Magnus could answer, Jamie calmly explained that he wanted to become a priest. Magnus was silent, then agreed to send the tuition. He felt he could no longer speak, much less argue with someone he understood so little.

Kristin kept the home in East Hampton open and welcoming for the children's weekends and holidays. But the war made travel difficult, and the times when they were all together were few. Christmas was one of them, but the warped emotional angles remained.

The first Christmas of World War II, Magnus used his workload to limit his visit to East Hampton. A special troop train was leaving Penn Station at midnight for Washington; Magnus planned to celebrate Christmas Eve with his children, drive into New York, catch the train, and spend Christmas morning with Iris before going to his office.

The children opened their presents before dinner. The tree in the living room just touched the sixteen-foot ceiling; the gaily wrapped packages covered the entire corner of the room. The fire roared with discarded wrapping paper as each child opened packages in separate areas of the room, spreading them around for a constant review of possessions. They exclaimed their appreciation with genuine excitement. Their gratitude had no objective, however. In spite of the words neatly written on each of the packages saying they were from "Fa" or "Father," the children knew that Aunt Kristin had chosen them, wrapped them, and that their father had only paid for them.

Each reacted to the others' gifts with proper appreciation. They carefully waited to express their real gratitude to their Aunt Kristin until later, when their father had gone. As Kristin sat under the tree handing out the presents, Magnus sat in a chair trying to share in the excitement.

"And here we have a gold package for young Eleanor Macpherson from Santa Claus."

"Not yet, please, Aunt Kristin. It's Jamie's turn."

"Oh, WeeDee, take it. Why don't you take it?" Magnus II asked impatiently.

"Because . . . I like this to last as long as possible. Give Magnus one, Aunt Kristin, please."

"No, it's Jamie's turn. And I don't think he can carry it alone. It's that huge red-and-green box over there."

Jamie walked quietly over to a large carton and carefully began to unwrap the paper. The package was obviously Jamie's "special" present.

Jamie unwrapped the box with great care, folding the paper and rolling flat the bows of ribbon. The process was too slow for Magnus II, who reached over from his area of floor and tore off a huge handful of paper. "Come on, Jamie, hurry up."

Jamie looked at his brother, instantly furious.

"You dirty stinking crud! Why did you do that? Why?"

The sudden intensity surprised everyone except Magnus II, who smiled at his younger brother and said, "Because we have to hurry, Jamie. Fa has to catch his train." He flicked a glance at his father, then turned back to Jamie. "So don't get mad at me. Why don't you look what you got, dummy?"

Jamie looked at his present: a crated set of new *Encyclopaedia Britannica*. He silently took a breath and started to take one of the volumes out of the box, but remembered his father and solemnly walked across the room.

"Father, I'm . . . Thank you so much, sir. I wanted them so much, I . . ." He glanced up quickly at his father. "Can I take them to school?"

"It's a great load, Jamie. Doesn't the school have a set of their own?"

"I could ship them. I wanted to have them in my room, to read."

"In your room?" Magnus II hooted.

"What's wrong with that?" WeeDee asked pleasantly.

"You know anyone who reads encyclopedias?" Magnus II snapped at her.

Magnus spoke quietly to his younger son. "I think you better leave them here, son. I got them so you'd always have them, here as well as school."

Jamie accepted the verdict. "Thank you again, sir." He went back to the crate, took out Volume I, and started to read.

WeeDee's special gift was a Victrola with an automatic record changer, and albums of Chopin and Gershwin. She, too, wanted to take it to school, but her Aunt Kristin reminded her that there was a rule against having phonographs at Ethel Walker.

"Oh, Father, *please*. Write them a letter. Tell them I have to have it in my room or . . . or I'll go blind or something. Please!"

"I don't think I can do that, WeeDee. You'll have it in your room here so you can play what you want whenever you want." They both looked at Magnus II, who pretended not to hear.

"I wish I could have it at school," but then the idea gave way to her joy and she threw her arms around her father's neck and said, "Thank you, thank you, Father." As he hugged his daughter, Magnus didn't see how he could have thought of leaving.

He was about to announce his intention of staying, until the next morning at least, when Kristin piped, "All right, then, I'm done. It's time for young Magnus' great present, and then we'll have some supper. So come along. For this one, we have to troop down to the playroom, and, Magnus, you have to be blindfolded."

It was certainly something big, not to be under the tree, and Magnus II enjoyed being the center of attention as he was led down the basement steps to the playroom.

Jamie and WeeDee both exclaimed their surprise before Magnus II had his blindfold removed. He didn't express any urgency, but stood waiting until WeeDee reached up and pulled the handkerchief away.

In the center of the room was a magnificent hand-carved billiards table with automatic ball return. A rack of pool cues hung on one wall, and a number of high observers' chairs were lined up on the other.

Magnus II allowed a smile as Aunt Kristin clapped her hands, tears of excitement overflowing her eyes.

"I had the best fun of any of you keeping *this* a surprise. Remember last week, children, when I sent you off . . ." She did not say where, for it had been to collect their presents from the Flemings in Manhattan. "*That* was the day they delivered this great thing. I feel I've been hiding an elephant under my bed!"

They all enjoyed the image, except Magnus II, who was watching his father. Then he went quickly to the cue rack, took two cues, walked over to his father, and handed him one. Magnus smiled, took the cue, and the two of them went to the table. The balls had been racked, and Magnus glided the cue ball across the table to his son.

"Your break."

"No, Fa. It's my table. You're the guest here; the honor's yours." He said it with genuine courtesy. The others took chairs to watch as Magnus lined up the white cue ball.

"I hope I don't plow a furrow in the green." He made a respectable break, but sank nothing. He turned to Magnus II to watch his shot.

But Magnus II just stood where he was, leaning casually on his cue.

"Well, Fa, I certainly can't take this to school, can I?"

WeeDee and Kristin laughed, but Jamie didn't. Nor did Magnus. As he had felt so often in the past, Magnus suddenly sensed a twist was coming, a painful twist.

"Why did you buy this, Fa?"

"I heard you were good at it and enjoyed it."

"Really?" He reached out with his cue and with the end of it rolled a ball into a corner pocket. "It's not just another 'thing' we have so we'll like it here and think of it as our home, is it?"

Magnus turned and put his cue back in the rack.

"What does it mean, Fa?" Magnus II shot across the table at him.

Magnus spun quickly and said, "It means it's Christmas, and I wanted to give each of you something you wanted."

Magnus II pondered that as he chalked his cue, leaned over the table, lined up a shot, and smacked two balls away.

"Is that what it really means, Fa? . . . I think it means you're rich. I think it's sort of bribery, so we won't blame you so much for not being here. Well, don't worry anymore; we won't notice, will we, WeeDee? Jamie?" The other children looked down at the floor and did not move.

Aunt Kristin stood down from her chair and said, "That's a vile thing to say, Magnus. When someone holds out a hand with a gift in it, you don't chop off the hand to take it."

Magnus II looked at her and gave a sharp laugh. "That's a funny picture, Aunt Kristin, Fa holding a billiards table in his hand." He turned to his father, all humor gone. "It'd be easier for Aunt Kristin, Fa, if in the future you just gave us . . . a check."

Magnus wondered what could be said in a moment to alter sixteen years of distance between himself and his son. He thought of asking each of his children what they wanted, not "things," but what they wanted of him. He looked at Jamie, who had not moved, and Wee-Dee, who was sneaking glances at what went on, then turning away, fearful of the conflict between her father and brother.

"Why don't we live with you, Fa?"

The words cracked against each other, readjusting the tension in the room. For the first time Magnus could remember, his elder son was asking him for something. His voice did not have its usual bitterness. The question was asked with a brusque pleading. Magnus looked at his son, whose lips were clenched tight against any expression of the emotion he apparently was feeling.

Magnus put out his hands, gesturing to include all his children.

"If you want to live with me, go right up and pack. We'll *all* go to Washington tonight."

The only reaction that he heard was Kristin, who gasped. But Magnus paid no attention to her, for he was watching his son's face lose its pain and wanting, and harden into a venomous triumph.

"Fa, we don't want to go to Washington. I just wondered why you never lived in our house. You never have, not in Canada, not here. . . . It'd feel funny to start now, wouldn't it?" He turned to the other two children, who were sitting on the high spectator chairs. "Wouldn't it be . . . strange, Jamie?"

"Yes," Jamie said firmly.

"It'd be kind of weird, wouldn't it, WeeDee?"

She looked up and smiled the smile behind which she hid.

"Well, we're all away at school anyway . . ." Then she quickly looked at her Aunt Kristin.

"Besides, Fa," Magnus II said, "there's a war on. We'd never see you anyway. . . . Come on, we better go have supper. Fa has to catch his train."

He dropped his pool cue with a sharp smack flat on the table, and walked out of the room and up the basement stairs. Magnus didn't move; he watched as first Jamie followed without looking at anyone, then WeeDee, who smiled at him, shrugged, and ran up the stairs after her brother.

Kristin took several steps toward Magnus, then stopped, confused by all she felt, and put her hands over her face. Magnus put an arm around her shoulders.

"It's too late for me to be their father," he said.

"You mustn't give up." She sobbed quietly and added, "In spite of the pain of trying."

"Mine and theirs, too. . . . Come along."

Supper was at first excruciating, but the turkey was excellent, the mince pie sublime, so they hid their emotions and enjoyed their food. Soon after supper, Magnus left for the drive to New York. Again his two youngest thanked him and kissed him awkwardly on the cheek. Magnus II shook his hand and with a mixture of humor and gall challenged his father to another billiards game.

Magnus' train was filled with soldiers returning from their last leave before being shipped overseas. As the cars sped through the night snow, they sang "Oh Johnnie, How You Can Love," "I Found My Thrill on Blueberry Hill," and finally, "God Bless America." Magnus felt afraid about Iris ever meeting his children, but he did not know exactly what it was he feared.

"Hello, Uncle Juny."

Magnus II stood before his uncle's massive desk at Fleming and Co.

"Holy smoke, Magnus, what are you doing here? Aren't you supposed to be up at school?"

"I'm on my way, but I wanted to drop off my Christmas present. It's a little late, but . . ." He put a small package on his uncle's desk, a money clip in the shape of a polo mallet.

"Why, Magnus, you're a peach of a kid to do that. . . . Did you and the others open our presents?"

"Yes, Christmas Eve, after my father left."

"Good." They shared the conspiracy. Magnus II then took out his wallet.

"I have a favor to ask, Uncle Juny. I've saved some money, and I wondered if you'd invest it in something for me."

"Of course I will, be tickled to do it. How much are you going to plunge?"

"Two thousand dollars."

"Two . . . ? Did you get that from your . . . ?"

"I made every cent of it."

Magnus II smiled beguilingly, revealing nothing, then went on. "I'd like to put it into a tobacco company. They're going to make a fortune in the war, don't you think?"

Juny Fleming looked at his nephew, marveling at his apparent aptitude for business. His own sons had not shown such talent. His frustration flared and diverted itself to the familiar hate of Magnus Macpherson.

"Does your father know about this?"

"No. I don't want him to, either."

"Good. . . . What are you going to get with what you make, Magnus?"

Magnus II shrugged, then smiled again, this time with a dangerous certainty.

"All I want is everything."

11

All Red and Blue stamps in War Ration Book 4
are worth 10 points each. Red and Blue tokens
are worth 1 point each. Red and Blue tokens
are used to make change for Red and Blue stamps
only when purchase is made. *Important!* Point
values of Brown and Green stamps are not changed.

—DEPARTMENT OF WAR

In April of 1943, Magnus II was eighteen and eligible for the draft. He was finishing his freshman year at Princeton and was doing well academically. The previous fall at the Big Game with Penn, he had gained a certain notoriety for bringing three New York prostitutes down to Princeton to share with his friends. Since then, he had become a campus personality, and was the accepted star of his own group.

For a while Magnus II thought he would try to avoid the draft, with his flat feet, but he was bored with Princeton, and sure there was much to be gained in a war by not fighting it. Two days after his birthday, Magnus II cut his classes, registered with the draft board in Princeton, and took a train to Washington to visit his father.

He arrived at Union Station in the late afternoon and managed to share a cab headed for Georgetown. It was his first visit since his father had begun living there. As the cab dropped its other passengers at government buildings, Magnus II noticed antiaircraft gun emplacements around various monuments, their crews slumped in place, bored with searching the skies. Magnus II smiled and shook his head.

"What's so funny, mister?" His remaining fellow passenger was a major in the army who carried a briefcase that was handcuffed to his wrist. Magnus II looked at the handcuffs, then at the major.

"It seems pretty useless."

"You better remember Pearl Harbor. Why aren't you in the service? You look old enough."

"I have leukemia."

"Oh, God . . . I'm so sorry."

They drove on to Georgetown in silence. Magnus II got out on Thirty-fifth Street, looked at the house, then went up to the front door and rang the bell.

Iris answered the door, all business. "Thank goodness you're here. Oh. . . . Are you the courier from the War Department?"

Magnus II knew immediately why neither he nor WeeDee nor Jamie had been asked to visit their father in Washington.

"No, I'm not."

"Oh. . . . Well, what is it?" She took on a slight presumption of power as hostess of the house. Magnus II smiled at it. She was a girl, with firm tits and ass, wrapped in cashmere, the perfect package for a lot of old guys who fantasized plugging daughters or child nymphs.

"I'd tell you what it is, but I think it'd scare you to death. I'm Magnus Macpherson, I'm looking for my father." He loved her flustered reaction.

"You are?" she said, blushing very red. "Well, golly, come in. He's not here, but . . . I'm Iris Fowler, your dad's assistant."

"His what?"

"Assistant."

"Oh." He smiled at her. She blushed again, uneasy rather than embarrassed.

"Don't you want to come in?"

"Sure."

As they walked into the living room off the foyer, Iris tried to be a hostess. It was her house, but somehow his being there took it away from her.

"Do you want a glass of milk or tea or something?"

"I drink vodka when I drink, but I don't want anything now. Nice house. Have you been here long?" Again he smiled, this time with apparent friendship, which confused her.

"You mean today?"

"No, I don't mean today."

"Well, I don't live here."

"You don't?"

"No!" She laughed too quickly.

"Oh. Too bad. Nice house."

He held her look, not letting it get away without an admission.

"Well, I live nearby." Relieved, she turned away.

"Nearby?"

"Over the garage." She made a throwaway gesture with her arm, as if the garage might as well have been in Tibet. She turned to look at him just as he began laughing.

" 'Over the garage'! Perfect. I love it." He walked over to her and took her hand, still laughing. "Fine. Don't worry. It's all right." He held on to her hand easily, not intimately, more like shaking hands with a friend. Iris felt relieved. She had not admitted to anyone that she was anything more to Magnus than his assistant. She knew people probably suspected something. But it was a forbidden subject, something unspoken, and the secret had exhausted her. Now she wanted to tell him everything and believe that she could trust him. He was Magnus' son; it was almost like having a brother.

"You're just not at all like I thought you'd be," she said.

"How did you think I'd be?"

"Well, younger. I keep thinking of you in prep school."

"You're exactly what I thought you'd be."

His hold on her hand changed; she took hers away and crossed her arms across her breasts, saying, "Did you know about me, before today?"

"No. I just know my father. . . . Whatever happened to Evelyn Lorraine? I thought that was still going on?"

Iris went to straighten the magazines on the coffee table. "They still have a kind of friendship."

"The screwing kind or the other kind?"

He sprawled on the brown velvet couch and put his feet on it. She could feel him looking at her.

"Iris."

"Yes?" She didn't look at him. Instead, she rearranged the flowers on the sideboard.

"Stop worrying."

"I'm not worrying. You just don't need to talk like that." She turned around and faced him, her lips tightening.

"Like what?" He put on a little-boy look and spoke with adolescent earnestness. "Holy cow, Iris, everyone knows there are screwing friendships and then all the other kinds. . . . Like ours, for instance."

The front door opened. From where she stood, Iris could see it was Magnus. He smiled, then noticed the tense look on her face. Again she crossed her arms.

"What is it, Iris?"

She tried to snap into some semblance of gaiety. "Look who's here. You have a visitor."

Magnus came into the living room and saw his son on the couch. "Hello, Fa." He didn't move.

Magnus glanced at Iris to see if he could tell what had happened before he came in.

"Aren't you surprised, Magnus? I thought he was the courier from the War Department, who never came, by the way. And what are you doing home so early?"

"It's quite a surprise. How are you, Magnus?"

"I'm fine, Fa. *How* are *you?*" The emphasis was careful but unpleasant.

Magnus turned to Iris.

"I have a meeting at eight that'll last forever. I need some food."

Iris was relieved to retreat into efficiency.

"A drink first?"

"Fine."

She turned to Magnus II and spoke as if she had never seen him before that moment.

"Would you like some dinner, too . . . ? Well, what am I going to call you two, with two Magnuses in the house?"

"Just call me Magnus, and dinner sounds fine." He then turned the smile to his father. "And vodka with ice, and a lot of olives."

Iris walked out of the room, her arms still crossed, her shoulders hunched up and rounded.

Magnus sat down across the coffee table from his son. For a moment he felt gratified that Magnus II was sitting there, no matter how contemptuous he was. Perhaps Princeton would meld him into a man who could be liked. That was why Magnus had taken all the trouble to get the boy admitted, donating the science wing, and having letters sent from the Church of Scotland attesting that Magnus Macpherson II was the grandson of a Presbyterian cleric. The boy also had received excellent grades, and one glowing recommendation from a particular headmaster.

"To what do we owe this visit?"

"I decided to give myself a birthday present."

"Did you get my check?"

"Yes."

There was a pause as they both remembered the significance of checks between them.

"Eighteen, isn't it?"

"Yes. I registered for the draft."

Magnus nodded. "I suppose they'll let you finish the school year."

"They might, they might not. The draft's a bureaucracy, and you know bureaucracies. That's what I wanted to talk to you about, Fa." He put his feet down on the floor, and with elbows on his knees, leaned into the conversation. "I know I'll make an atrocious soldier. I doubt if I can keep step, and if they give me a gun, I'll shoot six officers and blow off my own foot. But I don't think they're going to believe me when I tell them."

"No, I don't think they will." Magnus chuckled as Iris came in with their drinks and a small bowl of olives. Magnus thanked her; Magnus II did, too. He picked up an olive, dunked it in the vodka, and ate it. "I don't like vodka much, but it makes a great dip for the olives."

Iris looked at Magnus and went back toward the kitchen.

"She's very nice, Fa. Very . . . sweet." He fished for another olive and continued. "Where was I? Oh. Yes, me in the army, if you can imagine anything more *lu*dicrous. It seems to me I would be a walking disaster. I wouldn't be helping my country, or the army, or myself, if I were in the infantry. It seems to me my talents lie in other areas."

Magnus took a large swallow of his malt. He felt it go down his throat with the familiar burn. When it hit his stomach, it turned to acid and did nothing for the uncomfortable anger which spread through him.

"What is it you want, then?"

Magnus II was caught by the question with an olive held in midair. He dropped it in the vodka, lifted the glass to his father, and took a swallow. "I have to admit, Fa, you're very fast. . . . It seems to me that I could really be useful to the army if they found the right place for me. I've been looking into it, and I think I've found the perfect place: the Quartermaster Corps. I have a family background of pretty high-powered administration, and my record shows some impressive organizing skills."

"Yes. Group cheating, and running whores in Connecticut."

Magnus II blinked and smiled. "Oh, you heard about that. . . ."

"Yes, I did. Now, let's get down to it. You've told me your recommendation of yourself, but you still haven't told me what it is you want of me."

"Well, Fa," Magnus II said with amused exasperation, "I'm sure you can figure *that* out. I want to be commissioned and assigned to the QMC. You know everybody and can arrange it. That's what I want, obviously."

He grinned as boyishly as possible, then picked out another olive.

"No," Magnus said.

" 'No'? What's that supposed to mean?"

"I don't think you're a coward."

Magnus II scoffed. "No, Fa, I am not a coward." He ate the olive. "So what do you mean?"

"Then what are you, besides having 'impressive organizing skills'?"

Magnus II sighed deeply at the impending lecture.

"Oh dear, Fa. You tell me." He sank back into the couch.

"I think you have a virgin ass. Nobody's been smart enough to get around to kicking it yet. The army's a place where intelligence is no barrier against getting your ass kicked. And there's no one I know who needs it more than you."

"That's ludicrous!" Magnus II put his glass down hard on the coffee table.

"You like that word."

"It seems to fit this conversation. You're going to stick me in the infantry for the duration because you want me to have a little discipline? Now? My discipline was your problem a long time ago. Don't use me to make up for your failings as a father."

"I'm aware of those failings and regret them. You're spoiled, selfish, and, I think, indulgent. I'd be a worse parent if I helped you go on that way without getting your ass kicked for it. You're right; I should have done it. And I'll tell you something else: I hate privilege. There's no one in this world who deserves special treatment for doing nothing. Why should you?"

"Do you want to see me dead, Fa? Because that's what we're talking about. Any poor jerk can get blown apart if he's on the front lines. And that's where the poor jerks are." He sat back on the couch, picked up his glass, and put his feet up again. "Well, if you won't help me, I'll just find someone who will." He smiled. "And you know I can do that, don't you?"

"Find who you will and they can help you to hell. But I'll do nothing for you."

Magnus II stopped smiling and slowly pointed his finger at his father. "You're scared, aren't you, Fa? Do you know how scared you are, that sooner or later you're going to die and I'm going to have everything you've got."

"Please don't point your finger at me," Magnus said quietly.

"You're going to die. You're already getting old." He pointed toward the kitchen. "She's not going to change that. And I'm your oldest son, so you're working for me already. And that's why you'd like to get rid of me, isn't it? Isn't it?"

"Don't point your finger at me."

"I'm pointing at you, because *you're* my father, *you* forgot about me, and now *you're* scared shitless because *you* look at me and know *you're* going to die. *You* killed my mother; of course you're going to try—"

As Iris came in to announce dinner, Magnus reached over and grabbed his son's finger. He yanked him sprawling across the coffee table, which split and collapsed under his weight. Magnus switched his grip on the finger so he was able to bend it back to the point of breaking it, forcing his son to stay on his knees.

The pain was so intense, tears came to Magnus II's eyes. He opened his mouth, but allowed no admission of pain.

"Get up." Magnus jerked the finger, forcing his son to his feet. "Before you go, I want to tell—"

"Oh I'm going now, Fa?"

"You are. I wanted to throw you out when I came in. Not because of manners—I can't expect you to be considerate of me—but because it was my couch and I didn't want your feet on it."

"So sorry, 'Dad.'"

Magnus jerked the finger back; Magnus II yelped and fell on his knees in the foyer.

Iris called, "Magnus . . ." from the door of the living room and shook her head for him to stop. Magnus looked down at his son.

"I'll stop, but I want to tell you, never . . . never mention your mother to me again." His rage moved him to quickly open the door and shove Magnus II, still on his knees, outside. In doing so, he lost his balance, slipped on the top step, and fell after his son. At the bottom, they both struggled up, to find themselves sitting on the ground facing each other. Magnus abruptly reached out and grasped his son in his arms and hugged him. They were quiet for a moment until Magnus II began to laugh. His father let go of him and awkwardly got up and went up the stairs, where Iris was standing.

Magnus II remained on the ground, leaned back on his arms, and casually crossed his legs at the ankle. "Really, Fa. You don't think a quick hug will make up for it, do you?" He laughed. "For what you've done, and haven't done, Fa, I'm grateful. I like being this way. So does WeeDee. She's a drunk. And 'Jesuit Jamie,' oh, my God . . ." He let his head fall back, and lay there laughing.

Magnus watched from the top of the steps. He felt Iris' hand urging him inside; he followed her, having no sense of resistance. She walked Magnus into the dining room and sat him down in front of his dinner.

"I'll go see if he's all right," she said, and hurried back to the front door. Magnus stared at the place set across the table from his. Wee-Dee. What the hell did he mean by that? He pushed his chair back hard enough to tip it over and went to the telephone in the kitchen.

Outside, Magnus II was beginning to get up when he heard the front door open. Iris came down the steps.

"Are you all right?"

"I think so, except my leg."

"Here. Let me help you."

She reached down and took his hand. He pulled himself up, but did not release her hand. Then he pulled her to him and kissed her, forcing his tongue between her teeth. He pinched her breast. She beat at him, bit down at his tongue, kicked at his legs. When he let her go, she ran up the steps and opened the door before turning to see what he was doing.

He was just watching her, smiling pleasantly. "Good night Iris; see you again." Then he turned and walked away.

Iris went into the house, closed the door, and locked it. She hated him. He was a horrible person. Then she realized her excitement; she was damp between her legs. She heard Magnus on the phone in the kitchen and went to join him.

"But, Kristin, what did he mean? . . . Yes, he was angry, but that's the point. He wouldn't make up something to hurt me. He'd use the truth, don't you see? . . . You've never seen her drink? . . . Kristin, I'm not blaming you. Listen to me. I want you to go up to Ethel Walker on Friday and get her out for the weekend. Then bring her down to Washington. I want to talk with her. . . . No, I won't presume anything. . . . I just want to talk with her. . . . Good. Thank you, Kristin." He hung up and slowly put one hand over his eyes. Iris took a step; he heard it and quickly took his hand away. He turned around, and she came into his arms.

"Oh, Magnus, I love you so much. I do. I do love you." She believed it. So did he. As she clung to him, her excitement was forgotten.

When her Aunt Kristin arrived at school, WeeDee had no opportunity to stash any liquor in her suitcase for the trip. She knew something was up and was on her guard during the train ride. She pumped her Aunt Kristin for information, but learned nothing about why all of a sudden she was visiting her father in Washington.

When they reached the house, she understood Iris' presence as quickly as her brother had. Kristin, on the other hand, did not, or chose not to. She advised Magnus to find the girl another place to live or people might talk. Magnus spoke with his daughter, took her out to dinner, offered her a drink, and wine with meals. He saw absolutely nothing to indicate she'd ever tasted alcohol. In fact, at the restaurant, she asked to taste the wine, then scrunched up her nose distastefully and went back to her milk. Magnus exchanged a look with Kristin and smiled. They did not notice that WeeDee's napkin was knotted and damp with sweat from her hands.

By late Saturday night, WeeDee could not hold out any longer. She crept downstairs from her bedroom, took a bottle of Century and the keys to the car Iris used for errands. She went to the garage and drove out. Iris, sleeping in her room for appearance sake, heard the car go, and went to the house to tell Magnus. After several hours, Magnus called the police.

When she had consumed a third of the bottle, WeeDee decided she had drunk enough to last through the night and started back to Georgetown. Another third in the bottle remained for after breakfast, which she could cover up with mouthwash. The final third would get her through the train trip back to school. If Aunt Kristin went with her, she figured she could chew gum and drink in the john.

The pickup truck hit her when she was nearly home, spun her car around, then careened across the intersection and crashed into another car. WeeDee's car came to rest on its side. She did not know the pickup had run through a stop sign, that the driver had been drunk, and was dead from a fractured skull. She could see him rammed through the windshield. Her bottle of whiskey had smashed and soaked her clothes. She crawled out of the car before anyone took notice of her. Clutching her purse, she walked away, shaking from shock and fear of what she had done.

Within fifteen minutes the Washington police had contacted Magnus. He called Double Gibson and asked him to keep it out of the papers if he could. By the next morning Gibson had ascertained that there were to be no charges against WeeDee, as a witness had seen the accident, and the dead man's blood sample showed a high percentage of alcohol. Magnus again notified the police, this time about a missing person.

Gibson obtained a copy of the accident report and sent it over to Magnus with the following line circled in red: "Second vehicle had broken bottle of whiskey over front-seat area." The Washington papers barely made note of the smashup, their columns filled with news of victory, of Bradley and Montgomery pushing Rommel's troops out of North Africa. Magnus retained Washington's most prestigious private-detective agency to find his daughter, wherever she had gone.

She had not gone far. When she walked away from the overturned automobile, she needed a drink badly. She had three in the first bar she saw, then paid the bartender triple to buy her own bottle. Afterward she had barely enough money left to pay in advance for a room in a sleazy hotel. She drank half the bottle before she fell asleep. She finished the rest when she woke up. She felt better, went out, and bought a paper. She saw nothing about the accident, nothing about her. She felt even better and went into a liquor store. Using the false identification she had accumulated at school, WeeDee not only succeeded in buying another quart of whiskey but with a smile convinced the man to cash a fifty-dollar check.

She stayed in the hotel for three days, going out of her room only to use the toilet down the hall or to go back to the liquor store for another bottle. It was the first time she had ever had as much as she wanted to drink. On the third day, her hands began to shake, so she could barely pour from the bottle. She began to vomit anything she drank, and soon noticed that the bile she retched up had red in it.

She sat in the hotel room on the single wooden chair and cried, feeling stabbing pains in her stomach, which she could relieve only by bending over and lying on the floor. She could not stand the pain it took to go down the hall to the toilet, so she vomited on the floor where she lay. For a while the pain stopped. She lay quietly, surprised at the brilliance of the red color spattered in front of her. Then she saw the snakes under the bed and began to scream.

She had thrown away all identification that gave any hint of who she really was. When the hospital authorities checked the I.D. she did have and found it false, they notified the police, who notified Magnus.

At four in the morning he and Kristin found WeeDee, heavily sedated, in a ward with glucose injected into her arm. There were abrasions on her face and arms, and her skin was sallow. The ward was for violent patients, with mesh over windows and bars and locks at both ends. Because of the war, there were not enough nurses and some of the staff were too old for the overwhelming amount of work.

Magnus found two chairs, and they sat next to WeeDee's bed, each holding a hand. Many of the other patients were strapped to their beds. WeeDee didn't move, and barely breathed.

While he arranged in his mind how he would have her moved to a private room, and which doctors he would call, Magnus was also trying to figure some way to express his regret and sorrow. He did not blame himself for Magnus II or Jamie becoming what they were. But WeeDee, lying there, her red hair matted, was doing damage to herself for reasons which he was certain were directly involved with him.

"Magnus, I'm so very, very sorry." Tears pouring down Kristin's cheeks. "I failed."

"Stop it, Kristin." He said it sharply. "I was the one who neglected her, not you."

The sound of his voice disturbed WeeDee. She began tossing her head back and forth, a desperate frown on her face. Then her eyes opened, and she started to whimper at the sight of her father, putting out her arm to protect herself. The glucose needle popped out of her vein. Two nurses hurried up, one with a hypodermic. They injected her, and she was out before the needle left her arm.

The nurses asked them to leave. Magnus put his arm around Kristin, and together they walked out of the ward.

A day and a half later WeeDee returned to consciousness. She was in a private room; there were flowers. She rang for the nurse, who appeared quickly.

"Could you bring me some water and some writing paper and a pen?"

"Yes, of course. How do you feel?"

"I feel punk, but I'll live. . . . Please, the paper. . . ."

"How does your stomach feel?"

"It's sore, but it's O.K. Look, I've got to have that paper. If you won't get it, I'll have to—"

She started to get up. "You stay in that bed, young lady!" WeeDee felt too weak to move and realized there was an intravenous needle in one arm.

"Please. The paper."

The nurse nodded, then went out.

WeeDee had awakened with the pieces of her life in some kind of order. She wanted to get them down on paper before they became muddled again. She didn't know if she could write it; she wished she could talk to someone. She would write as if she were talking. But to

250

whom? The nurse arrived with the pen and paper, and WeeDee began to write in her square, precise handwriting:

Dear Father Montier,

I hope you'll remember me. You'll probably remember my parents, the Macphersons. You helped my mother a lot. But it doesn't matter if you remember or not, and please, don't feel you have to answer this. It's only important for me to write it.

I'm going to be seventeen in two weeks. I've been drinking since I was ten. I'm in a hospital now because I guess I went on a binge after getting into a wreck. I think the other driver was killed. That was about four or five days ago. I woke up just now, and realized there were some things I had to say to somebody. I feel like I've lived behind a log jam that kept getting more and more clogged. Nothing was flowing—except the whiskey that was flowing through me. Ha-ha.

Later. Some doctors just left. They don't have to operate on my stomach. They asked if I was strong enough to talk to the police. They said someone was killed in the wreck. I can't think about that now. I just woke up—the log jam had broken open. I know there's probably a lot of trouble ahead, but none of it matters, except one thing: the idea of it happening again. . . . Does any of this make sense? I'm tired.

Later. I went to sleep. The policeman woke me. A man *was* killed in the wreck, but it wasn't my fault. I know what caused the log jam and I have to tell someone. I chose you because you're a priest (I'm not a good Roman Catholic) and you're a doctor who worked with crazy people and I'm probably crazy so I have the feeling you'll understand. Also, you know about my mother. I've got to start writing fast because it's so clear right now. I've always believed my brother Magnus and I killed my mother. That was the log jam. It got thicker and thicker and scarier, too, and the only way to forget was drinking, because there wasn't anybody else except my brother. I felt like he and I were together, because we'd done it. I know she killed herself. But what nobody knows is that the night of the party when she died—were you there? I can't remember—before it started, Mother and I went up to get Magnus II. He was in his room dressed like Jesus on the cross, made up with fake blood and everything. He accused her of forgetting Him. That's why she did it; she felt she'd betrayed Jesus and that it would be impossible for her not to betray Him if she lived her life. So she ended it.

I just thought of something else. I went on this bender because I thought I might have killed someone in that wreck. Maybe I was trying to kill myself as punishment. Could that be so? If so, I'm really crazy.

I never told anybody about what Magnus did that night. That secret was the log jam, I couldn't move anywhere beyond it. I tried to stay close to my brother, but he scared me. (He still does!) So I was pretty much alone, with my bottle. Ha-ha.

But I didn't kill my mother! I'm not even sure if Magnus II really did. She killed herself, probably for more reasons than I'll ever know. But that secret was tying me to her. Yes! See? I'm writing so fast I hope you can read it.

I just thought of something else! The way I chose to do it. My father's whiskey. I never drank anything else. Since I killed his wife, I was killing myself with something he made, so it would be like he killed me, because—I *am* crazy—I wanted him to because I killed his wife! Can that possibly be true? I don't care if it's possible or not, I'm pretty sure that's the way it was with me.

So here I am. I just saw myself in the mirror and couldn't believe it. I must look thirty. That stuff works on your face. I don't know what I'm going to do, but I think I'm not going to drink anymore.

Thank you for reading this. I won't even know if you did or not. But thank you for being there.

Sincerely yours,
Eleanor Macpherson
(WeeDee)

WeeDee sealed the letter, bought stamps from the nurse, and waited until she could walk down the hall at the end of the week to drop it in a mail slot. As she was walking back down the hall, a woman came up to her, called her by name, and asked if WeeDee had ever heard of Alcoholics Anonymous.

Magnus went to see his daughter every day on his way to work. Their conversations were formal, distant. Every morning, he appeared at the door of the room carrying a small nosegay of flowers, determined to let his daughter know his regret. But though she greeted him pleasantly, she kept a careful distance. She had apologized for her behavior, but in the lifeless terms of a treaty. She thanked him each day for the flowers, the specialists, the psychiatrist. When the pauses became silences, Magnus would say, "Well, then . . . ," kiss her on the cheek, and hurry down to his car.

Aunt Kristin came once before she went back to East Hampton and made WeeDee promise she'd come "home" for summer vacation. WeeDee lied and promised she would. She never wanted to go back there again.

After ten days WeeDee was released from the hospital and went to her father's to stay until she was ready to return to school. She smiled to herself as she noticed that there were no longer any signs of liquor in the house. She was given a guestroom next to her father's. For the first few days Iris had made up all kinds of excuses for coming in to see how she was.

WeeDee went to two meetings of Alcoholics Anonymous. She was picked up and escorted by the woman who had come to see her in the hospital. In the second meeting, she stood up herself to admit as is the custom: "I am an alcoholic." But from that point on, she made no sense, and finally stopped trying. ". . . I guess I better leave."

"You don't have to," the moderator of the group said.

"Yes I do. I feel weak and thirsty, and being in here isn't going to help. Admitting I'm an alcoholic lets me off the hook of finding out *why* I'm an alcoholic. That's what I have to do."

She started out of the hall. The moderator stood and talked as she left. "We urge you to come back, Eleanor, as soon as you can. We'll call you. We'll pray for you. . . ."

Outside, WeeDee began to shake. She could feel sweat on her face; her blouse and underwear were soaked. Above all, she wanted a drink. The craving was unbearable.

The woman who had contacted her in the hospital came out and joined her on the sidewalk, but before she could speak, WeeDee said, "I don't want you to come with me. This is for me to do."

"You might want some help."

"Then I'll find it."

"I can't let you just—"

"If you follow me, I'll call the police."

"Call them. They understand about us."

WeeDee pushed her as hard as she could and sent the woman sprawling over the sidewalk. WeeDee started running, turned a corner, crossed a street. She could hear the woman coming after her, calling that strange name "Eleanor." She turned another corner and ducked into an alley, then a doorway behind some garbage cans. When she heard the woman run past, she jumped out of her hiding place and ran back the way she had come. She had noticed a bar down a street she had passed, and that was where she had to go.

After realizing she had lost WeeDee, the woman called the Macpherson home. Magnus answered and immediately phoned the police again. When he slammed the receiver down, Iris asked, "What happened?"

"WeeDee ran away from the A.A. meeting. The woman, Mrs. What's-her-name, thinks she might go drinking again."

"Oh, no. . . ."

"And this time when we find her, I'll put her in a place that'll dry her out and cure her. That's the trouble with weakness; it's unpredictable. Get me the detective agency on the line, then call Dr. Smedberg and get three names of sanatoriums for . . . drunks! Goddamn!"

"Magnus, wait, I want—"

But Magnus ignored her. "Iris, I am given children and I *can't see* them. There's a blind spot like I'm looking into the sun. I can see all around them, but when I look at them . . . nothing. I close my eyes and I see WeeDee's red hair, but not her. I have a weak child, and I know nothing about her weakness. I can make her sober, but I can't make her strong."

Iris, not knowing if she were interrupting or not, said quickly, "I don't think she's weak."

"Then what in all hell is she? Millions of people drink, Iris. Only a few of them are drunks. And if she runs away from A.A., I don't know what to do with her. I don't know who she is. . . . I know my foreman in Pittsburgh better than I know either of my sons. . . . I didn't even know Mary when she . . . died."

He stopped pacing and saw Iris watching him, leaning against the counter, her arms folded in front of her. They were in the kitchen again. They seemed to spend more time there than anywhere else in the house. Iris suggested once they move the bed down next to the icebox so they wouldn't have to leave.

"Iris . . ." He reached out his arms. She came into them, and he held her a long time before he said, "You know how much I love you."

"Tell me anyway."

"Very much. As much as I can love. . . . But don't ever want to

254

marry me, because if we do that, I'm afraid I'll lose you behind that blind spot with the others."

She did not move. They had never mentioned the subject of marriage. She had thought about it and had several dreams of an enormous wedding attended by President Roosevelt and several kings and queens. But she never believed it would really happen. She didn't mind hearing it never would, but she thought that she wouldn't have any more dreams, and she would miss them.

Magnus held her away to try to see what she was thinking. She smiled up at him and said, "You'll never lose me, Magnus. No matter what, I'm going to love you just like I do right now . . . always."

They went upstairs together for a time, but Magnus was restless and couldn't go to sleep. He decided to do some work, and went down to his study, hoping the phone would ring. Iris went over to her room to get a copy of *The Saturday Evening Post,* which had a new serial she wanted to read. When she switched on the light in the garage, she heard someone else breathing and almost screamed.

"It's me, Iris, WeeDee."

She was sitting on the steps which led up to Iris' room.

"WeeDee! What are you . . . ? Everyone's looking for you." Then Iris remembered and wondered how drunk WeeDee was. WeeDee saw her apprehension and smiled.

"Don't worry, I'm not drunk. I drew the line. . . . I drew the line. Iris, I don't know you very well, but I need a friend right now."

"You don't want me to tell Magnus you're here, do you?"

"Not right now. In about an hour."

"He's so worried . . ."

"He can take it; I need the hour."

The two women looked at each other. Iris said, "Come upstairs."

WeeDee sat very straight in the crewelwork armchair; Iris pulled up a stool and sat opposite her.

"What I meant by drawing the line—and I want you to tell my father this—I ran away from the woman who took me to A.A., I guess you know that."

Iris nodded.

"I went to a bar. I had to go there to draw the line, like standing on a cliff or holding a knife blade." She thought of her mother. "I asked the bartender for a shot of Century whiskey. He didn't even ask for an I.D. I guess I look old enough to drink." She looked at Iris and saw her lips tighten against offering an opinion.

"He put it down in front of me and left me alone with it. That's where we all stop, I guess, alone with the decision. You could have cut out my tongue so I couldn't taste it, pulled out my eyes so I wouldn't see it. God, you could have cut off my head, and my mouth would have still wanted that shot of whiskey. But if I drank it, I knew I'd go over. . . . And I figured this time I wouldn't be getting back. So I stuck my finger in the shot glass and drew a line in front of me on the bar. It was crooked as hell, because my hand was shaking. But I drew it, and I *know*—and tell my father this: I'll never go over it."

That truth catalyzed a friendship. She would never take a drink again; they would always be friends. There were no congratulations; they shared certainty.

"What are you going to do now, WeeDee?"

"I have to go away."

"Where?"

"Wherever they send me. The war. I have to get away from this family."

"I understand." She didn't really, never having had a family.

"Iris, do you have any money? I had to walk home because you guys took away all my dough."

Iris sprang up, and collected fifty-two dollars from her purse and several books where she kept secret cash.

"When can I tell Magnus?"

WeeDee thought a moment. "What did you come over here for?"

"A magazine."

"To read here?"

"I could have."

"All right. Give me about an hour. Then tell him everything, except about the money. I don't want you to get into any trouble."

"He'll keep trying to find you."

"I know. I'm ready for that. Tell him I came back to let him know I'm all right and that . . . I've missed him for a long time. . . ."

They hugged each other, and went down to the garage together. Iris watched WeeDee slip away into the darkness. Then Iris went back to her room. She thought a long time about her new friendship and decided that WeeDee was wrong about something. If Magnus knew she had been there, if he knew she was going to do something in the war, he might be able to find her before she was safely away. Iris decided to wait an entire day. And when the day passed, she saw no reason not to wait another. Magnus was worried, having accepted the inevitable fact that WeeDee was drinking herself to oblivion somewhere. But Iris wanted her friend to have the extra time. Besides, she loved secrets. Finally, after three days, she called Magnus at his office and told him WeeDee had just been there and had left.

By that time, WeeDee was at a Red Cross training center at Fort Dix, New Jersey, under a different name, learning how to be a recreation worker. She had been fitted with the gray-blue uniform and looked quite snappy (and old enough) in her visored cap. She had already heard that her group was going to be shipped out as quickly as they could be trained. According to the rumor, "Ike" Eisenhower was planning an invasion from North Africa to Sicily.

The letter WeeDee sent to Father Montier arrived at St. Bridget's Asylum in Quebec and remained unopened for several weeks. Father Montier had succumbed to what his order referred to as "a lapse of faith" over four years before. The stigma of a priest leaving the Church in those days was so great that Father Montier staged his own death by leaving his cassock, shoes, cloak, and suicide note on a quay beside the shore of the St. Lawrence River. He then disappeared. Such "suicides" were immediately suspect by the Church, and such priests were regarded as anathema.

The letter was therefore finally returned to the hospital in Washington on whose stationery it was written. There it languished for several weeks until an overworked secretary opened it. She read the first few lines and came to the name "Macpherson." She checked the postmark, found the patient list on that date, and forwarded the letter to its sender, care of Thirty-fifth Street in Georgetown.

Iris opened all the mail which arrived at the house. After the first few lines she knew she had another secret to keep. She was shocked by what she read about Magnus II; it made her remember his tongue in her mouth. She hid the letter in a book in her room.

12

Greetings. Having submitted yourself
to a local board composed of your
neighbors for the purpose of determining
your availability for training and
service in the land or naval forces of
the United States, you are hereby notified
that you have now been selected for
training and service therein.
                    —THE SELECTIVE SERVICE BOARD

On May 11, 1943, Albert Anastasia, previously of the Brooklyn docks, became a sergeant in the United States Army at the training center at Indiantown Gap, Pennsylvania. He had joined the army to escape the heat of prewar syndicate activity involving a Murder, Inc., slaughter of some thirty-five people. Three days later, he became a staff sergeant; one month later, his military career peaked and he was promoted to technical sergeant. In that position, Anastasia had unique talents which his superior officers learned quickly to respect. He was relieved of many of his duties so he could better service the officers' club. By the time Magnus Macpherson II arrived in Pennsylvania, Sergeant Anastasia had a firm hold on every operation on the base.

Magnus II was there for two weeks before Anastasia discovered him. Bitter and angry, the boy had pulled every string to avoid the draft. Now his only hope was his Uncle Juny, who was working through a congressman to have Magnus II transferred to Special Services, the USO entertainment division.

In the meantime, Magnus II managed to get his ass kicked, quite literally, by refusing to get out of bed one morning. He drew K.P. and became familiar with cleaning toilets, urinals, and other plumbing around his barracks. Even so, he soon found six yardbirds who understood that money could make the U.S. Army a better place. Four of them were from Jersey and two were from the Bronx, and they immediately understood that Magnus II was dealing in reefers.

Marijuana had been one of Magnus II's few business failures at

Princeton. At the time, reefers were too exotic for the Ivy League. The U.S. Army, however, presented a different consumer; any vice to relieve basic training was fine. Magnus II had a sizable delivery of raw materials made to him, and he set his six colleagues to work rolling cigarettes. Within a week they were in business, supplying a carefully screened clientele.

Two days later Magnus II was cleaning a urinal, considerably more content than he had been. As he was thinking about clearing ten thousand by the time Uncle Juny got him out, four hands grabbed him. They threw him backward onto the row of toilets, hit him in the gut, and pushed his face to the floor. They held him in that position with their boots on his spine and the back of his neck.

Magnus II was smart enough not to move anything except his head. He squeezed it around to look at two other feet coming across the floor. He had not mopped up around the toilets that morning, but he was too scared to worry about what his face was wiping up. He had never before been scared.

"Your name Magnus Macpherson?" There was an accent, but no emotion.

"Who?" he said through teeth clenched by the foot on his neck.

"The Second?"

"You think there's two like me?" He laughed weakly.

There was a silence; then the foot on the back of his neck was raised. Someone grabbed his hair and yanked his face over to a wet section of the floor, pressed his cheek in and pinned his nose down. Then the other heel went back on his neck and pressed.

"No more jokes. Your father. He makes whiskey?"

"Yes."

The heel lifted.

"So Macpherson's kid supplies the gongers in my camp. Pick him up."

He was yanked up and stared into a thick face with heavy jowls and small hooded eyes. Sergeant Anastasia's gut stuck out over his belt, and his hands were fat and wet. He looked at Magnus II for a long time before he spoke.

"I don't know. What'll I do with you?" He shook his head. "I'm gonna wise you up. We got a lot of oil burners come through this place. They'll take anything, and we get it to them. We got Dr. Whites in here, witch-hazel boys, gold dusters, and dugouts. And we got gongers, too . . . like you're finding out."

Magnus II didn't know what the man was talking about, that oil burners were addicts, Dr. Whites used heroin, witch-hazel men smoked opium, gold dusters injected morphine, and dugouts ate yen-shee, the residue of smoked opium. He could only figure out what gongers used.

The sergeant talked very quietly, as if he were bored.

"So listen good, Magnus Macpherson the Second. This is my camp. I run it. You don't come in here with your own ideas."

"I didn't know anyone—"

"That's the trouble. Right there. You come to a place, you don't look around. You take for granted you're the fuckin' king of any-place lucky to have you. You got to learn, Magnus Second. That's what I'll call you. Magnus Second. And learn this." He leaned into Magnus II's face and yelled, "You come into my place without look-ing around, your eyes they stop working good!" He grabbed Magnus II's head with both his wet hands and pressed his thumbs on his eyes. Anastasia expected him to scream or pull away; he was ready to grab his hair and shove his mouth down on the enamel urinal to chip out some teeth.

But Magnus II didn't flinch or scream. He stood rigid under the pressure, sweating and breathing hard, but he didn't make a sound.

Anastasia was impressed. He took his hands away.

"I'll give you sixty percent of everything we make," Magnus II said.

Anastasia was even more impressed. "That's very generous."

"It's your place; I didn't know."

Anastasia watched him, then nodded. "Let him go." The two other men released Magnus II. They were both privates, very large privates.

"I still don't know what I'm going to do with you, Magnus Sec-ond. Do your business. I'll hear from you. But be careful. The army catches you, they shoot you."

"Who do I ask for when I want to see you?"

"I'm Albert Anastasia. You want to know about me, ask your old man." He started out of the head, followed by the two privates.

"I don't talk to my old man." Magnus II knew the name of Albert Anastasia and had the wit to figure he and his father were enemies for some reason he did not know.

Sergeant Anastasia turned around and looked at Magnus II. Then he shrugged. "Too bad. I guess it wouldn't be worth a couple a mil-lion to him to get you back if you was kidnapped."

Magnus II started laughing. "You'd get about two bits."

Anastasia nodded. "When you come see me about things, don't forget to salute. I like it."

Magnus II immediately braced and snapped a flashy salute. Anastasia walked out between the urinals and toilets.

For the next two weeks Magnus managed to see Sergeant Anastasia at least once a day. He not only delivered payments, he delivered the news: new oil burners who came on the base, a certain major with a drinking problem, a colonel's wife who had a predilection for privates who weren't circumcised, and a captain who was spreading rumors about Sergeant Anastasia and expressing a personal determination to get the sergeant locked up.

Anastasia was amused and grateful for the information. He was also flattered by Magnus II's apparent admiration, but at the time he was suspicious of everyone.

Magnus II eventually convinced Anastasia that he could be trusted by suggesting a deal. It involved the subversion of officers' clubs, base by base, in order to procure a large supply of black-market liquor. Magnus II would make the arrangements; all he needed from Anastasia was some political help with arranging his transfer to the Quartermaster Corps in Washington, and a quarter of a million dollars for corruption.

Anastasia listened to the numbers and was impressed. Officers' clubs could be a national racket which didn't conflict with other syndicate members' present territory. The clubs could be serviced through those members, with a share of profit from each going to Anastasia. What Anastasia enjoyed the most, however, was having Macpherson's kid working for him.

Three days before Magnus II finished basic training, he received orders to transfer immediately to the Presidio in San Francisco for his new assignment in Special Services. Uncle Juny had come through with a plum, but Magnus II turned it down. He explained his choice with a mixture of self-sacrifice and patriotism, which his Uncle Juny accepted with further admiration. Another set of orders had come through asking him to report to the Quartermaster General in Washington. Arrangements had been made for a small apartment at the Willard Hotel with two private phone lines which did not go through the hotel's switchboard.

Before Magnus II left Pennsylvania, Anastasia asked one last favor. During the war, the U.S. Army had a special program allowing aliens in uniform to become United States citizens. Umberto Anastasia, who had jumped ship in New York harbor in 1917, had never become naturalized. He therefore took advantage of the situation and asked Magnus II to stand up as a witness.

A driver took them to the courthouse in Lebanon, Pennsylvania. As they drove, Anastasia seemed a little nervous. "I wanted one of my brothers to come stand up with me, but . . . it'd get too much attention." Anastasia was dressed in his best uniform. It was sharply pressed, and his shoes were shined.

"I'm glad to do it if this is what you want to do."

"What'sat mean?"

"If it's so important to you to be an American."

"It is. It's a great country. It's been good to me and my family. Freedom's a great thing." Magnus II looked to see if there was the slightest irony on Anastasia's face. There was none. "I come here jumping off a ship like a rat. Nothing. Now I'm something. More than something. If I was in Calabria, pfhh, another turd in the road. America gives me everything, or if not, I can take it. A lot of people think I'm the Evil One. I piss on them; let them think. They forget me when I'm dead, and my children will have a good life to live here in America." He looked at Magnus II on the other side of the back seat. "Another thing, if I'm a legal citizen, they can't send me back to Italy; they have to take care of me here. And here, in America, I take care of myself."

The car drove up to the courthouse, and the two of them went to the office of the local judge. Magnus II stood bemused as Anastasia sucked in his stomach and held up his left hand.

". . . Do you solemnly swear to uphold the Constitution of the United States and all its laws?"

"I do."

After the ceremony, Anastasia drove to the bus depot with Magnus II.

"Congratulations," Magnus II said.

"Thanks."

"How does it feel?"

"I feel . . . a little nervous. I always get a little nervous in front of a judge."

Magnus II laughed, reached down under the front seat, and produced a bottle of champagne and two glasses.

"What's this?"

"A little celebration." Magnus II opened the bottle and poured.

"Magnus Second, you got class. . . . Hey, driver, stop the car and take a five-minute walk. Here, right here."

The car pulled over and parked. The driver got out and walked away.

"Sergeant, let me propose a toast: to your first American partnership, may it see you through your old age and me to my first million."

Anastasia drank.

"You'll make your million, Magnus Second; you don't have to worry. Except about one thing: attention. Don't get any. Do the job, stay invisible. I'm not going to look over your shoulder; my people tell me everything I need to know. But I'll be reading the Washington papers. I see one mention of you, you're out. I see two, you're hurt."

"I know that. Why are you worried?"

"You're a charmball, Magnus Second. You'll be great at parties, and knocking up senators' wives. You'll do fine. But don't get your name in the paper. It's bad for business."

"I'll be careful. But if your people tell you I'm making a few strange friends, don't worry. I plan to make a lot of friends; it's Washington insurance. If I get my name in the paper with some Supreme Court justice, it won't be bad business. It'll make it easier."

Anastasia shook his head. "Only for a while, then everyone's watching you. You make your friends, but stay out of the papers."

Magnus II shrugged. "O.K."

Anastasia took an envelope out of his pocket. "Here's for petty cash. Count it."

Magnus II counted fifty one-thousand-dollar bills, during which time the driver returned and took them to the bus depot.

"Don't forget, Magnus Second. Don't use your phones for business. Hoover will have an ear on them tomorrow."

Magnus II laughed. "You sound like an anxious father or something. I'm not a virgin, you know."

Anastasia turned fast, grabbed Magnus II's tie, and jerked him across the back seat.

"This is business. Don't forget it. I ain't no nervous father, but I know your old man, and that makes it a lot easier to waste you if you fuck up."

He held Magnus II long enough to be certain his meaning was clear. Then he let him go.

On the bus ride to Philadelphia, Magnus II tried to figure out what his father had done to gain Anastasia's hatred; one did not ask questions about the past of the head of Murder, Inc. Magnus II presumed they had known each other during Prohibition and suspected that they were more than business acquaintances.

He was right. In spite of liking him, Anastasia had taken him on with the idea that if the officers'-club scam didn't work, Magnus II's connection to it could be used effectively to bargain for the gun and the pictures of fingerprints which his father had in a safe-deposit box. Even if Macpherson hated his kid, a scandal, involving the underworld with the family name, a name on bottles all over the country, would be bad for business.

Magnus II knew he had to figure out what his father had that Anastasia wanted. Someone close to Magnus would have to be corrupted. Who? WeeDee? No. Who knew where she was? Jamie? The little Jesuit would faint dead away at the thought of sin. Aunt Kristin? The idea of corrupting Aunt Kristin was ludicrous. Evelyn Lorraine would have been perfect. But she and his father were not close enough anymore for her to really matter. That led Magnus II without pause to the obvious solution: Iris. Iris would not recognize corruption. She might even be curious. Yes.

Magnus II did not see Iris until Thanksgiving Day of 1943. By that time he had established himself as an efficient aide to his superiors in the Supply Division in the Quartermaster Corps, and as a useful extra at Washington's more glamorous parties. Both duties took dedication, but both promised gratifying rewards.

Through the Supply Division, Magnus II was in direct contact with the branch depots where all army procurements were stored, as well as the Motor Transport Division. With a certain amount of careful observation, bribery, and paperwork, liquor was released from the depots and transported to various selected officers' clubs all over the country. These officers' clubs were run by a major who agreed to accept twice as much liquor as was needed at his club. The extra booze would be sold at cost to the black market and then marketed at excessive prices to otherwise patriotic citizens who were in need because of the liquor shortage. The syndicate people who sold the black-market liquor gratefully paid Anastasia a commission.

An added fillip to the syndicate members was the opportunity to occasionally hijack a large order. Information about truck movement in a certain area could be supplied, and the stolen liquor was worth twenty thousand dollars if sold legally; on the black market its value doubled and sometimes tripled. Since hijackings could be spread over the entire country, the pattern of corruption could not be followed to its source. Besides, everyone was too busy fighting the war.

Magnus II's other success was social. He was single and dangerous-looking, which titillated the females. He was bright and not fawning in his attention to men. He always had bad news about everyone in Washington. His stories were amusing, usually bitchy, and often scandalous. He was rich and somehow had managed to get an apartment at the Willard in spite of the terrible housing shortage. In short, he was a hostess's dream.

For Magnus II, the parties were very useful; they allowed him to discover the weaknesses of people in power. Many of the men wanted young female flesh. Many of their wives wanted young male flesh. Their desires represented a lucrative method of gaining friendship. Magnus II knew secretaries who had come to Washington for the excitement of helping in the war and had ended up living with five other girls in a boardinghouse. He also knew male nurses who were looked down on as being cowards or pansies. Some secretaries were delighted to be put up in some small but blissfully private apartment by a government man with the power and money to afford it. The male nurses were just as willing to screw a general's wife. Magnus II realized a need for matchmaking and excelled at it.

The growing realization of depravity led him to the congressman who wore black female underwear under his bulky suits. Through this congressman Magnus II was introduced to a unique circle of Washington bureaucrats who gathered together at a private Virginia estate each weekend to wear female attire. There he became acquainted with the son of a powerful Southern senator who hated his father. The young man had not become anything ordinary like a homosexual, but rather, a necrophiliac.

Through a friendly male nurse Magnus made an arrangement with several ambulance drivers. When the ambulance picked up a corpse which had nowhere to go but to the morgue, the driver would make a detour to the senator's house, pick up the son, and let him ride along for the rest of the trip. The ambulance drivers received a bonus should the corpse be a black male.

Magnus II saw Iris for the first time across the carcasses of three Thanksgiving turkeys. The hostess was helping her guests crank a homemade-ice-cream freezer. The idea was pumpkin pie with butter pecan à la mode, but it was taking longer than expected. A Supreme Court justice was rapidly exhausting himself; and the hostess had an admiral and the Persian ambassador lined up to relieve him. Iris had been talking to a nice marine major who was telling about "his" war, when she glanced around trying to spot where Magnus was, and saw instead Magnus II. He didn't smile, he just watched, and went on listening to a very earnest wife of an undersecretary. Iris felt a flow of sweat and adrenaline. She tried not to look surprised, felt the blush coming, and turned away. Sensing him still watching her, she finally excused herself and went around the table on which the ten pumpkin pies waited and walked up boldly to Magnus II and the undersecretary's wife.

"Hello, Magnus." Iris held out her hand. He glanced down at it as if it were a growth and turned to his partner.

"I'll see what I can arrange, Gertrude. . . . Do you know Iris Fowler, my father's . . . assistant?"

Some mechanism clicked behind the woman's face, producing a good-Washington-wife smile and a practiced babble as Iris and Magnus stood looking at each other.

"He*llo,* Miss Fowler, no, I haven't met you but I'm delighted to do so. Your 'boss' is quite a mystery around town; perhaps later you'll tell me all about him if the ice cream *ever* freezes. Excuse me, will you, Magnus? Let me hear from you soon. Good-bye . . . may I call you Iris? You know, it's my absolute favorite flower." And she shifted easily across them to another group without waiting for replies.

"You don't have to say 'assistant' like that."

"Like what? Like you're screwing my father?"

"Don't say that."

"Why not?"

"It sounds terrible."

"Iris, everybody knows it, so don't let it bother you so much. *I* don't mind."

"I don't care if you do or not. There's just more to it than that."

"Tell me what more there is than that."

"I love your father."

"Oh, dear."

"Very much."

"We all need a father, Iris. Some more than others. I need mine less than you need mine . . . or yours, or whichever he is to you at the moment." He laughed.

She didn't understand because she didn't want to understand. She flushed again.

"You're disgusting. I wish I could hit you."

"Really?" He smiled with interest.

"You're rotten. Already. You're eighteen and you're rotten."

"You're twenty-one, and"—he looked down over her body—"ripe."

"Don't you dare touch me, ever!" Quicker than instinct, she realized and regretted what she said.

Magnus II was delighted and spoke with sarcastic innocence. "Touch you? Why would I touch you, Iris? Oh, I know why. . . . Because you want me to." He quickly grabbed her hand. She pulled at it as she looked around to see if anyone was watching.

"Let go of my—"

"Feel it, Iris. It's all right. Feel my finger go across your palm."

She drew in a startled breath and yanked her hand away, looking down at it almost expecting to see a stain. Then she turned back to Magnus II. He was smiling at her again, this time with no guile, rather as if he and she were children discovering a secret.

"Feels nice, doesn't it?"

She didn't know why, but she wanted to laugh. Instead, she hurried across the room to get away from him. Magnus was talking in another room, and she went up to him, interrupting the conversation. "Magnus, Magnus is here. Your son," she added as an explanation to the others.

"Where?"

"Through that door, in the den."

"What's he doing here?"

"I don't know, I didn't ask."

"You didn't?"

She had to look at him to see if he were angry. He was not, but she noticed he looked old. Not old. But . . . older.

"No. I didn't talk to him much. I don't like him."

At that moment she hated Magnus II, and as she watched his father move through the crowd lining up for the dessert which was finally ready, she loved him more than ever, for all he had done, for all he had been to her. At the same time, she noticed she was gripping her opposite thumb with the hand Magnus II had stroked. She let go and crossed her arms over her breasts as she went to the table for homemade pumpkin pie with butter-pecan ice cream on top.

"Magnus . . ."

"Hello, Fa." He had left the den and gone to the front door, hoping to avoid the meeting. But since he was caught, he tried to make the best of it. For the moment he wanted no tensions between them; it could endanger his current work and make his future plans more difficult. When the time came, Magnus II wanted every bit of surprise at his disposal.

"You look well in a uniform."

"Thanks, Fa." He smiled proudly. "Just about everyone does."

"What are you doing in Washington?"

"I'm with the Quartermaster Corps." He said it with no tinge of triumph.

Magnus' look darkened. "So you got what you wanted."

"I'm doing a good job, Fa. . . . And you'll be happy to know I got my ass kicked regularly getting there." There was no sarcastic malice; he said it as a joke to share with his father.

Magnus smiled. "Good."

"I've got to get going, Fa. I'm on duty in an hour."

"Where are you staying? You have everything you need?"

"Yes, sir." Magnus II thought the "sir" a brilliant touch of military respect, but it was a little too much.

"Where are you staying?"

Magnus II wanted to get out without answering the question. "I was really lucky. I found a hole in the wall at the Willard that they let me have for the duration." He kept glancing at the door as he talked. "And it *is* a hole. But it's convenient, and I can catch a bus to the Pentagon, so . . ."

"The Willard Hotel?"

"Fa, I really have to run." The "sir" was a mistake; he'd have to be more careful. His father was looking at him from behind the old distrust.

"I'm sure you do. But whatever it is you're doing to get yourself a room at the Willard, don't depend on me to get you out of it. I'm not keeping you in school any longer—"

"It's a hole in the wall, Fa. Good night. Happy Thanksgiving."

That night, Iris dreamed of Magnus II and cried out in her sleep. When she woke up, Magnus was holding her and she was afraid he had caught her sexual excitement. She might even have said "Magnus," but their names were the same, so it didn't matter. She rolled over and relieved the confusion she felt with his willing body.

By dawn Iris still could not fall back asleep. She feared dreaming again and saying something which Magnus would hear. Finally she slipped out of bed and took a sleeping pill. Dreamlessly she slept through the morning.

But the next night she dreamed again, and the next. She began taking sleeping pills before going to bed, hoping they would keep her mind free. But she could not stop the dreams, and found excuses to sleep in her own room.

Three days before Christmas, Iris was in Garfinckel's department store doing some last-minute shopping when she saw Magnus II again. He was on the other side of the perfume counter. He had not seen her, and she turned to escape before he did, but in turning she knocked a large bottle to the ground; it crashed, and a piece of glass cut her leg. She felt nothing; she was staring almost dazed at Magnus II, who looked up at the sound of the bottle breaking and then smiled at her. Iris began to move away, going backward, knocking people aside.

Magnus II gave cash to a saleslady for the broken bottle and went after her. The old doorman barely had time to open the front door before Iris ran blindly out into the snow. The cold hit her and she suddenly felt ridiculous. Still wanting to get away, she began walking up Fourteenth Street as quickly as she could without falling on the ice. When she heard him call her name, she broke into a run, slipped, and fell to the sidewalk. She tried to get up, but he was already standing above her, reaching his arms out to help her.

"Iris. Did you hurt yourself?"

She stared up at him, suddenly unable to breathe.

"Are you all right?" He looked genuinely worried. She barely nodded her head.

"Can you get up?"

She nodded again. He leaned down, and she felt the panic rising, but then saw his concern and let him pull her to her feet. For a few seconds he held on to her; then she pulled away, almost lost her balance again, and finally stood looking at him.

"Careful . . . You're shivering, Iris."

"I'm cold, I guess."

"I'm going to get you a drink."

"I don't—"

"Think of it as medicine. You need it. Come on. I don't live far from here."

"The Willard."

Only then did the mean smile appear. "Oh. You've heard."

She was going to suggest finding a taxi, but she didn't.

"Yes. I've heard."

"Well, then, you know where you're going. . . . Come on. I'll give you a brandy and put you in a cab if there is one. Here, hold on to me. If you break a leg while you're with me, that would really give Fa a shock."

He said it so honestly, she joined him laughing, then took a firm grip of his arm and walked the few slippery blocks to the Willard Hotel.

The hotel was very popular with politicians and businessmen, who treated it as a men's club. Magnus II took Iris in by way of the freight entrance, which was the route he always used. He did not wish to call attention to himself in the lobby of the Willard; that day he did not wish it to be known that Iris was visiting him. They used a staff elevator, and arrived at his door on the fourth floor.

"As holes in the wall go, it's pretty nice," he said as he ushered her into the apartment.

"It's . . . well, it's *very* nice. How in the world did you find it, Magnus? I know a woman who looked for six months and came up with a basement room with a coal chute still in it."

"I was lucky. Cognac?"

"Just a little swallow."

"I'm the doctor."

He laid their coats on a chair. As Iris got out of her galoshes, Magnus II went to the bar. The room was small, but beautifully furnished with thick drapes over the windows. There was a fireplace which didn't work, and a tiny Pullman kitchen. Apparently the bathroom and the bedroom were through the door. As she sat down in a big comfortable wing chair, she noticed there were two telephones on the desk.

"Here you are." Magnus II offered her a glass. There was a light burning just over his shoulder that made her squint.

"Thank you."

She took the glass from him. He wasn't smiling, just looking steadily down at her.

"What about us, Iris?"

She flushed.

"Are we going to be friends, or what?"

She took a swallow of cognac; it began as a simple burn in her mouth and grew white-hot down her throat to her stomach.

"Yes, of course," and she began to choke.

Magnus II let her cough; he didn't try to help. When she had finished, he waited for her to look at him again.

" 'Of course' what?"

Iris took another swallow of her drink. The phone began to ring, but Magnus II did not move to answer it. She looked over at the desk.

"Of course we're going to be friends. . . . Aren't you going to answer that phone?"

"No." The light behind him glared into her eyes. His head moved closer as the phone stopped ringing. She felt him come very close to her, and she thought she should say something, but no sound came. When she opened her mouth, his lips were on hers and she stopped trying to struggle as his tongue ran slowly down her neck, and his hand, even more slowly, lifted her skirt. Finally she found strength to reach a hand up to caress his face. She wondered if she had known it would happen, if she had hated him so much to keep it from happening.

There was a strange buzzing noise. Immediately he stood up and said, "I *have* to answer that," and went to the desk. Iris realized the second phone was making the noise.

"Rita Hayworth," Magnus II said into the phone. He had a pencil and paper ready, and wrote something down.

"Repeating: Mayflower 2760, subtract two."

Then he hung up and turned back to Iris.

"I'm sorry, Iris. I'm sorry that came when it did. Let's forget it. Can I get you some more medicine?"

It was all clear to her, the two phones, having rooms at the Willard, getting assigned to Washington: Magnus II was engaged in dangerous spy work for the OSS. She felt ashamed of having thought of him as an evil person. His behavior was so obviously a cover-up for what he really was, a very brave man who was probably risking his life for his country even as they were sitting there. She wanted to tell him how proud she was of him, how happy the news would make his father. Oh, yes, particularly that. But she knew she could say nothing to anyone. She had seen the war posters of sailors drowning and the gold star in a window, "Because Someone Talked." She wouldn't say a word. She reached out her glass to him. It was going to happen.

"Yes, Magnus, I want some more medicine."

"Rita Hayworth" meant Magnus II was on the line and that it was all right to talk. "Lana Turner" would have meant to nix the conversation. "Mayflower" meant "Pilgrim," the exchange in Pennsylvania of a pay phone. "2760, subtract two" was the number of the pay phone when 2 was subtracted from the second number, 7. Anastasia would be waiting there for Magnus II's call at eight, the third number plus two.

At the end of the hour, she slowly dressed. They said nothing. She watched him lying on the floor, and they smiled as she held up a piece of underwear and remembered when it tore. Finally she sat in the chair fully dressed. Still naked, he leaned against her, and together they finished a glass of cognac.

"I have to go," she said.

"Yes. When will you come back?"

"I can't come back; you know that."

He looked away as if she'd said something stupid.

"Iris, I know you'll be back. Always call first. If there's no answer, don't come."

She remembered his mission. "I won't, Magnus."

"I'll write the number down." He got up and walked over to the desk. She noticed details of his body she had not seen before, the absence of a fold under the buttocks, the hardness of his leg. She felt herself becoming excited again, and wanted to go over and curve herself over the smooth rounded back as he leaned over, writing.

At that moment, she thought of Magnus. She was glad she was sitting down as a surge of nausea swept her body. She suddenly wanted to cry, loving the father as much as she did while at the same time desiring the son. Suspicions collapsed in on her, without order: he's my son, too, I wanted to be Magnus' wife, I am, and this is his son, and my son. But it's more like I'm Magnus' daughter, and he's . . . my brother. No, I'm not anything. I'm a stranger in this family, and I've betrayed . . . No. I love Magnus. I'll always love Magnus; he's given me my life. But this, oh, this! It's separate. It's completely separate. It's my first affair, it's. . . . he's the first man I've ever . . .

Iris stood up and went to the door. She watched the easy grace of him as he brought the slip of paper across the room, and was further stirred by the sight of his apparent excitement. He reached out and gave her the paper, then took her hand and put it on himself.

"I have to go, Magnus."

"Well then, go, Iris."

He was again the mocking man she had despised. She had wanted to say how wonderful she thought he was for his work for the country, but couldn't say anything to that hateful person, no matter how heroic he was being. She turned and went out the door.

As she went down the hall to the staff elevator, she heard him call after her, "Iris." She turned to see him standing in his doorway, still naked.

"Merry Christmas, Iris."

She went home and made Magnus' favorite dinner. She put on a very becoming velvet dress which he liked and laid a fire in his bedroom. Iris did not think about what she had done, but went about seducing Magnus that night with a sense of urgency. She had to make love with him without her diaphragm as quickly as possible; she had not worn it that afternoon with Magnus II. Iris didn't expect her period for another week. If she made love to both of them on the same day and if anything happened . . . who could tell? She made the evening memorable for Magnus in case it had to be remembered. Later that night, sleeping in Magnus' bed, she had no dreams for the first time since Thanksgiving. The next day, she decided to forget what had happened at the Willard Hotel.

Magnus did not have any member of his family with him at Christmas. In fact, he did not even know where his children were. He still had heard nothing of WeeDee; after six months the detective agency had given up. Magnus II was in Washington but had made no plans to spend the holiday with his father. Jamie had written the month before from school that he was going on a retreat with several other boys to a Jesuit novitiate seminary and therefore would not be joining him. Kristin decided not to come down, giving no reason beyond her decision. Both Magnus and Iris assumed their relationship made Kristin uncomfortable.

They therefore spent Christmas morning alone together. Magnus presented Iris with two pairs of nylon stockings which he had bought legally from friends; he refused to buy anything on the black market. Iris had knitted him a long scarf of Scottish wool in the Macpherson tartan. They sat in front of a fire reading in the newspapers of General Eisenhower's appointment as commander-in-chief for the invasion of Europe, and the Pope's prayers for a just peace "kept by a wise use of force." Iris cooked a mince pie and they had a wartime feast of chicken à la king and yams. Then Magnus decided to go to his office.

As she helped him on with his coat, Iris asked, "Magnus, is there anything wrong?"

"Is it that obvious?"

"No. I just felt, well, I just know you. What is it?"

"Christmas needs children, something like that."

Iris leaned over and hugged him, but could not quite look him in the face.

"I don't mind that they chose not to be here," Magnus said. "But

I wish they had reasons for coming. I suppose I've given them damn few."

She kissed him, and he went out to the garage to get her car. When he went by she was crying so hard she could barely see him wave.

The glass she was holding dropped to the floor; it hit perfectly on the keystone spot of its arc, and instead of smashing, bounced back up to her hands. She laughed aloud, and an idea snapped through her mind.

She would fill his loneliness. She didn't have to be married to him to give him the companionship he needed; so why couldn't she have his child as well? That was it! She would give him another chance to love and to be loved as only a child can love, the way she . . . no, the way she used to love him, maybe, but not any longer. She loved Magnus as a woman, as his lover, as his partner, as his wife, even though they weren't married. He needed another child so he wouldn't feel like a failure, and she was the only one to give him one. She took a sudden breath; she could have his child growing in her! She didn't think about there being just as much chance that she had his grandson growing in her as she walked through the house, planning which rooms could be turned into a nursery, how to transform the garage apartment for a nanny, and imagining the wonderful room she would make for their baby.

An hour later she realized her period had begun, four days early. She was devastated; she felt the child had been taken from her, somehow unnaturally, and sat in the bathroom crying uncontrollably, staring at her blood on her hand.

The sound of the phone ringing startled her to calm. She quickly washed her hands and ran to the bedroom.

"Mr. Macpherson's residence."

"Iris, I've run into a wall of cables. It seems the grand party General Eisenhower's planning is going to take a lot of gunpowder. I'm going to be here until late. I wanted to let you know."

"Thank you." She was staring at the prism on the reading table fracturing light into rainbows on the walls of the room.

"Iris, are you all right?"

"Yes."

"You sound . . ."

"Like a dumb cow!" She began to laugh. "I'm fine, Magnus." She laughed some more.

"I'll see you later, you madwoman."

He hung up. By then Iris had begun to cry again. She put the phone down. She had to stop crying. Maybe the sleeping pills would calm her. She went to the bathroom and took two, and realized she had to sit down again. She was flowing very heavily. She wanted to have a baby so much. She didn't want to be alone that night. She didn't want to be alone ever. What would happen if something happened to Magnus? She would be alone unless she had a baby.

She got up. The pills hadn't helped. She still felt a part of her had been destroyed. After a minute she went back to the phone and dialed the number at the Willard Hotel. There was no answer. She lay down and cried for ten minutes before calling the hotel again. Still no answer. She lay back down on the bed, empty and desperate, and began to think of Magnus II, of their lovemaking. A dull desire began to sharpen inside her. She picked up the telephone, dialed the number and waited, picturing the phone ringing in his room, on the desk across from the chair. The chair, his body over hers, his hands, his mouth . . .

"Hello?"

He was there; she forgot the usual trivialities.

"I want to see you tonight, Magnus." There was a silence. "This is Iris."

"You can't."

"Why not?"

"That's none of your business."

She hated him. But he was right, it was not her business.

"When can I?"

"What are you doing New Year's Eve?"

"We're going to the Rhinelander party."

"Then so will I. Have you been to their house before?"

"Once."

"Remember, up the stairs, down the hall, there's a big green marble bathroom. I'll be in it at exactly eleven-thirty. The door will be locked. Knock once, then three times."

"I can't do that. I won't."

"I'll have you out by midnight, don't worry. Think about it, Iris." He hung up.

Iris put down the phone, pulled the covers up over her, and fell asleep.

The invasion of Normandy took place in June of 1944 and Magnus picked up his morning paper from the front steps one morning to discover a picture of WeeDee on the front page. She was standing stiffly at attention, and General Omar Bradley was pinning a Purple Heart on a sling she had over her Red Cross uniform. The story identified her as "Lucie McFarland," but there was no doubt it was WeeDee. Magnus read quickly.

> Red Cross Recreation Worker McFarland went in with Bradley's First Army on Utah Beach, helping to set up field hospitals and evacuate wounded.
>
> On the drive toward Carentan, a machine-gun nest opened up, killing and wounding many of the men with whom she served. Pinned down by the German machine gun, McFarland saw that two men lay on the open road badly wounded. She ran out and dragged one man to safety. She heard the other man screaming with pain.
>
> In spite of being reminded she was forbidden to enter into combat by the rules of the Red Cross, she was heard to say, "There aren't any rules for that guy out there."
>
> She ran out again; this time the Germans were waiting for her. But the G.I.s with her covered her brave life-saving dash with a withering wall of hot lead.
>
> Miss McFarland dragged the screaming man twenty yards to a barrier before she was hit in the arm.
>
> General Bradley, when he heard of Miss McFarland's heroic action, insisted on awarding her the Purple Heart himself.

"Iris! Iris! It's WeeDee! She's a hero—heroine! Listen to this. . . ."

He did not notice Iris' reticence as he read her the article. Then he remembered he knew some people over at the Pentagon who could probably get a message to her and hurried into the den to make some calls.

Iris had been distracted for good reason. She was pregnant and had to tell Magnus. The day before she had told Magnus II, who had laughed and he said it was the best joke of all.

The correspondent who wrote the U.P. article which Magnus read about WeeDee was Jack Josephson, the only son of the publisher of the Pittsburgh *Star-Herald*. He was the one who had yelled at Wee-Dee that she was forbidden to go back after the second wounded man. Afterward he helped dress her wound and managed to check up on her as the Allied forces pushed across France. Three days after the liberation of Paris, on the twenty-ninth of August 1944, WeeDee and Jack Josephson were married. The ceremony was the first wedding in the synagogue since the German occupation.

13

We are now prepared to obliterate more
rapidly and completely every productive
enterprise the Japanese have above ground
in any city. . . . If they do not now accept
our terms, they may expect a rain of ruin
from the air.

—TRUMAN

It was over. Magnus sat in his office and wrote out his letter of resignation. He'd done his part, his duty, whatever anyone wanted to call it. He felt no sense of triumph, or even accomplishment, only relief. The celebration was for others. He wanted to go back to New York, to increase production at Macpherson Distilleries, and to forget Washington as quickly as possible. Roosevelt was dead, and without a war, the city would soon fill with generals and politicians looking for trouble in order to get back in the limelight.

Magnus faced numerous problems. A congressional report had accused the Big Five of hoarding the little whiskey they had while telling the public there was a vast shortage. The hoarding was for eventual sale at the end of the war, when price controls would be lifted and the distillers could sell at vastly inflated prices. To Magnus the report was pure political grandstanding. Whiskey had not been produced since 1942. At the end of the war, only 240 million gallons were left. Therefore, each distiller had to hold on to as much stock as he could.

Schenley and Seagram had continued their increasingly bitter rivalry. Schenley had bought "cane spirits" from Cuba, which made an inferior but palatable whiskey blend. Seagram's put on an advertising campaign stating its products were still made from grain and pointedly told consumers to check bottle labels for cane spirits. Rosenstiel screamed "betrayal of the industry," but Bronfman ignored him.

The temporary wartime excise tax on a gallon of liquor was nine dollars. Magnus never believed a tax was "temporary." Most Americans had money in their pockets from the war and were ready to spend it. His gamble was still the same: to know what they wanted to buy. Marketing would have to expand with new products. Magnus didn't want the company solely dependent on Century, as Hiram Walker was on Canadian Club. There was a lot to do, and Magnus itched for the gin games with Weiss. Also, living in New York would be less social and easier for Iris when the baby came.

He thought of the day Iris told him she was pregnant. Each time he remembered that scene, he cringed.

"How can you be pregnant? How did it happen?" He was more than surprised. He was angry.

"I . . . let it happen."

"You *what?*"

"I want to give you a baby."

"I don't want one, Iris."

There was a silence. Iris looked at him, her eyes glassy from lack of sleep and filling with tears.

"You don't . . ." she said hopelessly.

"Of course I don't. What gave you the idea? Iris, I'll not marry you, if that's what you're thinking."

"Oh, Magnus, no. . . ." She began to cry, and had to sit down at the kitchen table.

"Stop crying, Iris, and tell me what you were thinking, then, for I'm damned if I'll be held up for money with a cheap trick like this."

"It's not a trick, it's . . . not a—"

"Then what is it? You can't make a present of a child. It's something two people agree on, decide together. You know what I feel about marriage, about . . . children. I'll not have another!"

"Magnus, please, I *do* know how you feel. It's horrible; I wanted you to be able to love a child of yours again, and *be* loved again."

"You can guarantee that? Who the bloody hell do you think you are? You won't get away with telling me *your* child will love me. What makes you so sure you can produce such a thing? And what makes you so sure I'll love it? You're taking advantage of what you know of my children."

"No, I'm—"

"It's a filthy trick, Iris. I didn't want to lie to you, so I told you honestly I couldn't marry you. I *told* you that!"

"Magnus, I don't want—"

"You'll not have this child, Iris; you'll not have it!"

"What?"

"You'll have an abortion. I'll take care of it right—"

He started to go to the phone, but before he could reach it, Iris moved quickly from her chair across the kitchen and hit him in the face as hard as she could with both fists. She did not hurt him, but he stopped, watching as she cringed back from him, her arms raised to protect herself.

"You won't kill my baby. I lost it once before. I won't let you kill my baby, no matter how much I love you, no matter what you've done for me."

"That's not—"

"Yes! I know you can kill. I don't care, I love you. . . . But I won't let you kill my baby."

She ran from the house and locked herself in her room above the garage.

Magnus called his lawyer, Double Gibson, who spent the next twenty-four hours at the house acting as a negotiator. His conversation with Iris took place through her bolted door.

The next morning, there was simply a question of details. Both Magnus and Iris wanted to stay together, but neither wanted to be married (although Double Gibson suspected Iris had accepted her situation rather than preferring it). Iris would have her baby; Magnus would not legally accept paternity. That is, his name would not appear on the birth certificate. Iris insisted on that, explaining she did not wish to tie Magnus with the slightest moral obligation. Magnus would, however, accept a financial one and set up a trust fund in the child's name. When Gibson pointed out the social ramifications in Washington of living together and having a child out of wedlock, Magnus and Iris looked at each other and agreed that they didn't care. They didn't need society as much as they wanted each other.

Double Gibson's last question was, "Then why don't you get married?" In the surprised silence which followed, he was startled to see that it was Magnus who had been worn down overnight and might have been swung over, had not Iris said, "This is the only way for us." Puzzled, Gibson left them holding each other's hands across the kitchen table.

The baby was born on February 14. It was a boy. Iris named him Augustus because it sounded strong. A nanny was hired, as Iris insisted on keeping her job as Magnus' assistant. Each day, Magnus felt an obligation to go see the child. One evening the baby reached up, grabbed Magnus' finger, and smiled. The obligation dissolved.

Perhaps Iris was right; he could love his own child. Then again, perhaps she was wrong.

When the war ended, the house on Thirty-fifth Street, N.W., in Georgetown was sold. Magnus, Iris, and Augustus moved to New York.

Magnus II came out of the war not only unscathed but with a considerable tax-free profit from black-market liquor. He liked Washington, and the town seemed to appreciate his services. When the war ended, the army did not have any inclination to keep him so he set about readjusting to peacetime. He saw little need for change; he liked living at the Willard, and he liked his social position around town. He was making a lot of money, and he was regularly screwing his father's lover.

Magnus II set up three meetings in New York soon after VJ Day. He arranged to have morning espresso with ex-Technical Sergeant Albert Anastasia at Joe Adonis' restaurant in Brooklyn, luncheon with his Uncle Juny at the Brook Club on the East Side of Manhattan, and dinner with his father and Iris at their new house on Sixty-fifth Street. No longer was Magnus just his father; their relationship had thickened. Depending on who the real father of Augustus Fowler was, they could be, either the child's father and grandfather or his half-brother and father.

Magnus II's possible paternity was known only to Anastasia and the FBI. They were the two parties who had been observing Magnus II during the war and knew Iris went to the Willard two or three times a week. The FBI, however, was not as concerned with Magnus II's sexual activities as they were with figuring out whether he was just a crook or a spy selling information to Germany. They had been unable to tie down the code he used, and as far as they could tell, no incriminating information was passed to the enemy.

Magnus II took for granted the phones had been tapped and was very careful to mislead his listeners as much as possible. He let them believe, as Iris believed, that he worked for the OSS. J. Edgar Hoover and General Donovan, the head of the OSS, were personal enemies and intelligence rivals. Hoover was hoping to publicize the affair Magnus II was having if he were an OSS operative and contrast him with the moralistic purity of FBI agents. Therefore, no one from the FBI checked with the OSS to see if Magnus II were employed there for fear of revealing the director's plans.

Once the baby was born, Magnus II was the only one to attempt to check the actual paternity of Augustus Fowler. He learned that his own blood was Type A, his father's was O Negative, and the baby's and Iris' was AB, all of which proved nothing. He had also questioned Iris about the day of conception, but there was no way to calculate that exactly either. In any case, Magnus II continued to treat the subject of paternity as a joke. He knew that he had a volatile weapon against his father, but in the meantime, he really didn't care one way or the other about who was Augustus' father. The possibility was all that mattered.

On the appointed day of his New York visit, Magnus II was shown to a booth in Joe Adonis' restaurant. It was in a back corner facing the entrance. The night before, Magnus II had come up on a train jammed with sailors returning home. At Pennsylvania Station he made certain he was not being followed by doubling back at two stations of the subway. Then he took the Canarsie Line to Brooklyn and stayed in a hotel under an assumed name.

A battleship-gray Mercury drove up outside the restaurant and two men got out. Magnus II recognized them as the large privates who had handled his introduction to Anastasia between the toilets at Indiantown Gap. They looked over the room, made sure Magnus II was alone, then one of them went back outside to the Mercury. The other sat down at a table with a clear view of where Magnus was sitting.

Anastasia came into the restaurant. As he strolled over to the table, Magnus II stood up and flashed a proper salute. Anastasia did not respond, but seemed pleased.

"Sit down, Magnus Second. You look dumb doin' that in civvies."

"Old habits. . . ." They sat in the booth. The other bodyguard joined his partner. One kept an eye on the door, one on the booth. A waiter brought two double espressos.

"So, you make your million in the war?" Anastasia sipped the coffee.

"Not quite. But you did."

Anastasia blinked across at him, then looked idly out the restaurant window.

"Everybody makes a little money on a war, even the dead ones." He took another sip of his coffee. "But the war's over." He turned to Magnus II as if appraising an animal for further fattening or immediate slaughter.

"I've heard." Magnus II smiled at the threat and let the silence continue until Anastasia broke it.

"So I don't need you anymore."

"I know. I guess it's about time for you to use me to get whatever it is you want from my father."

Anastasia didn't move. He held his coffeecup halfway to his lips. "What do I want from your father?"

"I don't know. I tried, but I couldn't find out." He had corrupted Iris, but she had become more useful in other ways. He had never asked her to find out about Anastasia.

Anastasia took a sip from the cup and put it down.

"You know what you're saying to me?"

"Yes. I'm useless to you and might as well be dead, unless . . ."

Magnus II stopped talking and took the first sip of his espresso.

"Unless what?"

Magnus II put down his cup. "Unless I can be more useful to you doing what I want to do." He stopped talking again and let the silence irritate. He did not have to wait long.

"Don't make me ask questions, Magnus Second; I hate asking questions. You talk; I'll listen as long as it sounds good."

Magnus II folded his hands on the table. "I think two things are going to happen to the syndicate now: there's going to be a lot of shifting, and there's going to be too much money. I'll talk about the money first. In the next five years there's going to be between two hundred and four hundred million dollars in net profit for the syndicate. That takes everyone beyond being rich; it takes them into having so much money, they'll make mistakes with it. They'll not only lose it, they'll put it places where it will come back to haunt them. I know about Swiss accounts and safe-deposit boxes, but what does money do there but sit? So what can the syndicate people do with the millions they're going to have buried out in the backyard?

"I suggest you convince the syndicate to give some of it to me to invest. I'm well connected through my family to Fleming and Co. It won't be difficult for me to place money in legitimate business ventures which can then be taken over, manipulated, and used. What I propose is this: the syndicate makes a million dollars available to me for a year. If I successfully show a return of fifty percent, whether from merger or bankruptcy or manipulation of assets, my credit from the syndicate the following year will double, that is, I will be given two million to play with, and so on until 1950, when the credit line will amount to sixteen million. I will invest in companies where the syndicate already has a close operating relationship and can influence the company's decision-making, such as firms depending on trucking.

"Now, why should the syndicate go with me rather than someone else? Because I'm offering, among other things, blue-chip respectability. Fleming and Co. handles American investments for the Vatican. No one's going to check very hard where the money I invest comes from. When and if they do, it will be safely at work in legitimate business or in the process of legal liquidation. . . ."

"With the Pope fronting for us," Anastasia said.

"Exactly."

"You're crazy. How old are you?"

"I'll be twenty-one in April."

"You punk kid. What makes you think—"

"I'm the same age as you were when you were arrested for your first murder." He said it hard because he knew his age was a point which had to be dismissed. He didn't know how effective his comparison would be. "I did my homework. Joe Turino. You were twenty years old and—"

Anastasia grabbed Magnus II's lapels and yanked him up out of the booth. "You little prick, you trying to sucker me?" The pig eyes were hooded; Magnus II's genuine surprise convinced Anastasia that whatever he suspected was wrong. He threw Magnus II back into the booth, where the two men grabbed him and held him down.

"What the hell you know about Joe Turino?"

Magnus II didn't flinch, and spoke very evenly. "You were convicted of murdering him in 1920. On appeal, the case was dismissed. The four witnesses were dead by then."

Anastasia sat down in the booth again, studied Magnus II carefully, then dismissed his two men. "You know too fuckin' much. I don't like talking around in my past!"

Magnus II nodded. Anastasia bellowed, "Waiter! Two more espressos. Double!" He was still angry. "So what happens in 1950 when you get sixteen million? You join the country club, or what?"

"I use it to throw my father out of Macpherson Distilleries."

Anastasia's mouth dropped open and he began to laugh. It was a coughing phlegm-soaked laugh. Magnus II smiled but did not join in with a nervous counterpoint. He waited for the next question.

"So what else you learn doing homework?" Anastasia said finally.

"About the syndicate. The war helped a lot; it cleared the air of heat. Lepke Buchalter got the chair, so everyone is breathing easier. Lucky Luciano is still in jail, but I learned from a friend at the Pentagon there's a lot of pressure on Governor Dewey to let him be deported to Italy. After that, anything could happen. Meyer Lansky is down in Havana, and Bugsy Siegal is in the desert with his hotel.

Around here, you and Joe Adonis run Brooklyn, Joe Profaci and Vincent Mangano are in New York, and Willie Moretti and Longie Zwillman look after New Jersey. Frank Costello seems to be on top of things, but only because he's Lucky Luciano's ambassador. So for the moment no one's really at the top, everyone's making more money than ever, and they're going to make more in the next five years. The situation's ready for a lot of shifting."

"You done a lot of homework. Maybe too much. It ain't your worry."

"No, but you are. Because my plan depends on your ending up on top. Because with you as the *capo di tutti capi*—forgive my bad Italian—and with me at the top of Macpherson's, you won't just be as big as U.S. Steel, you'll be able to buy it."

"Magnus Second, you're crazy."

Magnus II shrugged. The second cups of espresso arrived, and Magnus II drank his.

"You hear me? You're crazy."

"I heard you. I'm not crazy."

"What makes you so sure this shifting is going to put me on the top?"

Magnus II counted on Anastasia's vanity. "Whoever runs New York runs the syndicate. Willie Moretti has an army of two hundred, and syphilis. Longie Zwillman married into society. Costello is somebody else's puppet; Luciano is going out of the country, Lansky is a Jew and knows the Italians wouldn't allow him to run anything. Profaci and Mangano will kill each other off; if not, they're too provincial to head the national syndicate. Joe Adonis is vulnerable; he's not a citizen, the government can deport him faster than he could reach the top. So that leaves only two of you, and I'm betting on you."

Anastasia listened with interest. Magnus II's ideas were not far from his own, but the last sentence had surprised him.

"I told you once, I don't like asking questions. Who's the other one?"

"Don Vito Genovese."

"Vito? He's dead, killed in Italy during the war."

Magnus II looked across the table, letting a smile grow on his face.

"Remember this. I can be useful to you, in more ways than one." Then Magnus II gave him a quick rundown. "Genovese will be back next month. He surfaced in Naples last year, acted as an interpreter for the American forces, turned in every black marketeer in southern Italy, then took over their operations. The army finally found out he'd been friendly with Mussolini and that there was a murder indictment against him. He was arrested and they're bringing him back to face trial. In New York."

Anastasia looked down at the table.

"I know Vito a long time."

"I know."

"You do, huh? You know a lot, don't you? I hope you're as good knowing nothing when the wrong people ask."

Magnus II did not respond.

"All right, I'll talk to some people about your investment plan."

"You can commit yourself to the first stage. You don't have to talk to the syndicate. It would be easier to go to them after a year with some results."

"You're pushing, Magnus Second. What if I tell you to go shove off?"

Magnus II shrugged. "I guess I'll just have to go live a decent life."

They both smiled; then Anastasia stood up.

"You'll hear from me." And he walked out. The two men preceded him, opening the door of the restaurant and the car. Magnus II watched them drive away. Then he hurried to the subway. Lunch with his Uncle Juny was in forty minutes.

"How are you, boy? Swell to see you. You look first-rate, absolutely first-rate. I've heard you did a whale of a job in Washington. Whale of a job."

"Where did you hear that? I was a PFC pushing papers around the Pentagon."

"Had a general friend of mine, nicest fellow in the world, General Stennisford, know him? He looked you up, found out your officers thought you had a good head on your shoulders. 'That one is no B-B brain.' That's what they said about you: 'That one is no B-B brain.' Come on in the house, here, come in the house."

Juny Fleming escorted Magnus II into the dark-paneled members' room of the Brook Club. Other men were having highballs before lunch, and Juny introduced Magnus II to them with avuncular pride. At the sound of his name, Magnus II saw their recognition and its underside. Their gentlemanly manner combined knowledge of the Flemings' hatred of his father with pleasure at meeting the heir to a large fortune, which confirmed once more that people would go on being young and rich, and that the world as they knew it would continue.

Their table was laden with Georgian silver, fresh flowers, and linen. A waiter older than stone served them Dover sole and salad.

"Well, boy, when do you start back at Princeton? I've been considering which club you should join, and I think you're an Ivy man, no doubt about it. I know some old Ivy men, I'll have them write a letter for you. Might as well get to know some of them. Can you get back in there in the middle of the school year?"

"Uncle Juny, I'm not going back to Princeton."

"You're not? Well, boy, where are you going?"

"Into business with you."

"What? Well . . . that's a peach of an idea, Magnus, and I'm . . . Boy, I can't think of anything that would make me happier. But I think it's important for you to finish your college."

"I don't want to waste three years having a good time at Princeton."

"What's your hurry? The college years are the best years of—"

"I'm going to take over Macpherson Distilleries in five years."

"You are?"

"As a matter of fact, we are."

Juny's face congealed from the enthusiasm of a proud uncle to rapacious ambition.

"What do you have in mind, boy?"

"I want a position with Fleming and Co., one that's nearly invisible, but one from which I can operate. I'll work out of your Washington office. I can bring a half-million dollars into the company right now, and I'd like you to make available to me another million. At the end of one year, if I haven't returned twenty-five percent on your investment . . ."

The lunch went well. Uncle Juny asked his nephew only one question: "Does any of the money you're bringing belong to your father?"

"No."

"Good. Go on."

"In five years I'll know enough about the distilling business to run the company. By then, my father will have made some mistakes; you can depend on that. We'll capitalize on those mistakes and we'll make a tender offer. We'll get control, and then we'll throw my father out."

"How much does your father know about your plans?"

"Nothing, and he won't know until it's necessary. In fact, he won't even suspect until it's beside the point."

Juny cut the end off a Monte Cristo Number 3 and lit it slowly with the gold lighter he carried in his waistcoat. Magnus II watched the busy distraction. He could see his uncle was perhaps the only person who wanted to throw his father out of Macpherson's more than he did himself. He waited, knowing that something more was needed to close the deal.

"Boy," Juny said, and puffed twice, checking the cigar's burn, "you're talking about an enormous undertaking. You'll only be twenty-five in five years."

"That's when you'll be able to decide, Uncle Juny. I'm not asking for anything more than a start right now. In five years if I don't take over Macpherson's, I'll have three other offers in my pocket. By then you'll beg me to do it. Besides, if I don't, who else is going to?"

Juny watched his cigar smoke go into the air. Then he laughed.

"We could whale the tar out of him, couldn't we?"

"Yes. . . . And Uncle Juny, there's one other thing I have to ask you. Could you suggest the name of a priest I can talk to? I miss my faith; I want to go back to it."

Juny looked at his nephew. He blinked back tears and closed his mouth to keep it from quivering.

"Boy . . . ah, boy . . . I can't tell you . . ."

At the same time Juny and Magnus II were finishing lunch, Iris was preparing for dinner. She had not seen the two Magnuses together since she began making love to both of them, and it would be the first time Magnus II would see the baby.

She hadn't seen Magnus II for two months, but she did think about him. Every day. That was why she had gone to the doctor to get a prescription for Nembutal. She would think of him all the time, when she was on the phone, while nursing the baby, when she was trying to go to sleep, even when she and Magnus made love. In a way, it was like being with both of them. In another way, it was like being alone. And increasingly, she was terrified of being alone.

Since the move back to New York, Iris' responsibilities as Magnus' assistant had virtually ended. During the day she would sit with the baby in the kitchen and talk to the cook. She would take long strolls through Central Park with the nanny and the baby. But on the day when the nanny was off and the cook went shopping, Iris became increasingly afraid. Of what, she was not sure, but being in the house alone seemed dangerous. The only thing which seemed to help was the Nembutal, though its effect didn't last very long. She needed to take more than the doctor suggested and felt lucky the prescription could be refilled.

Magnus II would be arriving in five hours. Well, fine, Iris thought. It's about time to settle things, to get it straight that he and I are never, ever . . . She remembered the afternoons in Washington, the excitement, the anticipation. She would arrive at the hotel so anxious, so aroused, would almost run down the hall to his room, and he used to tease her sometimes by pretending he wasn't there. It would drive her wild, and when he finally opened the door . . .

The baby screamed; she was putting on a diaper and had stuck him with a pin. Never, ever again. She picked the baby up, walked with him into the bathroom, held him over her shoulder with one hand, and uncapped the bottle of Nembutal with the other. She had to stop remembering like that. One more tablet should do it. He was coming to the house in five hours. Less. She started to laugh and couldn't stop, even though the baby continued to cry.

"No, no, it *is* funny," she said aloud as she laid the baby down on the bed and sat next to it, letting him quiet down and play with her fingers. Magnus' bed. What if he ever found out? How could she do such a thing? The father and the son. No, it wasn't like that at all. They were two separate people. She loved one, she almost hated the other. But could she hate someone whom she made love to? Yes, because of what he was doing to his father. But she was doing the same thing. No, not the same thing. None of it made sense. She only knew she desired Magnus II, despised him, hated herself, and was alone.

The front doorbell rang. Would the maid get it? No. The maid was doing errands for the cook; the cook was probably busy in the kitchen, and it was Nanny's day off. Iris hated to answer the door. She had begun to hate answering the phone, but the door was worse. If she didn't hurry, perhaps they'd go away, but when she reached the foyer carrying Augustus down the two flights of stairs, she could see an image through the opaque glass. She was about to back quietly away when the baby began to cry. The noise startled her to action, and she jerked the door open.

"Yes?"

A young man in a dark suit and clerical collar was standing on the step, looking first at the squalling baby, then at her. Iris knew who he was before he spoke.

"Good afternoon, I'm Jamie Macpherson."

At the Stork Club, most of the executives had eased back to their offices. Having finished with business, Magnus and Double Gibson were just enjoying each other's company. They spoke of politics, of motion pictures, of business in general.

Their captain, Louis, approached the table with a telephone. "For you, Mr. Macpherson."

Magnus was surprised. "I don't take calls when I'm having lunch with Mr. Gibson."

"She says she's your daughter, sir."

Louis held out the receiver. Magnus was stunned.

"Go ahead," said Double. "If she's still in France she may be calling collect." He got up and went to the men's room.

Magnus took the phone. She had written only once, one long letter filled with Paris, and Jack Josephson. That was all, nothing of why she had left, nothing for the worry she had caused.

"Hello?"

"Father?"

"WeeDee, where are you?"

"I'm somewhere in the Brooklyn Navy Yard. I waited in line for forty-five minutes to reach this phone, and you weren't at your office, so I had to borrow another nickel to call the Stork Club." She laughed.

"The Brooklyn Navy Yard?"

"Our ship just landed. Well, not just. About three hours ago. It's the first one we could get from Europe. Of course, I could have come back on a battleship, but mere journalists have to wait for cattle boats." Magnus could hear a male voice laughing objections. "So I waited around so the mere journalist and I could come home together." There was a pause as both of them listened to the vibrations of "home." Then: "Father, what are you having for lunch? We've eaten Spam and old K rations all the way from Calais."

"When are you going to be out of there?"

"I don't know. Probably another hour. Lots of lines to get through."

"In time for dinner?"

"At the Stork Club? I don't think we could take it, but we'd try."

"No. I thought I'd kill the fatted calf at home."

Again a pause.

"We'd love it, Father. I want you to meet Jack."

Magnus didn't care one iota to meet Jack and hoped the call wasn't just because of the formal necessity of that introduction. Husband to father. He wanted to see her, hold her, ask her about the two years he had lost.

"Bring him along, I look forward to seeing him. And your older brother will be there . . . and, Iris . . . and—"

Before he had time to tell her about the baby, she interrupted. "They just called our letter. Have to go. We'll come to the house as soon as we can. It ought to be quite a folderol. See you soon, Father."

He dialed the house to let Iris know there would be two more for dinner. He heard through her strained enthusiasm that Jamie had arrived and was waiting to see him. As Double Gibson returned to the table, Magnus hung up.

"What's the matter, Magnus?"

"I'm having dinner tonight with all my children."

Gibson looked away and said quietly, "WeeDee's back?"

"Yes . . . with the husband."

"He's a lucky man. Your daughter is an admirable woman."

They walked outside and shook hands.

"Why do you think WeeDee's admirable?" Magnus asked, beside his limousine. "Because she won a medal? She ran away for two years, and never let me know where she was . . ."

"Magnus, she did what she had to do. And I'd suggest it worked. I'd also suggest that what she did was more difficult for her than it was for you."

Magnus paused. "You may be right."

"Magnus, I *am* right . . . and she is admirable."

Double Gibson smiled and stepped into his car.

By the time Magnus reached the house that evening his three children had gathered in the sitting room on the second floor. All of them were being attentive to the baby. Iris rushed to greet Magnus and clung to his arm, chattering about all the facts she'd learned since each of his children had arrived.

Magnus first embraced WeeDee, who just shook her head as if she couldn't believe she was there, at home with her father and happy. Then she pulled back and said, "Father, I want you to meet my husband. This is Jack Josephson."

He seemed nice-looking, with an easy smile, sandy hair, round horn-rimmed glasses and a strong Semitic face. He was taller than WeeDee, shorter than Magnus II, who was standing behind him, holding the baby. Magnus felt Iris shudder. He said, "You're no 'mere journalist,' Jack; in fact, you look substantial to me."

"Well, sir, I am. It's just that Mrs. Josephson loves to keep me in my place, and if I keep her busy enough doing that . . . I'll keep *her* in my place as well." He delivered the punch line imitating Groucho Marx and received a loving slug from WeeDee. A nice young man. No, not so young. About ten years older than she was, Magnus guessed. Almost thirty. And WeeDee was only nineteen. He didn't like it; then he remembered Iris' age when he met her.

Iris was taking the baby from Magnus II when Magnus went over to welcome him.

"That's a beautiful baby," Magnus II said as he turned and shook his father's hand. "I think he looks just like me, Fa."

"Pity the poor child that. How are you, Magnus?"

Iris stumbled, and a nest of side tables fell over. Jack Josephson picked them up. Iris laughed, a high, piercing noise which was in the same register as a scream. Then she said, "Augustus doesn't look like anyone, except himself. . . . Have you seen Jamie, Magnus?"

Magnus saw his youngest son coming across the sitting room from the fireplace. He thought of Jamie as the real stranger, who had grown more silent over the years and who condemned merely with his presence. He had no masks like Magnus II, nor a smile to hide behind like WeeDee. To Magnus, Jamie had no face, only flesh over features which left a blank in remembering.

"Hello, Jamie. Welcome."

"Hello, Father," he said in a monotone.

"What brings you up here?"

Jamie tilted his head to one side. "You do."

"Magnus! Here's the camera!" Iris was waving a small brownie over her head. "Let's take pictures before I have to put the baby to bed. Then we'll eat."

There was a silence. WeeDee and Jack Josephson exchanged a careful smile. Magnus finally looked away from Jamie and saw Magnus II stifling a laugh.

"Well, don't you want to?" Iris said, looking desperately from Macpherson to Macpherson.

"Of course we do," Magnus II said. "A family portrait." He was mocking them all.

"I'll take it," Jack Josephson volunteered.

"No, you're part of the family," Magnus said, and smiled. "Iris, ask Miss Beales to come down."

The nanny was summoned and instructed on the intricacies of pushing the button as the family lined up in front of the fireplace.

"Smile, everybody," Iris said. No one did but Iris. The first flash went off wrong; the second captured the Macphersons for all time. Then they let out a collective breath of relief and went downstairs to the elegant pale apricot dining room. The baby was given to Miss Beales.

The table was set with memories; the three children recognized the plates, silver, and crystal from Quebec, which Magnus had put in storage, then exhumed for use in the town house.

"Where would you like us to sit?" Jack Josephson asked, and everyone looked at Iris, who had not given the seating arrangement a thought.

"Oh, sit wherever you want," she said, grabbing the chair nearest her. Magnus filled in.

"You sit next to me, Iris, down here, and Jack across from her. WeeDee, you sit up at the other head between your brothers."

"I think Iris should be there," WeeDee said, conscious of who the hostess ought to be, even if there was some doubt in everyone else's mind.

"Oh, no, that's all right." Iris looked from one to another with more doubt than any of them. Magnus II went to the chair at the foot of the table and held it out for her.

"Here you are, Iris." She walked the few steps to the chair as if to her execution. Everyone else took his place, and immediately the maid entered with consommé.

Magnus spent the main part of the meal speaking with WeeDee and Jack. He noticed that Magnus II and Jamie were involved in conversation and could not imagine what the two of them had to discuss. They both ignored Iris, who at first eagerly tried to add comments. Then she rearranged the food on her plate and glanced frantically up the table to Magnus.

As he talked with Josephson, Magnus liked the man more and more. Jack had wit, brains, and foresight. He said his father was anxious to retire as publisher of the Pittsburgh *Star-Herald,* and that he was going back home to take it over. He had gone to Harvard Business School, but had been a practicing journalist ever since, which he thought was as good a background as any for a newspaper publisher.

"Journalism as everyone thinks of it is like mildew," Jack explained. "The past glory is piled in a corner, and there's a sick sweet smell coming off it. And you know what follows mildew: rot. People's days are too short to look at more than two papers. So there's going to be a crunch. Radio will supply more and more people with the news. We'll always have the advantage of details, but the fact is, damn few people want detail. They want summary and a picture of a pretty girl."

Jack and WeeDee exchanged a loving look as the table fell silent, and Magnus caught the conversation between his two sons.

"But what do you think my penance would be?" Magnus II was asking. Then he realized conversation had stopped and everyone had heard him. "Oh, dear. The devil sneezed, I suppose. Well, I was asking my brother how a lapsed Catholic goes about returning to the Church, and he mentioned penance. Well, there is penance, and then there is penance!"

"I'm not a priest. I can't tell you what your penance will be," Jamie stated.

Magnus II turned back to him and smiled. "You're my baby brother and you've been a priest all your life. You can't fool us. You're not at seminary learning to be a priest; you're learning to be Jesus."

Jamie bowed his head.

"Oh, dear." Magnus II looked at the others. "This means more penance, I'm afraid. Jamie, forgive me. I'll say ten Hail Marys, I promise."

"The Church is *not* a joke!" Jamie spat out, then looked away, angry at his own words.

"Now, Jamie, there've been a few laughs since the Inquisition. How about Martin Luther and his constipation?"

Jack Josephson, unaware of the family politics, laughed. When Iris, who was aware of them, frantically joined him, Jack realized the pattern of stress and stopped, leaving Iris to laugh alone.

"Why so curious about penance?" Magnus asked his eldest son. Magnus II turned slowly to his father and smiled angelically.

"Fa, I miss my faith, believe it or not. Oh, no, I'm not ready for sainthood. I never will be. But what I miss is a kind of equalization of sin and forgiveness which the Church provides. My life has become messy and out of order." His smile became ingenuous. "I need confession, I need forgiveness, and I need the sacrament."

At the same time Iris laughed with her high-pitched hilarity, Jamie pushed his chair back from the table and threw his napkin down. "The sacrament is not for the convenience of making sin neat. You're not going to find a priest who'll let you get away with that!"

"We'll see, baby brother. . . . Uncle Juny seems to think I have a better chance for salvation than you think I do. He called Monsignor Sheen this afternoon, and I'm going to see him next week."

"You've had a busy day," Magnus said quietly.

"Yes, Fa."

"What about Uncle Juny? How is he?" WeeDee asked with an air of innocent curiosity, and hopes of turning the conversation. She knew what Magnus II was doing, and shot a warning glance across the table to Jack.

"Uncle Juny is getting 'a real bang out of life.' " Magnus II's imitation was exact, causing even Jamie to smile. WeeDee reached out and put her hand on her father's. Magnus allowed a grin, and the tension in the room eased.

"He offered me a job."

No one breathed until Magnus asked slowly, "What kind of job?"

"A very nice one. In the Washington office of Fleming and Co. Several accounts I already know, some interesting new ones." Magnus II looked casually from brother to sister and finally to Magnus. "I took it."

"You took it?" WeeDee was incredulous.

Magnus knew his son's game; there was more, he was sure. "He's using you."

"I know, Fa. He wants to take over Macpherson's in five years." Jamie, again emotionless, asked, "He told you that?"

"Yes."

"You can't work for him," WeeDee said, knowing Magnus II was capable of doing just that, and more.

"I think I should."

"Then do," Magnus said, "but get up from the table and get out of my house."

There was a stunned silence. Then Jack surprised everyone by saying, "Mr. Macpherson, excuse me, sir, but he could be right. It's not so bad having a family eye and ear on the other guy's head."

Iris, unfortunately, laughed, causing the others to glare impatiently and Magnus to frown.

"Thanks, Jack," said Magnus II. "We're all so emotional, aren't we? Dangerous stuff. They say if you have too much emotion, you go blind." He smiled at his family, then looked directly at his father. "I might as well tell you, Fa, here, when we're together, I want to run Macpherson's someday. I don't suppose there's anything unusual about that; you're my father, I'm your son, Macpherson's is a family business. But I'm going to have to be worthy of it. I don't want to just be the boss's son. When the time comes, I want to be as good as anyone you can get."

"What about Princeton?"

"What about it, Fa? The only degrees you ever needed were longitude and latitude off Rum Row." WeeDee turned to check her father, and noticed a softening. She laughed, and gradually the others joined in, all except Iris, who didn't understand why they could laugh then and not before, with her. Then she thought she understood: they were all Macphersons.

"Fa, I can learn more in a month at Fleming and Co. than I could in a year at Princeton. And as Jack pointed out, I can keep an eye on Uncle Juny. Sooner or later he'll fire me. But I figure that's the best qualification I could have to work at Macpherson's."

Magnus watched his son's easy charm as a calm quiet settled around the table. He knew a spy had a certain luxury in being able to jump either way. Of course, he did not trust Magnus II, and yet . . . And yet. He was amazed that hope would still so easily balloon inside him, hope that his son, his namesake, would one day . . .

Iris stood up and said, "Excuse me," as an accusation and hurried out of the room.

"Oh, dear, what *could* the matter be?" Magnus II shook his head.

"This is hard for her," WeeDee said.

"It's impossible for her," Jamie added with surprising sharpness, which brought him the table's attention. "She's being asked to live an impossible life." He caught his father's eye. "I have to catch a train back to Washington tonight. I came because . . . my rector suggested it, and gave me special leave. A Christian can't stand aside as two lives are being ruined. Even if I know I probably can't do anything about it, my conscience could never be clear unless I tried. . . . I didn't know we'd all be here. But I have to say this."

"Say it," Magnus said.

"You are destroying two lives, Father!"

"Which two, Jamie?" WeeDee asked, trying once more to dilute the intensity.

"That woman"—he indicated the door Iris had left by—"and her child. You're making her live without any social definition, without security as to who she is, or what will become of her and her child. You're putting them in a prison where their only view of the world is through you. And if you leave them, either by changing your mind or dying, no matter how much money you leave them, she will remain a whore and the child a bastard. Father, you cannot do this. You must marry."

The maid came in to clear the main course, but Magnus spoke as if she were not there.

"You came all this way, Jamie, to preach me a sermon and save my soul, did you? Well, save your chants for the seminary, where they'll do some good. My soul's already going one way or another, and there's not much you or the Pope himself can do about that. And you be sure to tell your rector that my soul mattered a hell of a lot *less* to you than the purity of your own conscience."

Jamie sat rigid, looking down at the table. WeeDee reached over and again put her hand on her father's arm. He did not look at her, but went on.

"All right, go back tonight feeling you've done what you can for me. You have, and that's that. Iris and I have made our choices. There's no prison here; *she* chose the life she lives with me."

"The child has no choice," Jamie said with quiet disgust.

"He's not your business!"

"He . . . is . . . my . . . *brother*." Jamie had turned to look at his father and did not see Iris come in behind them carrying the baby. Very deliberately Iris sat down, lifted up the corner of her blouse, and raised the baby to her breast.

The men looked away.

"But Jamie, all men are brothers," said Magnus II, glancing at Iris. "Aren't they?"

She did not answer or look up from her child.

The maid served ice cream in a silver bowl without taking the slightest notice of Iris nursing, even when offering her the dessert.

The men ate their ice cream in silence.

Only WeeDee noticed that Iris was crying silently. Her tears were falling from her cheeks onto the baby's bib. WeeDee looked across at Jack and shook her head slightly. It was not the evening for them to tell her father that she was pregnant.

In December of 1945, the Standard and Poor's index listed the five major distillers' stocks at four hundred. Before the war, they had hovered at fifty-five. Investors began to regard the liquor industry as a solid venture and started buying shares. Magnus' stock in Macpherson Distilleries, Inc., rose to a worth of eighty-two and a half million dollars. On Ted Weiss's advice, he began trading it off to develop a balanced portfolio.

Within a week, Magnus II set up three blind holding companies and in their names, discreetly began purchasing his father's stocks.

14

. . . These days, an American can get away with
saying absolutely anything, no matter how
trivial, preposterous, obscene, or even
treasonable, provided he begins and ends
by saying, "I hate communism."

—*France-Soir*

"Dr. Bromberg, did you ever know someone named George Crosley?"

"No, I did not."

"Or a woman named Elizabeth Bentley?"

"No."

"Franklin Victor Reno?"

"No."

"What about Laurence Duggan?"

"No. Who are these people? Why are you asking me about them?"

The two men in the dark suits sat across Bromberg's office at the Baltimore distillery. They had been very polite, one of them taking notes, the other asking questions.

"Dr. Bromberg, you signed a government clearance paper in December of 1941, stating you were not, nor had ever been, a member of the Communist party. We have information which indicates you were."

" 'We'? Who is 'we,' please?"

"The FBI."

"I see. And where did the FBI get this information?"

"Dr. Bromberg, that's not what we're here to discuss. Were you a member of the Communist party?"

"Of course."

"You admit it?"

"Yes."

"Then you admit the clearance paper—"

"I was never a member of the American Communist party. When I first arrived in this country, I subscribed to the *Daily Worker* for two months. I went to, I think, two party meetings, but they were ridiculous, attacking freedom, democracy, as well as capitalism. I was a Communist in Germany when there was nothing else to be but a Nazi."

"There were other political parties in Germany at the time, Dr. Bromberg."

"Yes, the Catholic Center party, the Christian trade unions, and the Labor Front. I am a Jew."

The two agents looked at him for a moment; then the younger man, who was doing the questioning, went on.

"Do you know a man named—?"

"Are you accusing me of anything?"

"No, Dr. Bromberg. We just want information."

"Then I will tell you something. You are scaring me. You are scaring me the way the Nazis scared me in 1930. Thank God we are here, not there. I will say nothing more to you unless my lawyer is present."

The older agent put away his notepad and said, "You have nothing to be scared of, Dr. Bromberg, as long as you tell us the truth."

The scientist smiled and shook his head. "There is plenty of room for fear in truth. For instance, think of all the space between your truth and mine. We're not so naive, you and I, to think that one truth cannot decimate another."

Without further words, the two FBI agents left.

Dr. Bromberg sat for a moment, shook his head, and sighed. Then he rang for his secretary. When she arrived, he said, "Please note in my appointment diary the exact time those two gentlemen stayed here. I'll dictate notes about our meeting; one copy to go to my lawyer, one to Mr. Macpherson. I'll deliver it when I go up for the board-of-directors meeting. . . . Date: May 1, 1946." He hesitated, then smiled to himself. "They came to see me on May Day."

Three days later, Magnus presided over the board meeting. There were sixteen members around the table, including Dr. Bromberg, Ted Weiss, and Jack Josephson.

"May we come to order? . . . I'm happy to welcome our newest board member, Mr. Josephson, president of Star-Herald Communications. He may seem a bit . . . excited today, but that's because my daughter just gave birth to a baby girl."

There was as much applause for Magnus being a grandfather as for the new board member's accomplishments. Then Ted Weiss took over.

"The Department of Agriculture has cut all the distillers' mashing days down to three for this month, and cancelled them altogether for June. Also, we're prohibited from carrying the unused wheat and corn over to the following months. We got to give it back so they can ship it to Europe."

An exasperated sigh went up from the members. "How long is this going to go on?" one of them, the president of a large Louisville bank, asked.

Weiss shrugged. "Dunno."

"We've got to mash," the board member continued. "The industry can't keep flooding the market with more and more blends. We're going to need a lot of whiskey by 1949."

"We got more of a problem than that. But let me give you some good news first. This fiscal year, the liquor industry is going to see around 230 million gallons of hooch." He waited as his listeners smiled. "Sounds great, doesn't it? Does to everyone else, too; Standard and Poor for distilling stocks is over six hundred. Fine; take advantage. But let me tell you, we *sold* that much; nobody *drank* that much. The wholesalers and retailers were filling their stocks depleted from the war. The truth behind the figures is, people ain't drinking the stuff like they used to."

"Mr. Weiss, excuse me," a suave Hartford WASP patronizingly interrupted, "but I have insurance figures that say per-capita consumption of liquor during the war years rose almost thirty-five percent."

Weiss snapped back, "Yeah, and per-capita income over that period went up a hundred and twenty percent. Those capitas are spending their fun money on something else but liquor."

The board members grinned. They enjoyed Weiss's presentation of facts, even when they were unpleasant. "You gotta remember," Weiss said, "people today aren't drinking as much liquor as they were drinking in *1917!* And there's a hell of a lot more people."

"Are we then considering a long-term trend away from alcoholic consumption?" asked the chairman of the country's largest sugar company. Weiss shrugged and looked at Magnus, as he always did, for exegesis of his figures.

"We sell a product that depends on the tastes and habits of the American consumer," Magnus said. "If the product isn't available, as it was not during the war, tastes can change and habits can diminish.

That's happened to some degree. But I have no doubt that we can now re-establish tastes and habits and improve on them."

"Mr. Macpherson, if we're in the business of taste, it seems we should consider expanding the range of Macpherson's products." The speaker was Bert Cavanaugh, the senior partner of a Wall Street investment-banking firm. He had helped put together the money to build the Baltimore plant before the war. Magnus suspected him of being close to Juny Fleming, even though Magnus II had told him there was no connection.

"Such as what?"

"It seems from the figures that during the war, American taste changed from straight whiskey to the lighter blends. That's where our emphasis on expansion should be."

"Excuse me," Jack Josephson interjected, "there wasn't much straight whiskey around during the war. There weren't any nylon stockings either; as soon as there were, women didn't keep drawing a stocking seam up the back of their leg with an eyebrow pencil."

Ted Weiss guffawed, but Cavanaugh ignored Jack and continued carefully. "That's a different point. There weren't any nylons. There *was* whiskey; people went on drinking. Most of that whiskey was blended, and people's appreciation altered slightly to that easier taste."

"Because we had to," Jack countered. "Give me a good straight whiskey, and I'm not going to choose a milkshake."

A heated discussion followed about which to develop: the straights or the blends. Seagram's 7 Crown, a blend which sold as much as the next three whiskeys combined, was an irritating fact to the members who propounded straight whiskey. The sales of Macpherson's old blend, Century, also countered their argument.

Magnus listened for a few minutes, then signaled for silence. "Bert, we have four blends and two straights. We have Macpherson's gin, and three Scotch imports. We're getting involved in rum. That's a damn wide spectrum. We'll stick with our blends until it's proved people want straights. Then we'll give it to them."

That night Bert Cavanaugh called Magnus II as usual at the Willard Hotel to tell him what happened at the meeting. Magnus II had learned to read statistics as well as Weiss, and knew there was a softness to the postwar liquor boom. He was depending on the false security of statistics to overextend his father's reliance on blends. He ordered Bert Cavanaugh to keep pushing, and to get Macpherson's decision on the record.

Magnus II knew that taste was going to change. In one of the companies in which he invested through Fleming and Co., using Anastasia's first million, he bought into Puerto Rican rum, Mexican tequila, and an industrial distiller who was branching into "Russian" vodka. Acutely aware of the times, he forced the distiller to drop any mention of the word "Russian" in advertising or labeling.

Magnus II was particularly aware of America's growing Communist sentiments because of his new friendship with Monsignor Fulton Sheen. Uncle Juny encouraged the connection, and as Magnus II had told Anastasia, you couldn't have a more respectable front than the Church. In the years from 1946 to 1948, Magnus made several major contributions to various Catholic charitable and political causes. When ex-Congresswoman Clare Booth Luce and Joe Kennedy teamed up to raise two million dollars to help the Christian Democrats in the Italian elections against the Communists, Magnus II donated a large anonymous sum.

Not long after, in the summer of 1948, he met a priest by the name of Father Crowley. Nondescript, diminutive, with half-rimmed glasses and a five-o'clock shadow, Father Crowley was something of a mystery around Washington. Magnus II met him at a Communion breakfast and was surprised to discover that Father Crowley was quite interested in finding out all about him. Magnus II immediately was suspicious of why the priest was being so attentive. They saw each other again at several functions, and spoke generally of Washington and Rome. Then one day Father Crowley asked Magnus II to join him for seafood and rumrolls at O'Donnell's.

Their meal passed in pleasant conversation on faith and politics, leavened with a little gossip. Then casually, over coffee, Father Crowley asked, "Were you with OSS during the war?"

The question was so unexpected that Magnus II did not know which lie to use.

"If I were, I wouldn't be allowed to say, would I? Why do you ask, Father Crowley?"

"There is a rumor. . . ."

"There is?"

"Yes. Apparently the FBI had taps on two phones you had at the Willard during the war."

Magnus II smiled. "What did they want to know, Father Crowley?"

"About the OSS."

"Why didn't they ask the OSS?"

"You know the FBI didn't ask the OSS much. Now that it's the CIA, Mr. Hoover asks them even less."

Father Crowley drank his coffee and wiped his mouth meticulously. "If you were not with the OSS, you might have been a spy, or involved in crime in some way. As a friend, I want to impress on you the considerable advantage to you of clearing up these questions."

Magnus II did not stop to speculate about the advantage. "I was not a member of the OSS, but the FBI knew *I* was aware that my phones were tapped. I didn't care. I figured if Mr. Hoover wanted them tapped, that was fine with me. As far as I'm concerned, Mr. Hoover should get anything he wants."

Father Crowley took off his glasses and wiped them with the napkin as meticulously as he had wiped his mouth.

"Your bank accounts show an amazing expansion during the war."

Magnus II smiled again. They'd examined his records; he knew along which angle to lie. "I'm a good businessman, Father Crowley. I'm unorthodox and secretive, but thank God up until now I've been free to choose my own style. Because if these Communists get any closer to control here, there won't be any choices or any profits. . . . We're losing the world, Father Crowley. Berlin cut off, Greece under attack. We'll lose our own backyard if we're not careful. That's why Mr. Hoover should get everything he wants. He seems to be the only man around Washington who sees what's going on."

"You approve of Mr. Hoover?"

Magnus looked as fervent as possible. "I think J. Edgar Hoover is the greatest American alive."

Father Crowley blew his nose on the restaurant's napkin, and they left.

Two days later Father Crowley called Magnus II, asking if he would care to go to the races. It was not a social engagement, and both of them knew it. J. Edgar Hoover's favorite and only public form of recreation was horse racing. Magnus II immediately went to a pay phone to ask Anastasia's advice about horses.

When Magnus II and Father Crowley arrived at the track, the box next to theirs was still empty. Then, just before the third race, the Director of the FBI and his party arrived. Mr. Hoover, with barely a glance in their direction, said, "Nice to see you, Father Crowley. Beautiful day, isn't it?" And he turned and looked at Magnus II.

"Mr. Hoover," Father Crowley said, "I'd like you to meet a friend of mine, Magnus Macpherson the *Second*."

"How do you do, Mr. Macpherson."

"Mr. Hoover, I am honored to meet you, sir."

Hoover introduced the two men sitting beside him. "This is Mr. Tolson and Mr. Dymally. You people know Father Crowley."

"Mr. Macpherson, who do you like in the fourth?" the director asked as he and his friends examined their racing forms.

"I'm afraid the dogs are running in the fourth."

Mr. Hoover chuckled. "Let's see, does anyone like the fifth?"

"Yes, sir," said Magnus II. "Black Lightning."

"He's forty-to-one," Mr. Tolson offered, amazed.

"He's never gone the distance before," Mr. Dymally added.

Hoover looked over at Magnus inquisitively. "I know the horse," said Magnus.

"On the nose, Mr. Macpherson?" Hoover asked.

"On the nose, sir."

Hoover spoke over his shoulder to one of the two agents sitting behind them. "Put ten down on Black Lightning in the fifth for me to win. If he comes in, I'll give the winnings to Father Crowley. If I lose, Mr. Macpherson, what then?"

"Losing a forty-to-one shot . . . I'll have to give Father Crowley my soul, or that part of it I haven't sold off already."

The field was strung out all over the track in the fourth race. While waiting for the fifth, Hoover turned the conversation to the nation's internal threat. Magnus II was as convincing with his sudden patriotism as he had been with his sudden faith.

"Who do you pick between Truman and Dewey?" Hoover asked.

Magnus took down his binoculars. "I never gamble, Mr. Hoover. I contributed to Dewey's campaign. He's a sure thing."

"Yes," Hoover said, glancing over at Magnus II, "fifty thousand. . . . Black Lightning looks spavined."

"Trust me, sir."

The Director did not put his glasses down. He followed Black Lightning to the gate and said, "I do."

"What about your father's company?" Father Crowley asked casually. Magnus II turned to him, surprised.

"What *about* my father's company?"

"If there were known Communists in—"

"They're off!" Mr. Dymally exclaimed, and all conversation stopped. Magnus II already knew the result, courtesy of Anastasia, so the race did not interest him. If Communists worked for Macpherson Distilleries, Magnus II could depend on millions of patriotic American stockholders' proxy votes. And if his father *knew* about the Communists in his company, Magnus II could probably depend on the board of directors.

When the race ended, Hoover handed Magnus II the winning ticket with a pleased smile.

"Would you pass that over to Father Crowley for me? You must have known that horse pretty well; certainly no one else at this track did. Yes, I'd say Mr. Macpherson was trustworthy . . . *after* we leave." The last was directed at Father Crowley.

At the end of the seventh race, an agent hurried up and gave the Director a message. Without any good-byes, Mr. Hoover and his party walked out of the stands. Seconds later, Father Crowley began to talk.

"Macpherson Distilleries is infested with Communists."

"Can you give me some names, background?"

"Yes, I have files."

"How many are there?"

"Three."

"Only three? You call that 'infested'? That's ludicrous."

"That's all that are *known*. There *have* to be more."

Magnus II went home that afternoon with the files of the three Communists working for his father. When he read them, he was disappointed. Dr. Bromberg had joined the party to fight the Nazis. The other two, a sales manager in New York and a foreman in Pittsburgh, had carried membership cards during the thirties but had given them up after only a few years. They were hardly cause to accuse Magnus of treason. Nevertheless, his father must know about Bromberg. Magnus II called his Uncle Juny and told him what had happened. Juny was delighted. He agreed that something could be made of it and that it was time to start planning for the takeover.

Magnus II never saw Father Crowley again. He read in the papers that President Truman had forbidden the FBI to help the House Un-American Activities Committee to investigate Alger Hiss until there was a reasonable case. One paper stated that Hoover was using a Roman Catholic priest to pass information to a member of the committee, Richard Nixon, but all parties denied the allegation.

Late that fall, Magnus II flew to New York and arranged to run into Iris as she was walking her son in Central Park. She had not seen Magnus II since the family dinner, more than two years before.

For Iris, that evening was a debilitating disaster. When the meal was finally over, WeeDee helped her upstairs to put the baby to sleep. They talked, or rather, Iris cried while WeeDee listened, trying to learn why Iris was so upset.

Afterward Iris felt any chance to become a real part of the family had died. She'd been too embarrassed to tell WeeDee she needed a pill; she couldn't tell her anything, not about Magnus II, not about the letter which she kept in a book next to her bed. The next day, WeeDee had gone on to Pittsburgh with her husband.

Since then, Iris' fear had grown. She went to a psychiatrist, who asked her what she feared, but all she could say was that she was afraid of everything. After three sessions she quit and bought a police whistle, a sharp letter opener, and finally a small revolver, which she kept with her at all times. Terrified the baby would be kidnapped, she had Magnus install security devices all through the house. She fired two nannies, a cook, and a maid, convinced that each was somehow harming her child. She begged Magnus to get rid of them and let her take care of the house, but he convinced her to keep at least a cook and a maid.

The only good thing which had happened to her, as far as Iris was concerned, was that she had finally met an absolutely wonderful doctor. A specialist in internal medicine, Dr. Jurgenson had taken her off pills completely and put her on his own vitamin program, which started with monthly injections at his office. Iris had never felt better; the shots completely wiped out her depression and even helped her "fear." She became such a faithful patient that Dr. Jurgenson taught her to give herself intramuscular injections, which saved going to his office. He sold her 30cc. vials of what he said was a mixture of hormones and vitamins, and prescribed disposable syringes. The number of shots had increased, but Magnus knew nothing about them.

When Iris saw Magnus II coming toward her in Central Park, she knew right away he had arranged to be there. She didn't care; she felt wonderful. She'd just had her shot. She pointed Augustus, who was riding a wooden horse, in Magnus II's direction and whispered to him, "There's Uncle Magnus. Now, go over to him and say, 'Hello, Uncle Magnus.'"

Apparently the child repeated the message correctly, for Magnus II smiled broadly, then took Augustus' hand and walked him back toward his mother.

"'Uncle' is the one thing I'm not," he said to her by way of greeting.

"What do you think he should call you, 'Brother Magnus'?" she laughed. "I doubt if you'll ever be a priest."

Magnus II sat down beside her, leaving a space between them.

"He could call me Daddy. I wouldn't mind."

"I would."

"How about Brother-Pops? That'd cover everything."

She couldn't help laughing, and said, "You're awful. You're just as awful as ever."

"Thank you, Iris, and I'll bet you still have honey between your legs. Remember I used to tell you—"

"Augustus, go play with your horsie, go on."

"—that I was a slave-drone to your queen-bee jelly?"

"Magnus! . . . Go on, dearest, ride your horsie." Augustus moved away, involved in an intricate conversation of his own with the horse.

"You remember, don't you, Iris?"

"Of course I remember," she said, smiling. At the moment, she believed she could control him.

"But no more of that, Magnus. I have a son, and I have a husband." She had never felt so confident in her life, and silently thanked God for Dr. Jurgenson.

"I know exactly what you have, Iris. . . . The question is, is it enough for you?"

"Of course it is."

"What about friends? What about fun? Do you have a lot of fun hovering around that dark house day in and day out?"

"What do you mean, 'dark'? It's a lovely house. It's a warm, lovely . . ." It was dark, though; she had never realized it before.

"Are you happy, Iris?"

"I don't . . . hover. . . . Yes. Of course I'm happy."

"Iris, I'm tickled to death you're a wife and a mother. But there's a lot more, you know."

"It's enough for me," she repeated.

"No it's not, and you know it. Iris, remember me? I *know* it's not enough for you."

She was losing control; she could feel it. She started to stand up, but he put his hand on her arm and held her down.

"Is this what you came here for, Magnus?"

"I missed you."

"You couldn't miss anything. You're too selfish."

"I miss making love to you."

"We *never* made love, we didn't love! You don't know what you're talking about!"

"Then I miss fucking you, Iris, and you miss fucking me, don't you?" he said, smiling calmly.

Iris was angry, but there were too many people in the park for her to make a scene. "Can you possibly believe with all your conceit and your vain . . . destroying . . . can you possibly believe that I've done without you for two years and I can go on doing without you?"

"I believe you *can,* Iris. But do you want to? . . . and what is it that you prove by doing it? That you can 'abstain'? You've already proved that. I remember what we did in Washington was very exciting. It added a certain edge to the day, remember?"

Iris remembered.

"Iris, what if there was nothing to remember? You know what that would be? A waste. A terrible loss. Because we had that sensational time together . . . and it didn't hurt anyone."

"Didn't hurt anyone! You're insane. I had a baby."

"You would have had a baby with or without me. And don't cry about not knowing who the father is. Augustus doesn't care, and never will, as long as he doesn't know."

Iris could feel fear flowing up her back. She turned to him. "You're going to tell, aren't you? Someday, you'll tell him."

"Why would I do a ludicrous thing like that?"

"Because you enjoy watching people squirm!"

She said it too loud. Several people in the park turned toward her. She hated to be looked at, and put her hand across her forehead as if protecting her eyes from the sun. "Magnus, stay away from me, stay away from all of us. I don't need you. I don't . . . want you. You're wrong about Washington. It hurt *me;* I was terrified all the time that somehow your father would find out."

"So was I. We took a chance together. But you have to admit, the terror added to the excitement." He reached over and took her hand away from her eyes so that she could see him. "And, Iris, lovely honey-thighed Iris, we spent all that good time together and he *didn't* find out."

Iris stood up. "I'm going home. Augustus! Come here! We're going home!"

As the child came toddling back to his mother, Magnus II said, "I'm going back to the Plaza. I'll be there for another three hours. Room three-thirty-three. Easy to remember."

She took her son's hand and walked out of the park without looking back. By the time she put Augustus down in his crib for a nap, her hands were shaking. When she gave herself another shot, the needle bounced twice before it pierced her skin. She knew it was the second injection in one day, but she felt panicked by what had happened. In a few minutes she felt a rush of excitement displace the panic, and was glad, glad the meeting with Magnus II had taken place. She was a woman, she could make choices if she wanted. After all, she wasn't really married, and Magnus was busy, and . . . he didn't have to know. She was free to do whatever she wanted, and she could handle the pressure. She had done it before. . . . And what if she hadn't ever gone to the Willard Hotel, what if she never had that to think about? He was right, it would have been a waste. A waste of time. It was almost three o'clock. Three-thirty-three. Easy to remember. She ran downstairs and told the maid to watch the baby. The maid looked surprised, having never been allowed on the nursery floor. Iris angrily commanded her to do as she was told, then ran out the front door and hailed a cab.

An hour later, Magnus II was asking Iris about the black-and-blue bruises he saw on her buttocks and was fascinated when Iris explained about Dr. Jurgenson. The next day Magnus II decided to become a patient. When Jurgenson learned Magnus II lived in Washington and couldn't get back to New York regularly, he prescribed a 30cc. vial of vitamin brew and fifty disposable syringes.

As soon as Magnus II left the office, he took the vial to a chemist. The analysis showed there were lots of vitamins and lots of hormones, but also a massive dose of Benzedrine. Magnus II had been to several "bolt-and-jolt" parties in Washington where Benzedrine was followed by barbiturates for a fast high and low. He considered telling Iris that she was close to being an amphetamine addict, then decided against it. If the woman his father lived with was the mother of an illegitimate child *and* a drug addict, so much the better.

During his weekly visits to New York, Magnus II introduced Iris to Benzedrine inhalers. He taught her which brand to buy, how to break them open, and how to chew the impregnated papers inside. The strips in one inhaler equaled two shots of Dr. Jurgenson's "juice."

"Iris." She didn't answer. She was lying with him on a down comforter on the floor of room three-thirty-three. Outside, the snow was packing into parabolic curves in the corners of the windows. "Iris."

She jerked up. "What? What's the matter?"

"Nothing. I want to ask you something."

"What?" She sat up and leaned against the foot of the bed, pulling the comforter around her.

"Does my father notice anything?"

"What? What would he notice? You're not making any sense." Magnus II noted her level of nervous irritation.

"He might notice your black-and-blue butt, for one thing."

She laughed. "No." The question was important; if his father suspected anything, Iris could lose her effectiveness.

"Iris."

"What?"

"Why doesn't he notice?"

"Because I wear clothes to bed, and because we like doing it in the dark."

"Always?"

"Yes, always. We like it that way. He enjoys giving me nice negligees, and I enjoy letting him—"

"I don't want to hear about that. I just want to be sure—"

"Why don't you want to hear? You want to hear about everything else. Does it bother you that your father and I enjoy—?"

"Not in the slightest."

She turned to him in amazement.

"You're kidding! It does, doesn't it? Come on, tell me why it bothers you that I fuck your father. Because I don't; *I make love* to your father! I don't care what you think, or what we do here, you'll never be what he is, to me or to anybody else. You may have the same name, but you'll *never*—"

Magnus swung and slapped her face as hard as he could, knocking her to the floor. He was surprised at the level of his own fury. He wanted to hit her again, but he suppressed the urge; to Magnus II, rage was weakness.

Iris lay there smiling faintly. "I've hated myself ever since I met you, haven't I?" She turned her head and watched the snow freeze on the window.

Magnus II forced his anger to subside, trying to examine it. He was not jealous of his father; that wasn't it. Iris was a tool; he felt nothing for her. He did not have to feel anything in order to hit someone. Anger was unfamiliar to him. . . . What did she say? Never . . . his father. "Never," that was it. She was a stupid goof-balled bitch. Never? On the contrary, it was going to happen quite soon.

A few weeks later, Ted Weiss noticed something was happening to

Macpherson stock. He didn't bother Magnus with it until he was sure; Magnus had enough problems. He was running out of whiskey.

The reason was success; people were buying Century and the other Macpherson brands in ever-increasing amounts. Magnus knew he didn't have enough aged stock to keep blending Century with the same high percentage of straight whiskey, but he could not cut back without losing his share of the market, and as Weiss had predicted, the market was shrinking.

In the end, Magnus made the only decision he could: he cut the amount of aged whiskey in all his blends. The board of directors split over his ruling. Bert Cavanaugh fought it down the line and forced Magnus to accept personal responsibility for the reduced percentages. Two days after Macpherson's new blends reached the retail market, Schenley began a high-powered advertising campaign, advising customers that they should check the back label on all liquor bottles to see the percentages of straight whiskey used.

Magnus accused Bert Cavanaugh of giving information to Schenley. Cavanaugh denied it, but Magnus threw him off the board anyway. He no longer had time for such dissension.

For the rest of 1949 and into 1950, the distillers engaged in a destructive price-cutting war, fighting each other for a greater share of sales. The effect on profits was devastating, and the dividend on Macpherson stock in the last quarter of 1949 was the lowest since the end of prohibition.

By January 1950 Weiss was sure someone was taking advantage of Macpherson's slump.

"Someone's buying up our common."

Magnus barely smiled. "Pretty dumb at this point, wouldn't you say? . . . Who is it?"

"Dunno. It's buried, lots of fronts. But it's going on."

"Fleming and Co.?"

"Could be. But . . ."

"But?"

"Something else. The clothesline . . ."

"What did you hear?"

"Not much. Something about the syndicate being interested in us."

"They've always been interested."

Weiss shrugged. "You're vulnerable right now."

"Not that vulnerable."

"Still like to know what direction they're coming from. Wouldn't you?"

"I'll call my son." He reached for the phone.

"No!" Weiss said it hard. Magnus looked at him a moment.

"Is it him, Weiss?"

"Donno. Might be."

"Here we go again."

Weiss nodded. "Might be messy."

"How?"

"Might have to spend some money, maybe some muscle, if it's the syndicate."

"Find out what we have to know."

Weiss started for the door, hesitated, and turned back.

"Macpherson, how come we do all this?"

"We like it. We're also damned good at it."

"Umm. Very successful, no doubt about it."

Weiss stood there, chewing his lip.

"You want something more, Weiss?"

"Donno." He shrugged.

"We're in for a free-for-all, we'll have a little triumph. That'll be fun."

"More success, yeah, I know that. But take it all away, what do you got?"

"What more can you expect out of a life than some success and a little fun?"

Weiss shrugged, then said, "More life." Then he shook his head. "Donno."

"Success *is* more life. So is winning."

"You sure?"

"Look at a failure; look at a loser."

Weiss nodded, not in agreement, but to acknowledge he heard. "We're mixing up the gods, Macpherson. Hope we never lose."

Two days later, before Weiss had time to pull in the clothesline, Magnus was served with a subpoena to appear in executive session before a subcommittee at the House Un-American Activities Committee. Magnus arrived at the hearing with William Wallace Gibson. They were shocked to find a swarm of reporters clamoring for a statement. Gibson handled them, but Magnus was angry, thinking the press had been tipped off by the committee in order to gain publicity.

The result was that he was far more rude to the committee than he had intended, finally walking out when one of the members questioned his patriotism. The subcommittee members recommended he be charged with contempt, and outside in the corridor, a photographer shoved a camera in Magnus' face, yelling, "Hey, Commie, look at me!" Magnus responded by slugging the man.

The next morning, pictures of the incident were on all the front pages, showing Magnus with a mean dark look on his face beside another picture of the photographer bleeding from the mouth. The papers all mentioned Magnus' testimony and its implication of Communist taint.

Five days later, when the SEC notified him officially that a tender offer was to be made for Macpherson Distilleries stock, Magnus knew that it had been timed to coincide with his appearance before the subcommittee. Against Weiss' advice, he called Magnus II to find out what he knew, but his son was "in conference and did not know when he could return the call.

Magnus hung up, feeling no regret; he had no time for reflection. His only thought was that when he defeated his son's attempted takeover, as he was sure he would do, perhaps Magnus II would decide to join rather than oppose him. Perhaps. Until then, Magnus would do everything he could to ruin him. He ordered Weiss to pull in the clothesline and find out everything he could about Magnus II's connections to the syndicate. Weiss already had something: he found out who was at Indiantown Gap during the war and began to weave the connection between Magnus II and Anastasia.

On January 31, the *Wall Street Journal* had a full-page advertisement announcing the tender offer of five dollars a share above the current market value. The ad listed a series of grievances with current management, including negligence, mismanagement, loss of profits, and "questionable patriotic practices." The management offered as a replacement listed a board of directors including Juny Fleming as chairman, Bert Cavanaugh, and Magnus Macpherson II as president. Listed under Magnus II's name were five corporations which he controlled, all involved in some aspect of the liquor business. Weiss recognized three of the corporations as the ones that had been buying up large blocks of Macpherson stock.

The same day, a blind item was planted at the top of a widely read gossip column which said, "Item: Which whiskey pays for Commies *and* a bam-basto-bino in a love nest of plush plumage on the East Side?" As soon as he read it, Magnus went home to be with Iris. She had not seen the paper. When he showed it to her, she first laughed. Then she glanced out of the sitting-room windows and pulled Augustus into her arms.

"Everyone will start looking for our house."

"I doubt that. Perhaps a few—"

"They will, Magnus. You have to get guards."

"Iris, no one's going to try—"

"You get guards! You get them. Or I'll take Augustus and go hide somewhere." The little boy, by then five years old, stared at Magnus, reflecting the fear in his mother's voice.

Iris jumped up out of her chair, and taking the boy's hand, went to look out the windows. Magnus walked over to her and embraced her from behind. She stayed rigid.

"Iris, I won't let anything happen."

"It's already happened."

"That newspaper will line garbage cans by morning. Don't let it—"

"No, Magnus. It's not . . ." There was so much she couldn't tell him. She began to cry, and turned to press her face into his shoulder. "I love you. . . ." The boy, released, wandered to the window and pressed his forehead on the cold glass.

"Iris, why are you so afraid? Tell me what's wrong."

"They'll come, Magnus, they'll come. . . ."

"Mommy, look, flash bubbles, flash bubbles. . . ."

At that moment, across the street, two photographers were taking pictures of the house. Magnus pulled Iris away from the window. Surprised, she turned and saw what was happening. "You see? You see?" she said with the hardest smile he had ever seen. Then she picked up the boy and ran out of the room. "Get guards, Magnus. Get guards!"

He called his security manager at the office and arranged for two men to be on the premises day and night.

As far as the press went, Magnus refused to comment, knowing the press was not going to be friendly no matter what he said. He still owned seventeen percent of Macpherson's common stock and knew it would be extremely difficult for an outside group to gain a controlling interest. As to the stockholders, he would let the Fleming group state their entire plan, then allow some time to pass. Wall Street sentimentality for the challenger would give way to the practical matter of power. He would counterattack just before the stockholders' meeting in April. By that time, he would have collected not only support, but enough information to decimate his rivals. In the meantime, he called a board-of-directors meeting to inform them of his plans.

On the night before the meeting, Jack Josephson boarded his corporate plane at the old City-County Airport outside Pittsburgh. From his seat he could see the slag pits of the steel mills glowing in the dark. The smoke from the mills clogged the sky, but he and his paper had just finished a massive campaign to end the pollution. Pittsburgh was about to become a grand, modern, and—for the first time—clean city. His children would have a great place to live and grow. He smiled to himself. Yes, children. WeeDee was pregnant again. They'd decided if it were a boy to name it after Magnus; Jack admired his father-in-law a great deal.

The plane crashed just after takeoff, veering down onto the pot-holed runway, exploding and burning. The firemen could not get close enough to do anything.

"Hello, Father." It was WeeDee; Magnus had been expecting Weiss to call with information on Magnus II. "Father, Jack's plane crashed. He died." She sounded as if she were in shock.

Magnus couldn't speak, until anger roared through him. "Oh, my God . . . Oh, God!"

"Father, I need you here."

"I'm coming. Are you alone?"

"No. People from the paper—"

"I'm on my way. WeeDee—"

"Come." She hung up.

He called his chauffeur, his pilot, and Weiss, who couldn't be reached. Then he went in to Iris' room to tell her. She had moved in a small bed for Augustus, and she was sitting beside it, watching the child sleep. He walked over and sat beside her on the bed.

"Iris, Jack Josephson was killed in a plane crash tonight."

She raised her head and stared into the darkness.

"I'm flying to Pittsburgh; can you get Augustus ready and come with me?"

She turned to him, terrified. "No."

Magnus expected it. "All right. I'll send the plane back tomorrow. Come as soon as you can."

"I can't."

"Why not? For the funeral? WeeDee's your friend."

"I can't. I can't."

She spoke too loud, and the boy woke up, instantly alert to the desperation in his mother's voice. She stroked his head as she talked. "Don't you see? You know that those newspaper people will be there. You *know* that. How can you want his picture, and mine, on every front page—?"

"My daughter's husband is dead. She needs any help her family can give her."

"But we're not family, are we, Augustus?"

Magnus' anger, which had little to do with Iris, exploded. "You come to Pittsburgh! If you don't, you can stay here and rot!"

Before the chauffeur arrived, he contacted his two sons. He reached Jamie at his seminary in Maryland, and Magnus II at the Plaza Hotel, room three-thirty-three. Magnus did not ask his older son to fly to Pittsburgh with him.

At three A.M. Magnus arrived at the Josephson house in the suburb of Fox Chapel. Numerous people introduced themselves and indicated the kitchen where WeeDee had asked to be left alone. She was sitting at the kitchen table with a glass and a bottle of Century.

She turned when she heard him come in. Her smile was in place but the tears poured silently down her face. She stood up and walked into her father's arms and he held her for a long quiet time.

"Thanks for getting here, Father."

He shook his head that it was nothing. Inadvertently he looked at the bottle on the table.

"Don't worry, I . . . I just had to draw a few more lines tonight. . . . Oh, Father," she suddenly cried, "what am I going to do when I start missing him?"

They stayed in the kitchen for an hour alone, saying little, much of the time holding each other as WeeDee fought her grief. Finally she made scrambled eggs and they both went to look in on WeeDee's four-year-old daughter, Ellen. She would have to be told in the morning. Then WeeDee showed her father to a guestroom. She slept in another, across the hall from the one she had shared.

The dawn came too soon. Magnus had not slept. Jack Josephson's death was bringing his children together, and this time he was determined to hold them. He would start with Magnus II. He remembered Iris; he would call New York and tell her she didn't have to come, that he understood her fear for her son, their son.

The funeral was crowded and dignified. WeeDee stood between her daughter and her father; Jamie was next to his father, Magnus II by the little girl. Three generations of Macphersons stood together, and as far as anyone noticed, not one expressed any emotion.

As the coffin moved out of the synagogue, Magnus II drew his father aside. "Fa, I'm not going to the gravesite; too much meat for the press. Tell WeeDee . . ."

Magnus looked at his son and nodded. "I want to talk to you

when I get back to New York. I want to settle the business between us once and for all. I want our family together."

Magnus II looked startled, then smiled gratefully. "Fa . . . When will you get back?"

"Tonight. About nine."

"I'll come to the house."

They shook hands; then, separately, they made their way through the curious crowds to waiting limousines.

Magnus stayed with WeeDee through the long afternoon. Finally he had to leave; the board meeting had been rescheduled for the next day. They said good-bye in her kitchen. WeeDee assured him she would make it. She walked him to his car and waved as he drove off to the airport.

Arriving at his house on Sixty-fifth Street, Magnus felt drained, but he had made a beginning with Magnus II, and was looking forward to seeing Iris and Augustus. The two guards on duty let him in the front door.

"I'm expecting my son in a few minutes."

"He's already here, sir."

Magnus nodded, and walked toward the library.

"Excuse me, sir. He went upstairs to have dinner with Miss Fowler."

Magnus was surprised, but said nothing and went up the stairs. He didn't know why he started to sweat, but when he was out of view of the two guards, he took the second flight two steps at a time. Iris' door was open. Augustus was asleep in his bed, but no one else was there. He went to his own room and found the door closed. He felt ridiculous knocking, but he did.

"Yes? What is it?" Iris said with considerable irritation.

"It's me, may I come in?" he said as he opened the door. The impressions came quickly: a fire in the fireplace, Iris screaming, naked, and Magnus II, naked. She ran to a corner of the room. "He said you weren't coming till tomorrow!" A tray of food was on the table uneaten; Magnus II was lying in the bed, smiling. The numbness around Magnus' fury cracked. He leaped at the bed and smashed his fist at the smile. Once, twice, then hands were around his neck. Magnus II began to fight back. He kicked hard at his father, and Magnus felt his rib crack. Then he began to squeeze at Magnus II's neck.

"Go on, ludicrous old man," jeered Magnus II, "it'll look lovely in the papers." He kneed his father again, this time in the groin, and they both fell to the floor.

"Stop it! Stop!" Iris could do nothing, and ran from the room. By the time she returned with her revolver, Magnus had dragged his son across the room. They were strangling each other, Magnus banging the head in his hands on the marble edge of the fireplace, Magnus II kneeing his father repeatedly, gripping at his windpipe with one hand and gouging at his eyes with the other.

When Magnus reached into the fireplace and picked up a burning log to jam into his son's face, Iris fired the revolver. The bullet smashed a mirror above the mantelpiece, and shards of glass fell down on them. The wood burned Magnus' hand, and he threw it across the room as both men let go of each other.

"Put it down, Iris," Magnus said.

"Real Russian roulette, Iris. Kill either one of us; it might be the father." Iris pointed the gun directly at Magnus II as Augustus came in the door. The guards had reached the second-floor landing. Magnus jumped up and knocked her down. The gun went off into the ceiling. Magnus II fell on both of them, and all three struggled for the gun. Magnus felt his own finger jammed into the trigger guard, but Magnus II held the barrel. Iris jerked at their hands, and the gun went off again. She screamed and put both hands over her ears. The gun fell as Magnus watched his son's eyes roll up into his head as his body sprawled on the floor. For the first few seconds the hole in his left forehead near the hairline didn't bleed. Then abruptly blood began to flow.

"Mr. Macpherson . . ." The guards were at the door with their revolvers drawn.

"Get out."

"Are you all right, sir?"

"Get out! Close the door and wait!"

They hesitated, then did as they were told.

Magnus was on the floor, propped up on one elbow. Iris was sitting, curled up against the wall, staring at Magnus II's body, her hands still over her ears. Magnus heard a noise and saw the boy standing over in a corner by the desk, scared, his black eyes fixed on Magnus.

Magnus stood up; his chest hurt intensely as he limped over to the bed, took the quilt off it, and covered Magnus II's body.

Iris suddenly stood up, pressing herself back against the wall.

"I have to go to my room."

"No. Stay here. Don't touch—"

She screamed, "I have to go to my room!"

Magnus saw her hysteria taking hold. He nodded, and she started to go.

"Wait." He went to his closet, took a dressing gown, and handed it to her. She slipped into it and went out the door, closing it behind her. Magnus glimpsed the two guards just outside.

When he turned around, Magnus saw the little boy holding the phone, dialing the operator. Only at that moment did he remember what Magnus II had said about Russian roulette, and realized the significance of what it meant.

"P'lice! P'lice! . . . Send the p'lice!" the boy was yawping into the phone. Magnus moved as fast as he could and yanked the mouth-piece out of his hand. Augustus cringed back against the desk, await-ing a blow. Magnus looked at him, not knowing what to say, unable to allow any emotion to surface.

Augustus didn't move; he watched Magnus dial the phone.

"Double? . . . Get over here. Magnus is dead . . . Here." He hung up.

Iris came back in and closed the door. She moved quickly to Magnus and handed him the letter.

"Read this. It's not your fault! He hated you! He was so horri-ble. . . . Magnus, I love you. . . ." Then she looked down. "I'm sorry!" Then she was distracted by her own needs. She hurriedly went over to a dark corner of the room, lifted up the dressing gown, and gave herself an injection. Augustus began to cry.

Pain moved quickly through Magnus down from his chest to his groin. It knocked him down, and he sat doubled on the floor near his son's body.

"Sweet dearest, don't cry," Iris said as she let the syringe fall and ran to her child.

As he waited for Double Gibson to arrive, Magnus opened the en-velope and began to read the letter.

"Dear Father Montier . . ."

It was WeeDee's writing. "I hope you'll remember me." Magnus checked the postmark, 1943. ". . . remember my parents, the Mac-phersons. . . ."

January 14, 1972

The Macpherson Industries jet came in over the Isla Vista campus of the University of California and landed at the Santa Barbara airport. It taxied up to the terminal and let out its single passenger.

From the plane, Gus had not seen anyone waiting for him. But as he stepped onto the tarmac, he saw Magnus standing at the nearest gate. There was no expression on his tanned face; his hair was still thick, still black. Only the familiar creases around his eyes were deeper. He was wearing a white muslin shirt, Levi's, and sandals.

When Gus had last seen Magnus at the hospital in Portland, his body drooped badly to the right. As they walked to the parking lot, Gus noticed a slight favoring of the right leg.

"Sandals?" Gus asked as they pulled out onto Highway 101, heading toward Santa Barbara. Magnus was driving a new Jaguar; the top was down.

"At the clinic, they call me California's oldest hippie."

"The clinic" was the Institute for Nutritional Research, where Magnus had been in residence for six months since he left Portland. He had arrived in Santa Barbara considerably improved, but dependent on a walker, and struggling with words. Gus had received positive reports on Magnus' progress, but was amazed to see him driving a car. And as far as Gus could tell, there was no speech impediment.

"How are you?" he asked.

Magnus glanced over at him, then smiled as he flipped the signal light.

"You're going to tell me."

The Jaguar turned off the freeway onto a dirt road. The ruts led to the edge of a cliff, where nearly a hundred cars were parked. Looking down, they could see a crowd of naked people on the beach.

"You brought running shoes, didn't you, Gus?"

"I got new ones for the trip."

Gus opened his suitcase and took out green-and-yellow shoes. Magnus put his on and they started down the path of the cliff to the beach. At the bottom, they stripped off their clothes until they wore nothing but socks and running shoes.

"How far do we run?" Gus asked.

"I'm under doctor's orders to do two miles, but if I can, I go a bit more. I'll do a little warm-up. . . ."

He proceeded to stretch the muscles in his legs, bending down, touching his toes, then putting one leg far out in front and bouncing. In the quick glances of one naked man looking at another, Gus noticed Magnus' body. There was no fat, and very little of the sagging flesh usually present on a man of seventy-two. The right leg looked slightly thinner than the left, but the upper torso revealed no imbalance of musculature.

"Ready, Gus?"

"Looks kind of silly wearing shoes, doesn't it?"

"It does."

After a half-mile, Gus lost his breath, at which point Magnus began to talk.

"So. How am I?"

The question was not an idle one. Magnus jogged along in the hot sun, the sweat trickling down his back, waiting for an answer, but Gus shook his head.

"I'll tell you when we finish. . . . Can't talk now."

Magnus smiled, and they ran to the deserted end of the beach, turned, and went back toward the crowd. Magnus knew the beach and announced each half-mile. His pace never changed, the limp on the right leg lessening as they covered the distance.

When he stated, "Two miles," Magnus didn't stop running. Gus did.

"All right, all right, Magnus. I'm impressed."

"Good. Come on, keep walking."

"I think I lost a lung back there." Then he asked abruptly, "How much longer do you need, Magnus?"

"I'm ready right now. . . . You can see that."

They glanced at each other, acknowledging a common purpose.

Gus smiled and said, "Then you can come back and give it all to me."

"You'll have to want it enough to take it."

"I want it."

Two girls jogged by. They waved and called, "Hey, Magnus, come on, run with us." Magnus waved back.

"I've just covered it with my son."

Both Magnus and Gus noted the use of the term, but did not react to it.

"What's the latest, Gus?"

"Sixteen trucks hijacked so far, three fires in plants, had to close down Baltimore for three days. There's a lot of pressure on the loaders at the wholesalers, lot of damaged goods. Last week three liquor stores were firebombed in New York; each one of them had a Century display in the window. The retailers are getting the message. But it's not the union this time; I've made sure. They're scared shitless they're going to get the blame, though."

"Any pattern?"

"No! All over the country. The syndicate's handling it. A lot of our drivers are getting busted up."

Magnus shook his head. "The police, FBI . . . ?"

"Diligently filling their files."

"Any good news?" Magnus asked.

"Nobody's dead yet."

Magnus looked over at Gus and shook his head. "They're hoping I'm too old and too tired—"

"Hell, they're hoping you'll die."

Magnus laughed.

"I've kept them waiting a long time. . . . Are WeeDee and Jamie for selling out?"

"They don't talk to me about their plans. But my guess is WeeDee wants to sell. Macpherson Industries isn't her interest, never was. She's got her paper and her politics. If McGovern wins in November, she'll probably be an ambassador somewhere. . . . She's never been too happy being a whiskey heiress, Magnus."

Magnus paused, then asked, "Jamie?"

Gus shrugged. "Damned if I know. I've never been able to figure what the hell he wants. His greatest joy is keeping you and me out."

"Is he the connection to the sabotage?"

"Oh, hell no. He's putting out big rewards for information, hoping to catch some dumb arsonist so he can 'smite' the poor bastard with righteousness or something. He really does want the world in order, you know."

"How's the board?"

"They're waiting, but they're itching. Every time Sonnencorp makes a higher tender offer, or another fire breaks out, they start doing a lot of fast math."

Magnus stopped walking and stood quietly for a moment.

"It's Juny."

"No."

"It has to be."

"He *is* too old and too tired. What's he want with M.I.? He has lunch with the Pope."

Magnus smiled. "I'm sure."

"He does. Big article in *Women's Wear Daily*. 'Look who's having lunch in Rome: Sophia and Cary, Bianca and the Earl of Snowdon, and right in the middle, Uncle Juny and the Pope.' I swear to God."

Magnus laughed, and they started walking down the beach again.

"I'll tell you why Juny's the connection, Gus. We know he brought Sonnencorp in to make the tender offer. They're heavyweights, and oil and whiskey look tasty to *any* conglomerate. It's all very neat, very legal. We could fight them off like we've fought off all the others. But there's the added elements of sabotage and violence, which makes everybody a little shaky, not so anxious to fight. And good money from Sonnencorp makes it easy to quit."

"You're telling me that Juny Fleming, the pillar of the New York Stock Exchange, is, in his old age, making side deals with the syndicate? What's in it for him? Money's not enough, revenge isn't enough. . . . What?"

"Eternal life. Come on, let's get our pants on. Your buttocks'll get burned."

They walked back to their pile of clothes, slipped into their pants, and sat in the sand. Magnus looked down the beach.

"All right. Now hear me, Gus. Juny Fleming *is* too old and too tired. He's spent his entire life guaranteeing his eternity; he's not going to lose his place at the last moment. And he can't go on to it until he's destroyed me."

Gus was uneasy with the ecclesiastical aspects of the explanation. "Come on, Magnus, so he wants to live forever with Jesus. That's not what this is about. This is business."

Magnus looked over at Gus and smiled wryly. "He's preserving his monuments, Gus. That's the difference between me and Juny; I say to hell with the monuments. And we'll get him because I trust death; Juny wants to get out of it."

"Death is getting so goddamned fashionable lately. Don't you die on me, Magnus."

"I don't plan to for a while. But Juny thinks dying is just getting into a better club. And I'm his initiation fee."

The explosion sent a shock wave over the beach. They heard a scream and turned in time to see a body falling over the cliff. It hit the sand, bounced once, and lay still. At the top of the cliff a car was on fire. Gus and Magnus looked at each other, dressed, and ran as fast as they could to the top.

By the time they reached the parking area, the first California Highway Patrol car had arrived and the siren of a fire engine could be heard approaching. The cars on each side of the Jaguar were scorching, and one of them began to burn. They could see a body underneath the Jaguar, but the heat kept anyone from trying to reach it. At the edge of the cliff a young woman was screaming hysterically. Several people tried to pull her back to safety.

A crowd gathered; the fire engine arrived and covered the hulk of the Jaguar with foam. Two firemen pried the body out from under the motor and dragged it clear. Two other Highway Patrol cars arrived.

Gus touched Magnus on the shoulder and signaled for him to move slowly out of the crowd. When they were clear, Gus led him behind a pickup truck.

"That was an accident, right, Magnus? It wasn't supposed to blow up until you got in it."

"It's pathetic. They're using punks who don't know their work."

"Lucky for you, unlucky for him. Stay out of sight, there may be some others around. I'll talk to the cops and get them to come over here."

"Gus, we both walk away, now. . . . They waited until you arrived to wire the car. They hoped for both of us."

Gus stared at Magnus, then nodded. Together they moved quickly into a stand of eucalyptus trees and headed toward Santa Barbara.

John Gianni sat in his office in Nassau waiting for the phone to ring. It was dark outside. He'd been waiting all day for his contact with Sonnencorp to let him know about the last five million he'd placed with the conglomerate. The money had been carefully washed through Switzerland into West German marks, and the executive would accept the money as an investment from a Luxembourg company, incorporated for the purpose. Gianni had placed one hundred and fifteen million dollars with the conglomerate in this fashion, working through companies set up in Hong Kong, Buenos Aires, Manila, and London. Having expanded too rapaciously, Sonnencorp desperately needed Gianni's massive infusion of laundered capital and agreed in return to buy Macpherson Industries and let Gianni control it. Gianni in turn would give that honor to Juny Fleming in return for Fleming and Co.'s umbrella of respectability.

John Gianni smiled as he looked out of his window over Bay Street to the harbor. The view had no doubt changed since the days Magnus Macpherson worked the wharves. Gianni remembered that Magnus had paid for his education, college, and law school. Then he shrugged. Business was business.

The phone rang.

"Yes. Gianni. Nassau."

"John, it's Meyer."

Meyer Lansky never used a phone. Gianni sat upright and began to sweat. It was Lansky's hundred and fifteen million that had gone into Sonnencorp. It was Lansky who was organizing the pressure on Macpherson Industries. Something must have gone wrong.

"Yes, Mr. Lansky," he said formally.

"I have no business to discuss with you, John." Lansky was covering him in case someone was listening in.

"What can I do for you?"

"John, your son, John Junior . . . he was killed today."

Gianni couldn't believe it; his first reaction was that it was done as punishment for some mistake he'd made on the Sonnencorp deal.

"Are you sure, Meyer?"

Lansky gave a long sigh. He was always sure.

"Yes, John. It happened in California. He was wiring a car. Something happened, an accident. I wanted to tell you, and say how sorry . . ."

Johnny. He was a demolitions expert; the Marines trained him, for Christ's sake! He had wanted to go to Vietnam. He'd enlisted and lived through four years of it. Afterward, he went into the Mob. The kid had hated school, hated the law, hated his home . . . hated his father, probably.

"Thank you, Meyer."

"Good-bye, John."

Gianni sat back in his chair, remembering his son. Johnny had always been contemptuous of his father's semblance of respectability, saying, "You can't keep your hands clean when you're shoveling shit, Dad." He was ashamed his father had never fought in a war, and he'd joined the Marines to make up for it. He came home a real tough guy, too smart to waste time in college. Dead, wiring a car. Gianni stared at the darkness over the bay as a light from a sailing yacht traced its way around Hog Island.

He wondered whose car his son had been wiring. It was strange Meyer hadn't mentioned it. Then he shrugged again. Johnny was dead; it was business.

He tried to cry, gave up, went home, and told his wife. She cried.

III
The Power
1951–1971

We live in an old chaos of the sun.
—WALLACE STEVENS

15

Queen Elizabeth was told on the eve of her
coronation that the British Expedition had
conquered the mountain. . . . Mount Everest,
the 29,002-foot giant, was the last main
outpost of the world unknown to man.

—THE NEW YORK TIMES

The Great Meadow Prison at Comstock, New York, was a maximum
security institution. Nevertheless, because it had been built more recently than other prisons in the state system, the facility was considered a "country club." Magnus worked in a basement, making and
repairing mattresses. The summer of 1953 was particularly hot, and
the mattress room was thick with humidity and human smells. The
day that Everest was conquered, Magnus watched an inmate bend
over the toilet and desperately search his own feces for a small
balloon containing heroin; his wife had passed it to him the previous
day in a kiss. When he found it, the man barely took notice of
Magnus, but mumbled, "Get your kicks, asshole," as he washed his
hands and the balloon in the sink. Magnus watched; he had never
seen so destructive a wanting. It made whiskey seem as pure as
prayer.

The man had everything he needed. He had made a syringe using
a lightbulb filament as a needle, with a fountain pen as a plunger. He
wrapped his arm, found a vein, and jabbed in the instrument. Blood
followed the filament out his arm before the jolt hit him. He gradually fell backward on the floor and rested, one leg twisted up under
him.

Magnus flushed the toilet and filled a mop bucket full of cold
water. He poured it on the man and helped him stand up and lean
against the wall. No one would notice the wetness of the blue-gray
uniform; everyone working in the mattress room was soaked with

sweat. Magnus urged the man to get back to his place as soon as he could, and left him there, mumbling something about snow.

Magnus went back to his stitching machine and shoved another mattress into place. He was still strong and used his job as a form of exercise; routine was boring, and worse, it didn't stop his mind. His thoughts ricocheted back and forth between past horrors and future time. Worst of all was remembering happiness. Magnus was grateful that he had not left much of that behind.

A guard came into the room and looked around. Magnus was a well-known prisoner. He had come in after a sensational trial with the connections and money to make his stay as easy as possible; a favor here and a Christmas present there made a great difference in attitude. The guard walked over and said, "Mr. Macpherson, you have a visitor."

Magnus looked up.

"Your counsel."

The prisoners had little freedom of movement and activities. Visiting privileges were regulated, but attorney's time was practically unlimited. For this reason, Ted Weiss had been anointed Magnus' "counsel."

Weiss stood at the end of the visitors' room, looking at inmates' paintings on the walls. He wore the same kind of fedora, the same kind of ill-fitting suit he had worn ever since Magnus first met him on the pier at Windsor. Magnus sometimes wondered what Weiss did with his money. With salary and stock options, he must have been taking home a hundred and fifty thousand a year, but he still lived in the same apartment over on the West Side. Its only advantage was that it was near Madison Square Garden, and he enjoyed boxing and hockey.

As soon as Weiss turned around, Magnus could see something was wrong. They sat down on opposite sides of a long table. The guards in the room stayed respectfully out of hearing.

"What's the matter, Weiss?"

"Got a problem."

"The parole?"

"No. That's all set. Just gotta keep you alive until then. . . . Anastasia decided to put out a contract on you."

Magnus automatically looked around the room, then back at Weiss.

"We should have blown his head off at St. Pierre. Doesn't the son of a bitch have enough problems?"

Weiss shrugged. "More than enough. . . . The clothesline says he's getting a little nuts."

"Can we get to him? Remind him of what we have?"

"The gun's too old; the stuff between him and your son ain't enough anymore. It worked at the time, but ever since the Kefauver investigations, Anastasia's been doing things for no reason. Lotta pressures on him right now."

"Why me?"

"He's hated you a long time. Everybody knows it, and he knows everybody knows it. If he doesn't do something about it, it looks like a weakness. He can't afford that right now. He's up against some rough competition."

"Can we get to them, give them our information in return for protection?"

"You could. Sure, Vito Genovese and Meyer Lansky, they'll be glad to help you. Then, when you get outta here, you're in bed with them and the covers are up to your neck. No. Just hope they get a chance to nail Anastasia before he gets to you."

"I'm a sitting duck."

"Yeah. You're getting a bodyguard."

"In here?"

Weiss nodded. "He's getting transferred from Sing Sing tomorrow . . . and don't think that didn't take some axle grease. He's one of Longie Zwillman's soldiers, in on a twenty for extortion, says he knows you. Guy named Johnny Gianni, something wrong with his face."

Magnus remembered him, the man who owed him a favor. But that kind of favor, getting in the way of a syndicate contract, didn't come free.

"What's he cost, Weiss?"

"College and law school for his kid. Anastasia's contract's worth fifty grand, so we're getting Gianni at a good price."

Magnus nodded. Three months of protection from Anastasia was worth it.

Weiss opened his briefcase and pulled out a thick legal document. "Brought the foundation papers." He handed them to Magnus.

"Have Jamie and WeeDee seen them?"

"Yeah. Just came from Pittsburgh. . . . Oh, yeah . . ."

Weiss scruffled around in the briefcase and pulled out some snapshots. "WeeDee sent these. . . . Says she'll see you next week."

Magnus took the pictures and put them with the papers. At that moment he didn't want to look at them.

"What do they think of the foundation?"

"Both say fine, if it's what you want."

"And Double says it works for taxes, and for my children to retain control?"

"Yeah. . . . But . . ."

"What?" Magnus already knew.

Weiss sighed. "Gibson thinks the papers you got are as tight as they can get, but there's no way he can protect you from a future claim—"

"Augustus Fowler is not my child!"

Weiss was silent. The guards glanced over, then away. Magnus lost his temper.

"What's the matter with you? Why can't Double understand this? There's a good chance he's not even my grandson; there's nothing to prove she was exclusively faithful to people named Macpherson. Can't you see that?"

"I ain't arguing on this, Macpherson."

"I'm paying for her sanatorium, her house out there, her platoons of private detectives. Good God! Am I going to spend the rest of my life waiting for that little bastard to step up smartly and say, 'I'm your son, give me mine'?"

Weiss said nothing. Magnus stood up.

"Tell Double this thing must not be vulnerable to that boy's claim. Tell him to go out to see Iris and make her sign something. If she refuses, I'll cut off her support."

"The newspapers would love it."

"I don't give a damn about the papers. There's nothing they could do to me that they haven't already done. You tell Double—"

"I'll tell him!"

Weiss's tone reminded Magnus of the impotence of anger in a prison visitors' room, and he sat down. They were quiet until Magnus said, "How's business?"

Weiss was glad to change the subject. "That kid of yours is a killer; if Jamie'd stayed a priest, the devil would be chopped liver by now. Tell you something else, he scares the hell out of me. Not because he does anything wrong. It's the way he does everything right."

"Go on." Magnus forced himself not to worry about Macpherson Distilleries. There wasn't any point. He could own the largest block of common stock, but as a convicted felon, he could only listen.

"The cost accounting he brought in is paying off: less waste, less loss. The new ad agency is applying the advertising-sales ratios to each product rather than across the board. Marketing research seems to be paying off, except those smart-ass kids with their Harvard Business School theories drive me nuts. . . . He wanted me to ask you about two things."

Jamie was very smart, Magnus thought. He was careful about informing his father. Jamie covered himself, making it difficult for Magnus to have any complaints about being left out, or giving him any excuse to come back.

"He wants to sell the hooch in a special glass decanter for Christmas . . . figures the customers will go for the package."

Magnus nodded. He thought it was a damn good idea. Get a good design, get it on the shelves on December 1, "The Century Decanter . . ." He stopped running with the idea, knowing he wasn't going anywhere but back to a cell.

"What else?"

"He wants to change the name of the corporation."

Magnus hesitated, trying to control his indignation.

"To what?"

" 'Macpherson Industries.' New board symbol: 'M.I.' "

"Damn. . . . Damn!" Magnus knew what Jamie was doing; he was opening the company to acquisition, a broader base of business. "We've had that name since before that boy was born."

Weiss said nothing. So much of business was staying quiet. Weiss knew Magnus intended to leave his company alone, to give up the day-to-day operation in favor of his son. He would become chairman after a suitable time had elapsed following his release from prison. That was the agreement, and Magnus would stick to it. But Weiss knew the man's company was being peeled off him like onion skin.

"Will I be told what's on his shopping list?"

"Absolutely. At all times. Jamie said that he'd never consider buying without your . . . knowledge."

"Knowledge" was Jamie's word, not Weiss's. "Knowledge" was one thing; "consent" was another. Magnus let it go. The times were against him, not to mention the place. He said good-bye to Weiss as quickly as he could, then suggested, "Weiss, you need a new suit."

Weiss raised his eyebrows. "You should talk."

That night in his cell, Magnus began reading Double Gibson's document establishing the Macpherson Foundation. It would be financed with an original gift of fifty million dollars of Magnus' stock, to be followed by five gifts of ten million dollars each at two-year intervals. Eventually the foundation would receive the bulk of Magnus' estate. The control of the foundation would be held by Magnus and his "offspring." The charter defined the term "offspring" quite carefully: "the natural and patrilateral issue of Magnus Macpherson, who are, as of this date, a son, James, and a daughter, Mrs. John Josephson (Eleanor)."

As he turned the page, the snapshots fell out on the floor. Magnus reached down and picked them up. His grandchildren were growing up without knowing him. Ellen was already seven. And Magnus—not "the Third" or "III"; thank God he didn't need a number on him. The little boy was almost three years old.

Magnus had never seen him and would not until he was a free man. Only three months, and it would be over, and he could begin to forget it all, Great Meadow, the sentence, the trial. . . .

Magnus knew that the timing of his trial had been lucky. As scandal, it did not get the attention it could have. The headlines were on the Alger Hiss trial, Senator McCarthy's announcement that there were 205 Communists in the State Department, the arrest of the Rosenbergs for atomic spying, the Kefauver investigations of organized crime, and the outbreak of the Korean War. What came to be known in the dailies as "The Macpherson Family Fandango" became macabre relief to the larger realities of the world.

Magnus was originally indicted for first-degree murder. His fingerprints were all over Iris' pistol. Double Gibson swiftly managed to change the charge to second-degree murder, then to manslaughter, and finally had Magnus plead guilty to involuntary manslaughter, thus avoiding a trial before a jury. He convinced the Justice Department to drop the pending contempt of Congress charge and settled out of court with the photographer whom Magnus had slugged. The photographer, however, attended every day of Magnus' trial, and his malicious pictures appeared in newspapers all over the country, though fortunately not on the front pages.

The emphasis on the reporting was slanted to the sordid; the stories did not hesitate to embroider, to speculate, and, simply, to lie. Magnus tried to contain his anger, but once he grabbed a reporter and said, "You pig, calling me a pimp for my son. Why don't you publish the truth? It should be enough for you." As Gibson pulled them apart the reporter smiled and said, "We're not after truth, Macpherson, we're after news. And I'm glad you're a reader."

Juny Fleming was called as a prosecution witness. To the press he had stated categorically that Magnus was a murderer, and that it was a miscarriage of justice to let him off with a plea of involuntary manslaughter. But the day before he was to testify, Double Gibson sent him a thorough outline describing how Fleming and Co. had been closely linked to Albert Anastasia through Magnus II. Gibson opined that if Juny insisted on expressing his righteous outrage in court, the Anastasia partnerships would certainly be discussed in the cross-examination.

When he took the stand, Juny was like a bottle of hot gas. He answered most of the prosecutor's questions, not to the judge, but to Gibson. The prosecutor, aware that a primary witness was fading to gray, began to press him. Juny, desperate to preserve his reputation, became clumsy and irrational, finally standing up and yelling across the courtroom, "You murdered my sister and now my nephew, Macpherson, and I swear to God I'll see you dead and ruined!"

The prosecutor was satisfied, but the judge, clearly furious, had the statement expunged from the record and reprimanded Juny for the outburst. Gibson could have gone after him, but felt the performance had helped his client and let Juny go with no questions.

The worst was Iris. For two harrowing days the prosecutor kept her on the stand. On two occasions a recess had to be called, once because Iris was crying uncontrollably and another time when she needed "medication." The press licked up every word she spoke. The complexity of her emotions was beyond her ability to explain in court. When the prosecutor pushed for some definition of her situation with Magnus II, she set her chin and spat out, "We fucked. That's all." The press arranged dots, dashes, and asterisks to suggest the unprintable verb to their avid readers.

By the end of her testimony, Iris had clearly defined herself in the eyes of the public as at least a whore, certainly an unfit mother, and worst of all, helpless.

"I loved Magnus Macpherson," she said at the end of her testimony in answer to the prosecutor's moralistic "Why?"

"I still do, but . . . ." She looked at Magnus for the first time since she took the stand. "I . . . couldn't handle it. People aren't equal, you know. I just stepped into a dream. It was all a dream, to live with him, and have his child. . . . He is your child, Magnus. I know he is."

Magnus looked up at her at that moment with such scorn she bowed her head and began to cry. The prosecutor said, "No more questions," but Iris did not move. The judge said, "Miss Fowler, you

338

may step down now." She looked up, startled, and tried to smile at the judge. Then she got up and walked quickly over to the press table. A bailiff jumped up to intercept her, but she reached it before he could stop her.

As she spoke, she looked at each reporter down the table. "Say anything you want about me. Anything; I don't care. But please leave my baby alone." The bailiff firmly took her arm and led her out of the courtroom. She did not look at Magnus again.

One element studiously ignored by the court was the constant reference in the press to Magnus Macpherson's Communist sympathies. The prosecution wisely never mentioned it, since it might have allowed Double Gibson to move for a mistrial on grounds that the political atmosphere was permeating the trial.

Nevertheless, Magnus was for a time the press's favorite "Comsymp"; hardly a day went by when the news of the trial did not include a reminder that Magnus had been cited for contempt by the House Un-American Activities Committee. Double respected the judge and believed he would not be swayed by innuendo, but the persistent invective made Gibson suspicious. He put two investigators on the case, who traced much of the information to a vehemently anti-communist organization called the Patriot's League. When they looked into the group's financing, they discovered that the principal backer was Louis Rosenstiel.

As soon as Gibson told him, Magnus knew exactly what Rosenstiel was up to: more market. Rosenstiel knew every bottle which Magnus had on the shelves was labeled "Macpherson"; therefore, every story in the papers tainted those bottles with "pink-Comsymp." In the first six months of the year, Macpherson's sales dropped an average of twenty-two percent.

The trial took longer than expected. The prosecution intensified the details of Magnus II's takeover bid in order to establish the motive for his father's act. Double Gibson's initial strategy was to put Magnus II on trial in absentia, but Magnus did not want the sordid facts of his son's life mauled over any more than necessary in the press.

Gibson therefore had to appeal to the mercy of the court and to emphasize the accidental nature of the incident. Iris testified she had tried to stop the fight with the first shot, and tried to kill Magnus II with the second. Anyone could have been shot as a result of the struggle for the gun. She said it was just luck that Magnus II was killed.

Gibson argued persuasively for probation, but the prosecution demanded the maximum penalty of fifteen years. The judge, in pronouncing sentence, expressed sympathy for the defendant, and cognizance of "the extreme emotional disturbance in which the defendant had found himself at the time of the crime." But the crime was felonious; death was not accidental. There had been intent on the part of the defendant to inflict serious physical injury to the victim. Though comprehensible in the heat of passion, the intent had resulted in the death of an individual. The law was clearly written, said the judge, though he handed down the minimum sentence, five years.

Gibson immediately moved to appeal; he was flabbergasted when Magnus refused.

"Magnus, with time the case will cool. You will *not* have to go to prison!"

Double and WeeDee sat with Magnus in a small conference room off the Court of General Sessions. Except for the week when she had given birth to her son, WeeDee attended every day of the trial.

"Magnus, if you don't let me appeal, you'll walk out of this room into jail."

"I know that!" Magnus sat in his chair, as he had sat throughout the trial. Each hand rigidly gripped an armrest. "But if I don't go, if I get away with it—"

"It's not getting away with anything. It's—"

"Be quiet, Double! Listen to me a minute. I know that if anyone could get me out of this, you could. But if you succeeded, I'd lose Macpherson's." He looked over at WeeDee. "We'd lose Macpherson's. Juny's just waiting for the trial to end to go after the company again. If I win the appeal, I'd be getting away with it because I'm rich and corrupt. That's what it would be in the minds of the public and the stockholders. They'd give Juny their proxies and they'd stop buying my whiskey."

"That's pure martyrdom. The public forgets everything." Double was angry and frustrated.

"Yes, they will with time. And I mean to give them time, and not let another trial give the press a chance to go on reminding them. Look what two trials did to Alger Hiss. Double, I know it's hard for you to lose a case—"

"I haven't lost! I haven't finished!"

"I know, Double. I'm not *letting* you finish. I'm going to prison!"

The three of them sat silently, all trying to accept the inevitability. WeeDee watched her father, then got up and moved her chair very close to him. She put her hand on Magnus' arm and whispered, "Father, do you think you're guilty?"

He stared at the ceiling for a long moment, until finally his eyes lowered to hers. "I read the letter you wrote to Father Montier."

WeeDee felt herself go cold. Magnus continued, "It was returned from Canada, the hospital sent it to me. Iris opened it, kept it, until that night. . . . With what I've learned since, your brother was filth, WeeDee. . . . I have no regret he's dead; I feel no guilt. But I *did* kill him. I meant to."

"He was trying to kill you, too, Father."

"Perhaps. I've tried to remember exactly what happened, not just the struggle, but what was going through my mind. I remember that the idea the little boy wasn't my son didn't occur to me until after Magnus was shot. I remember that quite clearly, so the question of whose son he was had nothing to do with it. But just after Iris fired the second time, trying to kill him, I stopped her; for a split second I wondered why I hadn't let her shoot him. Then he jumped on us both and we all struggled for the gun. There were just a few seconds, but I remember thinking, 'he *should* be dead already; only because I stopped Iris is he . . .' I knew my finger was on the trigger; I remember that. I have no doubt I was trying to point the barrel at him. I may not have pulled the trigger, or purposely aimed. But I did kill him, and I *meant* to do it. I wanted him dead."

He peered at WeeDee, wondering why he was so meticulously explaining his motives to her. He supposed because she had been at the trial every day, because she'd supported him, she seemed like his only family. Jamie had remained in seminary except for a single terrible visit; Kristin had come in from East Hampton, but the press had mobbed her, so she stayed away.

"Father, why are you telling me?"

"I was wondering myself."

She smiled as tears came to her eyes. "I guess it was going to take something as horrible as this for us to know each other again." She shook her head sadly as she took both his hands. "If *he* had killed you, I wouldn't have been here every day. I wouldn't have been here *at all* . . . unless it was to testify against him. I want you to know that."

Magnus nodded.

"I'm sorry about the letter, Father. I wanted to tell you—"

"I wish you had. Perhaps I would have known about him sooner. But don't punish yourself; you and I had walls between us."

"You don't need to punish yourself either, Father."

He didn't answer; he would have liked to believe her, but he didn't.

Noticing the silence, Gibson came back with another point.

"Magnus, do you think for a moment you'll keep the company if you're in jail? I can see an across-the-board crisis in confidence when a Macpherson isn't . . ." He stopped. All three of them thought of Jamie. It was a new idea to Double and WeeDee, but Magnus had already considered him.

"Yes, Jamie. His name is Macpherson; that should help with the stockholders and employees. He's Juny's favorite nephew, even more than his late brother was, and he's an honest-to-God Roman Catholic. It'll be up to Jamie to defuse Juny. There's no one else who can do that."

"He's twenty-two years old," Double said with hopeless exasperation.

"And everyone will be pulling for him. Young Henry Ford took over his company at twenty-eight. They were going to make Magnus II president, and he was only twenty-five. Jamie can handle it. Weiss will teach him."

"He's a Jesuit; he's taken vows," WeeDee said.

"There are dispensations, and he was a Macpherson even before he was a Jesuit."

"Father, . . . he hates the company."

Magnus smiled bitterly. "But somewhere deep in his Catholic soul where he can hate and not know it, he hates me more. Remember that, WeeDee, because it's going to be you who'll have to convince him. Tell him he can purify the evil from the company; he can keep me out of it. That should do it. But don't let him refuse."

Gibson repeated, ". . . 'he can keep me out of it'?"

Magnus nodded. "I'll retain control, but I will not interfere in his direction of the company. Tell him that, WeeDee."

"Even after you get out of prison?" Gibson asked.

"Even then. . . . 'Forever and ever, amen.' Tell him. He should understand that." Magnus stood up. "Now let's go back in there and get this over with. WeeDee . . ." She stood up and took his hand. "I'd have asked you to take over; I had no hesitance because you're a woman."

She nodded.

"But you've got your own responsibilities with Jack's company. . . . Double will help you out if you need him."

"Yes, of course," Double nodded.

"And I'll look after Iris," WeeDee said with certainty. Magnus looked away, not wanting to care.

The three of them stood for a moment, knowing there was nothing more to say.

"Come on," Magnus said.

That had been more than two years ago. His parole had been granted and there were only three months left of his sentence. He looked at the snapshots of his two grandchildren, Ellen riding her own pony, little Magnus at the wheel of a kiddie car. He believed he'd made the right decisions. The public already had forgotten the scandal, though his grandchildren would surely hear of it, probably in a cruel way. But their lives would not be infected with it; Magnus had paid his debt. And whatever the memory of it caused his surviving children, he knew they could take it. Besides, the Macpherson Foundation would put them in a position to withstand any residual criticism.

Magnus had thought about a foundation before Magnus II's death, mainly as a method to escape estate taxes. He was impressed how conveniently old Henry Ford had given up his stock but had assured control of his company for his offspring. Sam Bronfman had set up a separate corporation to run his children's trusts, trusts which retained voting control of Seagram's but which escaped the massive estate taxes when Sam died.

Magnus' intention was to withdraw from Macpherson Distilleries and dedicate his time to the foundation. At first his objectives were the usual lofty social concerns: world hunger, birth control, education. But as Magnus spent his time in prison, he saw the devastating effects of drugs and realized that alcohol, too, could be construed as a sedative. He told Double to add to the foundation's charter an additional organization dedicated to research, dissemination of information, rehabilitation, and eradication of problems resulting from drugs, alcohol, and tobacco.

In order to take advantage of the tax laws, the common stock which Magnus intended to give to the foundation would be donated irrevocably. But Magnus, as president of the foundation, would retain voting control of its stock and therefore of Macpherson Distilleries.

As he read over the charter, Magnus was pleased. It seemed to place him at a discreet distance, yet with no lessening of power. He anticipated the possibilities of his foundation and was curious to experience the transition from making money to giving it away.

Three more months. Actually eighty-eight days. He had to live one day at a time, or rather stay alive one day at a time. There was a guard outside his cell that night; Weiss must have arranged for it. Eighty-eight days. Tomorrow, eighty-seven.

Magnus put the charter down, lay back on his bed and allowed himself the luxury of thinking about "then."

When Magnus was on trial, Evelyn Lorraine had written him a letter. During those long weeks, it had given him his only moment of laughter.

Dear Magnus,

I can't tell from the papers whether you're Rasputin or Joe Stalin's cousin. What's happening to you is so horrible I can't cry, or even get mad, so I drink too much of your rotten whiskey and send my love.

How does it feel to be as famous as me? I'm beginning to know what it's like to be rich (but not as rich as ———). Also you'll be happy to know that I, too, have been labeled "pink." Those horny bastards from HUAC came to town for some free publicity and called me to appear. They asked if I'd been a Commie in New York before I came to Hollywood. What I was in New York was not a Communist, but it was none of their business, so I clammed up. One of those righteous prigs pointed at me and said I was "pink." I looked him straight in the eye and said, "There's only one part of me that's pink, mister, and I'm not going to tell you about that either."

I haven't lost any roles yet, but . . . (ominous background music) I was offered the part of a *mother* last week. So, if the crazy patriots don't get me, time will. And with that I'll get mad, have a drink of your rotten whiskey, end this letter, and send more love.

Evelyn

Magnus had called right away, and they spoke often during the trial. She had offered to come to New York before the sentence was pronounced, but they both agreed the proceedings were sensational enough without a movie star suddenly appearing on the scene. When he went to prison, they agreed to correspond. Since prison mail was thoroughly censored, such a correspondence could easily reach the press, so he wrote to a Hollywood post-office box, and she used a fictitious name.

Through their correspondence, Magnus learned that Evelyn Lorraine had learned about Iris from Bugsy Siegal, who heard from Longie Zwillman, who heard from a U.S. senator from New Jersey, who heard all the Washington rumors. She had accepted the situation and soon after married the son of a Fort Worth oil millionaire, who was hovering around Hollywood at the time. After six months, she divorced the boy and married another Fort Worth millionaire. That year, she had been the third most popular box-office attraction. After going through Fort Worth, Evelyn had two more husbands, making four in all. She was currently involved with a married U.S. senator, a black football star, and her latest director.

Her first visit to the prison was to celebrate his birthday, six months late. She came not as her famous self, but as his cousin from Scotland, complete with a black wig, granny glasses, and an orthopedic shoe. Her accent was the best she could do, having learned it for a forgettable film called *Highland Fling,* in which she starred with Sonja Henie.

During that first visit, they did not touch each other, because of her disguise and their awkwardness after ten years apart. They spent most of the time laughing. The second visit was easier and more relaxed. She came as the same character, but dropped the accent soon after they began talking.

"This time I waited for you, Evelyn. Last time, it was a lark. I have to warn you, I probably expect too much today. . . . Now that you're here, I have to ask you not to come again. The only way to get through prison is to wait for nothing."

"I'm sorry, Magnus."

"Don't be; I'm too glad to see you."

Evelyn smiled and took off her granny glasses. "S'funny . . . before the war, when you and I went our separate ways, I didn't think about it much. I don't know why, I guess I was busy, there was a war on and . . . well, I had all those Fort Worth husbands. I remembered you every once in a while. Nice memories, but the thirties seemed like another century. . . . I didn't know about you and Iris until later from Bugsy, and by then I was too full of Fort Worth to give a damn. But last time I came up here . . . Jesus Christ, how much time do I have? Are they going to throw me out?"

"You can stay until supper if you want."

"This is a damn hard conversation to have, sitting on either side of a fucking table."

"This table has heard it all."

"Yeah, I guess so. . . . listen, Magnus, I missed you. I missed you like I should have before the war. I feel like a script writer just came in and cut out ten years. After I left last time, I was madder than hell at you for throwing me over for some female you'd never seen before. And what really burned me up is that she was so goddamned *young!* You prick!"

Magnus shook his head hopelessly at the memory. He thought of his past with Evelyn, the first time he saw her in the Astor Bar, then in her yachting outfit at the Garden of Allah, the demure dress at the San Ysidro Ranch when he told her about her first movie. He turned away, and stopped himself.

"What's the matter, Magnus?"

"You're the only part of my past that's safe for me to look at. I don't want to wear it out."

"I hope you have a few more; I'm pretty poor pickings for you."

"You're talking to a hungry man."

"Well, you can't just think about now. You've got to have a few memories or something to look forward to."

"It's easier if you don't have either." He reached out his hand and touched her cheek. It was against the rules, but the guards at the far end of the room overlooked it. Evelyn turned and kissed his palm.

"What, Magnus?"

He took his hand away slowly, then shook his head. "I don't know."

"Magnus, tell me," Evelyn said softly. "You've got to know you're alive in here. You waited for me this time. I want you to tell me why."

Magnus tried to come up with words, but failed.

"I don't know why."

Evelyn looked away, not unkindly, rather to consider another tactic. Magnus mistook her glance as impatience.

"Do you want me to say 'I love you,' Evelyn? No, I don't. I loved two women. One's dead, the other's mad, or addicted, or whatever she is. . . . I don't trust myself with loving anymore; I've failed too greatly with it."

"Magnus, it wasn't only you. It takes two, they say."

"I've wondered about that; I've tried to believe it. All my explanations seem pathetic excuses. My love of Iris and Mary was . . . a kind of corrosion; it seems to have touched my children as well."

He paused and stared at Evelyn. "So consider yourself lucky."

"You don't scare me. That's all in the past anyway. I thought you were going to forget that."

"Yes. I was."

Magnus again was silent, then smiled slightly. "Since you were here last, I confess I've spent a good deal of time wondering what it would be like if you and I had more memory between us."

"We've got some; we can make more."

"New memories. . . . How old does something have to be before it becomes a memory?"

"Unfortunately," Evelyn snorted, "we're both old enough to be one now."

"I suppose I am." He smiled again at her, reached out, and took her hand. "I doubt if you are."

"Female movie stars hold the land speed record for becoming memories. And I'll tell you something: I'll be ready. I'm sick of being everybody else's dream. Dreams have to work too damn hard. Besides, I've just reached that point where I want to share pasts rather than futures."

She moved the hand he was not holding across the table, and they sat for a few moments with outstretched arms, smiling at each other. Then one of the guards started to walk toward them to warn them. Hearing his approach, they both took their hands off the table and put them in their laps. The guard said "Thanks" and returned to the far end of the room.

"What'll it be for us, then, Evelyn?"

She glanced at him, surprised. Then she shrugged. "I don't know. . . . Tell me what it is now, Magnus?"

"Back to that, is it?"

She nodded, barely smiling. Magnus looked down at the table for a moment, searching for words. Finally he looked back at her and said, "You're my friend, perhaps my best one. Nothing's ever been masked between us. I have to tell you that since I saw you last, a healthy lust has taken a firm grip on me."

Evelyn glanced down the room at the guards and said, "If they worried about us holding hands, what would they do if we just lay down here on the table?"

"The firing squad."

They both laughed, and started to reach for each other again, then stopped, leaving their arms in view.

"More than any of that, Evelyn, I trust you."

The smile left her face and she slowly arched her neck. Her posture was suddenly that of her film ethos, but the look on her face was of an unexpected discovery.

"When you're young, you fall in love, over and over; you lust and you hate and you crave and you ache. Then, when you grow up, you trust."

They sat for a while, quietly, and for the last half-hour of her visit, they dared to make plans.

Magnus kissed her good-bye with more than a cousinly kiss. Their correspondence increased and the plans became firm. On the day of his release, Magnus would step aboard a two-masted schooner at the Seventy-ninth Street yacht basin in New York, with a crew of two, a cook, and Evelyn Lorraine. Weiss had arranged for the ship; no one else knew. They planned to sail south around the Windward Islands as long as they could stand each other or until one of the crew talked in port and publicity caught up with them.

Magnus heard a noise at his cell door, slight, metallic. He opened his eyes, saw nothing. He didn't know what time it was, but he was sure he had heard something. He got up to ask the guard outside his cell what it was, but the man was not there. As Magnus pushed against the door to see, he felt it edge open and realized it had been unlocked.

Silently he backed into the dark cell and quickly stuffed clothes between his sheets in the form of a body. Then he slipped under the bed, the only place to hide. He pulled open the mattress and extracted the half length of broom handle he had previously sewn there. At one end of the broom handle, a steel mattress-stitching needle, about five inches long, was secured and braced with wire.

Magnus watched the cell door open and close silently. The feet came swiftly to the bed, and Magnus jammed the needle up into the groin. The man screamed; Magnus punctured him twice in the legs before he collapsed, wildly waving a hypodermic syringe in the air. Lights had gone on, an alarm was sounding. Magnus pried the syringe out of the man's hand and dragged him out of the cell. He threw the broom handle into the next cell and stood on the catwalk as the man lay screaming. Guards were all over him in the next second. One of them said, "What the fuck's going on here? Jesus, you, Macpherson?"

"I woke up and found him in my cell with this." He pointed at the hypo. "I don't know how he got in or what he wanted, but I fought him, got his needle, and stuck him a few times. Someone unlocked my cell to let him get in. I want the Hole until tomorrow morning when we can find out who did it." There were ten guards around him, holding shotguns. The one in charge ordered the screaming convict to be taken to the prison hospital. Before Magnus was led off to solitary, he glanced at the man in the next cell, who gave him an O-sign about hiding the broom handle.

The next day the warden conducted a thorough investigation, called Magnus in from solitary, and apologized. The inmate with the hypodermic had told them nothing, but the syringe had contained arsenic. The guard who had been outside Magnus' cell disappeared a half-hour after the "incident," and a bulletin was out for his arrest. Magnus was assured the "incident" would not affect his parole. He thanked the warden and went to lunch, where he saw his new bodyguard.

The secondhand skin had turned to rubber. Johnny Gianni's face had held its shape, but not its color. Where grafts had been made, under the right eye, running up into the right temple, it had developed gray ridges. Hair grew only where it had been surgically implanted on the right side of his head, for Gianni had gone naturally bald. He was sixty-five, an old "soldier" who'd been through more than wars, and was now living in "retirement."

He was exceptionally con-wise, having spent time in Dannemora and Sing Sing. He didn't speak to Magnus for a week after his arrival. He stayed close, moving into line behind him at the cafeteria, walking casually beside him to work or recreation, working his way to a position in the mattress room close to Magnus' stitcher. Gianni wanted to listen to what the cons knew, and try to discover who was up for the job. There was no doubt that someone would have taken over Anastasia's contract.

When he believed he'd learned everything he could, which was little, Johnny Gianni started a casual conversation with Magnus in the recreation yard. Gradually they established a relationship the other inmates would accept. Gianni was weird-looking. Only Macpherson, a notorious do-gooder, would want to talk to a guy with a face that looked like it could bounce. For the first few weeks the two of them never talked business except when Gianni gave Magnus some hints about staying alive: "Don't walk close along a wall, you can't get away from it. A shiv will come from the front. It's too hard to kill with a knife in the back. Don't let anyone give you food in the cafeteria; choose something you don't usually eat. Stay in your cell as much as you can, it's the safest place in the pen."

They finally began sitting at the same four-place table in the cafeteria, which other inmates avoided; they didn't like to look at Gianni while they ate.

"How does it seem to you?" Magnus asked.

"Can't tell. They know there's a contract out."

"What are my chances?"

"Yours are better than mine. I got longer to stay. We'll both stay careful, that's all." When Gianni chewed his food, the tension on his right cheek rhythmically pulled down on his eye, exposing red membrane.

"What makes you think you can get away with interrupting a contract, Johnny?"

"Who says I think that?" He smiled, stretching his lips so tightly they disappeared above his teeth. "Don't worry about it, Macpherson. What I'm doing ain't suicide. It's a gamble, like any investment, right? It's also a whole lot of politics."

"Politics?"

"Yeah, syndicate politics. Kefauver turned things upside down, shook everybody up. Frank Costello got mauled by that TV. A lot of people want him out as head of the syndicate, so—"

"Who?"

"Vito Genovese. I'll tell you something. Vito wants it all. He's been foul-mouthing Costello, trying to get him out. But Costello has too many friends. Your buddy Anastasia is one of them. Anyway, Costello's useless; he's too much a celebrity." Gianni smiled. "We work better under rocks."

"And Anastasia wants to kill me to show how tough he is and scare Vito Genovese? That's insane."

Johnny Gianni nodded. "Yep. Sure is. But you're famous; he'd get a lot of prestige. Also, he *is* insane."

"So are you, Johnny, if you get in the way. And it seems to me that his fifty thousand contract would pay for college and law school as well as I could."

Magnus watched carefully for Gianni's reaction. Johnny stopped chewing for a moment, then shook his head.

"If you don't trust me, Macpherson, you're dead. Listen. One, I'm Longie Zwillman's soldier. I knock off some joker who's after this contract, just in defense, I got some politics on my side. Longie and

Vito split up Jersey; they're very close. They got as much muscle in here as Anastasia does. All right? Two, I've worked for Zwillman forever. He's taking care of my wife and kid. He wants you alive; keeps Anastasia nervous. I kill you, my wife and kid starve, and I don't have no time to collect no fifty G's before Longie makes me pork. Three, I'm sixty-five, I'm gonna die inside. Sooner or later, there ain't much difference, except for the investments I can make for my kid. And four, I owe you a favor. Maggie wouldn't've married me if I hadn't of looked decent . . . at the time."

They didn't talk until they'd finished the meal and were walking to the mattress room.

"Do I have to live with Anastasia's contract, then?"

"You don't have to," Gianni said, and chuckled quietly at his own humor. "Let him forget you. You keep making him angry. Your son getting killed cost him a lot of money and a lot of face with the syndicate. Then your lawyer threatened him with IRS examinations of his business with your son. It should of kept Anastasia quiet for a while during the Kefauver thing, but it made him madder. Both ways, madder." He chuckled again.

"What's happening? The syndicate was always neater than this."

"I'll tell you what's happening. The Mafia families, the ones that go back in Sicily, they're taking over the syndicate and edging everybody else out. It ain't a good time to be a Jew or a nut. . . . Did I tell you to walk wide around corners?"

Magnus did as he was told and stayed careful; Johnny Gianni was always close. As Magnus' time passed, Gianni stayed even closer. Ten days before Magnus' release, Gianni moved into the next cell and set up his mirror so he could see anyone who approached Magnus' cell.

Magnus wondered which one of the inmates was going to do it. Maybe there was more than one. Maybe there was no one. Maybe someone had canceled the contract, scared off by Johnny Gianni and politics.

"Macpherson, you're getting messy."

"How? What do you mean, messy?" Magnus was washing his hands in the mattress-room toilet. Gianni was at the urinal.

"You don't come to the pisser without me."

"You're here."

"I want to be in here first when you come in. If I come in *after* you, sometime I'll find you stuffed in the sink."

Magnus was irritated. "Gianni, you don't need to be a hero to get your money. It probably isn't going to happen at all—"

Gianni turned and shoved Magnus backward against the wall, holding him there. "Listen, you son of a bitch, I'm too old to be a hero. I'm putting my kid through college keeping you alive, and goddamn if you're going to ruin it. Somebody's waiting for you to think he isn't here, for you to get relaxed, and messy. You stay careful until you walk out of this place. After that"—he backed off and zipped up his fly—"you owe me. So come on . . . and don't come in here to take a piss regular every day after lunch. Tie a knot in it."

The afternoon before his release, Magnus and Gianni were walking back from the library, where Magnus had returned his last books. The attack came from around a corner; an ice pick was aimed at Magnus' gut, tilted upward to puncture the heart, fast, quiet, making escape possible. Gianni lunged and took the thrust in his forearm. Magnus felt the ice pick pierce the skin of his stomach through Gianni's arm. He couldn't remember having seen the man before.

"Shit!" yelled Gianni as he kicked the attacker's balls and with a yell jerked the ice pick out of his arm, ready to stab the man. "Run, Macpherson!" But the attacker had already drawn a knife, jabbed at Gianni, who dodged back off-balance and fell. The man lunged for Magnus and dragged him down on his stomach. He was tremendously strong, held Magnus' neck down with his knee, and raised the knife up fast to slice into his neck. Magnus saw it coming and tensed for the pain, but it didn't come. Gianni's hand grabbed the blade from behind and held it back for a few seconds. Then with a cry he plunged the ice pick into the attacker's skull. Magnus wrenched himself around under the man in time to see his eyes roll upward. With a spasmodic jerk the man freed the knife blade from Gianni's hand and slashed a wide area behind him before collapsing on top of Magnus, the ice pick vibrating.

Guards were coming; whistles were blowing. Magnus shoved the body off him and looked at Gianni. He was holding his stomach, trying to hold in his insides. He collapsed to his knees, and as he fell forward, he never took his eyes off Magnus until his face hit the ground full force. By that time, Gianni was dead.

"Mrs. Josephson, Miss Fowler has . . . left us again."

In her office at the paper, WeeDee took a deep breath and snapped the gold earring from her ear to make way for the telephone. "It seems you can't keep her, Doctor." With her father vanishing after his release from prison, Iris was totally her responsibility.

"No, ma'am. We must suggest you find a high-security sanatorium. Also, having her child here is extremely difficult for the other patients. He wanders into their cottages—"

WeeDee interrupted. "I'll fly to New York tomorrow morning."

"We've notified the sheriff, as usual."

"I'm very disappointed."

"Mrs. Josephson, we're not a mental hospital. That's what Miss Fowler needs now. We have to suggest—"

" 'Now'? Has something changed?"

"We discovered a hypodermic syringe—"

"That's what she's there for."

"It wasn't used for amphetamines. We found traces of heroin. Apparently one of the special nurses you hired sold her—"

"Find her. I'll take a plane tonight. Did she take the boy with her?"

"As always."

"Find them."

16

Awopbopaloobop—Alopbam boom!
Tutti-frutti! Aw rootie! Tutti-frutti! Aw rootie!
—LITTLE RICHARD

Changing the name of the company to Macpherson Industries cost 1.2 million dollars and took nearly a year to finalize. By that time, M.I. was no longer exclusively in the liquor business. The diversification included chemicals, pharmaceuticals, an Oklahoma manufacturer of oil-drilling bits, and a growing string of well-placed rural newspapers. Each new acquisition eased Jamie's conscience; liquor was no longer the soul of his company. "What has been created can be purified. Creation is of God; contamination is of man. Life is purgation."

Jamie had left the seminary in body but not in spirit. He lived in a one-room studio apartment three blocks west of the Empire State Building. He always wore dark suits, black shoes, a dark tie. Unknown to his colleagues was the fact that two days a week he wore a chain of fence wire wrapped around his thighs, as he had at seminary. He shunned the opulent perquisites which his position provided. He reassigned the chauffeur, sold the limousine, and took a small office on the executive floor, which other employees referred to as "The Cell."

At five-thirty every morning he rose and attended Mass at a small neighborhood church. He ate breakfast at the same delicatessen and only changed his order when the owner's wife insisted. At seven-thirty sharp he arrived at his office and stayed in it at least ten hours every day. His visits to the washroom were regimented and his lunch was ordered in. He never went out to a restaurant, and checked the time taken by those executives who did.

When there were meetings, Jamie preferred them to take place at M.I.'s offices. He refused to sit at the head of the table at board meetings and instead sat in the middle of one side, placing those he wanted to watch opposite him. In business dealings Jamie did not negotiate or haggle. He studied the situation and made a single take-it-or-leave-it offer. The liquor industry had never known anyone like him.

At the end of his working day he would walk back to the delicatessen and have the special. If it were pleasant weather, he would walk around the streets of Manhattan, watching people. Few passersby took any notice of him, except when he stared too long or too intensely.

Later, he would return to his apartment, climb the three flights, and let himself in. The furniture was hardly more than he'd had at the seminary—a bed, a table, two chairs instead of one, and a small rug. He would bathe, read until ten, then pray; in cold weather, he'd use the small rug to kneel on. Then he would take "the discipline." He had brought his flail of cords dipped in wax with him, and twice a week he would flagellate himself.

Jamie had left the seminary because of a coincidence, not because of WeeDee's persuasion or the fate of the family business. By the time of his brother's death, he had reached his own spiritual crisis.

"The Church's ways are multifarious and are presently outside of the focus of your concerns," Jamie's rector stated by way of enforcing discipline.

Jamie believed in Jesuit discipline and adhered to it rigidly. He was then in the Philosophate, the second two-year period of training in the Jesuit order. His intellectual skills had been noted with growing solicitude by his superiors. This was the subject of his crisis, and the Rector knew it.

"I confess I feel impatience with my limitations of 'scope,' and will pray for help in controlling it. . . . Father, the Church is a great religion, but it makes infernal politics. Those politics can destroy the Church."

"The Church has survived a great deal, my son."

"No, it hasn't. It has totally changed and would be unrecognizable to Christ. In every century—"

"My son, your doubts are not original. I will pray that you will be able to overcome them. James, the intensity of your intellect is very great, but often it does not allow for human imperfection. The intellect has often seduced with its perception of purity. Be careful, my son."

Jamie prayed, too, but he kept inadvertently running across evidence which to him was an example of the Church's abrogation of Christ. He surreptitiously kept track of the Church's intense lobbying to have Spain included in the Marshall Recovery Plan to rebuild war-torn Europe. Spain was a fascist state and had not even entered World War II. But it was a Catholic state, so the Vatican worked for American aid. On the day Monsignor Fulton Sheen pronounced the invocation over the assembled congressmen, the measure passed the Senate.

It was just at this point in Jamie's self-questioning that his brother died and his father stood trial. A leave of absence from the Jesuit order was not termination. One could go out into the world and struggle with one's doubts in hopes of vanquishing them. Jamie had discussed going to Baltimore to teach in a private school, and just before Magnus II was killed, the Rector had agreed. Long before Wee-Dee came to see him, Jamie knew that there was going to be pressure on him to work for Macpherson Distilleries.

He visited his father just once during the trial. Magnus said nothing about Jamie's becoming involved with the company, but the subject lay just beneath the surface.

"To be honest, Jamie, I don't know how to talk to you. Even about all this."

"If there's nothing to say—"

"There's everything to say! Your brother's dead, for God's sake. Remember you once said I was destroying two lives? It's three: Iris, her son, whoever he is . . . and me."

Jamie looked up at his father. They were having dinner alone in the apricot dining room on Sixty-fifth Street. Iris had testified in court that day; WeeDee was upstairs with her children. Magnus had reason to feel sorry for himself, but Jamie had never seen it happen before. He was therefore wary.

"Do you think you're destroyed, Father?"

"Don't you?"

"I doubt it very much."

His father nodded agreement before he took a large bite of meat. He chewed and said, "There are a lot of people hoping you're wrong. . . . Perhaps you're one of them?"

"I don't want anyone destroyed, Father."

Magnus put down his silverware and sat back in his chair, chewing. His eyes held the dark stare which Jamie remembered from his childhood and into which he could never look for long.

"What would you have of me, Jamie? I've always wondered."

Jamie did not look up. He had never considered an alternative. His father had always been an unalterable presence in his life, like God and the Devil.

"I don't know, Father."

"Would you have me different?"

"Yes . . . although I don't know how."

"I'd appreciate it if you'd think about it. . . . And you might think about how you'd be different, if I were."

Jamie looked up momentarily, then back at his plate.

"I don't think I'd be different."

"Don't you? Jamie, do you think you'd be a priest if it weren't for the kind of man you think I am?"

His father knew nothing about Jamie's crisis of faith, but he saw Jamie's hesitation, and used it.

"You see me as some quintessence of evil which you have to make up for. . . . Nothing works that simply, I promise you. And what if I'm not as evil as you think, Jamie? What would that do to your purpose? What do you think you'd do without me and the Devil?" When his son did not answer, Magnus began to eat again.

Jamie didn't move. He sat absolutely still, his mind roaring with rage and reasons. But he felt something collapsing within him, and he didn't want his father to know. Carefully he folded his napkin, pushed back his chair, and stood up.

"I'm going to leave now."

"Why?"

"I have to get back to—"

"Come now, Jamie, the real reason for once. Just once, tell me how you feel. None of you children ever told me—"

"One of your children is dead!" Jamie blurted. "How do *you* feel?"

Magnus paused, then said, "Are you really interested, or are you looking for a confession?"

Jamie started for the door. When he heard Magnus begin to speak, he turned.

"Jamie, I don't feel the way you think I should. I'm sure of that. A man is dead, and I had much to do with it, and the man is my son. . . . But he was a stranger that night, in my bed with the woman I loved. He wasn't my son then, not even the snide liar who

was after my business. He was a cheap seducer who tricked and
cheated to destroy me. I feel no remorse for him, but neither do I
feel any triumph, so don't go off thinking that. What I feel is that I
killed a man who would have killed me, who had no qualms about
pimping in Washington and being partners with Albert Anastasia. . . . No, I have no remorse."

Incredulous, Jamie said, "He was your son."

Magnus glanced at Jamie from his chair. "Don't give me priest's
rules about love in a family. Each family makes its own. How the
hell would priests know? How would *anyone* know . . . about us?"

Distracted, Magnus waved away the subject as a digression.

"I used to be worried about what you children thought of me.
Now you know all there is to know. As for regret, I have it for what
I have become to you, what my business became in our lives.
Magnus II had to make himself a monster to destroy it, because it
was all so big, so . . . rich. . . . I can't tell what else I feel. But for
whatever reason, after this trial is over, I'm walking away from Macpherson's."

Jamie quickly walked back into the room.

"Dear Christ! Father, are you going to explain away killing my
brother in order to involve *me?*"

"Do you think I killed him? . . . And while you're at it, tell me
this: do you believe I killed your mother? Come, Jamie, what do *you*
feel?"

Jamie looked at his father, gripping the back of a chair.

"I *do* want you destroyed! I want all memory of you obliterated! I
want your 'success' annihilated so that it would be as if you were
never born." Jamie began to shake; he held on to the chair in front
of him as tears began to stream from his eyes.

Magnus smiled bitterly. "So now at least I know I have a son."

"I'm not taking Magnus' place!"

"You're taking your own, whether you like it or not, and you're
finding your own way to hate me."

Jamie left his father's house as quickly as he could, and did not
see him again until he was in prison. By then, Jamie had taken his
leave of absence from the seminary. He visited his father just once
with Ted Weiss, and then only to talk about business.

Jamie did not renounce his vows and had no intention of letting
his father's world affect his own. He regarded running his father's
company as the crucible in which his doubts would dissolve and his
faith would crystallize.

Well-disciplined by the Jesuits, Jamie quickly learned the business under Ted Weiss's diligent instruction. Although the predestined struggle between the elect and the damned in Augustine's *City of God* hardly applied to the fight between straights and blends, Jamie sometimes digressed into various exegeses. On such occasions, Weiss took to examining the upper corners of the room. As soon as Jamie concluded, they went back to worldly matters. Jamie even put to use much of what he had scorned about the workings of the Vatican. A dictatorship, whether spiritual or secular, was by far the most efficient way to run an organization. The business community, which had responded to Jamie's youth and brilliance with admiring curiosity, soon was referring to him as "The Holy Roman Emperor."

Criticism meant nothing to Jamie. He realized that to business people there was only one measure—profit. Uncle Juny had made that insight very clear when they had discussed Jamie's ascension to the presidency of Macpherson Distilleries. At the time, Uncle Juny had been angry and vengeful about Magnus II's death.

"Your father's wickedness is . . . is, well, he murders his wife, then his son, makes life a living hell for his mistress and bastard, and now he's getting you out of seminary and into his filthy rotten business."

They were in the bar at the Union Club; Juny had been in residence there during Lent. During his annual period of self-inflicted penance, he gave up the comforts of his hearth, home, wife, and cocktails at the Brook Club to show off his sacrifice at the socially subordinate Union. The sacrifice may have done something for his soul, but it did little for his personality.

"And it seems to me, young man, that you're betraying your sacred calling," Juny intoned as he lit up another Monte Cristo No. 3. During Lent, Juny chain-smoked cigars.

"I know, Uncle Juny; I'm as worried as you, sir."

"You are, huh?" Juny waved through the cloud of smoke which hung over him.

"Yes, sir. But at the same time, I can't underestimate what God's will may be. It's not beyond reason to believe I may have been called to do this."

"You've always wanted to be a priest, Jamie. You were always your mother's son."

"Yes, that's what *I've* wanted to be. But what if that's not what God wants me to be? What if all this has been preparation for what is happening now? One of the Jesuits' basic concepts is *Age Quod*

Agis, 'Do what you are doing.' Uncle Juny, I have faith that I can do this . . . as a Catholic, and as a Fleming . . . as much as a Macpherson."

Juny sat and scowled at his nephew.

"Your brother spoke with me about faith . . . once." He looked off through a window melodramatically as the betrayed martyr he felt himself to be.

Jamie let him indulge himself, then said, "My brother caused pain you and I are going to share the rest of our lives."

"Yes! Damn him to hell, yes!"

"We have to forgive him."

"Not until after Lent! Come along, I want my lunch. I thank God I can at least eat. . . . We go up a floor. . . . Do you know they want to let *females* in here? To *eat?* In the *Union Club?*" Juny led the way, trailing smoke.

When they were seated at a table overlooking Park Avenue, Juny put out his cigar stub and lit another. He watched Jamie through the smoke.

"As far as I can see, you're certainly all Catholic and certainly half Fleming. But you're no businessman"—he leaned across the table —"and that could be worse than sin."

"Uncle Juny, if I have to withstand your proxy fight or a tender offer, I'm not going to take on Macpherson's. So perhaps you'll tell me what you, as a businessman, want from Macpherson Distilleries."

"I want Magnus Macpherson out."

"As a businessman, Uncle Juny. That's emotional. In any event, he's in jail and I've been assured I would have complete control—"

"For how long?" Juny asked skeptically.

"As long as *I* choose to stay." Jamie let his uncle consider that for a few moments. "Please tell me what you want."

"I want control of the board of directors."

"I couldn't give you that," he went on before Juny could object, "and you couldn't get it; my father still controls the largest single block of stock. Your chances of a takeover either through proxy or tender are not as good now; you need the name of a Macpherson somewhere on your side. The company is demoralized, the stock is sinking, sales have fallen off. You could fight very hard and come up with a company ready for bankruptcy." Uncle Juny was too surprised to respond. He wanted a drink but mangled his cigar in his teeth instead.

"Uncle Juny, I'll need your help, and I will not take over Macpherson's unless I have it. I couldn't do it without your support in the business community and on Wall Street. And I want to feel I can come to you for advice."

"Advice is cheap. Maybe you should tell me what you're prepared to pay for it."

"I'd like you to assign two members of the board."

"Two?"

"Yes, sir. Any more would look dangerous. I don't have time to put down a board-of-directors revolt. Besides, if I take over, you'll have direct access to the president of the company. And I *will* listen to you, Uncle Juny."

"Access isn't control."

"Wouldn't it be enough for you to have that much of Magnus Macpherson's company?"

It was not enough, but was satisfactory for the moment. Juny agreed to appoint two members to the board of Macpherson's and to meet once a month with Jamie. Juny was enough of a businessman to know the company required a Macpherson at the head of it, just as his firm required a Fleming. He believed a company should be an extension of the family who owned it. To Juny, public ownership of anything was morally inferior and politically suspect. He would wait; Jamie perhaps would need more advice than expected, and the price for it would rise.

Jamie was elected president of Macpherson Distilleries four months after his father went to Great Meadow. Three months later, he was thoroughly in charge, having fired a quarter of the executives in a total shake-up of the company's management. Soon after, he felt sufficiently secure to begin to examine the company's position in the industry and look to the future. He called a meeting of Weiss, Bromberg, and the marketing-research staff and told them the great battle between blends and straights was a canard. What he had ascertained from his research was that public taste was adjusting, not to straights or blends, but to "something that was easier to swallow."

Such terms were blasphemy to whiskey men, anathema to traditionalists. The standard for excellence always had been based on hundred-proof whiskey, that is, liquor which was 50 percent alcohol. Even the law provided that bottled-in-bond whiskey must be hundred-proof. If a man couldn't taste his whiskey, he'd suspect it was watered down. But Jamie was adamant; he wanted a new whiskey developed with a lower proof which would be easier to drink.

He wanted it tested on markets as quickly as possible, and he wanted the testing to include women as well as men.

Confidence was restored in the "new" Macpherson Distilleries, and Jamie's success was soon apparent. The stock rose and sales made a comeback, but regaining Macpherson's former share of the market was difficult. The competition was intense; the advertising budgets of the leading distillers were climbing to annual expenditures of between five and twenty-five million dollars. Still, the liquor market did not expand, so the pressure for growth continued to invade the market with new products and further price-cutting. Some of the major distillers even went in for price-fixing.

From a businessman's point of view, Jamie's only failing was his inability to consider corruption. His blind spot in this area was total; if there were the slightest hint of improbity in business dealings, Jamie would withdraw from the discussion. Weiss had succeeded in confining Jamie's disapproval to an abrupt withdrawal rather than his initial desire to notify the proper authorities. In some ways his attitude made business difficult for Macpherson Distilleries. To corporate consciousness, "corruption" was considered a Sunday-school term (often used by aspiring politicians) for what went on in American business every day of the week. Worse yet, Jamie's principles intensified Macpherson's struggle with the labor movement.

The Distillery, Rectifying, and Wine Workers International Union was formed in 1940 with a charter from the American Federation of Labor. By 1942 most of the liquor industry was unionized, and the DRWW had twenty thousand members. A decade later, when Jamie took over the company, the union's welfare fund had three million dollars in it. Like other unions at the time, the leadership had been infiltrated by gangsters.

Not content with just dipping into the welfare funds, they extorted fees from airstrikes to get "smooth service" from the union's members. The fees, of course, never reached any of the workers. Most distillers paid the "grease," and regarded it as an inevitable business expense, but when Jamie was approached, he refused to consider the slightest payment. After finding out the extent of the practice, he sent a telegram to Senator Kefauver demanding investigations of criminal conspiracy in the leadership of the DRWW. The telegram was given to the press and appeared in full in the New York *Times*. Three days later, the first Macpherson truck was hijacked. A week later, a Macpherson warehouse in West New York, New Jersey, burned to the ground.

Weiss knew what was happening and tried to explain some facts of business life to Jamie.

"It comes down to dollars and cents. They'll do whatever they have to do, so it'll be cheaper for you to pay them," Weiss tried to explain.

"What happens if I take the loss?" Jamie asked.

"The game gets rougher."

"Doesn't anybody fight them, Mr. Weiss?"

"Weiss. Just Weiss. You're my boss. . . . A lot of people fight them. A lot of people get hurt. They have an advantage: they don't care about hurting people like I think you do. It's just part of business for them, like ordering new sales quotas is for you. They don't expect you to play by their rules, but don't expect them to play by yours."

"They expect me to *pay* by their rules. And I will not do it, Mr. Weiss . . . Weiss." Jamie was quiet for a time, then looked at Weiss and asked, "Is there someone I can talk to, someone who's somewhat reasonable, not the union, but one of the syndicate people, someone who would have control over the situation?"

"If you hadn't sent that telegram to Kefauver, I'd have maybe said yes. But you went public, and Kefauver's the one who made all these guys sweat battery acid on TV. The Distillery Workers usually work through two syndicate families, Longie Zwillman and Albert Anastasia. Anastasia never got on TV, but he ran scared, and still is, from any publicity. They all hate publicity. They're trying to dump Frank Costello now because he got too much. . . . And you send a telegram to Kefauver. . . . Look, Zwillman you might talk to, but I doubt if he'll see you now. Anastasia, you don't even ask. He ain't reasonable."

"Then we'll have to fight this out."

"It's a battle you won't win. They don't fight clean, you know."

Jamie looked at Weiss with bemusement. "I don't know how I'll fight. . . . When there's war, the rules are different. I'll have to think about it. But, Weiss, I'll never give in to that kind of extortion. If there's any reason for me to be here running this company, it might as well be this. And I intend to use every bit of power at my disposal here to do it. If Macpherson Distilleries spends every cent of its reserves on withstanding this kind of extortion, so be it. What better way for *this* company to—"

Weiss interrupted. "I can think of better ways. But . . . one thing: don't go into this depending on God. He don't help with fights like this. It's just us and them, and when it's over, God punishes the winner."

So it began. The hijackings increased, as did the arson. Jamie committed two million dollars to security, and put an armed guard in each truck. He began to fly to every Macpherson warehouse, distillery, and distribution center in the country, never using the company plane, always arriving unannounced, to look over the security himself. Whenever the insurance companies demanded further safeguards, Jamie doubled them. He spent a couple of nights at every Macpherson facility, making certain of the routine, and hoping that on the odd chance, they could catch someone connected to the syndicate.

Then Weiss learned that Anastasia had put out a contract on Magnus. When Jamie heard, he decided the problem was just one more area of careful security. He started to call the warden at Great Meadow and ask if he could fly up and look over the facilities, but Weiss interrupted him.

"Wait a minute. This ain't a warehouse situation. The rules just changed: now they're going to try to kill your father. You can put twenty guards in Macpherson's cell and they'll still get him. That ain't the way to do it."

"What is the way, Weiss? Is there one?"

"I'll take care of that. It'll cost something, but one guy on the inside to look after him is better than any amount of guards. Anyway, that ain't your worry. Anastasia's contract may have nothing to do with you and the union."

Jamie sat, coiled with tension. Weiss looked at the neat stacks of papers on Jamie's desk; he hated those neat stacks of papers.

"What is my worry, Weiss?"

"If they're getting ready to kill, they'll kill anybody. It won't make any difference to them."

"Is there a way to break a contract like this?"

"None that anybody knows."

"So my father will be murdered."

"No. He can protect himself, then disappear for a while."

"Then contracts are forgotten?"

"No. Not as long as they're out. But this one would cause a lot of heat on the syndicate if it comes off. Anastasia may get some discipline before the contract's filled."

"Discipline?"

"He may be convinced to call it off. Or he may get killed himself."

Jamie nodded. "And you'll see to it that my father's guarded, and that he . . . disappears?"

"Yeah. I'm already working on it."

"Good." Jamie allowed a smile.

Later that night as he was flying to the Kansas City rectifying and bottling plant, Jamie examined his conscience. Was he unconsciously opposing the union in order to prompt the threat to his father's life? No, he did not want his father to be murdered, of that he was certain, but the necessity of Magnus Macpherson's disappearance did give Jamie a sense of elation. If his battle with the union were somehow keeping his father away from the business, then there was already one positive result of the conflict. Jamie smiled. He would confess to such thoughts before his next Communion.

Jamie was never aware of the first attempt on Magnus' life. He did not hear about the second until Weiss had transported Magnus from Great Meadow to the Seventy-ninth Street yacht basin and seen the ship leave under sail. Weiss had hired a crew with impeccable backgrounds: a former Coast Guard officer and a former Naval Intelligence captain. Even the cook had been with the French underground during the war. Weiss assured himself and Jamie that Magnus would be safe to enjoy his freedom.

Then he called in the press and gave them the details of the two attempts on Magnus' life. He figured the headlines would increase syndicate pressure on Anastasia to call off the contract. Weiss also misled everyone as to Magnus' whereabouts, hinting that he had returned to his native land. For weeks after, journalists appeared in Dufftown, bothering the citizenry with useless questions.

Weiss did not even tell Jamie where Magnus had gone; Jamie asked not to know. He explained to Weiss that he believed the fewer people who had such information, the better. Jamie's real reason was that he enjoyed the idea that Magnus Macpherson had just disappeared.

A few days later, Jamie had even more cause to be thankful that he didn't know where his father was. WeeDee arrived unexpectedly in his office. She did not sit down before she started talking.

"Where's Father?"

"I don't know. I really don't. What's the matter?"

"Iris Fowler."

Jamie looked away and coldly asked, "What about her?"

"She's apparently a heroin addict."

If Jamie had known how to reach his father with the news,

Magnus would have perhaps returned. Jamie could not contain his relief.

"Oh?"

WeeDee misread his attitude, thinking it was Jamie's usual cold distance between himself and any human being.

"Jamie, I don't ask you to care, but I am going to need some help."

"Is she *our* responsibility now?"

WeeDee smiled an iron smile and sat down.

"She's mine. I'm asking you."

"Why is it your—"

"Because I made it that way. She's a friend of mine." She took off her gloves and ran a hand through her hair. She was tired and didn't want to have to moralize with her brother.

"She's our father's mistress, WeeDee. That's all."

"Jamie, there are some things . . . you'll never understand. Iris Fowler is a friend of mine. She did some things for me I won't ever forget. So will you help me?"

Jamie nodded barely. WeeDee went on. "I had to move her to Liggett's." Liggett's was a plush private mental hospital on Long Island used by the rich to dry out drunk relatives. Occasionally it took in addicts, and therefore had a maximum-security capability.

"She's there now?"

"Yes. We found her this morning in the Suffolk County Jail, screaming because they'd taken her child away, and needing her heroin. She ran away from—"

"I presumed. Where is the child now?"

"He's up at Father's house with the housekeeper waiting for me. I'm taking him to live with me until his mother's better."

"That's a mistake, WeeDee."

"It's not a—"

"What if his mother doesn't get better?"

WeeDee looked at her brother very steadily, still smiling. "I'm prepared to raise him with Magnus and Ellen."

"And in five years, what if she comes and takes him away?"

She didn't answer, knowing her ability to love, particularly her children. "There's no simple way, Jamie."

"He could be put up for adoption."

WeeDee stared at her brother a moment, then put her gloves on and stood up to leave. "If he were, I'd adopt him."

"Wait. You were going to ask me—?"

"I won't ask you anything, Jamie. She's at Liggett's; if you care to, you could visit her. But don't do it for her, or me. Do it for yourself." At the door, she turned before going out. "You're very smart, Jamie; you're smooth enough, and God knows you're ambitious enough. But you'd make a lousy priest." She tapped her chest. "No heart."

Jamie's jaw clenched quickly before he said, "We were born without hearts in this family so that we could survive. You think you can grow one now by rescuing Father's bastard?" He began to shake.

WeeDee watched him, then looked around the room. "We'll wait to see who the bastard is, Jamie." She opened the door and was gone.

Jamie dutifully went to Liggett's twice in the two years before Iris was released. Both visits were awkward, the first at Christmas being less so because of the season, and because Jamie gave Iris a small gift, unfortunately a woolen muffler in a Scottish plaid. It was not the Macpherson tartan, but close enough for Iris to remember the one she had made for Magnus. She remained silent throughout Jamie's stay. He talked a great deal and felt magnanimous.

On the second visit, the following autumn, Jamie met Iris in the lobby of the sanatorium. They put on overcoats; it was a cold but bright day. A groundskeeper was raking and burning fallen leaves. Jamie felt the familiar discomfort and embarrassment; Iris looked scourged, her body sagging in her coat, her hair hanging limply down her neck, her skin colorless, nothing about her indicating life except her eyes, which burned through the clouds of her sedation.

"Last time you came, it was Christmas, Jamie . . . but there's no holiday now. Why are you here?"

She didn't look at him when she spoke, and they kept walking at the same shambling pace.

"I wanted to see how you were getting along."

"How nice," she said with disbelieving sarcasm.

"WeeDee sends her love."

"How nice."

"She says that Gus is—"

"Augustus is his name."

"Augustus is doing well at school. He's already reading every book WeeDee has in the house."

"How nice."

They walked on, dead leaves moving before them in the breeze.

Jamie felt chilled and buttoned his coat over his muffler. Iris didn't seem to notice the cold.

"Jamie, I can see your obligation. I can see people's reasons coming off of them like sweat. Do you know how exhausted, how worn-out I get, seeing like that? No, of course not. . . . Well, I'm just too tired to pretend anything and be polite. I see your obligation. . . . When I can pretend again, I'll get out of here. . . . Right now, I'm too tired to talk."

"Do you want to go back to the main building?"

"Where's your father?" She kept walking.

Glad to be on another subject, Jamie decided to be as honest as he could.

"I don't know exactly. He was on a ship for a time, sailing in the Caribbean. He was in danger and had to hide. He went through the Panama Canal, and I think he's in California. He's still hiding from the—"

"Evelyn Lorraine."

Her eyes darted around and looked at Jamie. They softened for a moment of humor. "You mean you couldn't figure that out?" She then turned back to follow the path.

Jamie hadn't bothered to figure it out. When he heard his father pinpointed by the madwoman beside him, his impatience became intense. Any communication he'd had with his father had been through Weiss. Weiss only told him of his father's movements after they had been completed. He didn't want to know if his father was living with Evelyn Lorraine in Hollywood or anywhere else. It interfered with the idea of Magnus Macpherson's disappearance.

"You hate him, don't you, Jamie?"

"No."

"I can see it—"

"I don't like to think about him, that's all."

"I think about him all the time. I always have; I don't know how to stop. He was so important to me. . . . I know what happened. He was so many things to me, father, lover, best friend; I couldn't keep him straight. The psychiatrists here say that I was trying to destroy all that with Magnus II so that I could find my own self. . . . Do you think that's true?"

"I wouldn't know, Iris, I—"

She turned abruptly, clutching at his arms. "Jamie, tell me something: how do *you* forget? I still love him so much, and I don't think they'll let me out of here until I forget him. How do you forget?"

Jamie wanted to back away from her, but her grip was too strong. "I don't know."

"You must know! You must. I read the letter about your mother's death. Magnus told me you were there. You saw it all happen, Jamie. Please. Tell me. How did you forget, because my baby saw what happened that night and I have to teach him how—"

"You *never* forget, Iris!"

He shouted at her to make her let loose of him. She did, and he stared at her, wondering why she was considered any more insane or lonely than he was.

"How nice . . ." she said vacantly.

He would *not* think of his mother. He would not.

"What letter, Iris?"

She started walking; the letter was still a secret.

"Where's your brother now, Jamie?"

She kept walking, a bit faster as they had made a turn and were heading back toward the main building. Jamie kept up with her and began to sweat.

"My brother is, I hope, with God, and has been forgiven—"

"No! No! No! My son! My son, *your* brother."

She stopped and stared at him, then put her hands over her burning eyes at what she saw. Jamie was furious. The woman had forced him to hate her, and his soul would suffer for it.

"Your son is in Pittsburgh with WeeDee."

"Please don't hate me."

"I came out here to see—"

"Please." She slowly took her hands down from her eyes but did not look up at him. "I know why you came. You don't have to visit anymore. I'll get out of here soon. I have to get back to my son. I don't want *him* to forget me, too." She smiled, but her face couldn't hold it. "We better go back. I'm sorry, Jamie I'm just so tired. . . ."

Jamie never went to see Iris again.

In 1954, Louis Saperstein, the union insurance broker, and Sol Cilento, the secretary-treasurer of the DRWW, were indicted and tried for diverting $540,000 from the union's welfare fund. Saperstein was convicted; charges against Cilento were dismissed on a technicality. The trial was exactly what Jamie needed to bring his own struggle with the union to public attention and therefore to the law. He sent evidence to the Senate Labor Rackets Committee, and testified on two occasions before its chairman, Senator McClellan.

He spent most of his energies pressuring the AFL about its corrupt member. Big labor was merging into the giant AFL-CIO and could not allow its image to be tainted from within.

In February of 1955, George Scalise, a former pimp for Lucky Luciano and a convicted forger, thief, and tax evader, pleaded guilty to charges of conspiracy and bribery in dealing with the DRWW but blamed certain outside sources for framing him with false information. He was sent to jail for a year. Five days after Scalise was sentenced, a pipe-bomb exploded in the washroom of Macpherson Industries' executive offices.

Miraculously, no one was killed; several people were cut badly by flying glass, several others were in shock. Jamie immediately doubled security on all five floors and declared that all briefcases and handbags would be searched. Then he called Weiss into his office.

"Can we find out who did it?"

"Who ordered it, or who did it?"

Jamie glared at Weiss. "I want to know, Weiss, who is responsible for this."

"The guys that put the pipe in there are probably two ambitious punks from Jersey. They probably got the order from a captain in one of the New York syndicate families. The captain was contacted and had dinner with an underboss of another family, who was ordered to make the contact by his don, who's doing it because he's interested in Scalise, who's interested in the DRWW. You want to know all of them?"

"I know Scalise, he's in jail. The DRWW is under investigation. We've fought them, and we're winning. Now somebody wants to kill. Is it that 'don'?"

"Yeah, I suppose."

"Do you know his name?"

Weiss shrugged. He hated standing around in Jamie Macpherson's office; he hated sitting down worse. "Got a good idea; ain't sure yet."

"What's his name?" Weiss didn't want to tell Jamie much, but Jamie already knew.

"It's Anastasia, isn't it?"

Weiss shrugged again. "Could be." He was almost certain it was. Anastasia didn't need excuses to put a bomb in Macpherson's executive offices, but if a reason came along, he'd use it. Weiss decided to remain silent until he found out where Jamie was heading.

Very calmly Jamie began talking. "Weiss, I want to put a contract out on Albert Anastasia."

Weiss sat down. "Don't even think about it."

"Why not?"

"Don't even think about it! You don't put out contracts on Albert Anastasia!" Weiss felt ill; he took off his glasses and wiped his face. For the first time he thought of retiring.

"Why not, Weiss? Do we just wait for them to blow us to kingdom come? This is outside the law; the law has proved again and again that they won't or can't deal with this. Why should we put up with it? I won't allow this company to give in to extortion or murder. There's only one language they can understand: their own. And I want to send them a message: if any employee of M.I. or any member of the Macpherson family is touched, Albert Anastasia will be causing his own death."

"You'll be causing it."

"No, that's just the point. I'm trying—and you'll understand if you'll consider this calmly—I'm *trying* to prevent *anyone* being killed, including Mr. Anastasia."

"Nobody calls him Mr. Anastasia," Weiss said hopelessly. "I'm sorry you're thinking of committing suicide this way, but what really bothers me is you're gonna get me killed, too."

"Why can't we find someone just like they found two punks from Jersey to—"

"Because nobody, *nobody* is going to take a contract on Albert Anastasia!"

"Nobody connected to the syndicate or the Mafia or whatever it's called. But there *are* killers with no connection to them. So find me such a killer, Weiss, or I swear to you I'll find one myself. I'm asking you to do it because you have the resources to find a better man."

A drop of sweat fell into one of Weiss's eyes, and he had to wipe his face again.

"How much is your contract for?"

"What's the top syndicate contract?"

"The highest I ever heard was a hundred grand."

For the first time in the discussion, Jamie sat back in his chair. "I'll wire Switzerland tonight. Tomorrow there'll be a million dollars in a numbered account. The interest each month will go as a retainer to the man you find. Each year for ten years he will receive a hundred thousand of the principal. If anything happens to any of us, I'll cable the account number to a fictitious name in Geneva, after he has killed Anastasia. Our man will get a million no matter what happens, and we'll get ten years of insurance."

Weiss put his glasses on and blinked at Jamie.

"I gotta tell your father."

Jamie knew better than to order Weiss not to tell Magnus anything.

"If you set this up correctly, there's no need to do that. My father won't be in any more danger until Anastasia knows about the contract. Then my father will be safer than he is now." Jamie smiled.

"You know, this makes you just like them."

"No, Weiss, it doesn't." Jamie got out of his chair and came around his desk as he talked. "I've considered this very carefully. I'm fighting them in every possible way, and now I'm going to use their tactics. No. You know who is just like them? Who supports them and helps them survive? Every businessman who gives in to them, whether it's a bribe, a little 'grease,' or extortion. Those are the people who are as guilty as the punks and the dons."

He stood embarrassingly close. Weiss turned away and headed for the door, saying as he left, "Yeah, well, it just never occurred to me you'd be the killer in the family."

"Don't be melodramatic, Weiss; I'm doing what I have to do, to win and to protect my business and my family. There's no evil in that."

Weiss closed the door and hurried down to his office. He wasn't happy there, so he went next door. The chairman's office hadn't been used since Magnus went to prison, but it was kept spotless, as if he were expected at any moment.

Weiss walked around, touching the desk, a window, trying to figure out what to do. If he didn't get a candidate, Jamie would look for someone, Weiss didn't doubt that, and Jamie didn't know how to look, so Anastasia would hear about it. If Weiss told Magnus, Magnus would have to come back to control Jamie, and Anastasia would get a shot at him. If Weiss got out and just disappeared, Jamie, Magnus, and a lot of other people would get killed. Jamie was a fanatic, treating the union and the syndicate as a Holy War. Weiss hated wars; he'd been to the mattress twice when he was young in Cicero working for Capone. He knew what they were—massacres. The only chance he had was time; he would stall finding Jamie his killer. He wouldn't tell Magnus yet. He'd watch the syndicate politics; Vito Genovese wasn't going to wait much longer, and Anastasia was in his way.

Weiss opened a drawer of Magnus' desk and pulled out a deck of cards. He stood and shuffled them, thinking about how in hell he could keep everything from happening too soon.

In the fall of 1956, when Iris was released from Liggett's, she went immediately to Pittsburgh. WeeDee had bought a small cottage near her own home and turned over an old family car for Iris' use. The boy, Augustus, by then eleven, moved in with his mother. The plan was for Iris to settle down with her son, and then find a job. She had been, after all, the executive assistant to the president of a large corporation.

But Iris was scared. She believed that there was a world secret which everyone was keeping, a universal performance which went on everywhere, and she was the one who gave it away. People would often look at her strangely; they seemed to say, "Yes, of course, we know the secret, but we don't let it leak out like you're doing." Then they'd go back to checking the groceries or filling the gas tank as if nothing had happened.

Iris feared that if she continued to give away the secret, she'd be taken away from her son again and put back in Liggett's. She fought to control her anxiety; when the struggle was impossible, she took a pill.

A month after her arrival, Iris was invited to WeeDee's house for dinner. Twelve people were there, and she sat beside a nice reporter from WeeDee's paper. She found herself having a good time; not once did any of the guests indicate they even knew about the secret. The reporter made her laugh, and told her all kinds of funny things about the other people at the table.

During dessert, WeeDee smiled down the table at her. Iris realized what had happened: WeeDee had told them all, even the nice reporter, *not* to notice her. Iris thought she'd probably given the secret away the whole evening.

She excused herself from the table, went out to her car, and drove home. She forgot to take Augustus with her, but she didn't go back for him. She sat in the rocking chair in her own house, worrying and thinking. He would be all right. He was used to staying at WeeDee's house. He had his own room and was treated as one of the family. In fact, Augustus seemed to prefer to spend his time there.

Iris felt the panic begin to shake her; she got up and quickly took her pills. She had to get a job right away. She looked through the want-ad section of the Pittsburgh *Star-Herald:* waitresses, movie-theater usherettes, switchboard operators, all involving meeting people who would see that she couldn't keep the secret.

Since she arrived in Pittsburgh, Iris had gone to a clinic at the University of Pittsburgh Hospital. Because WeeDee was on the board of trustees, Iris saw one of the best psychiatrists.

"Iris, what *is* the secret?" her doctor had asked.

"I'm not sure. . . . It's like a level."

"A 'level'?"

"Another level. Under this one."

"What are these levels like?"

"Well, you know about this one where we are now. This one is how everything looks."

"And the other level?"

"That's the secret."

He smiled and looked quizzical. She liked him, but she knew he was the best performer of all. She said carefully, "Nobody can stand that secret level. You see too much, feel too much. So everybody covers it over. But if we give away the secret, they get angry. That's why people look at me; I'm leaking the secret." She laughed again, but she wanted to scream.

Heroin dissolved the secret level. With heroin, there was no secret, there were no levels. Iris had taken it before for the same reasons. But in order to get heroin, she needed money, and to get money, she began to bring men to her house on nights when Augustus stayed over at WeeDee's. Soon she found a supplier.

She met him in a park in the Shadyside area of town. The supplier naturally got curious; Iris' clothes were too nice. The day of his second sale, he followed her to her house, did some checking, and found out who she was. Within twenty-four hours the don of Pittsburgh's syndicate family knew about her. He remembered the connection between Magnus Macpherson and his colleague on the syndicate's ruling board. As a personal favor, the don sent a special messenger with the information to Albert Anastasia in New Jersey. The reply, which was returned to Pittsburgh and filtered down to Iris' supplier, was simple: "Sell her pure." Anastasia sent a postcard addressed to Jamie Macpherson, which was equally as simple: "You just started paying the price."

The postcard took two days to be delivered. On the first of those two days, Iris was arrested in downtown Pittsburgh for soliciting a police officer. WeeDee was called that night, drove down to police headquarters, and bailed Iris out. Iris had not been examined; the police had not noticed the recent needle marks in her arm.

When they arrived at Iris' house, WeeDee turned off the motor of the car. Iris talked first, very fast.

"I'm not saying I'm sorry anymore. It's too late for that. It's too late for anything. Just let me get out of here. I'll go pack and I won't embarrass you anymore, and thanks for everything."

"Never apologize to me, Iris. Never say 'thank you,' either. We know what we've done for each other, so that's that. The important thing is what's going to happen now."

"It's too late—"

"Are you taking heroin, Iris? And for God's sake don't be afraid or ashamed to tell me."

Iris tried to pretend. "Why do you think I'm—"

WeeDee would have none of it. "Because you're not a whore, and why else would you need the money?"

Iris gave up and put her hands over her face, saying, "Jesus, Jesus. . . . The police didn't even know."

"Iris! I was a drunk. I could be again, tomorrow. I know, so let me help."

Iris shook her head and took her hands away from her face. She spoke in a dull, defeated monotone. "You'll never be a drunk again, WeeDee. You know it and so do I. I have to get away from you people. It was all right when I was with Magnus. *That's* when I was crazy, not now, that day he asked me to go to Washington. I should have stayed in school; I should have stayed small. . . . WeeDee, all this, if I hadn't . . . it wouldn't have happened."

WeeDee reached across and took one of Iris' hands.

"Iris, you *know* that Magnus II would have found a way to destroy his father. He started long before you appeared in Father's life."

"I know. The letter you . . ." Iris hesitated.

"Yes, my letter. Father told me you'd kept it all those years. That's what I don't understand. You knew what my brother was, what he could do, to you as well as my father."

Iris sat silently for a moment. "You think *I* understand?" She shook her head. "No. I don't. I never knew what a man was until I met your father. I never loved your brother. I craved him. I knew what he was doing, some of it, not all. He was like a drug. I needed him. The doctors keep asking me, they keep trying to get behind Magnus II or drugs, to find out why I needed them." She laughed slightly. "I always thought it should be enough for the doctors that I took drugs or screwed Magnus' son. Jesus, what do they want?" She shook her head again, and covered her face with her hands. "But it's not, they keep wanting to find out *why*. . . . *I don't know*." She looked at WeeDee again. "Why would I want to destroy myself? That's what they keep hinting at. I was helping your brother destroy your father, but I was also doing a good job of destroying me. I didn't want to do that, WeeDee. I didn't want to hurt your father, either. He was the nearest thing I ever had to a father as well as everything else."

"Do you remember your father, Iris?"

"No, he was killed when I was two. All I had for a father was a picture on Mother's bedside table. He never even saw me; he was blind before I was born, and he was blown up in your father's still. . . ." Iris was speaking quickly, the words spilling out. "He never even *saw* me! Your father was making a hundred thousand dollars a month at that still, and my father . . . got blown to kingdom come. And you know why? One of *Magnus'* guards gave him . . ." She hesitated; she knew. "Oh, no! Good Christ . . ." She tried to open the door of the car. "Let me go! Let me get out!"

But WeeDee held on to her.

"Iris, what about Gus?" she said, knowing the boy was the only responsibility Iris could recognize, having so abruptly glimpsed so much.

Iris looked down at her hands and began to cry. Then she got angry. "Augustus! His name's Augustus! I'll take him with me."

"Where, Iris?"

"Then you keep him. He'd rather stay with you anyway."

WeeDee watched her begin to cry again.

"Iris, don't hurt yourself anymore. You're my friend. I've tried to hurt myself for some of the same reasons, and knowing's enough punishment. Now that you know, you can learn to live with it."

"Have you any suggestions how to do that?" Iris said bitterly.

"Yes. You never had a father. It's all right to be angry about it. You're not crazy for being angry with Magnus, even though you loved him. Iris, come home with me tonight. Tomorrow we'll go to the clinic."

"And they'll sedate me into mush, and keep me that way forever. No. I can't live with this. Magnus II was lucky. I ought to die, like Mary did or something. . . ."

"No, Iris."

Iris swung her fist as hard as she could and hit WeeDee straight on her nose. She grabbed WeeDee's purse, jumped out of the car, and ran into the darkness. WeeDee stumbled out of the car, trying to clear her head, calling for Iris. She put her head down between her legs, saved herself from fainting, then started to run. She looked everywhere. Everyone in the neighborhood knew who she was, and was glad to help, but they had no luck. Finally WeeDee gave up and called the police, advising them Iris Fowler was having a nervous breakdown. She did not mention the purse.

The next morning, Iris headed for the Shadyside park. She had WeeDee's money as well as the twenty she received from the man she'd stayed with overnight, enough for two jolts and room rent. She arrived at the park and met her supplier, who sold her more than she asked for.

The postcard arrived on Jamie's desk that morning at ten o'clock. Within the hour, a phone call came in from WeeDee; she told Jamie what had happened and that Iris was still missing. Jamie read her the postcard. When he hung up, he called in Ted Weiss and gave him one week to find their assassin, or Jamie was going to look himself. Ted Weiss had stalled, but he'd done his homework. He had a man, and told Jamie about him.

In finding a killer, Weiss had not used the clothesline or any other connection with the syndicate, either in America or Europe. For more than ten years Weiss had been contributing in excess of a hundred thousand dollars annually to the state of Israel. He originally had been asked by the Mossad, the Israeli intelligence organization, to help finance the flight of European Jews to Israel after the Second World War. Since then, he had given freely, if secretly, of his time and money, and had never asked a favor in return until then. The Mossad had pointed out Antoine Lescal.

Lescal was twenty-five, a *pied-noir,* the son and grandson of *colons,* the French settlers in Algeria. His father had been killed, as had a sister, by the FLN, the Muslim National Liberation Front. He was a driver and bodyguard for General Raoul Salan, a dedicated and, some said, fanatic believer in, first, the fate of France, and, second, the French Army. Lescal drove for him, but also killed and tortured for him. He was a superb marksman, but his specialty was a scimitar-shaped dagger said to have been favored by the ancient order of Assassins in ancient Persia. His colleagues believed that Lescal could carve his initials on the face of an FLN member before he slit the throat. He was brave, and more important, he was honorable. He had been decorated by the French government on four occasions. He believed in the honor of his cause, of the army, and of his family, those who were left.

As Ted Weiss told Jamie about Lescal, his own apprehension grew. When he finished, Weiss knew that the plan was preposterous.

"He sounds excellent, Weiss. Where do we send the interest from the Swiss account?"

"We don't. Forget this. It's crazy."

"Weiss, don't you dare—"

"Listen, I'm not going to hire any killers."

Jamie sat back in his chair.

"You're getting old, Weiss. I'm taking out insurance, not hiring a killer."

"This kind of insurance is too expensive."

Jamie stood up and started yelling. "Then what am I supposed to do, Weiss? Sit here and die, or let my father die, or my employees? You do this, or get out! I mean it! Get out."

"I'll get out." Weiss left the office.

Two hours later the police were called to a downtown Pittsburgh hotel. They thought at first, because of all the identification in the purse she carried, that Mrs. Eleanor Josephson, the owner of the Pittsburgh *Star-Herald,* had died of an overdose of heroin. They quickly discovered their error and brought WeeDee down to the morgue to identify Iris Fowler's body.

Jamie sent Weiss to Pittsburgh for the funeral, not out of any sympathy but to arrange for protection for his father, who announced his intention to attend. Weiss's absence for several days allowed Jamie to make a quick flight to Algeria.

Jamie met Lescal in a dark restaurant not far from the Algiers Casbah, which was barricaded by French soldiers. Lescal wore a full beard, large dark glasses, and a military hat with a visor pulled very low. Jamie drank mint tea; Lescal, Pernod. The disguise was always necessary, as he did not wish to have his face known to anyone. His English was adequate, and he accepted Jamie's arrangement. He told Jamie to have the interest from the Swiss account and the principal sent directly to his mother. He stated that he would take on the assignment for her sake, and because he could not abide "parasites" like those in the syndicate. Jamie told him about the inherent danger; Antoine Lescal said he would be happy to carve his initials on the face of Albert Anastasia. When he flew back to New York, Jamie was not only pleased; he was surprised to discover he was rather excited.

Out of professional courtesy to WeeDee, the other Pittsburgh papers did not publish the story of Iris Fowler's death. The wire services sent it out, but the item attracted little attention. The funeral, therefore, was not covered by the press. In fact, no one mourned the death of Iris Fowler except the Macphersons, and her son, Augustus.

Magnus flew to Pittsburgh on the day of the funeral. Ted Weiss had already arrived on the company plane with security personnel. He and WeeDee were waiting to greet her father. Neither had seen him since his release from prison. Magnus was sunburned; he looked thin, and hadn't seemed to age.

"I'm so glad to see you both," he said as WeeDee embraced him. "I'm sorry it has to be for this."

WeeDee put an arm through his and they walked through the terminal. Weiss watched the crowds nervously, as did the security people. If Anastasia had mailed that postcard, he might have done it to flush Magnus out of hiding with the hope of gunning him down at the funeral. Weiss found himself halfheartedly wishing that Jamie's "insurance policy" were already in effect.

As they walked, WeeDee said quietly to her father, "I won't be able to speak with you later, because of the children."

"How are they? Tell me about them."

"They're fine, just fine. Ellen is a beauty—"

"Like her mother?"

"More so. And little Magnus, well, he's a happy boy, and seems to have learned how to wrap most adults around his finger. What surprises me is that he senses a great deal more than a six-year-old usually does."

"Such as?" Magnus said, already anticipating seeing the boy.

"He seems to be kind. He's just a nice kid, that's all," WeeDee said proudly. "He's always been aware of Gus's problems and is a real pal to him, even though Gus is older."

Magnus glanced quickly at her, and WeeDee knew not to continue telling her father about Gus.

The security people led them to a limousine, helped them in, then went to a car which followed. They were quite expert, and Magnus felt he could relax a bit. Weiss sat in the front seat with the driver so that he and WeeDee would be alone.

"Father, Iris loved you very much. You mustn't think anything different."

Magnus frowned. "What difference does it make?"

"None to her; maybe it could to you."

"No, WeeDee, it couldn't. Whatever Iris did to me, once it was done, it was done. I had no wish to accuse or punish. I wished only that she would stay out of my life. But you kept bringing her back into yours."

"She had no one else, Father." WeeDee readied herself for an argument. Magnus, however, did not pursue the matter.

"When Weiss told me how Iris had died, then about Anastasia's postcard, I thought he obviously made the arrangements. . . . But then I realized he'd only helped her on her way. Without Anastasia, it might have taken a while longer. And then I thought of Mary . . . your mother, and I wondered why the two women I've loved most in my life—"

WeeDee began to shake; the memory of Iris' last conversation flowed through her mind, and she was terrified that her father would confirm Iris' final understanding. So she interrupted.

"Father, the only way I ever understood Jack's death was that there are no reasons. If I thought there *was* a reason, either human or divine, I'd go out of my mind. He lived; he died. So did Iris. So did Mommy. If anything killed Iris, reasons did."

She was again calm; her father took her hand and didn't talk again until they reached home.

They took the funeral home's limousine to the cemetery. The three children rode with them; Augustus was silent, his black eyes staring straight ahead, not sharing his grief with any of them. WeeDee put an arm around his shoulders; he did not reject it, nor did he react to it.

Behind them, the car followed with the security men. More guards were waiting at the burial plot. As a Protestant clergyman said the short service, Augustus caught Magnus staring at him; Magnus quickly looked away. He had not come to Pittsburgh out of love for Iris. He just didn't want WeeDee to have to bury her alone; Iris was not her responsibility. But now, that boy was.

When they returned to the house and the children had been sent off to change their clothes, WeeDee turned to her father and said, "This family meets over too many caskets."

Magnus and Weiss tried to disregard the statement by talking business. WeeDee went into the dining room. She excused the butler, and finally let herself weep for Iris as she set the table for dinner. Outside, she saw men guarding the house, and wanted to tell her father and Weiss to get the hell out. Instead, she made certain the butter knives were exactly angled on their plates.

That evening at supper, Magnus tried to get to know his grandchildren. The time, however, was too short, and the atmosphere of mourning was not conducive to any relaxed exchange. Augustus remained determinedly silent, refusing to display his grief except by an irritating passiveness.

Conscious of his silence, Ellen tried to cover it by talking about her favorite pastime, horseback riding. She successfully diverted attention away from Augustus to herself. Magnus could see her genuine excitement about the subject even as she balanced it against the day and the boy's feelings. She was a beautiful child, and her red hair inevitably reminded Magnus of Mary, the young Mary he had first loved. WeeDee recognized his expression, and they exchanged a nod.

But Magnus found himself most attracted by the little boy, another Magnus. At first, he took little notice of his grandson, being concerned with older members of the family. But gradually he became aware of the six-year-old who sat next to him at the table. The first exchange was a simple smile; Magnus had realized he was being watched, and glanced at Magnus Josephson in time to catch his stare. Instead of looking away, the boy continued his gaze, his curiosity about his somewhat mythic grandfather gradually giving way to an intimate smile of anticipated friendship.

Magnus was not only flattered; he, too, was curious. He watched the boy and noticed he was solicitously maintaining the conversation, asking Ellen a question about horses in those infrequent pauses when she ran out of things to say.

When the children were excused from the table, Ellen and Augustus went out quickly, but the little boy stepped over to Magnus' chair, no longer shy, and said, "Grampa, I love the hats you send me. I love the stetson the most. Thank you, Grampa," and he kissed Magnus quickly on the cheek before running out to play.

Magnus sat for a moment, hesitating to admit how much he was looking forward to knowing his grandson, to liking, loving him, and being loved in return. Then he pushed the thought from his mind. He was still in hiding. He couldn't afford such affection.

The next day, he left for California in the company plane in order to avoid being followed on a scheduled airline. Weiss flew commercially back to New York.

Upon his return, Weiss learned about the contract. Pleased with his own accomplishment, Jamie did not mention anything more about Weiss "getting out." Weiss knew that if he told Magnus the news, Magnus would come back to deal with it, and with Jamie. He also knew that syndicate politics and the DRWW were heating up, making business and staying alive difficult for everyone. Again, Weiss decided to hold the information from Magnus.

At its convention in Miami in February of 1957, the newly joined AFL-CIO threatened the distillery workers' union with suspension if it did not purge itself of corruption in ninety days. Jamie testified before the union's Ethical Practices Committee and supplied them not only with details of Macpherson Industries' years of struggle with the DRWW but also with a thorough picture of the leadership's close connection to organized crime.

Because of Jamie's pressure on the union, Anastasia made what turned out to be a serious mistake: he let it be known that the contract he had out on Magnus could be filled with Jamie. Weiss heard about it and told Jamie. Jamie ordered him to let Anastasia know through the clothesline that there was another contract, one involving a million dollars, a Macpherson contract on Anastasia.

To other members of the syndicate, Anastasia's contract against a father and son was indiscriminate; the fact there was a contract back on him implied weakness. Anastasia went into a rage, but until he found out more about the Macpherson contract, he could do nothing. Vito Genovese took advantage of the interval and did a lot.

On May 2, 1957, someone tried to shoot Frank Costello in the lobby of his apartment house on Central Park West. Costello ducked, bled a lot, and was arrested. The responding police found a week's receipts and skimming from the Tropicana Hotel in Las Vegas in his pocket, and he went to jail for tax evasion, still refusing to say who shot him or why.

Six weeks later, Frank Scalise, the underboss of Anastasia's family, was murdered. Supposedly he died because he was about to betray Anastasia to Genovese, and Anastasia found out about it.

That summer, Anastasia made his second serious mistake: by attempting to take over the Havana Hilton, he tried to muscle in on Meyer Lansky's gambling operation in Cuba. He did this as a show of strength, and for several months that strategy seemed to work. Anastasia became confident and let it be known that he planned to bring Frank Costello back from his "retirement" as the head of the syndicate. Such bragging was not meant to be subtle; rather, it was meant as a firm check to Genovese.

The politics worried Ted Weiss. He put a lot of money into the clothesline to make sure he'd hear if Anastasia were planning anything against the Macphersons. There had been no arson and no hijacking for almost a year; the DRWW was trying to stay on the good side of both the AFL-CIO and the McClellan Labor Rackets Committee. Anastasia was busy with Lansky and Genovese, but he wasn't going to forget the Macphersons for long.

What happened came with no warning. On the afternoon of October 23, 1957, the car driving WeeDee's two children and Augustus home from school was forced off the road and the chauffeur shot. The attacker, his face hidden by a stocking mask, first grabbed Augustus, who fought him as hard as he could. Then the man threw him down on the ground and took Magnus Josephson into his car. Ellen screamed, and Augustus threw himself across the windshield as the car drove away. The man reached out and threw the boy onto the road, skinning most of his right side.

Not knowing of Jamie's contract on Anastasia, WeeDee waited for a kidnap demand all night as the FBI took over the case. But in the morning, the boy was found stuffed in a trashcan not far from the place where he'd been abducted. His throat had been cut.

Jamie heard about it from a reporter from the Associated Press. He tried for twenty minutes before he could reach WeeDee. Finally he got through to her home, and the butler put her on.

"Hello . . ."

"WeeDee, I've just heard a horrible rumor."

"It's true." Her voice was lifeless. "Don't come out here for the funeral. Don't any of you dare come out here!" She hung up.

Weiss came into the office; he'd just heard what had happened. They said nothing to each other. Jamie told the switchboard operator he wanted to send a cable to Algiers, and Weiss listened as Antoine Lescal was activated.

Weiss knew that if Anastasia had dared to murder one Macpherson, he might be ready to murder them all in one of those syndicate slaughters which had proved so effective in the past. He convinced Jamie to stay in his office and to put guards he trusted on duty around the clock. Then he went to his office to call Magnus in California. Evelyn Lorraine answered.

"Miss Lorraine, this is Ted Weiss. I have to speak with—"

"He's already heard, Mr. Weiss. He left an hour ago."

"Where to?" Weiss asked, hoping he was going somewhere safe.

"To Pittsburgh."

"Yeah, of course. . . ."

"If course. . . . I tried to stop him, Mr. Weiss."

"Yeah. Thanks, Miss Lorraine."

Weiss made arrangements to have the company plane fly him to Pittsburgh, and had Security lay on a lot of manpower to meet him and Magnus there. He was careful to switch elevators, but when he went out on Thirty-fourth Street to catch a cab, two of them hit him from behind and dragged him into a car at the curb. He lay on the floor expecting to die at any moment. The ride was short, to a garage on the West Side. Weiss was pulled out, dragged between crates, and thrown on the floor. He looked up and saw Anastasia.

"Are you Weiss?"

"Yeah." He didn't move.

"You the one put a sprayer in my ear one night up at St. Pierre, remember?" He licked his lips.

"Yeah."

"I got plenty reasons to kill you. I ain't gonna do it. I take big chances snatching you off the street. The only reason you're livin right now is to deliver me a message. Get him up." They lifted Weiss to his feet. "You tell that Macpherson kid, the crazy one you work for, tell him I didn't have nothing to do with that little boy's killing. We don't kill children. I'm taking the trouble to tell him this because my boys are busy right now. I don't want them bothered with swatting flies. Right?" He looked around at his men, who nodded. "I got a lot of business right now. I don't want no bother from you people. All right, let's get out of here."

Weiss was hustled back to the car, driven back to the Empire State Building, and thrown out on the sidewalk. The doorman helped him up, and he limped into the elevator.

"I don't believe him," Jamie said.

"I do."

"Why?"

"Because I'm standing here."

"Did you tell him I'd already—?"

"No. I wouldn't be standing here if I'd've told him your guy is coming for him."

"Then we'll wait."

"Can't you—?"

"There's no way to stop Lescal, is there?"

"What if Anastasia really didn't—?"

"So what, Weiss? Isn't it worth the million to have him dead? It doesn't make any difference now. There's nothing we can do to stop Antoine Lescal. It's out of our hands."

Weiss blinked, stared incredulously at Jamie, then turned to the door.

"I'm going to Pittsburgh."

Jamie let him go. Poor Weiss, he thought, like a scared old dog, he runs to his master. Jamie ordered in rollaway beds for himself and his guards, feeling that he, too, was "going to the mattresses," as his enemies said.

The next day, October 25, Albert Anastasia was shot to death in the barber shop of the Park-Sheraton Hotel. Within the hour, the news was on the radio. Jamie had a television set wheeled into his office to watch for bulletins, and as agreed, sent the cable to Geneva with the number of the bank account. He was as ecstatic as he allowed himself to be, shaking hands with his guards, ordering massive meals in for his staff to eat in the boardroom. Weiss called from Pittsburgh; Jamie took it in his office.

"We've won, Weiss!"

"It happened too quick."

"Lescal flew here overnight. He could get here from Algiers in twelve hours," Jamie countered.

"But he couldn't set it up. Besides, there were two of them shot Anastasia."

"He brought a friend. They're probably on their way to Geneva now."

Jamie was still smiling, but the smallest doubt began to gnaw at him. "Weiss, don't worry me with your endless doubts. You're tired. Why don't you take a rest?"

But Weiss didn't. He pulled in the clothesline and heard that Vito Genovese and Meyer Lansky had agreed on Anastasia's death several months before. Genovese had contacted Anastasia's new underboss, Carlo Gambino, saying if something happened to Anastasia, Gambino would become head of the family. For diplomatic purposes, Gambino had included another New York boss, Joe Profaci, who gave the contract to Joey Gallo. It was a murder of syndicate politics. The Macphersons had nothing to do with it.

Within three days Weiss had pieced together what had happened. Because of the growing sympathy in France for Algerian independence, officers of the French Army in Algeria were planning to take over the country and rule as an independent military junta. They were led by General Raoul Salan, Antoine Lescal's boss. To make their plan work, the junta needed its own financial sources. Lescal had flown to Pittsburgh and killed seven-year-old Magnus Josephson in order to activate his contract. He then flew to New York to kill Anastasia, in order to receive the million, but the syndicate killers were ahead of him. Apparently Lescal was close enough to witness Anastasia's murder from across the street. He then disappeared, presumably on a false passport.

The money had been withdrawn from the bank in Geneva within a half-hour of Jamie's cable by a polite white-haired lady, who requested payment in Swiss francs, and disappeared. Weiss figured she was Lescal's mother.

When he heard all that Weiss told him, Jamie realized that he had bought and paid for the murder of his nephew. He put the phone down, knowing that no authority could give him legal retribution, understanding, or forgiveness. For the first time in his life, Jamie was unable to pray.

On February 27, 1957, Longie Zwillman, distraught over what the McClellan committee had done to his reputation as a Jersey philanthropist, hanged himself, according to official police reports. However, he was discovered in the basement of his plush home in West Orange, New Jersey, hanging by the neck, his hands tied behind him. Nothing was near his feet for him to have stood on.

On April 16, 1957, Johnny Torrio, former partner of Al Capone, died quietly of natural causes at the age of seventy-five, his wife by his side.

On May 2, 1957, Senator Joseph McCarthy of Wisconsin died in Tower 16 of Bethesda Naval Hospital of cirrhosis of the liver, two and a half years after the Senate censured him. Four bishops, one hundred and twenty monsignori, and seventy-five priests assisted at his pontifical requiem mass at St. Matthew's Cathedral in Washington.

In November of 1957, one month after Anastasia's death, one hundred of the syndicate's top leaders, representing every major city in the United States, gathered in the small town of Appalachin, New York, to pay their respects to Vito Genovese. Unfortunately for him, the meeting was raided by local police and the government eventually developed a solid narcotics case against Genovese, who was sent to prison in 1959 for fifteen years. He died in Leavenworth ten years later.

17

One of these days, General Motors is
going to get sore and cut the government off without a penny.

—MORT SAHL

Magnus did not go to the synagogue for Magnus Josephson's funeral
service; WeeDee forbade it. He and Weiss went out to the cemetery
in a company limousine; Weiss needed to be near the car phone at all
times, as he was still pulling in the clothesline. He had told Magnus
only that Anastasia was dead, that the syndicate had canceled the
Macpherson contract, and that Magnus no longer needed to wonder
if a gun were around the next corner.

But the relief was not compensation for Magnus' grief. His grandson, an innocent seven-year-old child, had been murdered. Magnus
knew nothing about Lescal; Weiss had not told him.

The limousine stopped and he saw the pile of dirt across the cemetery. Through a slow-falling snow, Magnus walked over to it and
looked down into the grave. The hole seemed enormous for such a
small child. For the first time in his life, Magnus regretted missing a
religious service. The ritualization of death imposed an order on
grief; without it, Magnus felt the chaos of sadness.

The procession of limousines arrived, and the rabbi preceded the
plain wood coffin to the grave. Magnus stepped back so he would not
be the first person WeeDee saw. She followed the casket, holding
hard to the arm of William Wallace Gibson. Ellen and Augustus
Fowler came after, holding hands. Following them were two hundred
mourners, the staff from the paper, friends who had worked with
WeeDee on the numerous committees she served. The mayor was
there, as were the owners and editors of the other Pittsburgh papers.
The press was restrained, and ignored Magnus' presence.

The rabbi read the Ninety-first Psalm in English rather than Hebrew in deference to the number of Gentiles present. "I will say of the Lord, He is my refuge and my fortress: my God, in Him will I trust. . . . For He shall give His angels charge over thee, to keep thee in all thy ways. . . ."

WeeDee took a handful of dirt and let it fall on the casket. She looked away quickly from the finality of the gesture, and, by chance, saw Magnus standing alone, back from the crowd. She tried to indicate that she at least allowed him to share her pain, but she had nothing to give. She turned away, took Double Gibson's arm again, and walked back between the other mourners to their car. Augustus Fowler looked at Magnus also, a dark blank look, then put an arm around Ellen, who had begun to cry, and followed after her mother and Gibson.

Magnus stood where he was and watched them leave. He expected nothing from WeeDee. She could not help but blame him in spite of her attempts to argue herself out of it. Her father did not kill her son; but her son was dead because of her father, his business, his money, his past. Magnus blamed himself far more than she did.

Just then he noticed that Ted Weiss was standing quietly behind him. Weiss looked pallid; Magnus knew he hadn't slept since arriving in Pittsburgh. They had stayed in adjoining suites at the Statler, and Weiss had been on the phone day and night pulling in the clothesline, figuring what Anastasia was up to, then, when news of his murder came, what the syndicate would do. Magnus overheard calls from Europe and North Africa, but paid little attention.

Weiss gnawed his upper lip; his whole body shook, leaving him limp. He shifted from one foot to another and said, "The shovels are under that phony grass over there."

They walked through the snow, and after a moment picked them up. "It wouldn't be sacrilegious?" Magnus asked.

"No. It's supposed to be filled by relatives . . . friends."

"I'll do it, Weiss."

Weiss shrugged.

"I'll help you."

They took off their coats and started to fill the grave.

By then, Weiss knew. He'd been responsible for finding the man who had slit the kid's throat. As an act of atonement, filling a grave wasn't enough. He knew there wasn't time in his life for anything to be enough.

"Macpherson, I'm gonna resign."

Magnus lifted the shovelfuls of dirt and let them fall. He glanced at Weiss once or twice, but said nothing until the grave was filled. Then he stuck his shovel down into the earth so it would stand and not be lost in the snow, and asked, "What is it that I don't know, Weiss?"

Weiss's face went white.

"You're gonna have to wait."

"For what?"

"For me to find out everything . . . and to see Jamie."

"How long?"

Weiss looked down at the grave.

"Not long enough."

Magnus nodded and asked no more. He would trust Weiss to tell him when it was time. They put on their coats and went back to the limousine.

Two more days passed before Weiss knew as much as was needed; he told Jamie the whole story on the phone. Jamie listened so silently Weiss finally had to ask if he were still on the line. He asked one question: "Does my father know, or my sister?"

"No, I thought I'd wait for you to—"

"Yes. Wait," he said, and hung up.

Magnus was already waiting. He spent his days at the Macpherson plant on the banks of the Allegheny River. With Double Gibson he put the final polish on the long-delayed Macpherson Foundation charter, and arranged for the transfer of funds. They made all transactions by long-distance telephone, since Magnus was determined to stay in Pittsburgh until his daughter would see him.

Aside from being Magnus' lawyer, Double Gibson was acting as a diplomatic go-between. He accepted both assignments, the foundation because it meant that Magnus Macpherson would return from exile, and the diplomacy because he was seeing a great deal more of WeeDee. A week after the funeral, she called her father at the plant and asked him to come over with Ted Weiss for dinner.

When they arrived, the butler escorted them to the den. WeeDee and Double were there waiting. As they entered, Double stood up and said, "Ah, Ted, I need to discuss a certain matter with you," and very obviously left Magnus and WeeDee alone.

WeeDee stood in front of the fireplace. Magnus did not move toward her.

"Damn him," WeeDee said of Double, and smiled, embarrassed. "He's good at it, but not so subtle."

"I have to say some things, Father."

"I'm here to listen."

"I can't help blaming you for this. I've tried not to—"

"I understand that, WeeDee, I blame myself."

"I know you do. I think I know how much you do. . . . But it doesn't make much difference to me. I want to love you; God, I want to. I need to love you . . . but I don't now. I can't. There's so much; not just Magnus. I've had to *try* to love you all my life, and I'm tired. I'm exhausted with it. I tried to explain to Double why I was so worn-out, but he said it was my mistake to think loving anyone was easy. And loving *you* . . . well . . ." She smiled, but only as a reference to Double's humor, not as an indication of her own.

Magnus didn't move, nor return the smile, and said, "I'll thank him later. I'm sure most people have an easier time loving than we do, WeeDee. I know what I've done, and what I haven't done. I was far away from all of you when you were growing up. That's perhaps the worst of it." WeeDee leaned on the mantel and looked into the fire. Magnus continued, "I could go on, but neither of us has a need of lists. I'm sure that we can find our way back to loving each other. The danger is, we'll give up and stop trying."

"I've given up, Father. That's what I wanted to tell you. I've stopped trying."

"Couldn't you—?"

WeeDee jerked around and glared at her father. "I don't want to!"

Magnus still did not move, but matched her tone. "I don't believe you!"

WeeDee looked totally surprised. "What?"

"We're never going to have it easy. We're a strange family, these Macphersons, don't ask me why—"

"The ones that are left."

"If you want to fight that way, I'm good at it."

"I don't want to fight."

"You don't want to try, because it seems harder for us than for others. Well, *we're* harder. We're not better. We may be a bit luckier in some ways and unluckier in others. But we have to love harder, and we have the strength to do it."

"God, Father, how can you ask *me* to go on trying after all this, when you've so totally and cruelly given up on Augustus?"

Both father and daughter heard the fire crackling, and the silence roar between them.

"That's a different matter, WeeDee."

"He's your son, you can try—"

"He's *not* my son."

"Then he's your grandson. Whatever he is, he's yours; his father, whoever he is, is *not his fault!*"

"So that's the deal, then. You'll try with me if I'll try with Iris' bastard. Double told me nothing of—"

"There's no deal. Your refusal of any compassion for that boy indicates to me that *you've* given up. How can I believe you about trying when you treat him so dreadfully? Father, if the odds were a thousand to one, if Iris had slept with a thousand other men, which she didn't, Gus still *could* be your son. What if he is? What if you're doing this to your own son?"

Magnus paused. "Doing what?"

"Punishing Iris with him. Punishing Magnus. Father, they're dead. You can't reach them through that boy."

"I don't punish him. I ignore him."

"You pretend he doesn't exist, and he does. You sent presents to Ellen and . . . and you never sent him a thing. Father, he's twelve now. He knows about his mother and you. And he knows you 'ignore' him."

Magnus stood silently in the middle of the room, feeling cornered. "Does he know about his mother and your brother?"

"He doesn't remember much, or he doesn't mention it."

"I'll try, WeeDee."

A sentimental gesture had no place; they were too cautious.

"All right. I'll try, too." She paused, then smiled, glancing quickly in the mirror above the mantel.

"You better let them come back in here. Double needs his second wing."

Magnus nodded, then asked, "It's not my business, just my curiosity: you and Double . . . ?"

". . . are just good friends. But we may get better."

Magnus nodded, then went to the door to call Weiss and Double, but the open door was a signal to the two children that they could come in to say good night to WeeDee, and they came in just behind the men. Ellen was all curiosity, Augustus all reserve.

"Hello, Grampa," she said, and smiled openly, as if she were engaged in a daring event. She was already a woman in her walk; her legs were too long, but there was grace in them. Magnus again searched her face for a resemblance to WeeDee's mother. But Ellen had a darker look, like his own, and she had Jack Josephson's crooked smile, which she lavished on him in her excitement. She stood on her tiptoes and kissed Magnus' cheek.

"Hello, Ellen. . . . I think you grow a little every day. I don't remember you having long legs like those."

"You don't? What did I have? Fins?" She laughed at her own joke, and Magnus joined her.

"Yes, you were a mermaid at the time. Now you're more a flamingo."

"Ew! I've seen them when we visited Florida. Their legs are awful, like orange celery."

Magnus laughed again as WeeDee said, "And here's Augustus. . . ."

Magnus turned and looked into the boy's dark eyes, which he admitted were a mirror of his own. He could not help hating the boy for having them, but he tried not to.

"Hello, Augustus."

The boy approached him and shook his hand. "Everybody calls me Gus, sir, except when things get formal." Ellen giggled and went over to Double.

"They do? I remember your mother preferred 'Augustus.' "

The boy's face hardened; he didn't let it show a thing. "I like 'Gus' . . . 'Gus Fowler.' "

"All right, it's 'Gus,' then." Magnus was wary; the boy seemed highly volatile.

Gus glanced over at Ellen, who was flirting with Weiss and Double and making them laugh, and, including WeeDee, said, "Don't worry. I don't want to change my name. I'll never change my name to Macpherson. And as soon as I can, I'll leave here and never bother you again—" He had been planning the speech for a long time, a child without a childhood, refusing substitutes for a home, a family, a mother.

"Gus," WeeDee interrupted, "you don't need to say that or think it." She looked at Magnus to check his reaction.

"You're very nice to me," Gus said quickly. "But I'm not part of this family, and I never will be. I want *you*"—he pointed at Magnus— "to know I know that." They gazed at each other.

WeeDee again interrupted. "You're a part of my family, Gus. You have been for some time, now maybe more than—"

"Don't do that. I'm not going to be a substitute." He said the word in definite syllables. "And you're not a substitute mother. . . . I don't know who you are. I only know I'm not a Macpherson. I'd be dead if I were."

By then the others in the room were listening. No one moved except Ellen, who hurried over to Gus's side and took his hand, saying, "Gus, you don't have to tell them about that."

He took his hand gently away, keeping his eyes on Magnus, who watched the boy, amazed at his persistence, angered by his presumption.

"The man who kidnapped Magnus picked me first, but he threw me away. He needed a Macpherson."

They all waited, hoping something would happen, a door would slam, a telephone ring, a log on the fire would roll onto the hearth. Gus smiled.

"It's funny. If you'd said I was your son before, you'd probably have gotten rid of me."

Everyone had words to avoid another corrosive silence. They all began talking, except Magnus, who watched Ellen pull at Gus's arm, urging him away.

"Gus . . ." Magnus said as Gus was going out the door. The boy turned, slightly crouched.

"It's true I don't know you. It's a fault of mine. But I intend to, if you give me a chance."

Gus watched, waiting for the twist he'd come to expect from Magnus Macpherson. When it didn't come, and he realized everyone was looking at him, he straightened up, shifted his weight and cocked his head at Magnus with careful defiance.

"We'll see," he said, and left the den with Ellen. WeeDee walked over to her father.

"Thank you." She leaned forward and quickly kissed his cheek.

"Now may I please have my second highball?" Double Gibson insisted.

Weiss watched the door that had closed behind Gus and Ellen. He turned and found Magnus looking at him. His eyebrows went up, and he tilted his head sideways at the door, impressed with the boy.

Magnus was impressed, too. He didn't want to like Gus Fowler. He didn't want him in WeeDee's house, in his family, as his son. But Magnus was impressed.

Dinner was almost pleasant under the circumstances. By the end of the meal Magnus and WeeDee were telling Double and Ted Weiss about Aunt Kristin, her flowing veils and scarves, and the cigars she kept up her bloomers. They were all conjecturing where she had acquired her vast repertoire of filthy songs when the butler entered. He whispered to WeeDee, who announced as he left, "Jamie's here."

"Where?" Double asked through the quick tension that followed.

"In the den. Apparently he's not well."

They all rose from the table and went out into the hall. Weiss followed last. He knew what was going to happen and would have chosen not to be there.

Jamie's face was blue with cold. His lips were purple; there were dark circles under his eyes, which were jaundiced and bloodshot. Magnus noted that his clothes were filthy and he had not given up his overcoat to the butler. They watched as he shivered uncontrollably, shocked to see dried blood between his tightly clenched fingers. He seemed surprised to see so many of them.

Magnus turned to see if this was what Weiss had been expecting. Weiss nodded once, then looked down.

"Jamie, what's the matter?" WeeDee said as she went to her brother.

"Stop. I came here to tell you."

He staggered and nearly fell. As he moved, it was obvious there was something wrong with his legs. He held out a hand to keep anyone from helping him. "No. I'm all right."

"No you're not, you're ill," WeeDee said.

"I have wished that . . . so much, that I'd be stricken . . . some pestilence. But God isn't as easy as that." He laughed eerily. "No, I had to come here and tell you, WeeDee."

"Tell me what?"

"I . . . hired . . . the . . . man"—his voice came bellowing out of him, as if such volume were the only way to force the words—"*who . . . killed . . . your . . . son.*" He looked up slowly from her astonished face toward heaven, but then shook his head.

"You . . . what?" WeeDee gasped.

"I thought I'd be protecting him, all of us." He began speaking quickly, as if he wanted to finish before he lost control. "Anastasia had threatened to . . . he might have done anything. I hired a French soldier, decorated, an expert, and honorable. Honorable! But his honor was owed elsewhere, and he killed for the money which would have been his reward to kill Anastasia. . . . God works his punishments in wondrous ways."

Double Gibson quickly went to the door, made sure no one had been outside, and closed it.

Jamie continued. "I won't dare ask forgiveness. I would be helped to go on living on this earth, as I must, by your unending loathing."

WeeDee backed away, her hands over her face. Double Gibson stood behind her and held her.

"You mean," she said, swallowing between phrases, "that you . . . that if you hadn't . . . done what you did, my boy would be alive?"

"*Yes!* Exactly," Jamie said, then blindly put out a hand for balance, fell to one knee, then doubled up and fell to the floor.

Weiss was the only one who went to him. Jamie had not lost consciousness, only the strength to stand up. Weiss undid Jamie's overcoat and loosened his tie and belt. He saw that Jamie's shirt was covered with large spots of dried blood.

WeeDee stood looking down at him. "I don't care what's happened to you. You can't equal or know the pain you caused. . . . I don't ever want to see you, ever, for any reason. . . . Get out of my house!" She looked at Weiss, then Gibson, and finally her father. The look of loathing softened to despair as she hurried out of the den. Again Double closed the door, then went over to Jamie.

"She's right," Jamie groaned. "I can't know it. God knows I've tried."

Magnus took several steps toward Jamie as if he were going to kick him and his voice grew to a roar.

"Don't waste our time with a list of your damned martyrdom. Tell me *who killed my grandson!*"

"We'll have time to find out about that later," Double interrupted. "The most important thing at the moment is who else knows about this." He looked down at Jamie.

"No one else, except I confessed it to my rector."

Double looked at Weiss. Weiss shook his head and said, "No one else."

"No one else must know. Ever," Double said. "Now, I'd suggest you two take Jamie to the hospital. I'll talk with WeeDee, and tomorrow we'll get together at the hotel."

Weiss nodded and helped Double pull Jamie to his feet.

"Mr. Gibson"—Jamie had to force speech—"tell her I've been at his grave praying for the last twenty-four hours. Tell her that I—"

"I'll tell her, Jamie," Double interrupted, "but I doubt if it will help."

Jamie nodded, smiled hopelessly, and with Weiss's arm supporting him, limped out of the den, leaving Magnus with Double.

Magnus had already contained much of what he was feeling. Dou-

396

ble had seen him suppress rage before and knew it was only a question of time before the fury would ignite.

"He didn't kill the boy, Double, in spite of what he wants to think."

Outside, the chauffeur was helping Ted Weiss put Jamie into the backseat. When he was settled, Magnus got in beside him, and Weiss perched on the jump seat. Magnus pressed a button which closed the partition window behind the driver. The limousine sped off to the hospital.

"All right, now. Jamie, you'd better tell us what you've done."

"I've murdered WeeDee's—"

Magnus interrupted sharply.

"Don't bother with your guilts. What are we to tell the doctors you've done to yourself?"

Jamie sat silently for a moment. "I haven't eaten for, I don't know exactly, since I left the seminary. . . . I went there to renounce my vows." He turned to see the effect on his father. There was none. Jamie went on. "I've been outside since I got to Pittsburgh last night. I went to his grave . . ." Jamie began to cry.

Magnus turned and slapped him hard across the face. "A man has a lot of reasons to cry in a lifetime, but self-pity isn't one of them. Where did the blood on your shirt come from?"

"It's mine," Jamie said. "I made a barbed-wire scourge—"

Weiss turned around in the jump seat. "Jesus, you *are* nuts!"

"When did you do that to yourself?"

"I . . . don't remember. Before I went down to the seminary."

"And they did nothing for you there?"

"I didn't let them. I just went there to sever myself from the order. I'm not worthy to be . . ." He stopped, sensing he might cry again, and turned to his father. "And, Father, I'm resigning as of now from Macpherson Industries."

"The hell you are!" Magnus said it so loud the chauffeur turned to see what had happened. "As of this moment, you are taking a one-month vacation. It'll be your first, if I'm not mistaken. And in that month I hope you'll get tired of feeling sorry for yourself, because that's what all this flailing and crying is about. You're out of the Jesuits. Well and good. You can't run a business with one foot in heaven and the other on earth." Magnus turned and stared out of the window. "You made a mistake, Jamie. A horrible, damnable mistake. But nothing you can do, self-mutilation included, will bring that boy back to life. So you damn well learn to live with it. It bluidy well doesn't give you an excuse to suffer away the rest of your life. You've got too much to do."

"You *want* me to stay?" Jamie gazed at his father wide-eyed.

"You have to stay. Weiss is leaving."

Weiss was watching Magnus as he said it. He was surprised to hear the statement, but he'd known Magnus a long time and was afraid he'd made a judgment similar to the one Weiss had made himself: Jamie was inexperienced, maybe nuts, and Weiss should have known better than to find him a killer.

They arrived at the hospital emergency entrance. Two orderlies took Jamie out of the backseat and rolled him inside on a gurney.

Magnus and Weiss stood by the automatic doors watching the cart roll down the hall and into a side ward.

"What will you be doing, then, Weiss?"

Weiss's head snapped up; Magnus had something planned. Accepting his resignation so quickly was part of it.

"No plans. . . . Thought I'd probably end up in Israel. They've asked me to come—"

"You found the killer, didn't you, Weiss?" Weiss had never been scared of Magnus until that moment.

Weiss nodded. Magnus looked at him with disgust.

"Do you know his name?"

"Yeah. Antoine Lescal . . . French-Algerian OAS soldier."

"Where is he?"

Weiss shrugged. "Disappeared."

"Find him again, Weiss. You have to find him again!"

Weiss felt the cold, and pulled his coat tighter. "I'll find him for you."

Magnus turned to the car. "Come on." Weiss didn't want to get in the car with him; he was afraid and ashamed, an old man who had failed the only man he had ever wanted to please.

The next week, Weiss closed up his apartment and flew to Israel. He made contact with the Mossad, who asked if he would be interested in joining them. Weiss agreed and began his search for Antoine Lescal.

For a month Magnus ran Macpherson Industries on a day-to-day basis. He had just enough time to reassure himself that Jamie had done an amazing job, particularly under the pressure from the union and the syndicate. Every idea Jamie had put into practice had worked. The acquisitions had proved profitable, and Jamie had per-

398

sonally supervised the realignment of their managements. Macpherson's liquors had held their own in spite of a continuing slump in the distilling industry. Diversification had made M.I. a consistently profitable company.

The foundation took up the rest of Magnus' energies. Only one event interrupted his intense concentration: a foolish studio executive had offered Evelyn Lorraine the part of "a fading movie star who falls in love with an out-of-work artist," quite obviously to copy Gloria Swanson's triumph in *Sunset Boulevard*. Evelyn had broken a lamp over the executive's head. Then she had "permanently retired."

Magnus had spent the previous three years with Evelyn. The six months they sailed around the Caribbean was idyllic in spite of the pressure of having to avoid discovery, either by Evelyn's fans or Anastasia's men. Magnus spent hours at the helm and told Evelyn long stories of Rum Row. One day when they were at anchor, Evelyn suggested that Rum Row would make a great film, with her starring in the role of Grace Lithgoe.

"She's a woman I understand," she said.

"And who do you see playing my part, then?"

Evelyn tilted her head to one side, then the other, and said, "Well, I see your part as being pretty small."

"Oh, you do, now." He grabbed her and pulled her overboard into a blue-green lagoon.

Their time on the yacht was like a honeymoon, but they had no inclination toward marriage. They were happy with no obligations of time or affection. Their future together would last as long as they both wished it, and not an hour longer.

The sailing ended because Evelyn had to return to Hollywood. Six months was a long time for a major star to be away. She contacted her lawyer each week, as Magnus contacted Weiss, in order to keep up with their respective businesses. MGM was exerting a great deal of pressure for Evelyn's return. The final straw was an ultimatum that if Evelyn did not return, the picture in question would go to another star—a younger star.

They didn't discuss living together from any emotional perspective, only the practical: Magnus was in hiding. He could keep sailing, but it didn't appeal to him without Evelyn. She offered her house in Beverly Hills. It was guarded, as most movie stars' homes were, and no one needed to know who he was or why he was there. She would make her movies, and they could live quietly together, he under an assumed name for the benefit of the servants. If there were public functions she had to attend, she would find another escort. They went west through the Panama Canal, thinking up a new name for Magnus. For no reason that either of them could remember the next day, they settled on Lothar Bandrio, and toasted him with champagne as they sailed into the Pacific.

As Mr. Bandrio, Magnus spent three nervous years hiding in California. He also invested in Orange County real estate, and investigated California's wine industry. When Evelyn went on location, Magnus would drive with a bodyguard to the Napa Valley and visit wineries. Then he set up a California corporation and began to buy. He was convinced that sooner or later American wine was going to take off and he wanted Macpherson's to be in a strong position. By the time Magnus returned to M.I., he had consolidated the third-largest wine company in the business.

When he left California for Magnus Josephson's funeral, Magnus didn't say good-bye. He and Evelyn were both excessively careful to avoid demands, plans, or emotional gestures. A week passed before either of them admitted they didn't like the separation. Their phone conversations grew more affectionate as time passed.

"Magnus, dammit, I don't like this. I don't want to miss you again."

"Nor do I you, but I do. I think what happened to us is habit."

"Um. You're right: I got used to you."

"They always say habits are bad for you."

"They're bad for parts of you, and fucking good for others. . . . Magnus, I've never been lonely before. It's like when I went to the dentist for my first filling: I didn't know what it felt like. Now I know, and it feels lousy."

"We can break the habit."

Cross-country static and silence.

"You're a big help. . . . I liked you better as Lothar Bandrio."

"And I liked you better on the yacht. But you're a movie star, and I sell whiskey. That means Hollywood and New York."

"Goddammit, I know it. . . . And I just hope Vito Genovese or whoever puts another contract on you, and then you'll have to come back out here!" She hung up.

Magnus put the phone down. He smiled, curious how they both avoided any reference to "love." "Habits," "used to each other," "missing" were about as close as they'd allow themselves to get.

The phone rang. He picked it up, and Evelyn started talking before he had a chance.

"Magnus, that was a rotten thing for me to say. I'm sorry."

"What did you say that was rotten?"

"About Genovese putting out a contract. If it wasn't rotten, it was at least bad taste, and I apologize."

"It was rotten."

"Oh . . . I'm—"

"I forgive you."

"You prick. I'm out here picking my toes and bouncing off walls, and you're obviously getting a big kick in the ass about it. Well, what am I going to do? What are you doing about it?"

"We're both going to wait and see what happens. We've put hooks into each other, Evelyn, so we know what we are to each other."

"I don't. You better tell me. Quick."

"You're outrageous and I'm impossible. Together, we're a smoother blend. We'll have to wait and see what happens."

More static. More silence.

"I don't have time, Magnus. Movie stars get old."

She hung up again.

When Evelyn Lorraine "permanently retired," Magnus tried for days to reach her. Her phone didn't answer, the studio only took messages, and finally he heard a recording saying that her number had been disconnected.

Later that day, he received a letter from her:

11/12/58

Dear Magnus,

I wrote you once a long time ago when I didn't want to use you. Well I'm not about to use you now. I just resigned from being an old movie star, but I'm not resigned to being old. So I'm going to Switzerland today to stop it (getting old). My lawyer says it's a good place for taxes, too.

I'm telling you so you'll know where to look for me this time. I don't know what this does to your pressures, but it makes mine ready to bust open. I miss you and I'm damned if I'm going to do anything more than tell you about it and hope you're ready to bust open, too.

I'll be in Gstaad. I've never skied in my life. If you want my address, ask the local chiropractor.

E.

Magnus found out the address of her chalet and her phone number. His phone bill quadrupled, but he and Evelyn made no plans. They often laughed at themselves being like two wary animals circling each other, waiting for a flood or an earthquake to force them closer. They laughed, and they kept circling, knowing instinctively that the first of them to move toward the other might get lost.

Early in 1959, Joe Kennedy called Magnus and asked him to lunch, not at 21 or the Harvard Club or any other public place, but in a private dining room atop Rockefeller Center. The newspapers had been filled with the "non-candidacy" of young Senator John Kennedy, so Magnus expected the purpose of the lunch to be money.

"Magnus, who do you think is going to be the next President?"

They sat at opposite sides of a small table drinking coffee and smoking Cuban cigars, which Kennedy had stockpiled in his humidor at Dunhill's, a block away. He had already figured Castro as a Communist, so he had bought up lots of cigars.

"Whoever can beat Nixon."

"I can't believe the Republicans will run him," Kennedy said, "but it's always a mistake to underestimate Republicans. . . . Jack Kennedy's going to run, Magnus. He could use your support."

"Joe, there's no one who can ask 'how much?' better than you can."

Kennedy smiled barely, but did not lower his eyes.

Magnus went on. "If I support him, and he wins, it'll cost more than our friendship is good for."

Kennedy puffed his cigar and said, "Not to repeat myself, but 'how much?' "

"Not very much." Magnus looked around the dining room. "But there are two questions. How much is my support, and how much do I expect. . . . I'll contribute fifty thousand now, and fifty thousand for each primary your boy wins. If he gets the nomination away from Humphrey and Johnson, I'll put in another hundred thousand. If he takes seven primaries, that will come to half a million dollars."

"That's very generous."

"I'm glad to do it. After eight years of Eisenhower, the economy is stagnant; the liquor business hasn't moved in a decade. Now, what I want—"

"Magnus, I don't want you to ask for something that can't be given. An ambassadorship is just not—"

"No, nothing as grand as that; nothing that would take a Senate confirmation. I want a quiet Executive appointment to some job where I can work and accomplish something. I don't want a salary or a lot of perks. Some title, an area of responsibility, and someone good to report to, that's all. It would let me balance my history a bit."

"Washington?"

"No. I don't like Washington anymore, and I'd be too visible an appointment down there. I think Europe, France perhaps. Some committee or other. . . ." He waved his hand casually, as if it were an unimportant preference. He wasn't sure he got away with it, because Kennedy watched him carefully for a moment before he responded.

"You really want this, don't you? What happens to M.I., the foundation, if you're in Europe?"

"The foundation is going to do a lot of work in Europe on the drug situation, so I can still be closely involved. M.I. is in good hands—my son's."

"I can't make any kind of promise, Magnus."

"Of course you can't. Promises are terrible things to have between friends."

They stood up and shook hands. Magnus went back to his office and had the first contribution sent to the Kennedy-for-President campaign offices, which had recently opened for the non-candidate. He looked on it as an investment. He did not know how long it would take to find Antoine Lescal, but if he had to go to Europe to do it, being an American official of some kind would be extremely useful.

As the fifties drew to a close, the industry became ever more aware of a restlessness in the drinking public. Two products in particular put a cold pause in every whiskey man's heart: one was vodka and the other, rum. In the late fifties, neither threatened the ingrained inclination to whiskey. But what caused concern in distilleries all over the country was that both products were being sold not so much on their own tastes, but for their ability to mix with other flavors to satisfy the specific drinker's diverse appetites. Whiskey, whether bottled in bond, or blended, or Canadian, or eighty-six-proof bourbon, had a taste which no one would ever mix with orange juice.

Traditionalists labeled vodka a flavoring rather than a real alcoholic beverage. Such epithets as "Russian sauce" and "soda pop" were applied to the clear substance, while rum was looked on as something akin to molasses, a sweetener to be used on pancakes.

Such aspersions may have comforted some whiskey men, but they did not seem to deter the public. By the end of the decade, a single vodka, Smirnoff, sold just under two million cases and controlled two and a quarter percent of the entire liquor market. Bacardi rum, though less noticeable, had sales of six hundred thousand cases.

Magnus didn't like the situation; like Seagram's and Schenley, he didn't want to expand into "the whites" on a gamble. Jamie, however, was adamant. His market-research people were certain that vodka was more than a fad. He barraged Magnus with demographics which indicated swings of taste to easily mixable products. Magnus sent them back with sales figures for Century Preferred. The conflict led to Jamie's proposal to begin marketing a Macpherson's vodka in three states as a test of its viability. The board of directors of M.I. was hesitant to commit itself, knowing that any issue between Jamie and Magnus always involved more than vodka.

Jamie had come to M.I. after his "vacation" with no noticeable change of style or habit. He lived in the same apartment, he kept the same schedule, he wore the same dark clothing. His attitude toward M.I. had not altered; running the company was still his life's cross. But he insisted that he bear it well, and without interference from anyone, particularly his father. By the fall of 1960, when the conflict with his father over vodka came before the board, Jamie had come to believe that without Macpherson Industries, it would be very difficult for him to find a reason why he should live.

At the board meeting to establish M.I.'s position on "the whites," Jamie sat in his usual place at the table, the center seat on one side. He watched the faces of the board members across from him as they listened to the statistics being presented by his market researchers, and thought those board members he could see had been favorably impressed. He did not look at his father, who sat at the head of the table.

As he always did, Magnus asked each member of the board for comments before he offered his own opinion. Jamie kept careful track of the directors' opinions, and was pleased that a solid majority favored the investment.

When the last member had finished, the table turned to Magnus. He looked at all of them, noticing Jamie was sitting straight in his chair, gazing down at his hands.

"I like to gamble, gentlemen, and this looks like a good one. But I like to choose the game, and vodka's not our game. Just because it's liquid doesn't mean it's liquor. From the president's marketing report, it looks to me like it's going to be more than a fad. It may be a trend. It may be the most popular thing since . . . Coca-Cola. But I'm damned if I want Macpherson's becoming the 'fifty-seven-variety' company of the liquor business. If we commit to vodka, we'll have to commit to rum, then slivovitz, then I imagine witch-hazel milkshakes. My feeling is, let these Smirnoff people have whatever they can make out of vodka. We're in the whiskey business; it's what we've done best for a long time."

Magnus missed Ted Weiss at such times. He didn't want to go into vodka, not because it didn't look like a good opportunity, but because he wasn't interested in it. Weiss could have turned the marketing research into whatever texture of mincemeat he wished. Magnus had to counteract such ideas with his own gut reactions, and he wasn't sure they meant enough to his board.

He looked down the table at Jamie, who, as chief executive officer, spoke last before the board voted.

"Does the president wish to comment?"

Jamie wondered for a moment if he even cared. The issue of vodka seemed to him as important as how many angels could dance on the head of a pin. It didn't make the slightest difference to M.I., the economy, or the world. But for the first time in his life Jamie experienced his own ambition, not for the glory of God or the triumph of the Church, not as his altruistic sacrifice of self for good over evil. He felt his own avaricious craving to take Macpherson Industries and have it for himself.

"Yes. I'll comment." He turned and looked at his father. "You oppose this because you're . . . content. Well, there *is* no gamble, because with the tax write-off, there's no possible loss. If Macpherson Industries does not investigate new markets, new products, any new opportunity that presents itself in as favorable a position as this one, then the company will start to die." He began to feel a provocative excitement like the dream he often had of being pushed in front of an altar without a missal and forgetting his Latin.

"I think the question of vodka, though certainly a minor consideration at the moment, is indicative of our will to stay vital and alive. When I came to M.I. eight years ago, I was assured that I would have decisional control over its operation. I feel if the board is not willing to commit itself to this project, it would indicate a lack of will and of confidence in me, and I will resign."

He delivered the entire speech directly to his father, and was delighted to see amazement come to his face. He glanced quickly at the other members of the board who apparently shared Magnus' surprise. A good many of them scowled their irritation with the dramatics, knowing they were facing a struggle in which they would have to commit themselves to Jamie or Magnus. That was exactly how Jamie wanted it. He stood up and walked out of the boardroom, closing the door carefully behind him.

Alone in the elevator, Jamie began to laugh. He believed his body was about to explode, and realized what had finally happened: he had experienced lust. He was not immediately ready to admit he liked it; a certain terror still infused the sensation.

He went straight back to his apartment, let himself in, sat in one of the two chairs, and waited. It seemed odd being there in the middle of the day. He could see so much better; the sun at that hour found a space between neighboring buildings and actually came directly into his window.

The apartment had changed little since he moved in. He had just thrown out the rug when he cleaned the apartment after his self-punishment. On the table was the straight-edged razor he had bought when he first considered killing himself. He remembered picking it out because it seemed to be similar to the one his mother had used. More madness. He spun the razor in its tortoiseshell case on the wooden table. It made a pleasant even sound as it turned, slowly stopping, indicating the door. Jamie spun it again and waited.

Jamie had no doubt Magnus would come. He smiled as he imagined what was going on in the boardroom as he sat there spinning the razor. He thought of Magnus being caught between an easy choice and his own stubbornness not to give in to such histrionic pressure as Jamie had created. But Jamie knew the board; they had grown to respect him, and they needed him as a chief executive, with the Macpherson name, without Magnus' tainted past. Magnus was still the man who had killed his own son. He could be chairman of the board, but if he were making the liquor or buying the new companies, the board knew there would be an adverse reaction, and Macpherson Industries would be vulnerable to a takeover. So Jamie sat and waited for his father to come and put M.I. into his now-willing hands.

The end of the business day came; by then, the ray of sunshine had been squeezed out. Jamie felt the vibrations of the commuter trains pulling out of Pennsylvania Station, a block away, and heard the traffic blare on Eighth Avenue. Finally he heard the footsteps coming up the stairs. He listened for the knock on his door, sensing and enjoying his exhilaration.

"Come in, Father."

Magnus had never seen the apartment. He was determined not to be surprised by it, but even with such mental preparation, he did not expect the austere darkness of the place. He looked around the room, presumably for a place to sit. He saw a chair at the same time he noticed the tortoiseshell razor on the table.

Jamie saw his father's hesitation, but left the razor where it was. Magnus sat down and examined the change in Jamie he'd seen rise in the board meeting as clearly as a cresting wave.

"Now you want it, don't you?"

"Yes."

"Good. I'd rather have you wanting it than making it one of your holy obligations."

"I want it all."

"You're welcome to try to get it."

"Not right away. Eventually."

"You can join your Uncle Juny in waiting for me to die."

"Everybody dies. You're sixty. I'm thirty-two. There's no hurry, Father. But eventually I want it all."

Magnus recognized the full extent of what had happened to Jamie. His son was ready to experience power rather than judge it. He wasn't going to run M.I. as Magnus had run it, with massive corporate force and the domination of the company with his own personality. Jamie was a different animal; he would remain unseen. Meanwhile, he would use power with quiet cunning by manipulating, seducing, and exploiting to get exactly what he wanted.

"The board voted for vodka."

"What was the vote?"

"Unanimous."

Jamie glanced over at his father. "I doubt if I changed *your* mind."

"Jamie, you might think you'll get M.I. one day, but don't waste your time thinking you'll ever change my mind. I voted for it because I want you to run my company; if that's the price it takes, I'll pay it."

"It's cheap. And I'll make you millions on it."

"You're getting greedy, Jamie. I'm glad to see it."

Magnus stood up and prepared to leave. He looked once more around the apartment. "Do you have to live here?"

Jamie followed the path of his father's examination. "No. I don't have to. And now that I've started to want, who knows what will happen? Wanting seems to be a voracious habit."

"A dangerous one as well. You might *get* what you want, so you have to be careful with the wanting."

"Have you gotten what you wanted, Father?"

He asked it with a cruel edge.

"Everyone gets more than they ever wanted, Jamie. You've learned that already." Jamie acknowledged the counterthrust with a nod. "But it's never enough. . . . All the riches and glory, Jamie, you go right on wanting more of it."

"More of what?"

"More of life. Any kind of life. . . . You know why there's a hell, Jamie? Because people who think they won't make it to heaven would rather fry than be nothing. . . . I'll see you at the office."

Jamie stood up and opened the door for his father. "You've become religious in your later years."

"These aren't my later years."

Magnus went out and down the steps. After a short time Jamie went to the delicatessen for the special, then walked over to his office and worked until midnight.

Three weeks after President Kennedy took the oath of office, Magnus was appointed a special adviser to the Tariff Commission, charged to negotiate with European governments under the General Agreement on Tariffs and Trade (GATT). He was stationed in Brussels with the Common Market administration, and flew to Brussels two weeks after his appointment.

He did not tell Evelyn he was coming. He wished no expectations, no conditions, no obligations, nothing which would unsettle the centrifugal balance that kept them in their careful proximity.

The second weekend following his arrival, after he had found a house near the Rue Ducale and moved into his offices in the Common Market complex, he went to Gstaad for the weekend. The season was in full flurry, and Magnus realized for the first time the advantages of being a diplomat; he got a room at the Palace Hotel. He knew where Evelyn would be; she had described her routine in her letters. He put on his dinner jacket and went down to the Maxim Room, where everybody went to dance.

Magnus saw her before she saw him. She was with a large party which included, he learned later, two other movie stars, a famous violinist, and the Aga Khan's uncle, with whom Evelyn was dancing when she saw Magnus standing at the bar. She did not miss a graceful step, and gave him no more than a vague nod, but she kept her eyes on him while laughing nicely at her partner's badinage.

When the dance was over, she excused herself and walked over to the bar. The crowd parted as it always did for her. Still she gave Magnus nothing until she stood before him, her dress of sequins shimmering.

"This is a corny scene, Magnus."

"How can you tell? It just started."

"You'd never get away with an entrance like that in Hollywood."

"I've heard Gstaad is less exacting."

Then she smiled. "What are you doing here?"

"I came for the weekend to see a friend. I just moved to Brussels."

She paused, and the smile faded.

He reached out, took her hand, and pulled her to a stool next to his.

"I'll tell you about it later. But first, tell me how delighted you are to see me."

She arched her neck, turned to the bartender, and ordered champagne.

"Brussels is very close, Magnus."

"It's as far away as we want it to be."

"I am not going to crumble. You know that, don't you?"

"Diamonds will crumble before you do, Evelyn; I've always known that. Besides, you don't look near to crumbling."

"You bet your ass I'm not." Her champagne arrived, and she lifted the glass. "Here's to the monkeys," and she took a swallow.

"The monkeys?"

"Yeah. There's a clinic near here that's giving me injections of all kinds of monkey glands."

"What for?"

She took on an air of dedication.

"Magnus, I'm going to conquer menopause and stay fertile forever. Not that I'd ever have a kid. Fertility keeps the skin young, and in the English words of my Swiss German doctor, 'ze scrotum tingling.' "

Magnus laughed, but Evelyn remained serious.

"I'm glad to see you, Magnus," she said quietly.

Ted Weiss sat at a table in a small Muslim café near the Algiers Casbah. By the summer of 1962 the native FLN had won their struggle for independence and had taken over the country. The fanatic

OAS remained, having taken their rage at De Gaulle's betrayal of their *Algérie française* underground in order to plot his assassination and begin again in Algeria.

At the Bassin de l'Agha, Weiss had slipped ashore from a Swedish tanker which he had boarded in Rotterdam. He had only a few hours before the ship sailed on for Genoa. His route to Algiers was complex, but a Jew did not travel there without taking elaborate precautions. He carried Dutch papers and was dressed as a ship's officer.

An Algerian came into the café and drank mint tea for a half-hour before he nodded to Weiss, then casually joined him. Their conversation was quick, the Algerian speaking in halting English.

"The man you look for, he is returned to Algeria, as the Mossad tell us. We are pleased to have this information. We do not know his exact location at this time."

Weiss did not reveal the slightest disappointment at having come such a long way for nothing.

"Will you contact us if you learn—?"

"We do not promise you such."

Weiss shrugged. "O.K., pal. But the next time we hear about a potential OAS assassin coming home, 'we do not promise you such' either. Get me?"

The black eyes of the Algerian burned with suspicion and prejudice.

"What is the Jews' interest in this man?"

Weiss corrected: "The state of Israel's interest is to offer the new state of Algeria any aid it can against fanatical terrorists, in hopes that the favor gets returned sometime."

The Algerian relaxed slightly.

"This Lescal, he is the slime of the pig. He tortures old ones, cuts up women, children."

Weiss said nothing. He knew Lescal's reputation, as well as his exploits.

"He kills with the pleasure, makes friends with Death, so Death never takes him."

Weiss squinted and put down his cup of thick coffee. He was tired, too old for spying and chasing. Then he shook his head. He had to find Lescal; he wasn't too old for that as long as Magnus Macpherson was still alive. He smiled to himself.

The Algerian saw it. "You smile."

"Nobody makes friends with Death. . . . Death gets you every time. It cheats."

The Algerian shrugged and left the café.

18

Let the word go forth from this time and
place . . . that the torch has been passed
to a new generation of Americans. . . .
                                        —JFK

Gus Fowler walked into Ellen Josephson's room without knocking.
She was sitting on her four-poster bed looking at her suitcase in the
center of the room.

"Packed?" he said.

She nodded. "I'm scared."

"So be scared. Come on." He took her suitcase and went out.
Ellen followed.

In the hall he picked up his duffel bag and started downstairs.

"Where is she?" Ellen asked at the bottom of the stairs.

"I don't know, the den, I guess."

"Do we have to tell her? Couldn't we just leave?"

Gus put the bags down and took Ellen by the arms. "I have to tell
her." He looked at her a moment, then kissed her. "Don't worry
about it. Come on."

They went into the den.

Gus graduated in 1963 from Shady Side Academy. He previously
was expelled from the Hill School and from Mercersburg Academy.
He went to a psychiatrist for five years, who succeeded in identifying
his rage and sense of rejection, but failed to discover a way for him
to safely express it, divert it, or be rid of it. He took up flying, he told
his doctor, because he could be alone and far above Pittsburgh. He
earned his pilot's license, but he also developed an ulcer.

Gus figured that he needed to get the hell away. His eighteenth
birthday gave him direct access to the trust which Magnus had set up
for him. He hadn't touched a cent of it; after five years with the

headshrinkers, he knew he wanted nothing to do with money provided by Magnus Macpherson. Knowing it was there, however, gave Gus the self-assurance to walk away from it.

Ellen had grown up exposed to every privilege. She was beautiful, seventeen years old, red-haired, and rich. She went to the Sewickley Academy, then to the Winchester-Thurston School. She rode in horse shows at the Rolling Rock Club and played an admirable game of tennis. Her mother was planning a debutante party for her at the Golf Club, and had sent off for applications to "The Seven Sisters" colleges. The surface of Ellen's life seemed to be attaining a quality gloss.

Ellen, however, was terrified of meeting people, of playing the role of her mother's daughter, and of being one of the most popular young ladies in Pittsburgh. She would cry or be sick to her stomach before a horse show, a dance, or a tennis match. But she would always appear, disciplining herself to do whatever she thought people expected of her.

The only person who was able to help her was Gus Fowler. Gus seldom went to the parties. He thought guys in their teens putting on tuxedos were dumb. He did watch Ellen ride in the horse shows, but avoided talking with her in the crowd, preferring to wait until they returned home. Ellen could hardly wait to be alone with him. Gus made her laugh. They would spend hours laughing about what Gus referred to as "the three-river social shit . . . The rich rise just like the turds in the Allegheny and the Monongahela. By the time they reach the Ohio, they're all floating on the top."

They had been lovers for six months. Discovery and the impending debutante party in the fall were the two most violent fears Ellen had. She was convinced that the only way to escape both was to leave Pittsburgh with Gus.

William Wallace Gibson was the first to suspect their relationship. On one of his frequent visits, he noticed that the usual conspiratorial attitude which teenagers have in their transactions with grown-ups was, in the case of Gus and Ellen, "tinged with intimacy." He mentioned this to WeeDee, who did not accept it. She reminded Double that Gus and Ellen had been raised as brother and sister. She had always been glad, and even relieved, that the two of them seemed to get on so well considering Gus's difficult past.

That week, however, WeeDee saw them holding hands. She was startled, but could not believe she had been so completely blind to have overlooked their liaison, whatever it was. The idea that they might be having sex in her house appalled her. She asked to speak with them. Gus's instincts were sharp to discovery. He knew the time had come to leave, and told Ellen he was going. He said that if she wanted to come with him, she'd better get packed.

Gus didn't look forward to confronting WeeDee. Through the years, he had carefully avoided it, keeping their relationship one of oblique emotional angles. She'd been good to him, had loved him and treated him as one of her own children. Gus knew it, but never had accepted it.

WeeDee had gone through some of the therapy with Gus in hopes of resolving some of their differences. They were not resolved, but had become clearer, at least to WeeDee. The psychiatrists explained that from Gus's point of view, any affection he developed for Wee-Dee would be a betrayal of his mother, whose death was still an unresolved trauma to the boy. He believed all the Macphersons were to blame, especially Magnus, and probably WeeDee.

WeeDee was sitting at her desk writing checks. When Gus and Ellen came in, she stood up and went to embrace them both with as much affection as they would allow. Gus stood, unyielding as stone, but WeeDee was surprised, then alarmed to feel Ellen as well give nothing to her embrace.

"Let's sit down."

Gus asked, "Is this going to be a long meeting?"

WeeDee smiled, adopting the careful tone she used with Gus. "This isn't a meeting, Gus. I wanted to talk to you, that's all. Come on." She set the example and sat on a couch. Gus hesitated, then sat opposite her, motioning Ellen to sit beside him. She did not look at her mother.

Noticing her daughter's lowered gaze and her proximity to Gus, WeeDee sensed that Double had been right. She felt devastated even before she began talking.

"Do you two have anything to tell me?"

Without hesitation Gus replied, "Only that we're leaving." Ellen looked quickly at him, then back down at the floor.

WeeDee heard what he said, but could not comprehend it.

"You're what? Leaving? What are you talking about?"

Gus gazed at WeeDee noncommittally. For the first time WeeDee thought she could hate him, not for all he had taken from her over the years and now betrayed, not even for whatever he had done with Ellen. She could hate him for his teenage superiority and coolness.

"You do know what I'm talking about," he said. "It's why you wanted to have this meeting. Well, whatever you think about us is probably true, and it doesn't make any difference, because we're leaving."

They glared at each other, but both were used to rigid control. WeeDee had more experience, but Gus had been a fast learner.

WeeDee spoke carefully. "You're doing this to hurt me, and you're succeeding all too well. But you're hurting yourselves more."

Gus cocked his head to one side, then leaned forward.

"You don't think staying around here is going to be *good* for us, do you? If we stay around here, we're going to be Macphersons, with a little class. Well, I'm not about to be that!" He caught himself and slumped back on the couch.

WeeDee hated being the grown-up. "Gus, I gave you all I could. Take it and forget it, and get out. But you're not going to take Ellen with you."

"I'm not taking her, lady. She's coming."

WeeDee stood up and shouted at him: "What . . . why are you talking to me like this: 'Lady'? You've never called me that in your life. What's the matter with you?"

Gus didn't move. He looked down, embarrassed rather than afraid of her anger.

"I guess 'Aunt WeeDee' sounded too weird. I guess it always has. You aren't my aunt. You aren't my anything . . . but you sure are a lady." He meant no compliment.

WeeDee stood holding on to the couch as if she were about to fall. "Ellen . . . Ellen, why don't you say something? Do you hear what he's saying? Talk to me. . . . Are you leaving?"

Ellen looked up at her mother, tried to speak, gave up, and shrugged. As she looked down again, she mumbled, "I love you very much, Mommy. . . . But I have to go with Gus."

"You don't *have* to! Ellen, does it occur to you he's taking you away just to punish me, my family, *your* family?"

Gus whistled and shook his head. "Well, there it is: I'm an outsider, right?" He looked accusingly at WeeDee.

"You *never* were, until you made yourself one this morning. I thought I knew you; I know I loved you. . . . But you're a stranger who's lived in my house all these years. You call me 'Lady' and seduce my daughter. I don't care who you are. I *want* you to leave. Now!"

Gus nodded and stood up. "Like I told you, Ellen, blood's the thickest milkshake. Come on, let's go."

"She's not going." WeeDee went to the door.

Gus rolled his eyes skyward. "You really need the gesture? That's all it is. You're not doing it to keep her here; you're doing it because it's what you think you *should* do."

WeeDee took a step toward him, ready to fight him, wanting to fight him. "She doesn't want to go. . . ."

Gus turned to Ellen, who was still sitting on the couch gripping her knees. "Tell her!"

Ellen didn't move. She barely looked at him. "Mommy, I love you and I know this hurts you, but I have to leave with Gus."

"You *don't* have to, no matter what's happened."

"I want to! *I* have to. . . ." She was quiet a moment, then shrugged. "I don't want to be like this, Mommy."

"Like what? I don't want you to be like anything, Ellen."

"No, Mommy, you don't see. . . . It's not real here; it's like concrete. It begins to harden, and you can't get out until you're just like everyone expects you to be."

"Ellen, that's *not true!* You've enjoyed it. You know you have. You can be anything you want here. . . . Don't let him do this."

Ellen shook her head. "I tried to enjoy it because I knew you wanted it so much." Again she shrugged, and gave up trying to explain. Then she looked directly at her mother. "And, Mommy, he didn't seduce me. I went into his room the first time."

By then, the detail made little impression on WeeDee.

"This has been a real home for you both. My love was *absolutely* real. You can't believe . . ." She was wearing down; she didn't trust her voice to go on.

"Mommy, we aren't what you want us to be, so there's no reason for us to stay."

Again WeeDee felt anger, but it was overwhelmed by loss.

"No reason? Of course there are reasons. Where are you going to go? Where are you going to stay?"

Before Ellen could answer, Gus interrupted. "We'll send a postcard."

Images came to WeeDee of police and private detectives, of calling for the servants to keep them there, at least to hold on to Ellen. But looking at her only daughter, the only child left to her, WeeDee saw that Ellen had already gone. No detective could bring her back, no servant could keep her. WeeDee put her hand on the door, opened it, and held it for them.

"You can always come back here . . . both of you."

She felt them move past, barely seeing anything of the children she had known as they disappeared. She closed the door and went back to the couch, remembering her three babies, Ellen, little Magnus . . . and Gus. Finally she concluded that children either die or grow up. Either way, she had lost them all. She went to her desk and picked up her briefcase. Her driver was waiting, and she drove to her office, realizing her father had lost his children as well, and wondering if she had the trait.

Gus and Ellen drove west over the turnpikes and freeways. The car was a new Chevrolet convertible, Gus's graduation present from WeeDee. They knew exactly where they wanted to go, and drove in relay to get away from Pittsburgh as fast as they could. Their goal was California, the farthest spot they could think of. They stopped only for gas and food, and in a little town in Kansas, Ellen bought a secondhand guitar with an instruction book.

The third day, as they drove across the plains of Wyoming at a steady seventy-five miles an hour, Ellen woke up, climbed into the front seat with her guitar, and practiced chords. After a time she said, "Gus?"

"Um."

"What if you are my uncle?"

"So?"

"That's incest."

"What's 'incest'?"

"You know."

"Yeah, I know. It's a word for fucking. There's a lot of those." He shrugged. "So what?"

"But what will people do if they find out?"

"They'll throw us in a pit and stone us."

"Oh, Gus . . ."

"Hey, what are you worrying about? It works, doesn't it?" Ellen giggled. "Doesn't it?"

"Yes." She strummed a chord triumphantly.

"And you're on the pill, so who's going to care? They call 'fucking' a lot of scary names to keep people from doing it."

"And fucking by any other name is just as sweet."

"Yeah, call it . . . 'incest-barph-ola,' I don't care. I'll still do it, won't you?"

"With you, yes. I'm not too sure about incest-barph-ola with anyone else."

Gus glanced over at her, then quickly back at the road. "Gimme a kiss."

Ellen hunched over the seat and kissed his ear, then stayed close to him and laid her head on his shoulder. He started clenching his jaw, and Ellen could hear him grind his teeth. "You're making that noise."

He drove on silently for a while. "I'm not your uncle anyway."

"Don't get hung up on that, Gus."

"What do you mean, hung up? I'm not hung up. I'm not your uncle, that's all!"

"Well, you're probably my something."

"I'm your nothing! You understand that? You're WeeDee Josephson's daughter. You're Magnus Macpherson's granddaughter. But you aren't anything to me. And I'm not anything to you, or to them."

They rode in silence, until Ellen said, "You're hung up."

"Hey. You want to get out here and walk awhile?"

Ellen moved away to her side of the car and practiced chords again on the guitar.

They headed south to Las Vegas, then drove a straight line to the Pacific, hitting the beach at Ventura just before dawn. When the sun flooded over the hills and washed the sand in warm honey-colored light, they ran naked into the water, both bellowing as they hit the cold.

They loved the Ventura beach, stayed a week, living in the car, sleeping on the beach, eating on the pier, and washing in gas stations. Then they started south, avoiding Los Angeles, staying near the beach in Oxnard, then Zuma, Malibu, and driving their last ten miles to Venice, California, at which point their cash ran out. So they sold the car, rented a run-down beachfront shack, and started looking for work.

Ellen looked in restaurants and bars; Gus hung around the small local airports. He finally picked up a job as a plane jockey for a flying school at the Santa Monica airport. He moved planes back and forth to their parking areas or ferried them to another airport. He would sometimes get stuck in the San Fernando Valley or over at Hawthorne Airport. The bus trip back to Venice took three or four hours even if it weren't rush hour.

Ellen worked first at a health-food store. With the devotion of a convert, she quickly inflicted on Gus newfound diets to cure his ulcer. He hated the food and he needed the ulcer; it was keeping him out of the draft. He didn't want to go to Vietnam.

When she turned eighteen, Ellen took a job as a cocktail waitress. The pay was worse, but the tips were better. Working from five to one in the morning, she was hassled by men, and came close to getting fired for being "unfriendly." The work was hard, the hours long, and there was never enough money.

Since Gus had to work in the early hours of the day when the air was best for flying, they began to miss seeing each other. He came home exhausted from trying to get around Los Angeles on buses, just as she would be hurrying out to catch the Santa Monica bus.

"Hey, how you doing?" Gus would say, opening a beer and collapsing on their only pillow.

"I'm late. . . . Damn, I miss you."

"Me, too."

"The toilet's stopped up again."

"Jesus, this place—"

"Sucks!"

"—sucks."

"Gus, we have to get a car."

"I know! Goddammit, I know!"

"I'll see you tonight."

"Yeah. . . . Look, wake me up, will you? I want to see you, you know?"

But she never did, because she'd get home around two and he had to be up at five. When they managed to have a day off together, which was seldom, they usually dragged out to the beach and slept all day in the sun. They didn't talk much. When they did, they argued about money. Gus refused to touch his trust fund; Ellen resented it. She felt she was working her ass off for his hang-up, which was stupid. His reaction was that she didn't have to stay. The argument would harden into sullen silence.

One night, when they had been in California about a year, Ellen came running into the house after work and woke Gus.

"Gus, wake up. I have to talk to you."

"Hey, what the hell is this?"

"Merle, my girlfriend at work. She knows this guy, I told her you were a pilot, and she told him, and he wants to meet you."

"What for?"

"He has a job for you or something. I don't know. But Merle says he has a lot of money. He drives a Mercedes and wears Guccis."

"He could be a pimp."

"Aren't you excited?"

"Not yet. When do I meet this guy?"

"Here's his phone number. He wants you to call him tomorrow morning at ten o'clock. Exactly ten, not a minute earlier or later."

The number was for a pay phone. The man who answered didn't talk long, only enough to make sure Gus knew about planes and navigation. He told Gus to expect five hundred dollars cash in the mail with which to rent a plane for half a day. Gus was to fly it down the coast to the beach just south of Carlsbad early the next Tuesday. On arrival Gus was to perform some low-level stunts, glides, and hedge-hopping for about fifteen minutes, then fly back to base. He would be watched, and could keep whatever was left of the five hundred. The morning after, he was to call another number at exactly ten o'clock.

Within a month Gus was flying planeloads of marijuana in from Mexico. He never met the man on the phone. He would be told which airport to go to, and the location of a plane. When he arrived, he would find his flight plan under the seat. He would then fly legitimately to an airport in Mexico, spend the weekend as if it were a holiday, be contacted there by phone and given his flight plan for the return trip. He would fly north, detour to a dirt strip somewhere near his route, land, be met by a truck full of silent Mexicans with marijuana. The grass would be quickly packed on the plane as the motor idled. Then Gus would take off, cross the border on course, and detour again to another dirt strip. If the signals from those on the ground were right, he'd land. The marijuana was unloaded, and Gus would be handed an envelope with two thousand dollars in it. Then he would fly on to his destination according to his flight plan, explaining any discrepancy in time to sightseeing or avoiding bad weather.

Ellen quit her job, and they moved away from the beach to a small bungalow in Laurel Canyon. They bought two old cars, a mongrel bitch which they named Merle, a stereo, a color television set, and a lot of marijuana. Ellen seldom went to the supermarket without taking a few hits. Soon, however, she began to get bored with having nothing to do. She sat around the house getting stoned, playing the guitar, playing the stereo, watching TV. She threw away all her bras and let her hair grow in her armpits. She was particularly unhappy when Gus was away, and asked about going with him, but he refused to even think about it. If he got caught, he didn't want to worry about what was happening to her in a Mexican jail.

But Ellen hassled him about it, and Gus began to reconsider. He was flying more trips, and saw that the job was relatively safe. The weekends in Mexico were long and boring, and having Ellen along with him would be a better cover if anyone were watching him. He suggested the idea to the man on the phone, who bought it. Ellen began to fly to Mexico regularly. She made him eat decently, which helped; when he was flying, the ulcer always kicked up.

On the morning of March 25, 1965, their twin-engine Beechcraft flew north over the Mexican border between Nogales and Yuma at an altitude of fifty feet. Ellen was smiling, a bit stoned, her hand pressed easily between Gus's thighs. She was watching the clouds.

Gus banked the plane and saw the car near the dirt strip below. A man got out, waved as expected, and held up a strip of red cloth to indicate air direction. Gus circled and brought the plane in, taxiing to the end of the strip near the car. Suddenly the man started to run.

"Oh, shit." Gus's fists clenched on the stick, the pain in his stomach jabbed again. He saw three other men jump out of the car and start shooting; another car he had not seen approached from the other end of the strip.

"Burn it!"

"What?" Ellen had been watching a cloud in the shape of a whale.

"Burn it! Move, goddammit!"

He turned the plane and accelerated directly toward the oncoming car. There were more shots. Ellen moved to the five-gallon container behind her seat, unscrewed the top, and poured the gasoline over the plastic wrapping. Something went through the fuselage just beside her. She screamed.

Gus gunned the motors, but the controls weren't right. The car swerved to miss the plane. Gus jammed the stick and ran the plane off the strip, tipping it onto one wing. Again Ellen screamed as she was thrown against the windscreen. Gus opened the door and pushed her out. He lit a match, threw it on the gasoline-soaked plastic, and leaped out. Ellen's mouth was bleeding. He picked her up off the ground and they started running. The blast from the plane's explosion knocked them down, and Gus covered her from the flying debris with his body as the agents ran across the desert toward them.

"Don't say anything."

"I'm scared shitless, Gus."

"There's no evidence."

"Mother, Grandpa. They'll kill us!"

He turned and looked at her, his jaw clenching.

"Don't worry, they'll take care of you fine. You're a fucking Macpherson, aren't you?"

"Don't move a muscle!" The first agent to reach them was mad as hell, sweating from his run, and wanting to do damage.

"So are you, Gus, you dumb shit. Why can't you—?"

Gus reached over and smacked her hard.

"Don't say any—"

The movement got him a solid kick from the agent and two broken ribs.

A week later, Gus was out of the hospital facility and in a maximum-security cell in the Pima County Jail. Tucson authorities did not take kindly to anyone involved in drug traffic, and they did little to make him comfortable. When Gus was told he had a visitor, he was not surprised that it was William Wallace Gibson. The room where they met was small and air-conditioned. Gus sat down slowly at the table in deference to his ribs.

"Gus, I would suggest we start with your side of the story."

"What for, Mr. Gibson?"

Double Gibson looked up from the papers in front of him.

"You're facing two to ten years in the Arizona state penitentiary, a facility not as pleasant as this one, I understand. They are setting a very high bail."

"I can't afford you, Mr. Gibson."

"I appreciate your concern for such matters, but I have been provided for. Now, I would suggest—"

"I'll stick with the public defender." He stood up and started for the door.

"Gus, stupidity is not an effective revenge."

Gus turned back to him.

"What the fuck's that supposed to mean?"

"It's stupid to choose the public defender before me. I'm motivated, and I'm better."

"No, what do you mean, revenge?"

"That really isn't my realm, but I'm sure your psychiatrists pointed out your inclination for revenge, for your mother, for your life, for Magnus Macpherson's gross and unjustified neglect of you. I understand your anger, but I question your method of expressing it. Smuggling dope is not a very effective way to punish anyone except yourself."

"I didn't do it for that. I did it to earn a living. I damn well don't *ever* have to spend any of his money. And I'm not going to use you for the same reason. So forget it!"

"All right."

Double gathered up the papers on the table and put them in his attaché case. He walked past Gus and was about to knock on the door for the guard. "Oh, yes. Ellen sends her love."

"Where is she?"

"Out at the women's detention facility. She seems fine."

"I hope she's kept her mouth shut."

"Apparently she has. Well, I'll be off—"

"Wait a minute. Let me just ask you one thing. And you can send me a bill. You got any good ideas for 'effective revenge'?"

Double smiled slightly. "Success, Gus. Right now, you're doing exactly what Magnus Macpherson expects you to do. If, on the other hand, you became successful, I'd think it would cause him considerable consternation." He turned and knocked for the guard to let him out. "You see, Gus, your amorphous connection to all things Macpherson could be quite interesting if you didn't feel the necessity of constantly thrashing at them. For instance, what if you accepted being a bastard, *and* a Macpherson in everything but name, and laid claim to your share of the manor?"

"Wait a minute." Gus stood up.

The door opened as Gus shifted uneasily from one foot to another. His stomach hurt and his ribs hurt. He glowered at Double Gibson and said, "You haven't heard my side of the story yet."

Double nodded, apologized to the guard, and went back to the table. Gus sat down and began to talk.

"All right. You hooked me. I figure you can get Ellen and me out of this pretty easily, don't you?"

"I have little facility to judge ease, but I never predict failure." He smiled sardonically.

"So what are you telling me?"

"You have some choices you should make."

"From in here, I don't see too many."

"Gus, you choose not to see because you're angry. Your first choice, and I would suggest you make it quickly, is whether you want to stay angry with the world, or take advantage of it. Of course I'll get you out of this, but that's not important. Are you going to continue indulging yourself in sullen anger?" He fixed Gus with a look he used to sway juries. "Gus, I would suggest that this is the only choice that means anything to you at the moment."

In Manhattan, it was lunchtime. Jamie Macpherson came up from the Seventy-ninth Street subway stop on Broadway and walked two blocks to the crowded offices of *West Side World*. At the first desk he approached, he asked to speak with the managing editor, Abner DeLong.

The paper was a weekly and not very rich. It prided itself on having the most intellectual and cultured readership in the country. The office was in an uproar, since DeLong had announced that morning that the paper had been sold out the day before to Macpherson Industries. In tense little groups the staff was discussing a mass resignation.

When word of Jamie's presence circulated, there was a staccato surge of voices, then silence. They stared at their new owner in amazement. All his clothes were dark, except his white Arrow shirt. His hair was neat, but he obviously didn't get it styled. And his face displayed nothing.

Janet Flanagan, DeLong's editorial writer, thought Jamie Macpherson would have been a happy Kafka character. She was fascinated by him from the first moment she saw him and wondered if her interest were perverse or perversion. She knew of her own carnal inclination to power, but the guy standing at the front desk wasn't your usual idea of power. He looked more like a limp Danish with no fruit *or* nuts. She liked her metaphor a lot, and decided to write an article about him.

Jamie watched as Abner DeLong strolled a little too casually over to him, noting that Abner wore custom-made shirts with his initials monogrammed on the breast pocket; also, that Abner pulled in his stomach as he gained attention. He concluded that Abner was vain and would have to make a speech for his staff.

"Well, Mr. Macpherson, we'd have rolled out the red carpet, but we didn't hear your limousine drive up," Abner said, expressing the contempt of a monogrammed shirt for a limousine.

Jamie just looked at him. No diplomatic smile. No need to say he'd come on the subway. This made DeLong nervous and no longer casual.

"Okay, listen, Mr. Macpherson, I don't know what *you,* and your *father,* and your accountants and lawyers do up there in your grand, big offices, and I never *wanted* to care. You could all go on making hooch and money until doomsday. But goddammit, now you're fooling with my life . . . with a lot of people's lives"—a pause for a long, emotional look to his people—"and what right do you have to come in here and screw them up? I have eighteen years—"

"I didn't come in here to screw anything up, Mr. DeLong."

Abner DeLong was not practiced in reacting to calm. His juices flowed at a level required in a pressroom.

"Goddammit, Macpherson, don't you and your father have enough blood on your hands without us?"

Abner knew right away he'd made a bad mistake. Some of his staff gasped. He tried to keep eye contact with Jamie Macpherson but couldn't.

"That was . . . I'm—"

"I came here to clear up a problem." Again the even tone, not a trace of reaction to what Abner had said. "I heard you and your staff were distressed about our acquiring your paper. We did so because it's a promising business venture. Five years ago New York had seven daily papers. Today it has five, and in a few years, we think, three. At that time, a well-written . . . and financially secure weekly paper could fill the void. You have a circulation now of forty-six thousand. By 1970 it should be three hundred thousand if you have the necessary financial backing. We are anxious to provide that backing. We don't wish to interfere in management or editorial policy at all." For the first time he looked around at the others. "Personally, I hope you'll all stay."

They all looked back at him. Suddenly there was no great corporate monster at which to be furious.

"Listen, I . . . ah, really, I'm really . . ." Abner needed to apologize.

Janet Flanagan said, "It sounds like you're not even going to read the paper."

"Probably not. But it might interest you to know I've never tasted whiskey, either." The smallest trace of a smile drew out laughter from all over the room. They didn't want to like him, but they did.

Once more DeLong tried to apologize. "Listen, Mr. Macpherson, I . . . I'm really—"

"I'm afraid I've got to get back downtown. I hope we can work this out. Let me hear from you soon."

He shook DeLong's hand and walked out. Janet Flanagan went over to her boss.

"What do you think?"

"He scares the hell out of me. He doesn't *feel* anything."

Janet smiled. "From what I hear, he only feels about God and his father." She would definitely do a story on him. She pictured a long interview in his penthouse or wherever he lived, and was pleased when Abner suggested it himself.

"You know, we ought to do an article on him. Jesus, did you hear what I said to him? God, I'm sorry I said that." Abner got his apology in to somebody.

A week later, Janet Flanagan was waiting for Jamie when he came into the delicatessen for his evening meal. That night, it was stuffed cabbage, of which the owner's wife was inordinately proud. As Jamie began to eat, Janet went over to his table.

"Hello, Mr. Macpherson. I'm Janet Flanagan."

He remembered that after his visit to the paper she had asked his public-relations people for an interview.

"Yes, I remember, and I believe your request for an interview was turned down."

"I'm persistent."

"So am I."

"If I get turned down twice, I get fanatical and become really bothersome. Look, Mr. Macpherson, I know just about everything I need, it won't take very long, no longer than it takes you to finish your cabbage."

She had short black hair and steady green eyes which matched the color of her sweater. She wore space shoes and Levi's and carried a bag large enough to contain foodstuffs for the poor of India. Jamie was curious.

"Please sit down."

"Thanks."

"Tell me first of all what you already know, so I don't repeat anything."

"O.K., you eat. First of all, you don't live in a penthouse. You live in a very strange place which I've only seen the outside of, don't worry. You were in the Jesuits when you came to M.I. during the, ah, family trouble . . . which doesn't get into the article, I promise you . . . The trouble doesn't get in, the Jesuits do. . . . You gave up your vows five years ago, but you still live like a 'monk,' which is your nickname in the industry. You've only taken one month's vacation in fourteen years, you have no hobbies or other interests that anyone knows about, you buy your suits at Klein's, you eat here every night, you don't see your family, Mrs. Josephson or your father, and nobody has ever seen you with any friends, boy or girl. You don't belong to any clubs, you don't even go out for lunch. In other words, you are nothing more or less than an emotional zombie."

Jamie hesitated with the cabbage, then went on and swallowed. "I must confess, Miss Flanagan, I'm not used to the press. Is this the way you elicit an outraged quote or two?"

"To be totally frank with you, Mr. Macpherson, that's not what I'm after."

"Be even more frank, Miss Flanagan. What are you after?"

"Ah, yes, well, since you ask, but first let me say that I'm your basic up-front, put-it-all-on-the-table kind of woman."

"The table awaits." The cabbage was finished.

"Yeah, well . . ." She took a deep breath. "O.K. Take as the given that you are a strange man. The reasons I don't want to get into yet, but you are, for whatever reason, a *strange* man!"

Jamie smiled. "My needs are just small, that's all."

"Wrong! Your needs are complex and many."

"Dare I ask what they are?"

"Do you?"

"I dare."

"Ask?"

"Yes."

"All right." Another deep breath. "I know as much about Catholic guilt as you. And you, I bet, are stuck in it up to your ass. What you need is some feeling in your life, emotions, you know? You need to get loved, and you need to get laid . . . not in any kind of specific order, but *a lot*. Now, you may think this is very bold on my part, but it's not. I mean, after all, what do I have to lose but my job? . . . Come on, you gotta say something. I'm the kind of girl whose mother taught her never to let the conversation sag, so I'll keep talking even if you stand up and leave, which would be embarrassing, me sitting here talking to chairs." Jamie didn't move, he didn't even blink. Janet got nervous.

"Well, what the hell, maybe *I* better leave. It's less embarrassing talking to yourself when you're walking. I mean, some of New York's finest people have arcane conversations with themselves strolling down Fifth Avenue."

"Just wait a moment." She wasn't sure his lips had moved. "Miss Flanagan, you just made me a proposition, didn't you?"

Janet thought and shrugged. "Yeah, you bet."

Jamie looked away, half-smiled, then glanced back at her. "I'm flattered."

"Oh, well, listen—"

"It's my first."

"After what I learned about you this week, I'm sure it is."

"Miss Flanagan, you have me at a disadvantage. You know a great deal about me, but I know nothing about you. Tell me everything I should."

"As my employer, as my interviewee, or what?"

"No . . . for a courtship."

"A 'courtship'? Jesus, doesn't that involve duennas and cotillions and little white gloves?"

"I don't know. I suggest it because I think I'm probably a pretty hard case. I doubt if a sudden frontal attack on my guilt-encrusted walls will bring them tumbling down. I think a certain investment of time will be necessary. It's not a bad investment for you. You'd get a lot of material for your story at least."

"The least isn't my worry. I'm wondering about the most. I don't want attachments. . . ."

"Thank you. What do you want, besides your story?"

Janet looked around, shrugging. "I don't know, exactly. . . . Just as a suggestion, I like to get laid once in a while, concerts, movies. . . . Jesus, I sound like a personal ad in the *New York Review of Books*."

"Miss Flanagan, I'm a virgin. . . . I just wanted you to know that."

"Oh, boy. . . . O.K. Here we go: I was born on a farm in Springsville, Missouri, twenty-seven springs ago. My mother thought the Pope was only an Italian, but that Father MacFee, our priest, was God. Father MacFee agreed with her. . . ."

They talked for hours; they walked for miles. At three in the morning, when Jamie escorted Janet to her front door, a brownstone two blocks from *West Side World*, Jamie said, "I like this; I hope you do."

"Like what?"

"Our courtship."

"I'll go to Bloomingdale's tomorrow for the white gloves."

"I don't know what will happen, and I think we have to be somewhat discreet about seeing each other."

"Fine. We'll wait and see."

"And I don't know when, or even if, you'll . . . 'get laid.' I want to be frank about that."

"Oh, fine. Thanks. But you just leave that to me."

Gracefully she clutched his balls, gave a squeeze, and said, "Good night, James," and went in the door.

He stood on the front step for several minutes. When he turned to walk home, Jamie was smiling.

It happened two months later at a convention. Jamie had never attended one, but he had been pressured for an entire year to be the keynote speaker. The occasion was the Licensed Beverage Industry meeting, held at the Beverly Wilshire Hotel in Beverly Hills.

The gathering promised to be exciting; consumers had started drinking again, and the liquor market had actually expanded. Yearly consumption increases had gone up four percent a year for five straight years.

Jamie summarized the reasons for the sudden expansion in his speech: "Today a steadily swelling adult population accept alcoholic beverages as a genuine part of their social life. There is more leisure time, and our economy continues to provide a rising standard of living to our customers. Perhaps best of all, our steady customers are living, and therefore drinking, longer." There was laughter and applause.

"We are not just in the liquor business," Jamie concluded. "We sell the consumer on *expanded product use,* and then get our share of the market. Our future depends on our ability to satisfy our customers' varied tastes."

Jamie's speech received restrained applause; what he said was true, but his opinion was unpopular with the older generation of distillers, who still yearned for a return to straight whiskey. Still, by 1966, most of the Big Five were preparing to market "the whites," and Smirnoff could no longer be overlooked as an upstart.

Most of the whiskey makers, however, were not counting on vodka but on the development and marketing of a new product called "light whiskey." The concept had been tried by Seagram's, who took its Calvert Reserve blend and reformulated it into a whiskey with a milder taste called Calvert Extra, which had sold very well.

No one was talking about exactly how they were going to make their light whiskey, but Jamie was persistent enough to find out that most distillers were going with a potion between eighty and eighty-six proof, with a lot of filtering to cut taste and color.

By the end of the convention he had learned that most of the distillers present were committed to putting 125 million gallons of light whiskey in their warehouses for aging. It would mature in the early seventies, and carry the industry through the new decade. If the sixties were the Vodka decade, the seventies would be Light Whiskey.

On the last day of the convention, Jamie received a telegram from New York which read,

Dear James, A friend of mine, Samantha Yost, is out there on business. I told her you'd buy her a drink. Call her at the Beverly Hills Hotel. She's a great person, a redhead, chemical engineer, knows all about mixed drinks. Do it now, do it now. I miss you. Love, Janet.

At first Jamie was irritated. He and Janet had agreed on certain rules guarding the privacy of their relationship. These did not include transcontinental introductions of friends. He also did not wish to be seen during the convention with any woman, much less at the Beverly Hills Hotel, where most of the executives made nocturnal pilgrimages to the Polo Lounge for a variety of sustenance.

On the other hand, Jamie had entrusted Janet Flanagan with expanding his social life, and she had done so with discretion and good judgment. He had gone to concerts and movies with her, and even had enjoyed having dinner with Janet's best friend and her husband. He therefore decided to call Miss Yost.

Miss Yost suggested on the phone they meet in the Polo Lounge. He could recognize her by the rose she wore. When he arrived, he asked the maître d' if a Miss Yost were present. The usual sophisticated sneer glazed into a look of anticipation as he showed Jamie to a corner table that commanded a view of the room.

The rose was lodged between two breasts of which Jamie had not really taken notice before that moment, perhaps because they were now dramatically revealed by the plunge of her black lace jumpsuit. Her hair was indeed red, a wig, but she was Janet, most definitely Janet, outrageously Janet, holding out her hand with fingernails painted a bright red to match her lipstick.

"Mr. Macpherson, I've heard so much about you."

For the first time in his life, Jamie stuttered.

"How do you do, Miss Yo-Yo-Yost."

"Some people do call me Yo-Yo, but my friends call me Sam."

Jamie checked the room and saw no one he knew from the convention. He looked back at Janet, just as the shoulder of her jumpsuit fell down her arm. She let it hang. Jamie stared, caught himself, sat up very straight, then stared again.

"Well, um, Sam, what brings you to Los Angeles?"

She poured him a glass of champagne from the bottle beside her.

430

"Just one reason. Guess what it is."

"I'm not very good at guessing."

"How do you know anything until you've tried it?"

Jamie felt her hand on his thigh. "It's probably too late—"

"The night is young."

"I mean too late in life, Sam."

"If you haven't tried it, your life is just beginning, believe me."

Her hand moved up his thigh. Jamie again checked the room to see if anyone, anyone at all, was noting what was going on under their table. He turned to her, determined to stop what was happening to him.

"You must be . . . completely . . . crazy."

"Just about you. I was the moment I saw you come in here and . . . Oh! Mr. Macpherson." Her hand had reached her ultimate objective. "As that great American philosopher Mae West said, 'Too much of a good thing can be wonderful.' "

At that moment, a large group of colleagues came into the Polo Lounge. Jamie turned his back to them as much as he could, considering the banquette and Janet's grip.

"I've got to get out of here."

"If you can walk with what you've got in your pants, I want to watch."

"Janet, I've—"

"Who?"

"*Sam,* we're leaving."

"Where should we go?"

"I don't care. Out of here."

"I know just the place."

Janet let go of him, and in sliding out of the banquette, managed to let one shoulder of the jumpsuit, then the other, fall to a strategic depth. Several of Jamie's friends spotted these movements and were quick to share their discovery with their colleagues. The entire party watched in astounded glee as the female apparition was followed toward the exit by the "monk" of the industry.

Jamie thought he had escaped until he heard a voice call across the lounge, "Evening, Jamie." His first reaction was to ignore the greeting and hope they would think they were mistaken. But he knew he'd never get away with it, so he called out with as much jauntiness as he could muster, "Good evening, gentlemen. Glad to see you're still drinking Macpherson's whiskey."

"Looks like you're buying, Macpherson," someone called.

Jamie stepped angrily forward, but Janet moved past him to their table and announced, "Don't be gross. . . . Mr. Macpherson gets it free." Then she pulled out her rose, dropped it on the table, and breezed out of the Polo Lounge, taking Jamie with her.

They laughed in the elevator and all the way to her room. When she closed the door, she said, "Do you mind if I slip into something more . . . convenient?"

"Convenient for who?"

"Both of us. Make yourself loose." She indicated another bottle of champagne on ice, with caviar, and pâté.

"Loose?"

"You know, your tie, your shirt, your belt, whatever feels tight." She disappeared behind a latticed screen.

Jamie sat down and folded his hands in his lap. It was going to happen, he was going to lose his virginity right there in that room, and there was nothing he could do about it. Any objection he might offer would certainly be overwhelmed by the kinetic energy of Janet Flanagan. He could see her through the lattice screen taking off the jumpsuit and putting on something else. He recognized his own excitement and wondered why he had such a resistance to sexual intercourse. Was resistance a habit, was the Jesuit vow still inflicting guilt?

She came around the screen wearing something black, which allowed whatever had not been visible in the jumpsuit to be seen explicitly.

Jamie's enthusiasm grew, as he sat on the couch, his hands still folded.

"You're very beautiful."

"Thanks."

"I'm afraid something's gone wrong."

"What's the matter?" Janet had never made love to a virgin and was determined to be very careful and take it very easy.

"It's gone," Jamie said.

"You're just a little nervous. . . . No, not a little: you're a lot nervous."

"I can't stop feeling this is . . . well, wrong."

"What's wrong with it?"

"I don't know. We're not married, we're not having children. We're doing it for no other reason than animal craving."

"Umm-hmm, sounds good to me. Get your clothes off."

"It's filthy, Samantha."

She realized he was serious. Then slowly Janet Flanagan recognized certain unique needs.

"You're right, Jamie Macpherson, it's filthy." She went over to him, calmly unfolded his hands, undid his buckle, and pulled his belt out of his pants. "It's filthy and dirty. It's carnal and disgusting. Now, take your clothes off. Stand up and take them off."

Jamie looked at her, amazed. He stood up and said, "I'm sorry, I'm so sorry . . ." and undid his tie and shirt.

He took his pants off and started to fold them. She yanked them out of his hands, and in a tone which combined her own excitement in the command, said, "Get your clothes off, Jamie. Don't waste time apologizing. All of them. Get them off."

He hurried, and in a moment he was naked. His problem, however, still remained.

"You see? It's no use. I'm sorry, Samantha, truly sorry."

"Don't apologize!" She slapped the belt across his buttocks. "It's all right, Jamie."

Jamie appeared to be shocked; the belt had hurt. At the same moment, he felt a stirring in his groin. Janet whipped him again.

"I'm sorry, Samantha . . ." Then he looked down. Janet had never seen him smile quite so diabolically.

"Don't apologize!" The belt smacked across his thighs.

"Forgive me." He started moving toward her.

She began to laugh.

"I'll never forgive you!" She whipped him across his stomach, then his ribs, moving backward across the room. "You're a dirty, filthy, rotten sinner!"

"Forgive me!" He sank to the bed on top of her, watching walls come tumbling down.

Afterward they lay silent, the belt tangled around her arm, Jamie thought, like a rosary. He reached over and unwound the belt and lifted it away. Then he laid a hand gently on her stomach.

"Nice," she said as she put her hand over his.

"What do we do now?" he said expectantly.

She smiled as she rolled over into his arms. "Recover."

"But . . ."

"What?"

"Shouldn't we *do* something?" He laughed at himself.

"What?" She smiled, curious.

"We should commemorate it somehow, write about it in stone, or across the sky with comets!"

"You liked it."

"Of course I did. But it means more than liking it, doesn't it?"

"We had a great fuck. What's it supposed to mean?"

"Is that all?"

"Jamie, be grateful. Great fucks don't come easy."

"But it's more. It was such a . . . quintessence of giving and taking, all the way from the animal to the holy."

"S'funny, Father MacFee never mentioned that."

He laughed. "Janet, I feel like I've given you my soul. I feel like I've discovered a new continent."

She stared back at him, then reached over and pulled herself close to him, pressing her head against his neck. She held him silently until he felt her tears against his skin.

"What is it, Janet?" he asked, stroking her hair.

"I'm scared."

"Why?"

"I don't want your soul. It's too big a responsibility."

"Ridiculous."

She pulled away from him. "What do you know? You think you're the only one who can cut himself off from everybody? I don't know *my* family either, and they don't know me, just like nobody knows you."

"You do, now."

She smacked a hand over her eyes and started to get up. "Oh, boy, so this is what it's like to fuck a Jesuit virgin." She stood and smiled sadly. "Jamie, a fuck is a fuck. With us it's good, which I always knew it would be, and that's all the reason it needs. Want some champagne?"

She went over to the ice bucket and started to pull out the cork. Jamie shook his head.

"I can't believe that. A . . . 'fuck' . . . is too fundamental. You can pretend it's casual or sophisticated, but it isn't. A fuck is *always* more than a fuck, and you're kidding yourself."

"Listen to him. He gets laid once and he's a philosopher. Well, Jamie"—she poised, holding the champagne bottle at forty-five degrees—"I can only say for sure that a fuck is never *less* than a fuck."

She let the cork fly across the room and poured two glasses of champagne.

"Cheers for fears," she said, handing one to Jamie.

"Still scared?" he said, smiling.

She nodded. "What if you're right? What if it means something and I don't even know what it is?"

Again Jamie laughed. "I don't know what *usually* happens with you, but it occurs to me that we might find out by further developing our relationship."

Defensively she said, "Don't get your hopes up."

"All right. . . . Tell me how you knew that . . . fucking would be good with us."

"Well, you never know for sure, but you can get a pretty good idea. You turned me on, just standing there in your priest suit and tie in *West Side World.*"

"Why? Was it my body?" He struck what was, to him, a particularly erotic pose.

"No! Who could tell about a body in that outfit? In fact, I didn't begin to even know you had one until the night I copped a feel." She laughed. "Remember?"

"Then what was it?"

"I've always had a thing about power," she teased. "It started with a policeman when I was ten, a real crush, then, when I was a teenager, singers and movie stars from afar, not because of their voice or that they were sexy, just that they could do what they did to crowds. I had my first affair with a guy who was running for president of the sophomore class at college. It lasted until he lost. Then a guy in uniform, a major—"

"What do you mean?" Jamie interrupted.

"About what?"

"About me." He was no longer smiling. Janet felt jittery.

"Well, there you were, you'd just bought my whole world. You controlled my whole life, and a hell of a lot besides. And then when you shot down Abner—"

Jamie stood up abruptly, went over to his clothes, and began to dress.

"Jamie, what're you doing?"

He didn't answer until she came over to him. Then he spoke with the same icy precision he used to address members of his staff.

"It's too bad, Janet. Apparently this fuck *was* less than a fuck for you. I'm not Macpherson Industries. You were probably thinking of my father."

"Oh, God, Jamie, I didn't mean that."

"Didn't you?" He continued dressing. Janet watched him a moment, then walked over and stood in front of the door.

"All right. You can walk out of here all hurt and hung up on your father and contemptuous of me and women and relationships. I've been walked out on before, and you've been hung up on your father *forever,* so nothing will have changed. But it's phony, Jamie; you're using it as an excuse to go on being a goddamn monk. . . . Maybe you're as scared as I am. Change is scary, they say, any change, even giving up pain. . . . Look, I made an honest mistake with you just now. Somewhere along the line I learned to react to men by what they could do. I mean, after all, most men don't give a damn about *who* they are; what they care about is what they do, their business, their golf score, their titles, their money. If that's what they want appreciated, why shouldn't we appreciate it? So you tell me you're different, you don't care about Macpherson Industries or being the president and chief executive officer. Then you tell me there's something special about us fucking, which scares me. You think I was fucking your power, not you, which scares you. So we're both scaring each other. Why *is* that? . . . You know why? Because when you walk out of here, we'll both have succeeded in not changing again. You'll stay tied up to your father's company, and I'll go on fucking power and never getting close to anyone."

He wasn't certain she was finished speaking for several moments. Then he said, "Janet, if I say what I've been thinking since we fucked, would it scare you?"

She kept her back to him, her hand on the doorknob.

"If it's something nice, probably."

"Then what can I do?"

There was a long silence.

"Don't leave," she said, terrified.

Another silence.

"Now *I'm* scared," Jamie said.

"Join the crowd," she whispered.

"I'll stay."

"Oh, God . . ."

The cases of the *State of Arizona vs. Fowler* and *Josephson* were both dismissed for lack of evidence. The experience of jail and the trial affected Gus and Ellen in different ways. Ellen was shaken and wanted to go home to Pittsburgh. Gus was not ready to do that, but that summer he used his trust fund for the first time and paid for his tuition at UCLA.

Ellen stayed with her mother, attending a few classes at Carnegie Tech in art history. She avoided her old social life.

At first, WeeDee was glad to have her daughter back, but soon she realized that the distance between them had expanded.

In 1967 Ellen turned twenty-one, and came into her own trust fund. The day after her birthday, she took a plane to New York, then flew to London. From there she began a hedonistic pilgrimage around the world, to Ceylon, Nepal, the Seychelle Islands for a time, then on to Greece, restlessly searching for better sex, better drugs, and the ultimate experience, whatever it might be.

Once she wrote Gus from Sardinia, asking him to join her, but never mailed the letter.

19

We can't return, we can only look behind
From where we came
And go round and round and round
In the circle game.

—JONI MITCHELL

Gus Fowler idly flipped through the "Beverage Industry Report" and came upon a paragraph which held his interest.

TOP-RANKING EXECUTIVES IN THE INDUSTRY 1970
Magnus Macpherson
Chairman of the Board, and Consultant, Macpherson Industries; Honorary Chairman, License Beverage Industries; Chairman, Macpherson Foundation; Honorary Life Director, Distilled Spirits Institute.
INDUSTRY HISTORY: President, Macpherson Distillers, Ltd. (Canada) 1925–1933. President, Macpherson Distillers, Inc., 1933–1950 (company changed name to Macpherson Industries in 1953). Recipient of the "Edgar" award as "Industry Man of the Year," 1959. Appointed by President Kennedy to the Tariff Commission as Special Representative to the Common Market, Brussels, 1961 (Current). B. 1900, Dufftown, Scotland. Education: Public School, Dufftown.
Honorary Trustee, Columbia Presbyterian Hospital.
Honorary Trustee, Princeton University.
Trustee, Museum of Modern Art.
CLUBS: Racquet, Knickerbocker, New York Yacht, Sulgrave (London), Metropolitan (D.C.), California (Los Angeles), Jockey (Paris).
SERVICE RECORD: His Majesty's Forces, WWI.
PERSONAL: Married the former Mary Fleming (dec.). Three

children: Magnus II (dec.); Eleanor, current president, Star-
Herald Communications (Pittsburgh); James, current president,
Macpherson Industries.

He threw the magazine aside, thinking how impressively it read,
while exposing so little. Gus Fowler had arrived unannounced in the
executive offices of Macpherson Industries. He was amused as various secretaries rushed in and out of Jamie's office with directions. He
was asked to wait, to sit down, to move to a conference room which
was already occupied. Finally he was shown to the boardroom. He
walked to the head of the table and stood beside the chair, enjoying
the long mahogany view. Jamie discovered him there. Neither admitted any awkwardness.

"Hello, Gus." Jamie surprised Gus by smiling.

"Hello." He didn't know what to call Jamie. "I hope this isn't a
bad time."

"I wish you'd called. Things are busy, as I'm sure you saw. But sit
down, I'm delighted to see you."

Gus moved quickly from the head of the table, and the two of
them shook hands and sat opposite each other at one end.

"What can I do for you, Gus?" asked Jamie, apparently interested.

"I was in New York and I thought while I was here I'd try to get
reacquainted with you, so I could ask you about getting a job at
M.I." Gus had always heard that Jamie was the coldest member of
the family. He knew little about Jamie's life and thought if he'd
called for an appointment, Jamie might not have seen him.

"I've heard you've done very well at school," Jamie said. "Your
Aunt WeeDee is very pleased."

"That's good. I've liked California a lot." Gus overlooked the
"Aunt" WeeDee. He hadn't come to refine family genealogy. "I'm
going to be finished in the spring, so I'm trying to make some plans."

Jamie nodded, still smiling. "I'm surprised you'd think about coming to M.I." They both were aware of what lay between Gus and
Macpherson Industries. "I would think an honors graduate would
have better opportunities than working for a liquor company."

"Well, it's a good company, and I have some connections." They
both smiled, but neither of them took it as a joke.

"You see, Gus, the future of the liquor business looks very shaky.
No one knows what's going to happen—"

"It sounds like you're trying to talk me out of this."

"Not at all. I'm curious about your other opportunities, and your motives. After all, your interest is something of a surprise to me."

"O.K., I understand that, but the future of the liquor business isn't that bad. You'll have to get through this light-whiskey thing, but then there are a lot of possibilities."

Jamie's lips tightened. Gus didn't want to alienate Jamie, but he did want to get his attention.

"What do you mean, 'this light-whiskey thing'?" Jamie asked, still attempting a smile.

"I think it's a hundred-million-dollar bust."

"And why do you think that, Gus?" He was patronizing, and Gus knew it.

"Because it's strictly from desperation. Whiskey won't change into something else. It's like putting fat tires on Edsels and calling them dune buggies; you still got Edsels with fat tires that nobody's going to buy. If people don't want whiskey, they're not going to buy it because it's lighter, thicker, or pink and perfumed."

Jamie felt a cold sweat begin in his armpits. Light whiskey was his gamble, and what Gus had just described was his nightmare. Gus knew the figures; one hundred million dollars was being spent by the industry on light whiskey, and Jamie was spending fifteen of it. He began getting angry at Gus's presumption, but all he said was, "I hope you're wrong, Gus."

"I doubt if I am."

Again Jamie smiled patronizingly. "Where do you get all these ideas, Gus? You seem well-informed about liquor for someone who's been on a campus."

"Thanks, I was hoping you'd notice. I started getting interested when Louis Rosenstiel sold out. He was a real whiskey man; straight bourbon ran in the guy's veins. Why would he sell Schenley in 1968, just when everybody started laying away light whiskey? I think he knew it was a bust, and he wanted out."

"Mr. Rosenstiel was old; he wanted to retire."

"Aw, come on. These guys never get old."

"Rosenstiel's fourth wife testified to a New York legislative committee about his connections to Meyer Lansky and the syndicate. You may not have known that."

"I knew it. I also knew he put a million bucks into setting up the J. Edgar Hoover Foundation. But he's been fighting both sides of that battle all his life, and it never got him out of the business. . . . Look, who cares about light whiskey? The fifteen or twenty million you lose, if I'm right, you can write off over five years. Your stock-holders will bitch, but they won't lose much dividend, I figure a dime a share for a couple of quarters." He shrugged. "Big deal. What I care about is a job. I wanted to let you know I'm interested and I've done some homework."

Jamie spoke carefully. "I'll certainly keep it in mind, Gus. But I should tell you that I don't share my father's inclination toward nepotism. I'm not so sure a company should be run by a family. I'm wondering if it might not be a good idea for you, after you finish school . . . to travel."

"I might just do that, Jamie." The lips compressed again; Gus stood up. "And thanks for including me in the family."

Jamie smiled appreciation at the fast move, then went to the door quickly and opened it.

"Merry Christmas, Gus."

"Happy New Year, Jamie. I'm sure I'll see you again sometime."

Gus found out what he wanted to know, that Jamie accepted Gus's bastardy and was not about to let him get close to the Macpherson homestead. Gus wasn't surprised, nor was he angered. He could wait. From New York he flew to Pittsburgh to spend Christmas "at home."

While he was in college, Gus had started writing to WeeDee, and on two occasions when she traveled to Los Angeles, she took him to dinner and they had made progress toward a more civil relationship. In their unspoken truce, they censored the subject of Ellen. To Gus, Ellen was a nagging leftover to a bad scene; to WeeDee, she was a lost daughter.

When he arrived in Pittsburgh, both Gus and WeeDee admitted their nervousness. They agreed to take the visit as it came, one day at a time. Because WeeDee was as usual very active socially, she asked Gus to accompany her, but he begged out of the charity balls, cock-tail parties, and dinners, saying he had to study. During his visit, Double Gibson flew in twice, but each time he had to return the next day to New York. He had little time to speak with Gus, except to comment on the meeting with Jamie: "I would suggest, Gus, that you not consider M.I. as an 'equal-opportunity employer.' "

Gus scoffed. "I'm the minority of one."

"For the moment." Double Gibson smiled trenchantly. "The time will come for your assumption to a different role. I have great confidence you will seize it."

"I will."

"As to Jamie, word has it that he has discovered love—not generally, but specifically for a lady journalist."

"She must be a penguin to like all that ice. I don't believe it."

"It's an interesting turn of events, although I don't speculate on the reasons for the lady's attraction. There is a part of Jamie Macpherson which detests M.I. But the far greater part revels in his genuine ability to run it well. That is what you threaten, for what would happen if you *were* another son?" He smiled again before he went on. "Then again, what would happen if Jamie had a son?"

"Yeah. An 'interesting turn of events,'" said Gus.

On his last night in Pittsburgh, WeeDee and Gus had dinner together in the kitchen. The staff was off and WeeDee cooked omelets. They both agreed their visit had been a good one and that they were more relaxed with each other and less wary. WeeDee beat the eggs, then said, "We have to talk about Ellen."

"O.K., let's do it."

She took a moment to begin as she poured the eggs into the pan. "I don't know what to do about her."

Gus watched her from the kitchen table and said nothing.

"The last time I heard from her, last *July,* she was at Hydra. Her correspondence is . . . strange. She usually writes on the back of candy wrappers or napkins, and there's a lot of drawings mixed in. What she says makes absolutely *no sense.*" She felt herself losing control, so she stopped talking and sprinkled cheese over the eggs.

"Sure it does," Gus said. "It means she's thinking of you, loves you, wants you to know where she is and that she's O.K."

"She's not O.K. She's flying around the Mediterranean taking any drug she can pop into her pretty little face."

Gus was silent; he figured WeeDee was probably right.

"What am I supposed to do, Gus? Send the police, detectives? Try to cut off her trust, get Father to take it away from her, or Double to . . . Gus, what am I supposed to do, besides let her brain fry away in the sun?" She had to wipe the tears from her eyes before putting the salt and pepper on the omelet. She slid it onto a plate, cut it in half, and sat down at the table.

"Probably nothing, WeeDee."

WeeDee put her head in her hands and wept. "She's the only child I have." She snapped her head up, her eyes wide. "Oh, Gus." She reached for his arm and clutched it, unable to verbalize an apology, then went on crying.

"Hey, don't worry about that, for Christ's sake. I know whose kid

I am and whose I'm not. And in spite of a good try on your part, I ain't yours." WeeDee looked up, started to laugh, and coughed. Gus watched her drink some water, then he said, "Listen, WeeDee, I don't know about Ellen. I haven't heard a word from her since we broke up. Our relationship was more frantic than crazy, but it *was* pretty crazy. I worry about her sometimes, but I doubt if there's anything you or I can do. But I'll tell you what. I'll write to her and see if I can find out anything."

WeeDee reached out and took his hand. "Thank you, Gus. I'd be grateful."

Gus smiled and ate his omelet.

By the time he received an answer to his letter, Gus was graduating. Ellen had enclosed the envelope of his letter so he could see the places it had been on its route to finding her. Around the stamps of Greece, Italy, and Spain she had drawn the petals of flowers with colored ball-point pens.

Dear Gus,

Far-out! Your letter was wonderful! And it's had the most *wonderful trip!* It reached me here, finally, and I'm hurrying to get this written in time for the mail and before the evening blast begins. Tangier is, oh wow, I can't begin to tell you, it's fantastic! The colors will burn your eyes out. It's hot, dry, we watch the sunrise from a purple tent on the beach, sleep during the day, get up for the sunset, then eat, then drink, then dance, then go down to the purple tent.

Come! Yes! Yes! Yes! What a fantastic idea! You've probably become horribly straight in *school!* Good God, Gus, far-fucking-out! I can't believe it. But you have to come! We can put you up. We is me and Benny. I met him in Majorca. He has this neat place high up in the Casbah, as in, "come wiz me to the." I smoke hash and watch miles of laundry blow and listen to the muezzins on the minarets calling Muslims to prayer, and way off over the blue straits is Gibraltar and Spain. It's so far-out. Don't tell Mom about the hash. I think she worries a lot.

But you have to come! Give yourself a present! Spend your trust money on joy and love like I do. The women here are beautiful, so are the men, so are the boys! What are you into these days besides studying? How's your ulcer? Come and tell me *everything*. I'll meet you at the airport.

Love and love,
Ellen

Gus didn't take long to decide. The ulcer was gone and he'd worked his ass off for three solid years. He wanted a vacation. Ellen sounded all right and Tangier sounded spectacular. Besides, traveling and looking after Ellen would please two Macphersons. As soon as he finished his last exam, he flew over the pole from Los Angeles to Paris. There he caught a flight to Tangier.

Ellen was waiting at the airport. He hadn't forgotten how lovely she was, but was surprised that she still attracted him. She fell into his arms. The embrace was so familiar that it seemed impossible three years had passed.

"Gus! Gus! Oh, wow, this is just too much. Just in time for the sunset. I'm so glad to see you! It's fantastic."

She was deeply tanned and looked radiantly happy. Gus nodded, "You're worth the trip."

"We're going to have the best time! I can't wait for you to meet Benny. He's fantastic."

"Who is Benny, besides your roommate?"

"He's a merchant, sells Moroccan wine all over the Mediterranean. He'll be back tonight, and meet us at the party. He was born on Majorca, went to the Sorbonne . . . and he treats me like a princess."

"You came to Tangier to be a Jewish princess? You could have stayed in Pittsburgh. What party?"

"You're the guest of honor. I've told Pepe all about you."

"Pepe?"

"His real name's Maurice d'Ambord, but I call him Pepe, like in 'Le Moko.' Fantastically rich, owns tankers or something. You're going to love Tangier! Oh, wow, I can't believe you're here."

As they walked to the baggage-claim area, they were followed by a native man. When his bags arrived, Gus was not allowed to touch them. Ellen explained, "This is Sala, Gus. He's one of Benny's servants. He'll do anything you need to have done." Sala nodded and hustled the bags out to a Citroën which was waiting at the curb.

Gus's jet lag helped him adjust to Ellen's nocturnal schedule. After dropping his bags and changing in the Casbah apartment, Gus and Ellen were driven by Sala out L'Avenue d'Espagne along Tangier's ten-mile beach, the Plage. Near the end of it was a large purple tent belonging to Pepe, who met them as they arrived.

"We are delighted to have you here, Monsieur Fowler. I have heard nothing but the good things of you from chère Ellen. I look forward to discovering the bad."

Pepe was a tall, attractive man with a devastatingly white smile.

He was losing a bit of hair at the top, but it did not detract from his aquiline good looks.

About twenty guests were feasting on squab and rabbit. The local wine flowed; sumptuous fruits and spicy pastries were served throughout the night. A tape deck supplied the latest *ye-ye* music as couples danced, then went outside to undress and plunge into the sea.

Gus had an enervating, if indistinct first night. Ellen introduced him to the guests, who included two English sisters, one a blonde, the other a deep brunette. Their faces were brightly painted and they wore caftans and gold slippers. They danced with each other, not with incestuous inclination, but with European style and enjoyment. Early in the morning they lay down on some pillows beside Gus.

"Have you tried the local wine yet?" the blonde asked him.

"As a matter of fact, too much."

"It's quite super, really," the brunette said. "Muslims aren't allowed to touch alcohol, yet they make it so well, don't they, Fiona?"

"Super! Do you know how a Muslim winemaker tastes wine to see if it's good?"

"No, Fiona," said Gus, all earnest student. "Tell me about it."

"They use poets, for their magic tongues."

"Yes, the Muslims are allowed to taste a tongue. That seems to be quite kosher, isn't it, Teeta?" The sisters went into their own intimate laughter, and called for wine in order to illustrate. Sala brought three goblets and put them on the carpet. He stood pouring the wine from a silver urn held at his eye level, and did not spill a drop. Gus noticed his steady hand and smiled his appreciation.

"You see, the only way a Muslim can taste the wine he makes is with three people. Teeta, you be the Muslim and I'll be the poet." The blonde took a deep swallow.

"What does that make me?" Gus inquired.

"A silent sieve," Teeta said. "Pay attention to Fiona, now."

Gus turned to look at the blonde who planted her lips on his, begged his teeth open with her tongue, then slowly let the tangy red wine flow into his mouth. They stirred it around together; Fiona's tongue was then withdrawn, and replaced by Teeta's. Gus felt their hands all over him.

"Ah, you're enjoying the wine tasting, Gus."

Pepe stood above him, holding a smoldering pipe. "Perhaps you like to try some hashish. It will turn the purple tent to many colors. Of course, the dawn helps very much."

Gus hadn't smoked anything for a long time.

"Sure, why not?"

The two sisters took the pipe and held it to his mouth. Gus saw many colors quickly. He also saw Ellen run across the carpets of the tent and embrace a tall dark-haired man with a mustache. She took his hand and pulled him over to where Gus was lying between the two sisters.

"Gus! This is Benny." Gus stood up with difficulty, lost his balance and started to fall. The two sisters propped him up as he greeted Ellen's lover. He looked about forty, but seemed in pretty good shape.

"Hey, how are you, Benny?" Gus sank back down on the pillows. "I guess we better meet when I get back from Mars."

Benny nodded, put an arm around Ellen, and kissed her on the cheek. She knelt down next to Gus and said, "We're going home now. Sala will come back here for you." He felt her breath on his ear. "Enjoy, dear uncle." She kissed him; then she and Benny were gone. Gus's hashish-infused vision was of ceremony; Ellen's breath had been a baptism, so naturally Gus needed water. He floated out of the tent, and was astounded to feel the universe in each grain of sand under his feet. He accepted that he was stoned out of his gourd and exultantly raced the sisters down the beach. Later they undressed and bathed in the sea, watching the moon come up from the other side of the world. Gus felt the warm salt water and saw in it, among other things, the center of the earth. He floated on the swells until the sisters pulled him into shallow water to finish what they had started. Then they ran into the sea like basilisks and disappeared.

Gus lay there for a time, letting the waves wash off the warmth of the new sun. Gradually he became aware of a man squatting about ten yards away from him. Sala was waiting to take him home. Gus stood up and attempted dignity, which he soon had to abandon as he staggered, stark naked, up the beach. Sala slipped a caftan over him and led him to the Citroën.

Sala charged through the crowded streets with the horn blaring steadily. Gus said, "Stop!" which had no effect until he bellowed the command into the servant's hirsute ear. When the car slowed, Gus explained to Sala that he preferred to walk for a time. He was, after all, a tourist. He got out and began to stroll, concentrating on making his feet hit the center of the cobblestones rather than the cracks between them. Each time he came to a corner, a slight toot sounded from the car and Sala pointed which way for him to turn.

Gus began to feel a little better, but he could barely wait to return to the apartment and collapse on his bed. He heard the car horn start tooting, then blaring, but he was not at a corner, so he did not turn around, figuring Sala had seen a pretty girl. The Citroën had been blocked on the narrow street by a water cart whose owner was screaming at Sala. Shuttered windows were opened and the street in front of the Citroën filled with Arabs in fezzes, flowing robes, and yellow slippers.

Gus paid no attention, intent on his bed. When he reached the next corner, an Arab came up to him and indicated a direction. Gus turned to check with Sala, but saw only a crowd in the distance. Believing the Arab to be another of Benny's servants, he went where he was told, around a corner and into the waiting arms of two other Arabs, who helped him into the back of an old Peugeot panel truck. The truck started up, causing Gus to fall as he finally became suspicious of what was happening.

"Hello, Gus."

Gus looked up. He hoped that the hashish was still working, and that his eyes would adjust. But as he became used to the dark, he saw it was Magnus Macpherson.

"What the hell are you doing here?" he gasped.

"I'll ask you the same thing."

"I'm on vacation, visiting Ellen."

"Your vacation is over." Magnus was sitting on a steel bench at the front of the truck. He slid a small panel open to the driver's compartment. "Is the car still blocked?" An affirmative answer was given, and Magnus closed the panel. He looked at Gus a moment before he spoke.

"Listen very carefully; we don't have much time. The man Ellen is living with, 'Benny,' is Antoine Lescal. He murdered Magnus Josephson. He's keeping Ellen as a hostage because he heard rumors I was getting close. Ellen knows nothing. She believes he's a wine merchant. He is not. He oversees a drug operation for his friend Pepe, bringing morphine base in from Marseille and distributing it to South America. Lescal came back tonight from Brazil, carrying seven hundred thousand dollars. He uses his share to finance terrorism against the Algerian government."

Gus was astonished, but he knew there was no time for it. "What do you want me to do?"

"This isn't the time for me to tell you what I think of you for running off with Ellen. You should have been horsewhipped—"

"You're right, Magnus, this isn't the time. Tell me what you want me to do."

"Don't call me Magnus."

"I'm not going to call you anything else! What about Ellen, for Christ's sake? We've got to get her—"

"We are. Neither Lescal nor Pepe knows I'm this close, or what's going to happen. But they're very careful; Lescal doesn't let Ellen out of his sight unless one of his natives is with her. I suspect you'll be used; if we move on him or on Pepe's operation, he'll hold Ellen hostage and kill you."

A knock sounded on the panel; Magnus opened it. Gus could see the man in front was holding a walkie-talkie. He said in English, "The car is moving."

Magnus nodded and closed the panel. "We're going to let you out on the street so Sala can find you. Just act lost, and sleepy from the wine and hashish." Gus was startled to learn that his activities of the previous night had been monitored so carefully. "We're going to move as quickly as we can; the Moroccan authorities are in on this, so the organization is complex. You stay close to Ellen. Sala and the other servant are killers. We'll get a gun to you, which you must tape inside your thigh. Keep wearing a caftan, and keep any hands but your own away from it."

"How will I know when you're going to move?"

"We'll tell you. Two more things: Lescal is addicting Ellen to heroin. He started it three weeks ago."

"Bullshit, I know an addict when I—"

"He's doing it slowly. She's hooked, but not badly enough for her or you to notice yet. You can check the tracks on her thighs. She thinks she's injecting amphetamine."

Gus remembered his mother. "What's the other thing?"

"Sala, like Lescal, uses a dagger, but in the back."

There was another knock on the panel. Magnus moved to the back door of the truck and opened it.

"Hurry."

Gus crawled to the entrance, looked up at Magnus, then dropped into the street. He began to walk along, looking around, asking directions. The Citroën roared up and Sala jumped out. Gus looked furious and yelled, *"There* you are! Where the hell have you been, Sala? I want to get to bed." Sala had no time to wonder. "Come on, let's move it, for Christ's sake." Sala opened the car door for him, then drove him to the Casbah, apologizing effusively until Gus told him to shut up.

Gus didn't sleep very much that day. He wandered around the apartment, noting where Lescal and Ellen slept. Sala's counterpart was outside Gus's door, sitting in a chair. Gus explained that he had jet lag and couldn't sleep. Finally he returned to his room, barricaded the door, and lay down. He began worrying about how he could refuse wine, hash, and those sisters without making anyone suspicious. He had to find a way, because he had established his inclinations the night before.

An idea occurred to him. He wrote Ellen a note saying he couldn't sleep and was going sightseeing, went out of the apartment and into the streets of the Casbah.

He had not gone far when Sala rushed up behind him, looking sleepy and irritated. As graciously as he could, the man offered his services as guide and suggested starting at the Sultan's Palace. Gus expressed his appreciation, but explained to Sala that what he really wanted was to get laid. In fact, he had an itch to do it that moment. The request was one which Sala could easily and quickly fulfill. He led Gus down several dark streets to a particularly rancid hole in the wall. There he introduced Gus to a Turkish madam whose appearance would terrify maggots.

Gus had hoped that he could bribe and fake from that point, but apparently Sala and the madam were old friends. If Gus did not make proper use of the facilities, Sala would hear of it. So Gus followed the madam down some damp stairs. Upon introduction to his chosen one, Gus engaged himself as quickly and as daintily as possible, despite the woman's attempt at various Turkish contortions meant to impress American tourists. On his way out, Gus noticed his change and keys were in the wrong pockets, meaning that Sala had searched his clothes. He did some more sightseeing, bought a roll of adhesive tape, then returned to the apartment and finally slept.

That evening's plan included a restaurant called Café Maure, various nightclubs in the new town, and a visit to Pepe's tent on the Plage.

Gus met "Benny" again with Ellen over drinks before the evening began. As they watched the sunset, Lescal spoke very little, excusing himself with his bad English. Ellen immediately discussed Gus's sightseeing, which had apparently been reported in detail.

"You're crazy going to a whorehouse, Gus."

"Well, damn, I didn't want Sala telling you about that."

He looked at Lescal, who shrugged that it didn't matter.

"Why am I crazy?" Gus asked.

"They don't have Public Health in Tangier," Ellen said. "I mean, you could catch a case of almost anything in those places."

"That must be it."

"What?"

"For about the last hour, I've been scratching and fanning—"

"Oh, no, Gus."

Gus shrugged. "I'm afraid so."

The doctor at the Hôpital Anglais diagnosed the case as crabs and provided a noxious blue salve. Gus talked him into a penicillin shot as well. When he went out to the car, Gus berated Sala for having guided him to such a house of contagion. He arrived at the Café Maure just before dessert and told Ellen, "No booze and no dope; they'll react badly with the medicine. And no fooling around unless the lady in question wants to rot." He turned and smiled at Lescal, who was watching carefully.

"Oh, no, Gus. Shit," Ellen said sympathetically.

"Shit," Gus agreed, smiling stoically at Lescal. For a moment Lescal gazed suspiciously at Gus. Then he ordered dessert.

At the third nightclub, the two English sisters caught up with them and joined the party. Gus danced with them both, then rode in their Triumph convertible to the Plage, behind Lescal's Citroën. The sisters learned of Gus's condition and sympathized by keeping their hands to themselves. The evening went on, however, much as before. Not surprisingly, the sisters looked for other diversions. Soon Teeta, the brunette, was investigating the caftan of a Spaniard whose jaw seemed to protrude farther than his nose.

"Whew, can she get off on that guy?"

"Of course she can," the blonde, Fiona, stated. "You see, Teeta is a twit. . . . But you're a very clever fellow, aren't you?"

"You think so?"

"Going to a Turkish brothel. . . . So, no liquor, no hashish, and no Fiona and Teeta." She laughed uproariously as Gus watched her. "A sacrifice, but such a clever one. Now, come here, I want to whisper something. . . . My little gold bag, which I'm going to leave here when I go, has a small revolver in it." She stuck her tongue in his ear. "We're being watched, so you must say something pleasant to me."

Gus smiled and reached for his glass of mineral water. Pepe was smiling across the tent in their direction. "Known Pepe long, Fiona?"

"I've worked for him for years, but now I'm better paid. So kiss me enthusiastically, and remember this. The *chergui* comes tomorrow morning at exactly dawn. Kiss me."

Gus did as he was told with enthusiasm. "Dear Gus," said Fiona, "I do hope you'll get rid of your sacrifice soon."

"Thanks. You're pretty well informed, aren't you? . . . What's a *'chergui'?*"

"It's a desert wind, very dangerous they say. It can wipe out nearly everything in its path. The safest thing to do when it starts is to lie very flat on the ground."

Fiona went across the tent to join a pilot for Air France who had spent most of the evening talking with Pepe.

Gus sat alone, watching Ellen, watching Fiona, watching Lescal, and watching the gold purse beside him. He couldn't think how he was going to get the gun unobtrusively out of the purse and carry it. His caftan had no pockets, and he had left the adhesive tape at home. As he was conjecturing, Pepe sat down and sprawled on the pillows next to him.

"Your little cousin is very dear to us, Gus," said Pepe, looking at Ellen, who was obviously far gone on hashish or whatever else Lescal was giving her.

"Is she? Glad to hear it, Pepe. She is to me, too."

"It may seem to you I live a very . . . exotic life here. But there are dangers; but then, there are dangers everywhere, *n'est-ce pas?*"

"*Oui, partout,*" Gus said with a flourish to cover his reaction to Pepe's veiled warning.

"*Ah, monsieur, parlez-vous français?*"

"*Non.* I studied it for three years in college, and you just heard it all."

Pepe laughed charmingly and nodded at Ellen. "We would feel very sad if anything were to happen to her."

"Who's 'we'?"

"All of us love her." Pepe smiled his most devastating smile.

"What could happen, Pepe?" At that moment, Gus realized a plan for the revolver and said, "It's beautiful out here. The Casbah's the place I'm worried about."

"Why, Gus? The Casbah is a wonderful place."

"Well, first of all, I probably got the clap today—"

"No, Gus." Pepe feigned amused shock.

"Yeah. And if I'd had any money, Sala would have stolen it."

"Stolen?" Pepe's eyes turned to him like a rapier.

"Yeah, he went through my pockets when I was in a Turkish whorehouse. Luckily I wasn't carrying enough for him to steal."

"Mon ami, je le regrette beaucoup. I tell Benny; Sala will be whipped."

"Aw, don't do that, Pepe. If I were Sala and he were me, I'd steal his teeth if they were any good."

Pepe nodded and looked back at Ellen and Lescal. "I understand why you aren't dancing. Are you uncomfortable?"

"I'm all right, and I get a lot of pleasure watching, you know."

"Oh, yes, watching is next best to doing." Pepe laughed and went over to join Ellen and Lescal. He whispered in Lescal's ear and laughed.

Gus spent several hours being a thoroughly good sport. He waited for Fiona to leave the tent for a swim with the pilot. Then he rose to go relieve himself. He started out of the tent, but then turned suddenly, glared at Sala, and hurried back to pick up the gold purse.

The facilities were a rather elaborate outhouse with carpeting and drapes. Gus made use of it as he took the revolver out of the gold bag, checked its size, then slowly put it up the only bodily orifice which could contain it, and hoped his sphincter muscles would last. He held the gun in place until he arrived back at the tent, then went in and sat down carefully on one side. He assumed a desperate expression; Lescal and Ellen saw it and came over.

"I hate to tell you this," Gus said to them, "but it must have been something I ate. What do they call 'tourista' in Morocco?"

Disgustedly he threw Fiona's purse back on the pillows.

"Oh, no, Gus."

"Oh, Ellen, yes. And I don't think I can dare walk very far."

Pepe had two of his men carry Gus out to the Citroën on a chair; Sala drove him to the apartment. Alone in his room, he quickly freed the revolver, and amidst numerous flushings of the toilet for effect, cleaned and examined it. It was custom-made and held only three cartridges, but their tips had been filed down to make them dum-dum bullets, the kind which went in small and came out big. Gus taped the gun to his thigh and went to sleep. He woke up once from a nightmare: he was bringing the gun back in the car and it went off. He got up and flushed again.

Through the next day Gus stayed in his room and tried to sleep. He found it difficult. At one point Sala was loudly berated in French for stealing. Later, Gus could hear other voices arguing with Lescal in French and Italian. He dozed off, but was awakened by loud banging on his door.

"Who's there?"

"It's me, Ellen, let me in!"

He moved the furniture away from his door. She came in, dressed for the evening in her usual sheer caftan. Her red hair was tied on top of her head with gold rope.

"Gus, are you all right?"

"I'm all right and you're beautiful. Why?"

"I . . . I don't know. I was getting dressed and I got so worried about you. How are you?"

"The plumbing here works well, thank God. The troop movements around my balls seem to have dug in."

"Oh, Gus." She laughed and hugged him.

He affected martyrdom. "Be gentle with me."

"You know, I love you. I think incest is great. When you finish fucking, you still have a relative. . . . What do you think of Benny? I'm in love with him."

"Yeah? Well . . ." He considered telling her everything so they could get out during the *chergui* together. But at that moment she went over to the bed and pulled her caftan above her knees. From what appeared to be an elaborate garter belt she pulled out a hypodermic needle, smiled, and said, "He gives me this fantastic dope. It gives you such a buzz." She went on talking as she injected the needle in her thigh. "He's really neat, and sex is sensational." She finished and put the needle back. "I mean, Gus, what more could a girl want?"

"If I think of anything, I'll let you know. What are we doing tonight?"

"Having dinner with some groovy friends. They have a screening room, and we'll see a new dirty movie, which the guy makes. . . . Oh, God! That stuff is *so groovy!* . . . Then down to the beach, I guess. You can have fun, can't you?"

"Sure, just sit me close to the john."

The evening progressed as expected. The food involved lamb; the pornography, young Arab boys. Gus fled occasionally to the washroom to check the revolver taped on his leg, and flushed. By two, the party had settled in on the Plage. Gus missed the two sisters, who did not appear. He would have enjoyed more of Fiona's insights and support; he didn't know what the *chergui* at dawn involved, or how he should be prepared. He stayed as close to Ellen as possible, suggesting with a kind of manic abandon that they show Benny all the dances they'd learned in Pittsburgh.

As dawn approached, couples wandered out of the tent to the beach. Gus realized that nobody was coming back. He tried to keep Ellen dancing, but she was sleepy and lay down beside Lescal. Gus sprawled beside them and started explaining some of the more complex philosophies which he'd studied, babbling on until Lescal said, "We go home now. You join us, *n'est-ce pas?*" Lescal helped Ellen to her feet.

"Now? Oh. Is it time to go home already? I love watching the dawn."

Lescal turned toward the tent's entrance. "It is here."

Outside there was a yell, then silence. Lescal looked at Pepe; the guests remaining sat up on their cushions, curious. There were sounds of a scuffle, then a shot. Lescal threw Ellen to the ground and from the back of his waist drew a scimitar-shaped dagger. Pepe had a gun in his hand and was yelling to his men. Lescal was about to grab Ellen, but Gus tore his revolver from his leg, leaped at Lescal, and wrenched the dagger back. With his other hand, Gus jammed the revolver barrel as hard as he could through Lescal's teeth.

Fortunately, both of them fell to the ground, for at that moment the entire top of the tent was blown off, riddled with bullets. Gus glimpsed Pepe crawling away. Several people screamed. Lescal started choking on his own teeth as Gus jammed the gun in farther and said, "Let go of the knife or I'll blow your neck open!"

Lescal did so as Ellen struggled free of a piece of the tent. She saw Lescal and Gus, got up, and started kicking at Gus.

"What are you doing? Leave Benny alone!"

"Ellen, goddammit, this is the guy who slit your brother's throat! This is Lescal."

Ellen staggered backward, fell, and started screaming hysterically as Moroccan police and soldiers swarmed into the tent. Gus, still lying on top of Lescal, holding the gun in his mouth, saw the Arab's eyes flicker, and turned to find Sala ready to plunge a dagger in his back. He pulled up the gun and shot Sala in the face. The dum-dum bullet hit, and bits of his skull flew through the air.

Lescal used the distraction to gut-punch Gus and kick free of him. He jumped up, and dodging between the screaming guests, slipped out of the tent.

Gus looked around for Ellen, and saw her being helped to her feet, still screaming, by two of Magnus' men. He got up, hurting from

Lescal's punch, and hurried out. Even though he was carrying a gun, the Moroccan soldiers seemed to know who he was and let him go.

Outside, Gus saw Pepe lying on the sand being searched. Beyond him, three natives had caught Lescal. His body fell limp between them, and they dragged him to the panel truck in which Gus had ridden, threw him in the back, jumped in, and closed the doors. The truck immediately started moving, churning sand.

Gus ran toward it and leaped on the hood. He grabbed hold of a windshield wiper and pointed the gun directly at the driver's head, yelling for him to stop. When the truck stopped, the three natives came around to see what the trouble was. Gus jumped down, and keeping his gun on them went around to the back.

Inside, he could see Lescal spread-eagled, facedown, his arms and legs chained to the sides of the truck. Above him on the steel bench sat Magnus.

"I'm coming with you," Gus said.

"Get in, then. Hurry." Gus jumped in. The three men followed, the doors were shut, and the panel truck started moving.

"What the hell are you doing?" Gus demanded.

Magnus turned toward him, then looked back at Lescal. "You'll see."

"What's happening with Ellen?"

"An ambulance will take her to the airport. My plane is waiting with a doctor, and her mother will meet her in Pittsburgh." Gus watched Magnus reel off the details, his attention never wavering from Lescal.

The drive was a short one. When they stopped, the three natives opened the back doors, undid the chains, and dragged Lescal out. Magnus and Gus followed them into a large warehouse. It had a dirt floor, several wooden pens, and a table and chairs.

"What is this place?" Gus asked.

"It used to be a slaughterhouse. . . . Give me your gun, Gus."

"I'll keep it, thanks." He stepped backward and felt something hard in his back. The driver was there holding a shotgun. Gus let his revolver fall to the floor. The Arab picked it up as Magnus went over to where the other natives were chaining Lescal.

Two posts which were part of the pens had been prepared previously. Lescal was already hanging between them, just able to touch the ground with his feet. He was groggy but conscious, his mouth still bleeding.

Gus walked slowly over to Magnus.

"How did you find him?"

"Ted Weiss found out he was in Tangier. We were closing in on him when he went after Ellen."

"What are you going to do with him?"

Magnus turned to him. "I didn't want you here, so don't interrupt." He turned to the natives, who appeared well-rehearsed. One held Lescal's head back by the hair, another forced his mouth open, the third fitted a wooden device into it and strapped it around Lescal's head. The device forced Lescal's mouth to stay open and kept his tongue in place, allowing only enough movement to let him swallow.

From one of the pens they lifted a spool of what looked like white string. Magnus went to the table and put on surgical gloves. He cut off the end of a finger from a third glove. Very carefully he put several drops of what Gus could see was mercury into the finger-end. Then, using black silk thread, Magnus tied the tiny pouch containing the mercury to one end of the white string and took the whole spool with its attachment over to Lescal. His voice was harsh.

"Lescal, I want you to know exactly what's going to happen to you. This looks like string, but it's actually rope-stranded copper wire about a twelfth of an inch in diameter. It's been coated with white rubber. This little bag is filled with mercury. It acts as nothing more than a weight, but if you struggle and it breaks inside you, you'll live for two or three days as your insides burn out. So don't break it; I'll kill you sooner than that."

Magnus nodded to the strongest of the natives, who stood behind Lescal and bear-hugged him around the solar plexus, compressing Lescal's lungs. Magnus covered the wooden mouthpiece with his hand and jammed the pouch of mercury and wire up one of Lescal's nostrils. When the native man let go, Lescal sucked air into his nose, forcing the wire down his nasal passage into his throat. Lescal gagged several times, but the mercury bag weighted the wire down into his esophagus. Lescal, who had been sullen and contemptuous, now appeared terrified.

Gus watched, not daring to say a word. Magnus unwound about twenty-five feet of the spool and left it in front of Lescal. "We're going to wait for this to go through you, Lescal. The rubber coating on the wire will keep it from cutting your intestines." Lescal tried to talk, but could do nothing but bellow noises as Magnus unrolled some more of the spool, tied it securely to an iron pillar, then looped the wire around a railroad tie and knotted it securely to the back bumper of the panel truck. The driver got in and started the motor.

"The breaking strength of the wire is approximately five hundred pounds, Lescal. Watch."

The truck started moving; the loop of wire around the railroad tie tightened, then cut through the wood.

"It will take about eight to ten hours for the wire to pass through your guts, Lescal. We'll wait, and then we'll tie the ends to the pillar and the truck, and straighten the wire out again."

Lescal bellowed, trying to talk. Magnus carried the two pieces of railroad tie over in front of him and dropped them so Lescal could see what the wire had done. Then Magnus sat down, trembling slightly, and ran a hand over his face. One of the natives cut Lescal's pants clear of his body. Another stood in front of him, slowly feeding the wire into Lescal's nose.

Gus watched. His first reaction had been to run for help, but he knew he'd never get out of the warehouse. He thought about talking to Magnus, but realized it would be useless. He waited. The natives watched Gus; one of them held the shotgun. Occasionally Lescal would struggle and cry out, but Magnus remained motionless.

An hour passed. Casually, Gus moved across the warehouse, pulled up a chair beside Magnus, and sat down.

"Don't waste reasons on me."

"I won't," said Gus. "I'm just curious. Why don't you just kill him?"

"That would mean nothing to him. He's a torturer; he only understands torture."

"Yeah, but you're not a torturer. From what I've heard, you're not even a murderer."

Magnus turned sharply and said, "We're whatever we have to be."

"I thought we're whatever we *want* to be. Nobody's making you do this."

"Don't give me reasons!"

"I'm not! I'm just wondering what your reasons really are. What's this going to prove?"

Magnus didn't answer. The warehouse expanded in the daytime heat, making sudden cracking noises. The sounds of traffic increased. Gus tried to think as, inexorably, the white wire went down Lescal's throat. Then he noticed the revolver he had used lying on the table beside Magnus. Gus waited as Lescal, with violent shakings of his head, indicated he needed to relieve himself. The natives spread papers underneath him, and after Lescal dropped on them, removed them.

"What happens if he faints?" Gus asked.

"They'll stake him to the ground until he recovers."

"Then hang him up again?"

Magnus glanced at Gus and said, "You're thinking that I'm insane. I'm not. I'm doing this for my grandson and for Ellen. This animal damaged my family. What I'm doing to him is nothing compared to what he's done to others."

"Magnus, it's positively ceremonial, but I still don't get it. You've been chasing this guy for more than ten years. . . . What if you get caught?"

"I won't. It's taken care of."

"Of course. I'll bet you've bought every goddamned official in Morocco. . . . So who's going to apply justice to you? I mean, you're killing a man—"

"No further justice is needed for killing such a man."

"Says you. You do to him what he did to you, and poof, it's like neither of them ever happened. But it doesn't work like that. You're still a torturer and a murderer."

"I don't want you here. Get back."

Gus didn't move. "Sure, you're the magician. The law didn't get him, and God didn't do a damn thing, so you figure you'll be judge and God. Well, enjoy it, Magnus, it may be your big moment." Gus felt the adrenaline jolt through him. "You *want* to kill this guy; don't kid yourself that you have some divine duty. . . . Yeah, now I get it. You've been looking for this guy all your life. It's not for Magnus Josephson or Ellen; it's for you. You can load him up with all your shit, just like you loaded me with all the shit about my mother. Goddamn you, you might as well kill me!" He swung, bashed at Magnus' head, and leaped for the gun.

Magnus was stunned for a moment, then grabbed at Gus's arms as the two of them rolled to the dirt floor, the gun in Gus's hand. The natives ran up, but Gus fired wildly, and they kept their distance, watching Magnus and Gus kick and punch each other. Finally Magnus rolled on top, jammed Gus's chin up, and started to pry the gun out of his hand.

Suddenly Gus laughed. Magnus froze.

"Yeah," Gus said. "Familiar scene." Magnus hesitated, and Gus rolled quickly free, aiming the gun at Magnus' head. He gestured for Magnus to stand up.

"Tell that guy to put the shotgun down," Gus said, still lying on the floor.

Magnus glanced over to the natives and nodded. The shotgun was put on the ground.

"You owe these guys any money?"

"It's been arranged," Magnus said, barely audible.

"Yeah, of course. Tell them to get out. Fast."

Again Magnus nodded. The natives hesitated.

"Move it!" They hurried to the far end of the warehouse and went out.

Gus stood up slowly, still holding the gun on Magnus' head. He backed up halfway to the exit where the panel truck was parked.

"All right, you have some choices. I plan to put this gun down and go for the cops. You can get to that shotgun before I reach the door. If that's the choice you make, this time there won't be any doubt in your mind, or mine, who's killing who, and for what reason. Next choice: if I get out of here, you can blow Lescal's head off. But by God you'll pay for it!" He dropped the gun on the floor and walked to the truck. "So take your pick, Magnus." He started the motor and prepared to ram the truck through the warehouse doors in case the natives were waiting outside.

"Gus! Stop!" But Gus couldn't hear. The truck had started moving. Magnus picked up the shotgun and fired broadside at the truck. The two charges blew off a tire and knocked the rear axle loose from the chassis. The vehicle lurched and stopped as Magnus hurried over to the cab.

Gus was staring straight ahead, gripping the steering wheel. Magnus propped the gun against the fender. He was trembling again.

"What you said . . ." Magnus was trying hard for control.

"About what?"

"My reasons for this seemed clear, until you said . . ."

"He's your scapegoat, Magnus."

Magnus looked down at the ground for a time, then said, "For the last few days, I felt something was wrong. But it was too late. I'd worked for this . . . I had the power to do it."

"Scapegoats are phony, Magnus. You can bury Lescal in the desert, but you still haven't gotten rid of who you really blame."

He met Magnus' gaze, and watched his face alter from astonishment to despair.

"I've thought about this day for so long. Now, I need more time . . ."

Gus got out of the panel truck. "Time for what?"

"To be rid of . . ." He stopped. He glanced at Gus; Gus shook his head.

"Rid of what? A lifetime? . . . We're stuck with our lives, just like everyone else." For the first time, Gus saw Magnus not as an onerous shadow, but as a man who had been as alone as he himself had been.

"Goddamn, Magnus, I wish you'd stop hating yourself long enough to take a chance on somebody."

They stood quietly; then simultaneously Gus and Magnus reached out their arms and hugged each other.

Both felt immediate alarm, and embarrassment. But they held each other until Magnus said, "I'm sorry, Gus."

"Don't be. It gets in the way."

"All right. But I owe the apology for having used you for my own hates."

Gus cocked his head to one side, ready to disbelieve and protect himself. But instead he smiled.

Magnus turned and went over to Lescal, opened the manacles on his wrists, and let him fall. He looked quickly at Gus and said, "I'll warn you, Gus; I'm not good at loving sons." Then he started tying Lescal up with the white wire.

Gus watched a moment and realized that one day Magnus Macpherson would die; by calling Gus his son, Magnus had made himself mortal.

At sunset, Antoine Lescal was dumped at the back door of the Algerian consulate. He was alive and yelling. A note explained the delicacy of the white wire and its weight, which by then was near its conclusion.

A half-hour later, a charter jet arrived at the Tangier airport. Magnus and Gus boarded, and the plane took off for Inverness in Scotland. Gus had said he was on a vacation, and Magnus decided to use this time to show the boy his heritage.

They spent the night at the Station Hotel, sharing a room and talking of what had happened. Magnus admitted to feeling relieved of a madness. Gus laughed and said he felt like he'd just been born.

From Inverness they went to Dufftown and visited Kristin, who had returned from America when "her brood" had grown up, and was living happily in her old cottage. Magnus led Gus past the house where he grew up, along the Dullen Water to the Mortlach Kirk, where Magnus' father and mother were buried. Magnus told Gus the stories of how The Creation was made. As they walked up the braes of Ben Rinnes, Magnus tried to find where his father's wee pot had been, but the heather had long since covered it.

When they reached the tor where Magnus used to look down on the town, Magnus said, "Gus, I want to adopt you. I don't mean it as a burden, only as a choice. It's just a legal matter. . . . If you choose, I'd like you to be called Macpherson."

Gus watched the course of the River Fiddich between its limestone banks. "I told you once, Magnus, I'll never be a Macpherson. I'll stick to that. It's not resentment; it's just the truth. Whatever you and I are to each other, we'll find it out . . . but not with names and legal papers." He looked at Magnus. "But I tell you what you could do: give me a job at M.I."

Magnus smiled. "I'll give you a job, Gus."

As they walked down Ben Rinnes in a warm summer sun back to Dufftown, Magnus explained his plans. He would put Gus in M.I.'s international-sales division, working out of Washington, where he would become familiar with the legislative process as practiced by industry, and he would be separate from Jamie. In six months Gus would take a place on M.I.'s board of directors. Jamie would be furious, but that would be good for him, good for M.I., and good for business. Neither Gus nor Jamie wanted to accept being his son, but both were. Magnus no longer had any doubt about Gus.

"Jamie, I'm pregnant." Janet Flanagan stood at the window of her apartment, watching the rain. "I thought you'd want to know."

Jamie gazed at Janet a moment, then smiled. Spring had refused to come that year; the days had gone straight from winter sleet and cold to wind and rain. Probably summer would start momentarily with its wet heat and heavy air.

Pregnant. His first reaction was that he wanted a son; he would name the child Magnus Macpherson. No number would be attached, out of deference to WeeDee's murdered child, as well as to the infamous memory of Magnus II. Jamie had no desire to honor his father but would do anything he could to strengthen the sense of family against the steady aggravation of Gus Fowler. Gus had gone on the board, then become vice-president of the International Division, in less than a year. He was too young, only twenty-six. Jamie knew what Magnus was doing; the setup of a rivalry was irritatingly unsubtle.

If the baby were a girl, Jamie did not have an idea for a name. He looked back at Janet, who was glaring at him.

"Will you please say something? You're always silent just when I need you to talk. I mean, I don't need you to talk often, but now—"

"Congratulations."

"What? . . . Who to? Me?"

"Us. We're getting married."

Janet's irritation softened. "That's what I thought you'd say. Well, look." She went to her writing desk and picked up a folder. "I thought it'd be a good idea to write up some notes so that we could stand being married. I mean, we aren't your basic matrimonial types. The idea turned out so well, Abner's going to run it in the paper, and it got me an advance for a book. Also, I had a lawyer read it, and she said it would work. So why don't you look it over? If it makes any sense to you, we can get married and live happily ever after."

Jamie took the folder and read what turned out to be a thirty-eight-page marriage contract. Among its many points were total financial independence and no obligation should the relationship terminate, except a fifty-fifty responsibility for any offspring. They would find a "mutual dwelling" together. Janet would not change her name. If the child were a girl, she would take the surname Flanagan; if a boy, Macpherson.

The phone rang. Janet answered.

"It's long distance, for you. . . . I thought you didn't give anyone this number?"

"Only for emergencies. I don't want to talk to anyone right now."

"I'm afraid Mr. Macpherson is busy just at—" Janet was interrupted. She listened, then covered the mouthpiece.

"It's Evelyn Lorraine, in Paris. She says your father just had a stroke."

January 22, 1972

Long distance static and silence.

"I don't believe you, Magnus."

"Come and see for yourself, Evelyn."

"Where are you?"

"Lenox Hill Hospital in New York."

"What the hell are you doing in a hospital?"

"I thought you'd ask. I just became a grandfather again. Jamie and his wife had a son this morning."

"Congratulations. You'll be a goddamn patriarch in no time."

"Evelyn, how long are you going to be in Nassau?"

"I think another week. I don't know. This junket is poison; the food's too rich and the sun's too hot."

"What the hell are you doing on a junket? You and your friends are all over the social page of this morning's New York *Times*."

"Well, good for us. That's why this resort flew us here; a few faded stars, a few deposed titles, to give the place class. Ever since I went to Hollywood, I've been giving class to tacky." She laughed.

"Would you like a visitor?"

More long distance static and silence.

" 'I've grown accustomed to your death.' "

"And have you been enjoying yourself?"

"No, but I don't want to have to get used to it again. It takes too long."

"Then I'll have to outlive you."

"You bastard, you probably will."

"I will, Evelyn, I promise you."

"Magnus, I feel rotten about walking out on you in Paris."

"If I'd died, like we thought I was going to, you would have been doing the right thing. Your leaving was part of our understanding; I didn't want you to stay."

"It still was rotten."

"Yes, dirty rotten, you're right. . . . What's your room number in that tacky place?"

A long pause followed.

"Eight-thirty-two," Evelyn said and hung up.

Magnus smiled, put the phone down, and opened the door of the telephone booth. A nurse came up to him.

"Mr. Macpherson, there's a call from Washington for you."

Magnus followed her down the hall to the nurses' station and took the phone.

"Magnus? Gus. Call me on a pay phone. It's busted wide open."

"I'm supposed to go view the baby."

There was a pause.

"Your sudden grand-paternalism will have to wait."

Gus hung up. Magnus went back down the corridor to the phone booth and called their private number. On the first ring Gus answered and started talking.

"I just got a call from a guy I know at the Securities and Exchange Commission. He told me a certain executive from Sonnencorp has been singing about how a hundred million dollars plus has been pumped into Sonnencorp to keep it from falling on its conglomerate ass. The money is from the syndicate, and this executive has already pointed to the corporations all over hell-and-gone, Hong Kong, Switzerland, London, where the cash was laundered."

"Wait a minute, Gus. Why is the Sonnencorp man talking to the SEC?"

"His name is Hudson, and it seems he's scared shitless. The guy who got killed rigging your car in Santa Barbara was the son of a lawyer in Nassau who laundered the money going into Sonnencorp. Hudson could handle risking larceny, but not conspiracy to commit murder. So he's—"

"Wait. What's the name of the lawyer in Nassau?"

"Both the lawyer and his kid are named John Gianni. Anyway . . ." Gus went on with corporate details, but Magnus was thinking of generations. Johnny Gianni died in prison protecting Magnus. His son and namesake went to law school, for which Magnus had paid. That John Gianni laundered syndicate money to get control of Macpherson Industries. And the third John Gianni was blown up rigging Magnus' car.

"Magnus, you there?"

"Yes. Where is this Sonnencorp executive?"

"The SEC called in the Justice Department, so the FBI's guarding him night and day. Hudson's dealing for immunity, but there's got to be a leak sooner or later."

"Don't leak it to anyone. Get as much of this documented as you can, details, amounts, corporate entities, everything. I'll fly to Dulles from here in the company plane. Meet me there at six. Then we'll fly to Nassau and see Gianni."

"Gianni? What for?"

"I want to get to him before the syndicate does. The more potential talkers we have, the sooner they'll stop hijacking our trucks. Is the SEC going to have trading of our stock halted?"

"Not until Hudson finishes singing and they can get a grand jury together."

"Good. Bring a stenographer along with a typewriter."

"To Nassau? What the hell for, Magnus?"

"Gianni's the syndicate connection to Fleming and Co. He has to be; Juny brought Sonnencorp in to take over M.I. If Sonnencorp was broke, Juny had to know where to get them money, not only to buy us, but to save them. Somehow Juny knew about Gianni. . . ."

Magnus heard Gus flipping through papers.

"And I can tell you how: Gianni went to law school with one of Juny Fleming's sons."

Magnus had to laugh.

"What's so damn funny?"

"I'll tell you when I see you at Dulles. Six o'clock. You and I are going to save Juny Fleming's ass; it'll probably kill him."

At first, Evelyn Lorraine was not pleased to have anyone banging on her door at two in the morning. When she found out it was Magnus, she was furious.

"You get a room and I'll see you tomorrow morning," she said through the door.

"I'm leaving tomorrow morning."

"What's the hurry?"

"Business."

"I don't like being fitted in, Magnus."

"I do."

She laughed. Her professional trademark of royal dignity was always perforated by her "sewer laugh," as she called it. Magnus stimulated it more than anyone else she knew.

"You wait a minute, Magnus. There are things I have to do to my face."

"I know all those things, and they don't make any difference to me. Just open the door, or I'll get arrested."

The door opened, and Evelyn stood imperiously in a peignoir. Magnus smiled and said, "How could you improve on that?" He noticed her careful scrutiny, and asked, "How do I look?"

"A hell of a lot better than in Paris."

"Can I come in?"

"I don't know." Evelyn was serious; her decision had nothing to do with spending the short night, and Magnus knew it.

"You gave me your room number, so you knew I'd come."

She was beginning to feel awkward standing at the door. "Sure you can come in, Magnus, but tomorrow you leave, because nothing's starting between us like it did in Gstaad. From here I'm going to Paris to buy clothes, to Sardinia with friends, and then home for the Gstaad winter follies."

"Why tell me your plans?"

She blurted, "Because I'm selfish. I don't want to watch you die and get stuck again with missing you. You're fifteen years older than I am, Magnus, and next time something happens I won't have the strength to get over you." She shook her head and walked into the room, leaving the door open.

"I'm going to give you a head start," Magnus said. "You go off to Paris, and Sardinia, and Gstaad; run away as hard as you can. But you'll run right into me. Good night, Evelyn." He stepped inside and closed the door behind him. At the sound, Evelyn whirled around, and the look on her face told Magnus everything he wanted to know.

"You son of a bitch. You sneaky son of a bitch," Evelyn shouted, furious at having revealed so much.

Magnus went to her and said, "In forty years I've never asked you for more than one night." He kissed her.

They were quiet for a time, Evelyn leaning her head against his shoulder. Finally she said in a whisper, "After the stroke, when I heard you were better, I laughed, then I cried, the first time I've cried without a camera in front of me for . . . well, forty years. . . . But I couldn't call you; I couldn't even write. I gave up on you in Paris like we agreed. The trouble is, our agreement didn't cover rising from the dead."

"I wasn't dead."

"Well, you sure looked it when they carried you out of the Crillon on a stretcher."

"Here I am; forget all that."

They kissed again. "I've been thinking about you ever since you called today," Evelyn said, going to the window. "Wondering what made me want you to come: habit? missing? loving you?"

"We're both old enough to admit it."

"Smart enough; don't say 'old enough.'"

"I'm old enough and smart enough to know I want more than a night with you, and I'm here to ask you for it."

"You're leaving tomorrow morning."

"That'll give you time to consider."

"Is this a proposal?"

"Yes."

Magnus walked over to the window and stood behind Evelyn. They could see each other half-reflected in the dark glass. Magnus spoke softly in her ear. "Evelyn, we've had careers and marriages and lovers. We've both paid a great deal for being rich. We got lost in our lives. We got power, and with power we shaped our dreams, and corrupted them. You were a 'garbage can' in Hollywood; I was convicted of killing my own son. But we found each other and somehow led each other back. Evelyn, I want to wake up every day and know you'll be there when I need you."

She stared back into the dark reflection, barely breathing.

"I need some time, Magnus."

"All that I have."

She turned to face him. "Somebody told me, flying down here on this junket, that people over fifty weren't really fit for love, but only to be friends. Their bodies aren't right for it, their passions are 'dulled,' he said. It made me mad, but it had me worried . . . until you called." She kissed him. "So take my hand and lead me back to bed. . . ."

The next morning, Gus and Magnus went to Government House and met with the crown prosecutor. Then they drove to John Gianni's investment-banking firm overlooking Bay Street. They walked straight through the reception area, alarming several secretaries, and into Gianni's private office.

In spite of never having met him, Gianni immediately knew Magnus.

"Well, Mr. Macpherson, what a surprise." Gianni tried to force a grin.

"Let me begin by expressing my sympathies about the death of your son last week. You know, of course, he died wiring a dynamite bomb to my car."

"Yes, sir, I've learned that." Gianni began to sweat. "But I had nothing to . . ." He stopped talking; Gianni knew he had a lot to do with it. The syndicate was cooperating in forcing Macpherson Industries to sell out, and Gianni was the connection to their methods and their money.

"Now, John, we know everything you have accomplished through Mr. Hudson at Sonnencorp."

Gianni didn't respond; he barely breathed as Magnus continued. "We have shared our knowledge with the local authorities, who should arrive here with a warrant for your arrest in, I'd guess, twenty minutes."

"Arrest? What for?" Gianni could barely speak.

Gus answered. "Her Majesty's government looks unkindly on questionable corporations established in crown colonies such as Nassau and Hong Kong for the purpose of washing money from organized crime. Mr. Hudson, who is currently spending time with the SEC and the Justice Department, is pointing the big finger at you."

Magnus said, "This is my son, Gus Fowler."

Gianni wiped his face with his hand. "Why are you here, Mr. Macpherson, to watch the slaughter?"

"No, to offer you some time. Our plane is at the airport. We're flying to New York."

"I doubt if you're offering the trip for free."

"You're right, John. I want the file on your dealings in this matter with Fleming and Co. And I will want you to sign a statement on the plane explaining Juny Fleming's involvement in detail."

"I've got a wife and children, I can't just leave."

Magnus looked at his watch. "I suggest about fifteen minutes now."

Gianni sat with both hands gripping his desk.

"I've got to make some calls."

"We can't allow you to do that. You come with us or we wait with you." Gus had a gun, but he didn't move to touch it. Gianni hesitated, then stood up and went to an English hunt picture on the wall.

He swung it open and worked the dial of a safe. Out of it he took a file and gave it to Gus; then he stuffed an attaché case full of cash.

Downstairs, they got into a car. Gus drove down Bay Street on the way to the airport. Magnus had not been there since his Rum Row days. The city had changed beyond recognition. He couldn't even tell the corner where the old Lucerne Hotel had stood, but he didn't have time for nostalgia.

On the plane, a stenographer took down John Gianni's statement. Gus went over the file; Juny Fleming had written nothing down, but Gianni had records of phone conversations and meetings which could be corroborated. Juny could probably escape conspiracy charges; he only acted as a matchmaker between Gianni's money and Sonnencorp's need. In any investigation, however, Fleming and Co. would be dragged through the worst of it. And Gianni was seriously implicating Juny himself.

When the secretary had typed the statement, and Gianni had signed each page, Gus sat down across the table from him as Magnus picked up the phone and gave the pilot permission to land.

"We can't be in New York already," Gianni said.

"No, John," Magnus answered. "You're not going to New York. We've been circling; it's midday, so you didn't notice where the sun was. We're landing back in Nassau. If we didn't, we'd be accessories. . . . You're a lawyer, John, so you understand that."

Gianni started to get up, but Gus shoved him back down. "Sit down, Gianni, and fasten your seat belt."

Gianni didn't struggle. The plane landed and taxied to the end of the runway, where Nassau police were waiting. As Gianni started down the steps, Gus handed him his attaché case filled with cash. Magnus watched from the window, already anticipating his meeting with Juny.

"Gus, I want you to set up a meeting," Magnus said when they were back in the air. "Jamie, WeeDee, Ellen, you, and me."

Gus cocked his head. "Ellen?"

"Yes. Her mother tells me she's doing very well. I want to see for myself. If it's true, I want to find a place for her at M.I., if she wants it."

"With that crowd, you'll need a judge," said Gus.

Magnus smiled. "I suppose so. I'll get Weiss to fly over. And you'd better invite Double. I'm going to put Weiss on the board and make you a trustee of the foundation. . . . And I'll give you stock equal to theirs. Jamie stays president of M.I., you stay vice-president of the International Division."

"That includes Mexican oil?"

"It does."

"In five years the International Division will dwarf the rest of M.I., I promise you."

"I'll be interested to watch that happen. I plan to sell a lot of liquor in the next five years."

"*You* do?"

"I'm not coming back from the dead to molt, Gus. The only hope you have of getting rid of me is if I work myself to death."

"You'll dance at our wakes."

"And, Gus, you have no hope at all of getting rid of Jamie."

"I know that," Gus snapped, "now that there's a little Magnus to get it all."

"That has nothing to do with it. Jamie is good at running M.I. It's as simple as that."

"No it's not, Magnus; don't kid yourself. You've got two sons who both want M.I., and I'm going to be as good as Jamie any minute. You can't just die and leave us to fight it out; we'd destroy the company. Sooner or later you're going to have to make a choice. I'll give odds right now that when the time comes, you'll choose me."

Magnus didn't answer. Gus smiled confidently, then shrugged and looked out of the window. He was very smart, this son, Magnus thought, a better diplomat in his tough straight way than his priest brother. Gus at least presented the idea that Magnus would have to choose. Jamie had never suggested any choice, rather that M.I. had been thrust on him and was his for the keeping. And there was a grandson, another Magnus Macpherson. Gus was right: he would have to make a choice one day. Magnus sat back in his chair, smiling, thinking of the new Magnus Macpherson, who might by chance have a son born in the year 2000.

Gus caught the smile and misinterpreted it. "Am I right?"

"About many things, and wrong about others."

"I'm not wrong about this."

"If confidence were all. Gus, you're right about the choice: I'll make it. But don't waste your time on guessing games."

"Magnus, as long as you're committed to making a choice, the race is wide open. And if the race isn't fixed, I'll win it."

"What if I give it all to Jamie?"

Gus looked at him and cocked his head to one side. "You'll live long enough to regret it even if you die the next day. And then I'll take it away from him. But don't worry, Magnus, you won't give it all to Jamie."

They shared a look, then both glanced away. Magnus was moved by an unfamiliar emotion, one that he could only guess was pride.

Their cabin attendant approached, telling them they were coming into Kennedy Airport and that the landing might be rough, as there was a storm.

The snow began to cover the roads. From their limousine, Gus checked his sources in Washington. His contact at the SEC didn't want to talk over a car phone, but mentioned that the Justice Department was already issuing subpoenas on the case. Apparently two FBI agents had delivered one that day to Juny Fleming at his office.

"It's gotta be in the papers tomorrow morning, Magnus. The Stock Exchange will stop trading on M.I."

Magnus nodded and told the driver to take them immediately to the Flemings' apartment on Fifth Avenue. Telling Gus to wait in the car, Magnus walked past the doorman without a word. He stepped into the elevator and asked for the Fleming apartment.

The apartment door was opened by a maid. At the mention of his name, there was a commotion, and Mrs. Fleming appeared. Magnus had never met her, but was familiar with her stretched smile and her chic lion's mane of hair from the society pages. Mrs. Fleming had always kept up with fashion, but at that moment she was obviously scared.

"What is it, Mr. Macpherson?"

"I was hoping to speak with your husband, Mrs. Fleming."

"He's not here."

"Perhaps you could tell me where I could find him. I would say it's urgent."

"I can't tell you. I don't know. He left about an hour ago. He told me to see no one, answer no phones. He said he didn't want me to know where he was, so that I didn't have to keep a secret. Mr. Macpherson, please leave him alone. He's not well."

"I'm not here to cause him any harm; in fact, I believe I can help him. If you hear from him, please tell him that." He turned to go.

"Do you know what's happening, Mr. Macpherson?" Magnus looked back at Mrs. Fleming, who appeared uncharacteristically wistful.

"I'm not the one to tell you anything, Mrs. Fleming. I'm sure you'll hear soon enough." He stepped back into the elevator.

Gus was waiting on the ground floor and hurried him into the limousine. "New York doormen know everything. Juny Fleming left an hour ago for Southampton."

Magnus nodded. "Gus, I want you to go up to the hospital and bring Jamie up-to-date."

"Now? Thanks a lot."

"What's wrong?"

"Janet Flanagan does *not* like business to be discussed when she's around. And God help me if little Magnus wakes up. The pussy whips will fly!"

"I'll leave that to you. This is important: I don't want the press to get any negative reaction from us about Juny or Fleming and Co. Let Sonnencorp collapse around us. I want M.I. to appear too strong for a takeover, in case someone else has the same idea."

"It isn't the time to be Mr. Good Guy. We can kill Fleming and Co. with this."

"We'd be stepping on empty shells," said Magnus. "Juny bought up a lot of M.I. stock for this takeover. I'm about to make a deal for it."

Gus shook his head and got out. Magnus told the chauffeur to stop at a liquor store. He bought a bottle of the Glenlivet. Then they drove through the snow to Long Island.

Magnus opened the bar compartment beside him and poured some malt into a glass. He added water from a small thermos, sipped it, and let the taste flow over his mouth. He had wanted Juny Fleming in just such a corner for a long time. Yet Magnus felt little triumph, less anticipation. His only thought was business.

The Long Island Expressway was tied up by the snowstorm, and the drive took hours. They did not reach the Fleming compound until four in the morning. Magnus noticed a chain-link fence had been constructed around it, barely concealed by hedges. Two new houses had been built beside the drive, but the rest of the compound seemed to be much the same.

Juny's car was parked in front of old Joseph Fleming's house; only one window showed light. Magnus and the chauffeur went up the steps, Magnus carrying his bottle with him. The doorbell didn't work. Magnus knocked; when there was no answer, he tried the door. It opened and they went in.

Juny's driver was asleep on a couch. Magnus told his own chauffeur to get whatever sleep he could, and took the flashlight.

Down the hall was the study. Magnus pushed the door open and went in.

Juny sat in front of a dwindling fire, still in his overcoat. He had nodded off to sleep. On a table beside him was a bottle of Macpherson's Century, an empty glass, and a candle. Magnus looked around the room at the portraits of Fleming horses, and smaller portraits of Flemings themselves. Behind the desk was old Joe's portrait in the full regalia of a Knight of Malta. Magnus clicked on the flashlight to see if the painter had got it right. Yes, old Joe's eyes were still lofted up to heaven.

"What . . . who's there?" Juny stood and turned, recognized Magnus, stumbled backward against the mantelpiece, and crossed himself. "Thank God. I'm dead and I've gone to hell."

"Not yet, Juny."

"Oh, no! I'm still alive? . . . I thought the Devil looked just like you, Magnus."

"He may."

"What are you doing in my house?"

"I was hoping to have a drink with you."

Juny looked down at the bottle of Century on the table. "I was drinking your filthy hooch, presuming it would poison me."

"I've brought something better for the occasion."

"What occasion? Get out of here and let me die in peace."

"You're not dying in peace, Juny. I doubt if you're even mortally wounded. You're out here thinking up how to be a martyr."

"You've always been poisonous. What are you talking about?"

"You committed a big sin, Juny. But if you come up with a bigger sacrifice, you think everyone will forget. It doesn't work, Juny. You'll just have to accept yourself as a self-righteous, hypocritical snob who managed to stay rich. . . . Shall we have a drink?"

Juny walked slowly over to the bar.

"You've always hated me for my money, haven't you, Magnus?"

"I've hated what being rich allowed you to be. I never minded you having money; it came in handy on occasion, if you remember."

"I remember, and I'll rot in hell for giving you money . . . and for letting you take *my sister* away." Juny stood at the bar, holding two glasses, his hands shaking. "God, I want to die so I can at least forget about Mary."

"Give up hating me about Mary; you've enjoyed it so long, you're depending on it for righteousness. If the God you believe in exists, she's in His hands, so you shouldn't worry. And if there's a God, He knows I loved her and what I thought of myself for what happened."

Magnus walked over to the bar and poured the malt into the two glasses. "Your house is freezing."

"The furnace is off."

"Any water?"

"The pipes are drained."

Without being asked, Magnus sat down. Juny threw more wood on the fire and poked at it.

"What are you here for, Magnus? Helluva time to come calling."

"Business."

Juny jabbed with the poker. "Don't tell me a thing about Mr. Hudson. I know all about him."

"And I know all about John Gianni."

Juny slowly put the poker back in its brass stand and gripped the mantel for support. "I thought probably you did. That's swell . . . just swell. And which sleazy newspaper will have the pleasure of reaming me and my family?"

"I'm not going to help you up on a cross, Juny. Hear me, now. You can beat anything Hudson says about you; he'll go down with Sonnencorp. I doubt if Gianni will talk very much in public; the syndicate doesn't like talkers, and he has to stay alive. He gave me a signed statement, but it won't be shared with the press."

"So what's the name of the game, Magnus—a little private torture, or your usual blackmail?"

Magnus took a long sip of his drink. He saw Juny's smile, the same snide smile he'd had when he stood with his polo mallets. "I want your son, Juny, the one who's running Fleming and Co., to come on M.I.'s board of directors."

"You dare . . ." Juny staggered quickly to his chair and sat down. He waited for the thump of his pacemaker, which hurt him. He gasped twice for breath, then took a drink from the glass, which shook in his hand.

"You want to go on destroying us in the next generation, don't you, Magnus? My sons and your sons. Well, my sons don't pal around with liquor men . . . or bastards!"

Magnus let it go by.

"They'll learn, Juny, or the SEC gets what I have and they'll close Fleming and Co. down. You won't be a suffering saint to anyone; you'll be a pariah. . . . I don't care about your sons except that Fleming and Co. can be useful to Macpherson Industries in the future. My sons have a lot of plans; they'll need a lot of investment capital. Besides, I hear you own some Macpherson stock, which I'll want voted my way."

"How nice for you, Magnus. What a peach you are."

"When I announce that your son is coming on our board, it'll do a lot to dispel rumors that you finally tried to have me killed in order to take over M.I."

"I *never* knew about—"

"Juny, I know better, so don't bother to lie to yourself. You knew where Gianni got his money; you knew what the syndicate was willing to do to guarantee their investment. The law could never prove it, but you *know* you rubbed up close to murder. . . . Your conscience won't let you die for a while. You'll have to wallow in your guilt, wailing and gnashing your teeth. You make me sick with your guilt, Juny, but I'll have your son on my board this morning."

Juny drank again and coughed. "What is this?"

"It's pure malt whiskey, the water of life, Juny. Drink it slowly, not like a bluidy fish in a desert."

They were both quiet for a time, staring into the fire.

"How can you face this without God?" Juny asked. "All this chaos without Him. At least I had a reason—"

Magnus turned slowly toward Juny and began to laugh. "Juny, you poor sod. Now you're going to excuse what you did with divine faith. Juny, you and God deserve each other. You use Him as your excuse, and He uses you as an example of His faithful."

Gradually Magnus stopped laughing and watched Juny, who was breathing with difficulty.

"Magnus, you have no faith at all?"

"Oh, yes, in Macpherson Industries."

"But faith in God . . . ?"

"I envy the certainty of faith but I despise all the deception."

"I pity you." Juny smiled his superiority.

"I'm sure that makes you feel better, Juny."

"Worshiping your company—"

"No, I just have faith in it."

Juny turned and glared at Magnus. "You need humility, Magnus. Your conceit is grotesque."

Magnus considered the opinion, then shook his head. "I have a deep respect for the chaos, Juny." Magnus stood up. "I'll expect your son to contact Jamie Macpherson before the Stock Exchange opens."

Juny looked up at him, coughed, and said, "God cursed my life the day you walked into this house."

"Believe in that, Juny. You'll live forever." Magnus picked up his bottle of malt and went out of the study.

His chauffeur was snoring softly on the couch. Magnus went to the front door and let himself out. The snow had stopped, and the wind had died to an occasional gust. He crossed the lawn, passing the bare tree under which he and Mary had stood so long on his first morning in America. No, Magnus remembered, his first morning in America was spent in jail. He took a handful of snow and ate it. It melted in his mouth, and he took a swallow of malt whiskey. Standing near the boathouse and looking out over the ocean, Magnus watched the dawn appear east-southeast.